FICTION   Earls, Nick,
EARLS   1963-

          Perfect skin.

WITHDRAWN

Perfect Skin

Perfect Skin

NICK EARLS

ST. MARTIN'S PRESS ☙ NEW YORK

www.stmartins.com

Library of Congress Cataloging-in-Publication Data

Earls, Nick.
    Perfect skin / Nick Earls.— 1st U.S. ed.
        p.   cm.
    ISBN 0-312-28056-4
    1. Fathers and daughters—Fiction.   2. Dermatologists—Fiction.
  3. Single fathers—Fiction.   4. Australia—Fiction.   I. Title.

PR9619.3.E22 P47 2001
823'.914—dc21   2001034945

    First published in Australia by Penguin Books Australia Ltd.

            First U.S. Edition: September 2001

        10   9   8   7   6   5   4   3   2   1

I didn't think my life would be like this. As naïve as it seems, when I was in school, I think I assumed that everything would be sorted out long before I was thirty. . . .

Perfect Skin

I

You'll be under a drape, a green paper drape, and you'll have to lie very still. You'll hear some zapping noises, and something that sounds like a vacuum cleaner. That's just the sucker, and it's there to suck up the smoke that we get when we zap the cancer with the laser. That's all totally routine. And we'll have someone else in there, probably Nigel, our nurse, holding the sucker so that I can concentrate on the zapping. Okay?

Yeah.

Good. Any questions at this stage?

No.

Okay.

And every time I get into the preamble to minor laser skin surgery, I try to stop it seeming totally routine. I try to take myself by surprise, as though each idea is occurring to me for the first time, and then leading me to think the next. Rather than the whole thing coming out as a long and tedious list of effects and side effects, personnel and noises and what we can hope for. All lost in a drone as even the patient loses interest.

I check that we've got time to do this one now, and that Nigel has the treatment room prepared.

Okay, Brian, I tell the now well-informed patient,

sitting there with his skin cancer on his ear. We're ready to roll.

I put my surgical glasses on, and my mask, and I scrub. Meanwhile, Nigel checks where the lesion is and sets everything up. I prep the skin, drop the drape into place so that the ear and not much more is left exposed. I inject the local and fix a sterile handpiece to the laser.

How are you going there, Brian?

No worries, he says, from under the drape.

Can you feel this?

I touch the ear with a needle tip.

No, he says, and shakes his head.

Can you feel this? And this time, if you could try not to shake your head, that'd be good. It could be a bad habit to get into if I'm lasering your ear and I have to ask you questions.

No problem.

Could you feel the needle?

No.

Okay, let's get to it. Let us know if there's any problem under there, but I don't expect there will be. You'll feel me fiddling with your ear. That's normal, since the whole ear's not supposed to be numb. The top bit should be, and you shouldn't feel any pain. So let me know if you do. And remember there'll be noise—zapping and sucking. So don't be put off by that, and just stay nice and still. Okay?

No worries.

I get started, holding the foot pedal down and passing the red guide light along the edge of the tumor, dropping circle after circle of Silktouch CO_2 laser on there, ablating the skin to a depth of one hundred microns each time. I lift off a sample to be sent for analysis, and I work away, working down through the tumor, lifting the debris off with a cotton swab. I clear the malignant tissue and some normal epidermis around it. Thinking of skin, the layers of skin. Knowing skin well enough that I know what's happening at a microscopic level as I follow the tumor down through the dermis until I can be sure that what I'm seeing is normal deep tissue.

And then it's done. The same preamble for each skin cancer, but a different job each time as I face each specific tumor and work my way to its tidy elimination.

Looks pretty good, I tell him. Nigel will put a dressing on there, and he'll explain everything you've got to do to look after it. We should get results back by the end of the week. Okay?

Yeah.

Any questions?

Do you think you got it all?

Yeah, I do. Like I said before, there's a small chance it'll come back, but just a small chance. So if you notice a lump developing like the one you had, get it looked at. But it's very unlikely. That all went just the way it should.

I wash my hands and I leave it to Nigel to finish. Sylvia, our receptionist, is in the corridor when I walk out of the treatment room.

So now can I check my e-mails? I ask her. Once I've written the file up?

Once you've written the file up.

Thanks.

I was late today. Not late by much but by Sylvia's

reckoning that's still late, and patients take priority over e-mail. Mornings don't always organize themselves easily for me—the multitude of baby rituals, the run around the college campus, the shower before starting work. Before my first patient. Today, Brian and the skin cancer on his ear. I seem to have found myself a lot of things to fit in before eight-thirty, but babies do wake you early, so it works most days.

Back in my room I hit the On key and my terminal kerboings into life as I make notes in the file. Something called a Window Weasel pops up on screen. It looks pretty cheery, but it says:

> Hi, Jon. Your trial period is up. We hope you're enjoying your Window Weasel software. Click YES!! I LOVE MY WEASEL!! and you can register to use Window Weasel for life for only $30! Click LATER to register later.

This mystifies me. Where this crap comes from I have no idea. I really don't have a clue about the software that might be lurking among the vast numbers of megabytes that George said were essential to make the system worth having. Not that it'll be completely worth having anyway until everything's on there, but some of us are still more attached than we should be to the practice of scrawling a few notes on paper after each consultation.

So, if I'm to be honest about it, I'm at best AMBIVA-LENT ABOUT MY WEASEL, and clicking LATER seems the only option.

And then all I've got when I check my mail is a bunch of jokes from George, yet again putting his share of the megabytes to great use. Ten blonds conquering a jigsaw puzzle, important things Mariah Carey has said about life. Why do I get my hopes up? Why do I have it in my mind that there might be something interesting waiting for me? Why do I treat the process of checking my e-mails with any kind of enthusiasm, when the paper mail in my in-box gets nothing but disdain and has to wait its turn? It can't be because George only sends me jokes electronically.

George, meanwhile, is no further away than the next room. I can hear him talking through the wall, the word-less murmur that I know is his voice explaining something to a patient. There is no actual need for George to e-mail me anything, he's just having a love affair with the elec-tronic transmission of text. What I don't get about it—and I'm sure George isn't even aware of this—is that he's never actually told me a joke in his life.

Seventeen years I've known him—half his life, or thereabouts—and never once has he verbally told me a formally constructed joke. We get e-mail access, and in minutes he's zapping me things about dogs, mice and el-ephants going into bars, or various famous people on fish-ing trips together or dying simultaneously and confronting a very droll Saint Peter at the pearly gates. There's a vaudevillian lurking in George that, sadly, in the real world will never be done justice.

Jon, your next one's arrived, Sylvia says. *No hurry. Here's the file.*

Thanks.

And your running clothes are still in the change room.

Yeah, sorry, I had to move a bit quickly when I got here, didn't I?

I hand her the file I've been writing in and I go to load my running gear into a plastic bag before the room takes on the smell of this morning's sweat. The theme song from *Porky Pig* comes back into my head, the way it has done the last few days when I've been out running. Why is it that I always seem to run with a rhythm that takes my mind to something crappy like that? Is it that way for everyone else too? I can't believe my timing's so different that they're all out there with something interesting and contemporary in their heads, and I'm the only one stuck with a cartoon theme song. And I can't believe I can remember so many of the words.

My running gear is particularly foul today. My run finished at about eight and it was already too hot then for running in comfort, and rank with the steaming wet smells of a lifting monsoonal low as the sun hit the ground for the first morning in a week. Not that there's any good time of day to run in an Australian February.

So I wasn't at my best when I had the conversation that made me late. Conversations, two of them, a few minutes apart. Me with sweat stinging my eyes and my shirt slapped wet across my chest and the theme song from *Porky Pig* still bouncing through my head in its jolly way as a student pulled up in her car to ask directions. Just as I was spitting, but managing a neat, professional runner's spit so I don't think she noticed anyway.

First she drove past me slowly down the street, obviously looking for something, her old red Pulsar loaded with junk and going slowly enough for me to notice it and to see a bumper sticker advertising tea, and another with the name of a Cairns car dealer and a phone number two digits too short to be up-to-date.

College starts in a week or two. And the bumper stickers stuck in my head because they were part of—maybe even the basis of—my assumptions about what she was doing. Moving cities, a thousand miles, to study. I still don't think I'd find that easy, even though I'm twice as old now as when I started college. I still don't know if I could drive a thousand miles with everything I own in the car and set up a new life somewhere, away from everything I'm used to. Of course, that's an assumption too, the untested assumption of an idling mind, out running along a street it's been down plenty of times and that doesn't often present something new to think about.

She got to the end of the street, U-turned and came back and stopped to ask me for directions.

Oh good, she said, *I was worried for a second,* when I told her there was another section to the road, just over the creek, and that whatever high number she was looking for was probably there, and three easy left turns away.

Near my car, coincidentally, I realized a couple of hundred yards later as the path dipped at the end of the street and I hit the concrete ramp and saw her car again, stopping, behind mine. And I can remember seeing the water flowing out from under the ramp as I ran over it, and seeing that it actually looked like a creek today rather than an empty open drain. Somehow I couldn't tell her she'd rented a place near an open drain. That doesn't seem like a fair introduction to the neighborhood.

I watched her get out of her car as I ran toward her.

She swung her legs out, lifted herself from the driver's seat and stood there, looking at the house, her hands on her hips. She didn't even shut her door, as though she might still have changed her mind, driven off. Turned north again, and gone.

With our cars parked end-to-end, conversation two was unavoidable. But maybe I would have said something to her anyway.

I said something like, It's not what you were expecting, is it?

And she said, *It does look a bit more condemned than I'd hoped.*

I told her there were students living in it last year, and it looked just as condemned then. She laughed, but in the polite way of someone whose situation has not been improved by the joke. The house is in bad shape, and the fact that I park near it often enough to know that it's in a relatively stable state of decay wasn't going to be much help to her. There are tiles missing from one end of the roof, the veranda leans like an old man badly in need of a walker and the only new feature is the large rezoning application sign at the front.

She said, *Maybe it'll be lovely inside,* knowing it wouldn't be. *I'm not paying anything for it, at least. It belongs to a family friend. I think he hasn't been down here for a while. They're putting apartments up. Sometime.*

She was hoping for more, for something different. She'd driven a long way with a different house in her mind, a different beginning to the year. And I felt sorry for her—I still feel sorry for her—but it didn't seem to be my place to do anything. I couldn't think what to do. It would have been easy if there had been some emergency going on, but this was just bad luck, disappointment.

But the moment might have been handled slightly more sensitively if I hadn't right then pressed the button that unlocked my car doors. The doors of the navy BMW parked in front of her old red Pulsar. And they unlocked with a flash of the lights and a smug electronic tone that made me feel like a big middle-aged Beemer wanker.

I remember she looked at the car, then at my hand. I always run with the keys in my hand. I didn't mean to press. I probably press all the time, and spend my whole run locking and unlocking the car, if it's in range.

Mine looks a bit incongruous parked behind that, she said. *But at least it goes with the house, I suppose.*

And that's when I said the BMW wasn't actually mine—which I figured I could, since it wasn't and it won't be, even though I'm driving it now. And conversation two became about that.

No, I wasn't the MLB on the vanity plates. I kind of inherited the car when some things got sorted out. There's a gray Corolla at home. Which I actually own. I just can't see any reason to add distance to its odometer until the lease runs out on this one and I hand it back. And the gray Corolla's got regular plates.

How I came to be explaining this in any detail at all to someone I'd never met, I don't know, but that's what made me late for work. A student who'd found the falling-down house she was to live in and didn't want to face it, and wanted to talk about anything else instead. And the inexplicable lie she thought she was being told about car ownership was simply the first topic going.

And no, MLB doesn't want the car back, or the plates. Vanity plates are so . . . eighties. Anyway, I think she got them as a twenty-first present from a bunch of people she'd stopped liking by her twenty-second. Something like that. Something very MLB.

That's what I told her. And then I said I thought she must have a lot to unpack and I was going to be late for work if I wasn't careful. I wished her luck with the house, as though that's a thing you do with houses, and as though her luck with the house hadn't already declared itself to be bad, and I got into the car.

Got in and drove without stopping to arrange the towel on the seat first, in the way that I usually do. Drove and sweated right into the BMW upholstery and took the first corner faster than I meant to, while pushing the Lemonheads CD into the player. Getting my head into work, singing along and wondering why the Lemonheads fell out of my brain the moment my feet hit asphalt. I would have felt quite good about myself, running with the Lemonheads going through my mind.

And the running's easier now, much easier than it was when I started months ago. I pass more people than pass me now. I get the chance to be amazed at just how slowly some people can run. Not that the fast people aren't still way out of my league, and that won't change. But it doesn't have to. That's not what this is about. I'm fitter. I've never been this fit. That's good. It's enough. This is about fitness.

So it's important to make time for it. Around the baby things, around work. And it's enough that I have to try to make time for all that, without getting into conversations about liscense plates, or whatever. Useless attempts to offer some kind of reassurance to someone whose luck you can't change.

It's strange. That was probably the first time in months that I've had a conversation with someone I don't know, other than a patient or one of the day-care people. And that seems like it should be a bad thing—keeping to your own small world to that degree—but why should it? It's having a baby around, partly. It changes things, particularly how you spend your time.

Sylvia's at my door again, wondering what's got into me today, but making her point with nothing more vocal than raised eyebrows. But they make it clearly enough. I'm well used to interpreting her eyebrows now. Not that there's anything subtle about them. They're a pretty fiendish pair of eyebrows, but that's Sylvia. From certain angles she looks a little like Robin Williams in *Mrs. Doubtfire*. From other angles she looks more like the regular Robin Williams, but with a well-tended bun and, fortunately, less arm hair. She's fifty-something, and treats us all like children who aren't quite behaving. Particularly George, who gave her the job in the first place. It's a system that works better than I might have expected.

Sorry, yeah, I'm ready, I tell her. Let's have him. Her.

Her. The name's on the file. Like the others.

I've seen my twelve o'clock patient before.

It's not getting lighter, his mother says, about the red lump of a strawberry nevus on his forehead just above his nose. *And I've thought about it, and I'd really like to do something before he starts school.*

I take the photo from last year out of his file, and we compare. I go around to their side of the table and crouch down next to Tom. I hold a mirror up to let him see his lesion, and I hold the photo next to it.

Okay, I tell him, what we hoped was going to happen was that this would just start to fade away. And then we wouldn't do anything. But it doesn't look like it's going to, does it? So we can do something to make it go away. How does that sound?

Tom looks far from convinced.

Remember? his mother says. *Remember what we talked about if you promise to do everything the doctor tells you?*

McDonald's? Suddenly things look up. *Okay.*

So we can make it go away?

Yeah.

Good. Well, I'd better tell you how we're going to do that. And it's pretty clever, and it should all go fine. First—and this is the funny bit—I'm going to put a sticker on your head.

A sticker?

Yeah. I'm going to squirt something on there, then put a sticker on. And we'll leave that there for a little while, then when you come back and I take the sticker off, it'll be numb. Do you know what numb is? Numb is when you can't feel anything. So I can fiddle around with the lump, and you won't feel it. And you just have to lie really still for a little while, then it'll all be done. And we might have to get you back a couple more times to do that all again to make sure it's finished. But all you have to do each time is stay still. Sound okay?

Yeah.

And how does it sound to you? I ask his mother. Can we get you back in an hour or two, once the local's taken effect? What I want to do is use some local anesthetic cream, rather than anything that might be uncomfortable.

That sounds good. And coming back would be fine. We go into the treatment room for me to put the local on and she says, *How's your baby? You were going to have a baby not long after we were here last time.*

She's fine. She's really good, actually. A lot of fun. A lot of work too, but a lot of fun. She's six months now.

What's her name?

Lily.

That's a nice name. You should have a photo on your desk. You and your wife and Lily.

Yeah. I keep thinking I should take more photos of her. She's only this old once, I guess.

The first thing I do at lunchtime is call my mother. I ask her how Lily is and she says, *We've been having fun. Lots of rolling round, some sucking of feet.*

I think that started a couple of days ago.

Could be teething.

Do you think so? She seems pretty calm, most of the time.

She is six months.

Yeah, I know. And that's kind of hard to believe, isn't it?

George sticks his head around the door and tells me lunch is here.

There was a time when Lily would almost fit on my hand. It wasn't long ago, but now that it's gone it almost seems like something I've made up.

Salad roll, large, George says, when I get around to the lunch room, and he throws it to me like a quarterback.

Would you treat your own lunch that way, Porge?

Would it ever be a salad roll, large? They GladWrap them good and tight, Jon Boy, just for throwing. George has three pies in front of him. He picks one up, takes a bite, and through a full mouth says, *Lentils,* as though he's therefore got the healthy food pyramid totally under control.

Wendy comes in and takes the other salad roll (small) without having to demonstrate her catching prowess. She sees me as a convert to the salad roll now, though all it actually shows on my part is a lack of imagination. I decided a while back that I could do better than cheap Chinese and sloppy lasagne, and suddenly I was a regular with the salad roll (large) simply because I hadn't given lunch enough thought to come up with two healthy options. And it's such a retro-feeling choice.

Oscar claims the last pie—the other lentil pie—and starts on it carefully with a knife and fork. Despite having seen him eat plenty of times, it can be hard not to notice his neatness as he goes about it. Particularly when he's sitting next to George, who treats each pie like a mortal enemy and attacks. It's like eating in a Hall of Mirrors— each of them embarking on the same process, but one of them turning it minute and the other enormous. Wendy knows it, I know it, and they don't.

Oscar lives at George's place and they always split the take-out bills evenly, since each of them gets a whole meal from his portion. Two satay sticks would do Oscar most nights, but it really is as though they haven't noticed the disparity. Oscar is the definition of compact, the last person I know to wear panther-print Bata Scout school shoes. He got so annoyed when they stopped putting the compass in the heel—when he was in his twenties—that my father made him write to the company and complain. *There's a lot you can do with a compass, lad,* I think my father said, backing him up. Not that any of us could ever think of a second thing you could do with a compass. But I think the letter scored Oscar a free pair of compassed shoes that someone found in the warehouse. They wouldn't reverse their decision, though.

Today, mid-pie, he says, *Hey, check this out,* and takes a very small phone from one of his pockets. *Pretty cool.*

Oh god, you've gone and bought it, George says in an exaggerated groan. *I knew you would. Why couldn't you get one the size of a phone? Nanotech as virility symbol, episode sixty-four. A definite step beyond the big car for the small-penised man.*

Hey, I'm a small man. A small phone works for me. It's a simple matter of scale. Nothing to do with my penis. And, anyway, look at me. I weigh 106 pounds. I wear schoolboy-size pants. Who's going to look at me and think there's a big penis?

Come on. George has got a point, I say, deciding to take him on. You weren't offering it that way. You were being size-ist again. Going down that "small is sexy" track. And how does that phone work style-wise for the guys who fight out of the flyweight division?

Medium-to-large guys, for instance, George specifies.

Or large guys who used to be medium.

Without making this personal.

Hey, you were never medium, Porge, Oscar says.

This is the phone equivalent of the small, sleek, throbbing red sports car that's all engine. And I can't get one butt cheek into those. This is what I'm saying. You're turning small and sleek and intricate into something desirable, and where's the room for the big simple people in your new millennium? The people whose hands work best with a house-brick-size phone, who biologically need the Landcruiser-equivalent vehicle.

You big guys have had it your way too long.

And can I get a date anymore? I'm emasculated by this. This phone, George says, taking it between thumb and forefinger, *this is the new millennium penis. The "wow" penis. That's what it's about. Wow factor. And big things don't have it. Big is passé now. It's all about neat little things with flair, presentation, cutting-edge applications.*

What, the penis that's also a corkscrew and nail clippers?

No, that sounds like the Swiss-army penis. And those applications, while they broaden the scope of the instrument, aren't exactly cutting edge. Maybe I'm thinking more about slinky contours, a funky range of colors.

Yeah, that'd be it, Wendy says. *A funky range of colors'd be enough for me. That'd fix all the design flaws. How about we vote for penises in all colors and move onto the next agenda item? I think improving the penis is probably beyond us since, for a start, you'd have to try attaching it to some kind of brain. It does usually operate without much input from the cranial one.*

You don't mean Steve? George begins.

No, Steve's the exception. Now that he's trained. I'm talking generally. The people who think their idea of—what was it—flair? Who think that flair is some substitute for a second's consideration. And if it turns out that it's not biologically possible to attach the penis to a thinking body part, some delaying device would be okay. A warning signal even, so you knew there was, like, a minute to go.

Or a seven-second delay, like live radio.

Now there's a very male time frame. Why does it so often get treated like speed reading? It's not better if it's faster. That only means you get to roll over and sleep sooner. And how do you think it is for women, reaching their prime at thirty-five when you reach yours at eighteen? You were all appalling when you were eighteen. No reasonable woman went near any of you.

As opposed to now, you mean? George says.

Wendy stops, looks at us and laughs. *Good point. Nice phone, Oscar. That's what I meant to say.*

Thanks, Wend.

So we begin our meeting. The four of us. Three of us associates in LaserWest, Oscar the hired-hand part-timer. It's a Wendy MBA strategy, regular meetings. Not that you need a degree to see the sense in it but, since Wendy's the one with the MBA, it's the kind of policy she gets to set.

Today, she talks through budgets and billing, how much we're spending on disposables, patient numbers, which have been down a little for this month and the last, exactly as anticipated with Christmas and the holidays.

But it's at least as busy as this time last year, she says, *which means it should be busier over the next couple of months. So it's probably time to be looking seriously at getting another dermatologist in to take some of the load from George. What do people think about that?*

She looks at me, and I nod.

Yeah.

It's easy to agree with. The numbers show we'll need someone else, and with George the only one of us who's a specialist dermatologist (and referral patterns as they are), it's another dermatologist we need. But I'm tired today and I can't concentrate, and I'm looking past Wendy's head and out the window. So I agree and I tell her I'm happy if she starts asking around, and I leave it at that. It's still hot outside, from the look of it, and the window tint makes the sky a deeper blue. Lily didn't sleep so well last night, and she's on my mind today.

When the meeting is closing it's as though Wendy's aware of that, and she says to me, *Day care's back on for tomorrow. The runny-nose emergency is over.* As though it's the last item of business.

Then she and George have their two o'clock patients to see and I have Nigel telling me, *The strawberry nevus from this morning's back and ready to go.*

After work I go to Coles supermarket. At the start of the day I was carrying a list of things to buy, but it's elsewhere now. And when I lose my list I usually buy toilet paper, just to be sure. Sometimes I end up with an awful lot of toilet paper that way, but I never run out.

But I usually buy Designer Collection gray, which seems to be absent today. So I stand there, thinking about the cupboard under the bathroom sink. Trying to visualize it, to put a picture in my mind of its stock levels. Meanwhile, singing along to 10CC's "The Things We Do for Love" on the Muzak, and only becoming aware of it a couple of verses in.

Can I help you, sir? a woman's voice says next to me, just as I realize I'm putting in a significant subconscious effort to portray a mad bastard, standing quietly singing a seventies hit to an empty toilet-paper shelf.

Yeah, I can't see the Designer Collection gray, I tell her as I turn, figuring that the singing's made it too late for dignity already and I might as well not hide my toilet-paper preference from the Coles staff.

Designer Collection gray? Toilet paper has names like that? the student from this morning's run says, smirking at me, and then deciding what the hell, why not laugh?

Maybe.

She laughs again. If it wasn't at me, I think we'd both be having fun here.

You have to put thought into toilet paper, I tell her. You don't just pull off a six pack without slowing down on your way past, you know. And, if you'd seen my bathroom, you'd understand why it had to be Designer Collection gray. This peach, for instance, it'd send out all the wrong signals, design-wise.

Really?

Yeah. See?

I point to the package.

This bit here. "Complement your bathroom," it says. Peach would be a radical departure for me.

You read toilet-paper packaging? She takes it from me. *Hey, it also says, "Try the unexpected and be adventurous. Use*

*colors and objects not commonly found in bathrooms." What's
that about?*

I don't want to know. I'm happy to go no further than
point one—complement your bathroom. But it's possible
that I could be a creature of habit. People might have said
that once or twice.

So, is the running a habit too?

Yeah. It'd happen most mornings.

*I might see you out there. I run a bit myself. I'm Ash, by
the way. Ashley.*

I'm Jon.

And I've never met anyone while standing next to this
much toilet paper before. Maybe that's what suddenly
makes me feel awkward and wonder what I'm doing here.
Standing with this student who must think I'm at least
eccentric, hung up on very specific toilet paper and singing
to the shelf when the toilet paper isn't there. I'm not sure
what to do, where to look, where I should look at a time
like this.

So I look down into her shopping cart and I find myself
saying, No one can eat that much sour cream . . . as though
it's any of my business at all.

I've really lost it this evening.

It's those months without meeting new people. That's
what I put it down to afterward. After Ash has emphat-
ically told me sour cream goes with anything. After she
has asked my advice as to whether she should buy toilet
paper based on complementing the peeling paint on the
wall or the dark fungus on the ceiling. After she has
thrown a six pack of peach into my cart and told me,

Vibrant and contrasting—you'll thank me for it, and we've both suddenly realized we don't actually know each other, and reeled off in opposite directions. And then, I suspect, scuttled up and down the aisles, doing our utmost to stay well apart.

I should concentrate so much more when I'm out. You change the way you operate when you're the only adult in a house with a six-month-old child, and I should remember to change back to my previous well-monitored self in public. It's a critical age for communication—I have a book that says that—so you find yourself verbalizing any thought that comes into your head, so that she gets to learn what words are about. You wander around the house talking about trees and birds and dog hair. About putting that dirty plate in the dishwasher. About tucking your own shirt in. All without any inhibitions.

You find yourself singing a lot, because all your life you wouldn't have minded singing a lot but you were so obviously crap at it that you didn't, and finally you've met someone who's far too young to know. So it's Lily's fault, all this. I have no qualms about scapegoating an infant.

And my workmates have adjusted to the fact that I almost always tell them when I'm going to the toilet now, and I try very hard not to get into the specifics of the trip. There are too many diapers in my life, and that and too much unmonitored commentating make for a dangerous combination. Somehow Wendy seems to have gone through this with two children and hardly blurred things at all. She's obviously better with boundaries than I am. There have been a couple of times when I've pulled up not more than a microsecond before telling Sylvia, when she's trying to thrust a patient on me, Hang on, I've just got to go and do a poo.

Things, therefore, could actually have been worse in Coles. Sometimes, in fact, they are worse in Coles. One of the checkout people is called Eileen, and what chance have I got of avoiding at least humming the only big hit of Dexy's Midnight Runners as I'm unloading my groceries onto her conveyor belt? Sometimes I start to hear words muttering tunelessly out of me before I realize what I'm doing. And she looks at me. She knows I'm doing it. I'm sure of it. So I avoid her line entirely now, even though she's a pretty slick operator.

When I park at my parents' place and open the car door, the heat slurps in and shows me the kind of day I've missed while I've been in air-conditioning.

Just having a sleep, my mother says. *So I'll make us some tea.*

I go into the bedroom to take a look at Lily while the kettle's boiling, and she's curling and uncurling her fingers as though, somewhere off in a dream, she's doing something purposeful. Explaining the double-helix shape of a DNA molecule to someone, something like that. *No, Watson, no. It goes like this.*

Then my mother's next to me, with a pot and two cups and a plate of mixed biscuits on a tray. We go back to the den, and through my father's study door I can see his computer toiling away, its cursor having been set off in the morning on another chase around the Mandelbrot set, or whatever. Programmed to do something shapely and mathematical, so that when he finishes work and gets home at the end of the day there's something new on the screen. Now there's a man who knows how to live.

And it's not as though it has anything to do with his job. Management consultants simply have no need for recreational mathematics. He's even happy to call it a hobby, though that only makes other people think it stranger. I'm sick of telling him to stop bombarding people with his Jim's Fractal Gallery home-page address. And I wish Oscar hadn't once sent him a polite e-mail in reply, but he wasn't to know that my father would call it fan mail and take it as encouragement.

I think it started with an interest in chaos theory, years ago—when chaos theory was a concept still owned by mathematicians—but with improvements in technology it's got way out of hand.

Of course, he said, a couple of months back when displaying that day's screen marvel, *now chaos theory's just some advertising term. Gives you better air-conditioning, and the like. What are they going to grab hold of next and turn into a buzzword? The Feigenbaum period-doubling cascade?*

Which only demonstrates that my father, for all his science and surprising Fractal Gallery marketing flare, doesn't have much of a grasp of advertising, and doesn't realize what it is about buzzwords that appeals. That it's the simple juxtaposition of two paradoxical but normal words that sells. "Chaos" and "theory." Fuzzy and logic. And the notion that there might truly be science that creates the buzz (however insurmountable the science might be for the everyday non-postgrad brain). And Feigenbaum won't get a look in. Heisenberg never quite fired the public imagination with his uncertainty principle—despite following the paired paradox rule and combining it with a

solid German boffinesque name—so no way does Feigenbaum stand a chance.

*So, any idea what's happening with the day-care place to-
morrow?* my mother asks me.

Oh, yeah, didn't I tell you? Wendy said things are okay
now, apparently. So everyone can go back tomorrow.

Lily, like her father, is a creature of routine. Except I
get to decide the routines for both of us, at least in principle. Monday and Tuesday she spends half the day with
my mother (and sometimes my father) and half with me.
Wednesday, Thursday and mornings on Friday she's at
day care. Wendy's daughter Emily goes there too, and it's
through that connection that Lily got in. It's small, it's
expensive, it's unduly cautious when there's anything viral
about, but she seems happy there, and that matters more
than most things.

By the time I check on Lily again, she's awake and
being quietly amazed by her own hand. It's as if she's
trying to work out whether she's controlling it or not. Or
maybe it's some wriggly pink thing someone else left there.
She flaps it around, sees me, says, *Haaa,* as though I'm
something worth sighing about.

Hey, Bean, I say to her, using the name George gave
her when she was a day old and he was the first to comment on her kidney-bean-shaped head. I pick her up and
give her a bit of a toss in the air and she laughs in her
gurgly, drunk-person-drowning kind of way. A glob of
cheery drool swings down onto my right cheek.

Fortunately her head is much less kidney-bean-like than
it was. The birth canal is merciless when it comes to head
shape, so it's lucky babies' skulls are designed to take it.

But I think it meant that George (himself morphologically many sizes above conventional beauty) took to her the first time he saw her, and he bought her a series of toys with affirming strange-shaped heads during her first week. But he couldn't let go of the name, so it's stuck. I even tried to put him off by telling him he was just copying Kurt Cobain and Courtney Love, but he said, *They were basing it on ultrasound, and have you noticed the special temporary shape of your lovely daughter's head?*

In the car on the way home we play the Lemonheads. I sing. The baby book didn't specify that I should sing the Lemonheads' "Into Your Arms," but it didn't specify anything else, either, and I'm planning to dodge nursery rhymes as long as I can. The Bean flaps around, grabbing handfuls of air. I'm going to assume that's appreciation.

I'd get a toy out of your bag, I tell her, but I'm driving. So the best I can do is sing. You can join in any time, by the way.

Blah blah blah. I talk about our evening, walking the dog, mashed pumpkin.

Mashed pumpki-i-in, I sing, to the irresistible phrasing of "Into Your Arms." I know a place where I can go eat mashed pumpkin.

On to the weather, my day at work, how we both like having a bit of a drive around in the car, the coincidence of meeting that student twice in one day. But she had to buy groceries, I suppose. It's not that improbable that she'd find herself late afternoon in the nearest supermarket.

Let's talk about the word "coincidence." Have we done that one before?

As soon as I open the car door at home I can hear Elvis

approaching, the click-click of hard whippet toenails on the concrete under the house. It's too hot for him to jump around today with the usual small-brained glee that comes with us arriving home, so he gives me a stare instead, and I try not to misinterpret it as meaningful.

It's something, I think, that he learned from my father, who has a great capacity for the apparently meaningful stare. He's an indisputably clever man and there are times when the stare really does mean he's deep in thought, but once at a wedding he broke from a very meaningful twenty-minute gaze to say only, *I'm sure those two women are related, because they have identical teeth.* But he could just as easily have come out with something about number theory. As far as I know the same can't be said for Elvis, but they're both prone to keeping things internal.

I take Lily in one arm and her voluminous baby bag in the other and we all go inside, to room after room of stifling, closed-in heat. I get the fans going and the windows open, and the evening rituals start. Elvis asking for Bonios in his big grumbly feed-me voice. Jumping, begging shamelessly, saying something that sounds very like Bonio, nudging at the container with his nose. Me sounding him out first to see if he'd prefer a cheeseburger, the way I do every night. Running the whole routine and making him progressively more excited so that, when it comes, the Bonio's like a gold ingot and he clunks it into his mouth and jogs off somewhere to hide it. Then I can move on to a few slow spoonfuls of apple puree for the Bean, followed by an attempt at the last bottle of formula in the fridge.

We sit on the back veranda, since it's less hot, but that

doesn't seem to help much. Despite all my friendly talk and the attention I draw to the lorikeets in the trees, Lily's not in a great mood for feeding.

See the birds. Look at the colors.

Thanks, but no thanks.

We walk. I push her in a stroller and Elvis trots along beside us, stopping to sniff at weeds other dogs have marked, sometimes giving them a squirt of his own signal. I have a sense that he has some map of the world in his mind, his world, a small, insular medieval kind of world with an absolute perimeter and these pheromonal sign-posts along the way. A smaller world than mine, even.

Later, Lily seems a little more contented in the bath, but maybe it's her first chance in a while to get cool. We get involved in a game that has me whipping up a current and sailing several plastic ships around her, but somehow I end up singing 10CC's "The Things We Do for Love" again, just when I should be singing Nick Cave. Damn that muzak. She gives a red tugboat a joyful whack that splashes us both, then picks it up and gnaws on its funnel.

I think we'll dress light, I tell her afterward. Even though we're having company, it's far from formal.

George and Oscar come over with Thai take-out. It's a pretty regular Wednesday night thing, eating at each other's houses. It started a few months ago, and I think it began with a misunderstanding of Wendy's. There's a par-ticular Wednesday night each month when she goes to a book club, and on one of them George and Oscar and I happened to plan to get together for take-out on the same night. Either she wasn't concentrating or she misheard something, but she referred to it as *your book club*. So now we do it regularly and that's what it seems to be called. No books, though. George told Wendy we like the modern classics. So much, in fact, that we get together nearly every Wednesday. He said he asked her if her book club had done much Proust yet, and told her, *He kept us going for weeks.*

I start serving the food, since George and Oscar want to have a play with the Bean.

Don't get her too worked up, I tell them, or she'll never sleep.

And George says, *Nag, bloody nag. That's all I ever hear from you,* and he throws her in the air again, until I tell him to watch out for the fan.

Hours after they've gone, the Bean still isn't settling. I'd quite like to blame George, but it's probably the heat. I mix formula with robotic non-enthusiasm. Another day draws to a close.

In med school, I wouldn't have picked that the three of us would be doing this in our mid-thirties, being single and sharing take-out together. I thought we'd all be married, settled down with the next generation made and growing. It's as if school synchronised our lives by giving us exams together twice a year and I thought they'd stay synchronised, and just as predictable. But we've each found our own way to LaserWest and Wednesday night take-out and the lives we lead, and the overlaps aren't the obvious ones. Thai food, for example, rather than having children who play together on weekends.

I'm surprised that I had such a rigid view of the world. Surprised that it didn't cross my mind that Oscar was gay until he told me. That I didn't realize George might find himself simply going out with no one, and structuring his whole life around the expectation that that's how things'll be. And then deciding, since he's got that sorted out, that there's probably plenty of advice he can give other people about their lives.

What am I supposed to do? Get a hobby? I found myself saying to him tonight to shut him up. My guess is that all the good stamps have been collected by now.

But I'm being harsh. He's actually not that bad. So I'm glad I didn't keep going and tell him I was years away from a genuine understanding of the Feigenbaum period-doubling cascade, or even a passing interest in any of the other things people I know call hobbies. And, as Wendy once explained to me, *Advice is a guy way of letting someone know you care.* Maybe.

There's still fussing from Lily's room, so I get her out of her crib to see if I can settle her down. We lie on the sofa with the fan on above us, the voices of the late news talking in the background and her heavy head on my chest. She's making snuffling noises, checking, checking, looking up at me to ensure all's well. Without meaning to I start singing and she looks at me again, her big blue eyes somehow reassured, dopey, diverging as her sweaty head thumps down on my sternum, and she's asleep.

It's ridiculous that I once thought my medical degree meant that I understood something about babies. I now know that it prepares you well for everything except the ninety-nine percent of the time that they don't have an actual disease. As a med student I became the slickest in my rotation group at checking for congenital dislocation of the hip. And that's handy. On each baby, once. It doesn't count for much as a day-to-day management skill.

Now she's quiet, I put her to bed again.

You're okay, I tell her, in that reassuring voice that comes in just above a whisper. You can sleep now. Great hips, by the way.

I go to bed myself, and Elvis begins his usual routine of restless sleep alternating with night patrol. Shuttling between my room and the Bean's to keep a check on both of us. Folding and unfolding his bony limbs down at the end of my bed, until he's arranged like a collapsed director's chair across my feet. Nudging Bonios into any available armpit with his long nose, knowing they'll be safe there. Occasionally he posts them through the bars of the Bean's crib. Sometimes she finds them and I'll walk in there in the morning and she'll be clutching a Bonio in both hands, like a dense, wheaty dance partner, her hands on its hips. Sometimes gumming away at it with her mouth, drooling all over its head.

Tonight we don't get that far. The fussing starts again, and I want her to be years older and amenable to reason. Decades older and off somewhere, having a great grown-up time and hopefully not feeling the need to cry at night at all. Not a minute older, just the age she is now, but taking things slowly, peacefully, and sleeping when it's time to.

Please, please sleep, I say aloud as I lie there, willing her to stop the noise. Please.

She doesn't.

———

We don't have many nights like this. That's what I tell myself while we're out in the car, driving around the dark suburbs in the early hours. Driving—the rhythm of it—is usually good for putting Lily to sleep.

Driving, the cool of the car air-conditioning and me singing doggedly along to the Lemonheads. What more could a girl want? I ask her between tracks.

Eventually it works, or something does. She tires of the upset and sleeps, and I can put my fears of a drastic un-diagnosed disease aside once I see her back in the crib and calm. I lie on my bed, listening to every breath on the monitor.

Then it's dawn, and the light surprises me, shocks me into realizing I've slept for a couple of hours.

She's still snuffling. I can hear her, asleep and breathing. Maybe even dreaming. It's all okay.

2

Teething, Oscar says confidently, after giving her the once-over. *See that little incisor about to come through?*

Just teething?

A life-threatening meningitis would be quite a way down the list, he says, thereby inviting me to shut up and trust him. *It's a long time since you've done the general stuff, hey? Haven't you even read one of those books? You know, one of those groovy best-sellers written by some cuddly pediatrician with a British accent.*

Yeah, I've got one of those. I just . . .

Teething. Despite any recent articles that might doubt the syndrome, that's what I'd call it. There's certainly no evidence of anything else. She'll be fine. You know what to do for teething?

Yeah. I'm not sure about taking her to day care now, though. You know how paranoid they get about the possibility of anything being contagious.

So much for my professional credibility.

It's Sylvia who suggests keeping her at work, and takes her from me as I fetch the port-a-crib from the car and battle with it in the filing room.

We'll be all right, she says. *And soon that nasty tooth'll be through and everything will be fine. And we'll be back to being lovely with everyone again.*

I go into my room, press my terminal's Start button, and the Window Weasel appears again.

Hi, Jon. Your trial period was up yesterday and you haven't registered yet, but we're sure this is just an oversight. We hope you're enjoying your Window Weasel software. Click YES!! I LOVE MY WEASEL!! and you can register to use Window Weasel for life for only $30! Click LATER to register later.

If the weasel loved me back it would have helped out with Lily last night. I click LATER.

I pick up my e-mails. The first two are joke forwards from George. A list of forty things that show you aren't drinking enough coffee. Another called "Does a Bear Shit in the Woods????" that I leave unopened, and that sits on my priority list somewhere below gratifying the weasel. Would the bear shitting in the woods be any less hilarious if it had only one question mark, instead of four?

There's also one from Wendy's sister Katie, a reply to one of mine from a couple of days ago called "On the versatility of the wok," in which I suggested that my new wok-based approach was the ideal way to a low-risk, smoke-free risotto:

> that if I leave something alone it solders itself to what-
> ever it's cooking in. So one of my main strategies is to
> keep things moving. That way you see your mistakes
> good and early. And something with the elbow room of

> a wok makes it all much easier. It breaks all the rules,
> but we get to hear the smoke alarms a lot less this way.

Jon,
To be frank, I hardly see the versatility at all. What is it
with men and this attachment to woks? Master one tool, and
you think the kitchen's yours. I bet you think you can give
advice about everything that goes on in there. When you bake
a cake in your wok, save a piece for me.

And, hey, I think you told me once work keeps you pretty
busy, but W tells me you're prone to slacking off. Or maybe
business has slacked off at the moment. One or the other.
Anyway, I do sessions out your way sometimes. We should
have coffee, or something.

Slacking off . . . This deserves a quick reply.

Katie,
The wok is the Sensitive New Age Barbecue. Things are way
better than they used to be. There was a time when men could
only club stuff, then burn it. And that was only a few years
ago. I can't claim the wok does EVERYTHING, but since it
easily extends to balti curries, noodle dishes and now risotto,
what else could you need?

But coffee could be good. I'm actually a very busy man, but
I try to do coffee semi-regularly. Can't devote all our time
to the service of others, can we? And I thought you learned
not to listen to W back when we were all much younger than
this.

That should do it. A final defense of wok mastery, an invisible lie about going out for coffee. Half-lie—I only claimed semi-regularly. But why shouldn't I go out for coffee? It's a thing people do.

Sylvia's in my doorway, saying, *You're all playing today. George is sitting next door with jokes coming in from all over the world, he tells me.*

And they're all going to be bad, aren't they? That's the tragedy of cyberspace. That so much can travel so far and yet mean so little.

Your first patient's here. When you get the chance.

Thanks.

I read through the e-mail once more, click Send and it flies off to Kate. Or, to be more specific, to ktnflag—a username I haven't yet decoded. Why do people get fancy with these things? What would have been wrong with something more obvious, like katiewatts?

This exchange with Katie began a couple of weeks ago, after we'd talked at a barbecue at Wendy's place. I've met her on and off for years, usually at things at Wendy's place, and she's never been particularly animated. More the kind of person you get used to saying "Hi" to at kids' birthdays, while you're both fumbling a piece of brightly colored cake around a paper plate.

E-mail seems to suit her better, which is something I hadn't expected. It seems too contemporary, for a start. Katie, we suspect, has a peculiar thing for the eighties. Which is partly about music, but mainly about hair. The music we can go with (just), but Katie has eighties hair and, as the years go by, it looks more and more wrong, and like something that could hold her back in life. It's like the hair Meg Ryan had in one of the early parts of *When Harry Met Sally,* except of course it'd now be the hair from the movie *When Harry Met No-one Because the Only Single Woman at the Party Had Eighties Hair.*

Oh god, as if I'd know why, Wendy said, when I once made a subtle attempt to put the words "Katie" and "hair" in the same sentence. *And as if I could ask her. I think she thinks it's okay.*

Katie and Wendy's relationship hasn't always been easy, but I think they've settled better into being sisters now that they're both in their thirties. And part of that, perhaps, is knowing the questions you never ask.

Katie's three years younger, and Wendy used to treat her as a bit of a hanger-on. Which I don't think she was. That might have started at school—their relationship low point, apparently—back when Wendy was being a prefect and her fanatical ability to juggle many things with competence was starting to emerge. And Katie was being a rather clumsy fourteen and spending most of the time with Band-Aids on her knees and her hair maddeningly out of control, and the unwelcome challenge of dealing with a rather insensitive older sister who decided it would be fun to call her Mess. Something Wendy only gave up when Katie was in her mid-twenties, and the name came to reflect her life more than it did her appearance. They were going through their last bad patch when Katie got her PhD in clinical psychology. Apparently Wendy's first response to the news was, *I can't believe how old I must be. How terrifying.* Wendy got her MBA not long after and Katie apparently said to her, *I can't believe how old*

you must be, and told their parents there'd be no congrat-
ulations unless there was an apology first.

But a second child (Wendy's) and a couple more relationship disasters (Katie's) down the track, things seem
much better. Wendy still claims the big-sister turf, but
more benevolently. I think she's more protective than Katie would like sometimes, but she's like that with everyone
unless they stop her. She's certainly like it with me. And
I haven't worked out how to stop her yet.

At school she had several years when she got to be sad
that no one seemed to want to go out with me, and she
was around to cushion the blow just about every time.
And you reach a stage when you need to move away from
friends like that, but some of them just track you down.

So what chance did Katie have? Maybe it's no surprise
she resorts to text-based conversation, and conducts it
away from Wendy's view.

The part I still don't get about it is her e-mail address
and, after a quick and unrewarding check for e-mails, it's
the bit I'm still trying to work out when Wendy comes
into the kitchen at lunchtime.

Katie's e-mail address, I say to her, figuring I might as
well ask. The ktnflag part, what's that about? Is it to do
with someone she works for?

No, she's in private practice.

That's what I thought.

Wendy flicks her tea bag into the trash. *Say it carefully
and you get it. K T N flag, Katie and Flag. Flag is her cat.*

Flag. As in bit of cloth up a pole.

I did tell her it already stood for something.

Why Flag?

To which Katie's answer is, why not? But forget that for a second. Have you noticed they're sharing an e-mail address?

I think I was trying not to.

She shakes her head. *How is she going to turn things around when she does things like that?*

She's not a football team having a bad season.

Really? You think Katie's okay? she says, missing the point.

Sure. There's nothing wrong with Katie, I tell her, but only because Wendy's her sister and I know the lines you just don't cross. Maybe she's not looking for a guy, or human partner. Maybe she's got things just the way she wants them. Anyway, I thought there was some guy . . .

There always was some guy. There rarely is a guy. The guys don't last. It's the post-guy grieving periods that have the staying power. The last guy was months ago, and she's back at that sworn-off-men-for-life stage again. You know that stage, that goes right up until she meets the next one? And then she zeroes in like a kamikaze pilot. She stalls then, re- alizing she's said too much. She stirs her tea.

It's all right. She bags the shit out of you in e-mails.

Yeah. I never said kamikaze pilot, okay?

Come on. I've been one myself. I think we both know that.

Shit, Jon. Ages ago. Back in the eighties. Mid-eighties, even.

Back when Katie . . . was too young to do herself that kind of harm, I manage to say, realizing just in time that "Back when Katie got the hair" wasn't the way to go.

Hmmm. I think she might be lining herself up for it again.

Just from something she said a couple of days ago, I think her radar's picked up something on the horizon. And why is it that that worries me? Why do I assume the next one's going to treat her badly? There must be some okay guys out there. And Katie, in her own way, is quite a catch.

Sure.

It's just going to take the right guy.

You could say that with more conviction.

K T N Flag. Katie is one of the smartest people I know, and she and a cat have gone halves in an e-mail address. He's holding her back, Jon.

It sounds like you think she should drop him.

Better off without him, I reckon. She spends far too much of her time talking cat talk. But you never heard that from me. Anyway, I'm notoriously anti-cat, apparently, so, you know . . . Katie's okay though, really? Isn't she? You're a guy. She's okay, isn't she?

Sure.

I press the plunger, pour my coffee. And I'm most of the way to the door before Wendy says, *Bags the shit out of me in e-mails? What do you mean she bags the shit out of me in e-mails?*

3

Thursday night, with the teething-relief measures in place, goes better. Lily sleeps, I sleep, and we're the first at day care. All back to normal.

Which means a run. I park in the usual place, and I notice that the student's red Pulsar is in the driveway of number 176 and one of the windows of the house is open—probably a bedroom window, from the look of the curtain that's hanging out of it.

The student. I've forgotten her name already, and I think I'm only assuming she's a student. Did she ever tell me?

Her name was a noun—like Flag—that much I remember. Started with an A.

Ash. That was it. As in short for Ashley, I suppose. I suppose, or was that something she did tell me? She told me. There by the space marked Designer Collection gray.

It takes about two miles to work this out, most of my three-mile lap around the college campus, running unattractively in time to a jumble of 10CC songs. By the end of it I can see her saying it, saying her name. I can see neat teeth that I didn't look at, blue eyes that I've borrowed from someone somewhere. She's starting to look like someone on TV. Standing next to her car. Standing in Coles with all that sour cream. Standing in a film clip in a half-empty house, looking straight at the camera and singing. By the three mile mark I have no idea what she looks like, but I can visualize a substitute version of her perfectly, dressed to pack things in boxes, standing there with the studio lighting glistening from her lower lip as she offers me guacamole in a rather disconsolate way. As though she has now lost heart when it comes to her theory on the universal applicability of sour cream.

Most of this, definitely, is from TV, from watching late-night music shows during the Bean's restless times. With the probable exception of the guacamole.

I finish my campus lap and move onto the part of my run that is in my mind as "the street circuit," as though I'm a Formula One car. But my mind is idling along again, wondering if the Bean's tooth will come through today, wondering if there's anything I'm supposed to do or change when it does come through. Wondering if Katie has no idea that Meg Ryan's hair is now pretty good, and that Katie's version was already from another era when they made *When Harry Met Sally.*

Wondering what Ash the student is doing today, as I approach her house. And she runs past me. She waves without turning round, and keeps going until she gets to my car.

You were being smart and warming down, weren't you? she says when I get there, and I notice that her tank top says "Gold Coast Half-marathon Finisher."

Not that I'm aware of.

I get a bit competitive when I see someone ahead of me.

Sure. I pass people sometimes. I know what you mean.

I bet you do.

Of course, some of them get a bit pissed off and take a swipe at me with their walker, but . . .

She laughs, puts her foot up on her fence and does a hamstring stretch. She stretches with such ease that she's probably one of those people who never really needs to. She takes her foot in both hands and leans forward till her head touches her knee. Which means I don't stretch today, since I'm not one of those people. It'd be a mistake to mention walkers and then struggle my way to my best quarter-hamstring stretch in front of her. But I've never been flexible. In fact, I'm better than I used to be. I've tested myself, and I've gone from "poor" to "below average" with all my work over the last few months. But I think that's still something to keep to myself.

She stretches the other side and says, *Where were you yesterday? Did you run?*

No. It didn't work out yesterday.

And her teeth aren't quite as neat as I'd imagined in the film-clip version of her, but her hair's the same. Dark, naturally dark, black or close to it, straight and quite short, but irregularly short. Pushed back from the sweat on her forehead, and it's her shiny, sweaty forehead that's glistening in the sun, rather than a glossed-up lower lip catching studio lights. And she's breathing normally, while my breathing's still catching up from the run. She's swapping her weight from one foot to another as she's standing there, as if she isn't finished, her lean and restless runner's body maybe ready for another lap.

Do you know if there's any running group around here, or anything?

Yeah, there are plenty, I think.

But you're not into that?

Not really. I spend a lot of time with people, so I tend to run by myself. Actually, that's not really it. I've only been doing it for a few months. Everyone I know's gone to lard, so it's really just about making sure I don't. It's pretty casual. Non-competitive.

Groups don't have to be competitive. I usually run with people. It's not bad.

So where are they?

No, before. I've just transferred here. To do an honors thesis.

Well, I'm not sure I'm a group runner. I don't think I've got enough event-related clothes to wear. Plus, you've seen me. I look so not like a runner that on two occasions buses have actually stopped for me.

You're kidding, she says, and laughs, clearly not sure if I'm kidding.

Well, one stopped. The other just hung around at the bus stop a bit longer than usual. But I waved him away. I wasn't going to stand for shit like that.

At work, the Window Weasel says:

Hey Bud! We're having fun aren't we?? So go click YES!! I LOVE MY WEASEL!! and you can register to use Window Weasel for life for only $30! Click LATER to register later.

I click LATER, send the weasel off and decide I don't like much of the false bonhomie people program into automated messages. The weasel is a minor irritant. It is not my "bud."

There's another e-mail from Katie.

Re coffee—another weak spot for the wok, by the way (and
if you make it in a wok at your place, I don't want to
know)—my best breaks tend to be middle of the day, so how
about lunch? Which I assume is at least semi-regular for you,
too. So suggest a day, if feasible.

And Monday would be feasible, since I start work after
lunch on Mondays, so I suggest it.

Today at lunchtime I go to Coles again. I've got diapers
to buy. And, yes, disposables, even though I have cloth
diapers at home. I'm very over them now. My baby book
tells me to expect four thousand nappy changes before the
Bean can get better organized sphincter-wise, and I have
a serious attraction to convenience. No, a need for it.
We've thought it through—the Bean and me—and we
choose disposables.

I know all about the landfill issue. I know that I'm
responsible for a couple of cubic kilometers of it, and I
know that the plastic parts of the Bean's disposables might
outlast us both by thousands of years, but that's the way
it is. Build on it.

I imagine that I'm not the only parent in town who's
made this choice. And that in the outer suburbs, new
housing developments are being built on quietly settling
piles of grungy diapers, plus non-biodegradable packing
material, betamax VCRs, lava lamps (from both times they
were in), toasters that were fine until the catch stopped
staying down, fungoid futons, coffee makers that seized
up because no one ever cleaned them.

I can imagine aliens landing quietly by night, core sampling this in someone's backyard and leaving, analyzing

what they've got and wondering if it's a treasure trove or a very sad fallen civilization (stricken by bad appliances and worse bowel control). And I'm thinking this while I'm gazing at the diaper shelves, imagining the aliens deciding that our planet sucks, and I'm quietly singing the Lemonheads' "It's a Shame About Ray." Great song, but I've really got to lift my game.

I pick up a couple of thirty-six packs, and go to meet the Bean at day care.

4

On Saturday I take the Bean down to the campus lake. I want her to see the ducks, but when we get there she's less excited than I'd hoped. I'm not sure that she's up to wildlife yet.

There is one thing I like about that, though. An upside to her not giving a shit about the ducks. It shows that she can tell me apart from them. She looks at the ducks with a minor version of her straining-to-poo face, and she looks at me as though I'm one of the good guys. The reality-checking device, the one that'll see her right. An entity she can trust. Of course, I'm not unique in that. I think she trusts Elvis, too, and while I'm tossing bread to the ducks he's going insane about a medium-sized stick.

Soon he's flopped beside us, panting, since it's simply too hot to keep up any reasonable level of stick madness today. He looks at me with his big eyes, checks all's well.

I think you've got them under control, buddy, I tell him.

Then I talk more about the ducks, the trees, the buildings, as I hold the Bean in a standing position and use one of her hands to point. One day the content will count for something, and there's plenty I'll be able to tell her, all kinds of things to explain that she doesn't understand yet.

And about much more than scenery, when the time is right. But for the moment she's just propped up there, bowlegged and pale and passively pointing. The Bean and her silly flowery hat and her perfect skin. Her chubbed-up pale limbs, yet to be shaped by any serious function. Soft all over, other than when she head butts. The Bean and that excellent musty baby smell.

I try to mop up some drool and she puts my hand in her mouth and bites. There's something tiny and sharp in there, and when she lets me look I can see the white point of a tooth coming through a raised, red bud of gum. I get a little excited, she thinks I'm an idiot, Elvis jumps up and comes back with a stick.

I've brought the camera with me, so I sit her down and try to line up something that will capture the moment of tooth discovery. Even though I know it'll probably end up as nothing more than a picture of a baby with spit down her front. But I guess you can never have too many of those.

Smile. Smile, I say, and earn a look of great curiosity. You have to smile now, I urge her, but she reverts to the straining-to-poo face.

No, smile. Just a quick smile first. Please. What can I do to make you smile? Okay, there's three bits of string and they go into a bar . . .

I lift up her top, blow a big raspberry on her front and get a whack on the face and a gurgly laugh. I get the shot—the gurgly laugh, the hand reaching out for a second whack, a big drool-string from the lower lip to the left shoulder.

Nothing like physical comedy, is there? I say to her, and pull her hat over her eyes.

She waves both arms, rolls backward like a scuba diver leaving a boat. She's not brilliant at the sitting yet, and visual input clearly means more to her than I'd realized. I'm near the end of the roll of film, so I take a few more photos to finish it off. I've taken far more photos of her over the last few months than I would have expected.

There seems to be much more to photograph now than there was, but perhaps I'm also better at noticing it, more used to watching her. She seems to turn older almost every day. She amazes me sometimes. Not so long ago she was a pair of orifices with an unsophisticated mulching system in between, now she knows a thing or two about the world. Not much, but a thing or two, and more all the time. The Bean takes things in, sizes them up. I can tell. And I think she's very clever doing that. Dote, dote. I think there's part of me that genuinely believes I'm a co-inventor of the smart beautiful baby.

I'm looking forward to things with her. Stories, making her laugh with words, telling her about things that she might never get to see. Typewriters, for instance. She may never see a working typewriter. That struck me yesterday, as I shut my computer down for the weekend. Not so long ago it would have been unbelievable.

I want to tell her about typewriters and how, with them and other old machines, you could actually see how they worked. How you would push down on a key and it would make a tiny hammer hit a piece of ribbon with ink in it, and hit the ink off the ribbon and onto the page. And I can tell her about paper money, stamps you had to lick, the time before bar codes. It sounds like I went to school with Dickens. It sounds as though I'm going to bore the shit out of my daughter. When has a child ever thanked a parent for a long dissertation on the artifacts of the industrial age? Bad luck. That's how it's going to be. She's not just going to be bought a Nintendo and left in a corner.

And I can tell her about laser surgery, for that matter. By then it'll be far less special. I can tell her that laser surgery and the Internet and CD players and a lot of other things weren't always around. That I know how things were before them and when they were new, before they were commonplace and merged with the background. I knew them when they were part of current affairs, before they were history, part of the set of things already in the world. And history seems weighted somehow differently to the events of your own time. It's as though you're given it, and the things you store as your own memory are put somewhere else.

I was too young to get Watergate at all, so I inherited it. I watched the Clinton impeachment day-to-day and it unraveled as a current event. They're both impeachments of American presidents, but in my head they couldn't be more different. I received the Nixon story afterward, end first. I heard Clinton's from the beginning, from the first denials.

The death of Marilyn Monroe was world history. As a sixties child, one of the first things you got to know about Marilyn Monroe was that she was dead. So that affected every frame of her that you ever viewed. Before Kurt Cobain died, I owned two Nirvana albums. I think I can remember the first time I heard "Smells Like Teen Spirit," the street I was driving on, not far from here. Even though I probably can't, I think I can.

I wonder when Lily will speak. Not for ages yet, but I still wonder. My first words were spoken to dogs, perhaps since dog affirmations get so much repetition. Maybe she'll be the same. Maybe her first recognizable sound will be *Elvis.* Maybe her first sentence will be, *Go away and leave me with my Nintendo,* some day when I barge into her room to tell her about the world, and some useless ancient notion that's offering me a moment's fascination.

And I wonder where Ash is today, if she's around. We're near her house. What's she doing on her first weekend in Brisbane? I'd like to think—not that it's any of my business—that she's got friends here, even if she's new and I already know she's got no one to run with in the mornings. A big, lumbering, sedentary boyfriend even, or one who sleeps in and gets athletic later. She looks very fit, so my guess is that's the kind of guy she'd be with. Maybe they even transferred here together.

But enough mindless speculation. I'm in need of adult conversation, and we're due soon at Wendy and Steve's. A swim and a barbecue. Wendy and Steve mastered suburban summer weekend rituals a while back. After lunch the Bean can sleep there, and as long as I don't run any theories about history by them, or reach a point where I'm unable to suppress my urge to explain the typewriter, everything should be fine.

5

We can't run together, I tell Ash on Monday morning. You've no idea what it'll do to my self-esteem.

I'll be gentle with you, she says. *Promise.*

We run, she chats. And that alone is enough to tell me there's only disgrace for me out here. She chats, and I can't find a fraction of a second when I'd fit a word in around the mechanics of breathing.

And I'm wondering, did we organize this? Did we arrange this last week, or is it just happening? Is it a simple overlap of habits? Of her habits with mine, technically, since I've been running here for months now.

I know now why I run by myself. Why I don't buy special clothes for it. Why I boast about my running only to the morbidly sedentary and the genuinely elderly and people with chronic lower-limb ailments. I'm crap at it. Sure, I'm the fittest I've ever been in my life, but I'm coming off a very low base.

And I need to spit. Runners spit. I spit all the time when I'm running. It's okay to spit, isn't it? But suddenly, probably since I've never run with someone before, this seems as much like a social event as it does like running. Ash helps that along by talking, of course. Long, effortless unpunctuated sentences of talk, damn her. Pointing things out along my running track and talking about them—the City Cat ferry, the huge riverbank houses at West End. This is the kind of activity I usually conduct with someone who's six months old, but I get to be the talker then. And there's no simultaneous running going on.

So, with the talking, it seems wrong to spit, as though it could kill the mood or something. Not that there should be a mood. Suddenly, though, it would feel strange to spit. No matter how much I need to. No matter how much saliva has built up in my mouth. No matter that I'd normally be at least six spits into my run by now, and there's no way I can swallow it all. But she's made a mood out of all this chat, and spitting now would be like sitting under the umbrella of a street-side coffee shop and hoicking one over my shoulder.

She turns to her right at the end of a sentence. Spits. Neatly, onto the base of a palm tree. She really is a runner.

And I'm in the clear. I turn to my left. I spit. Or, rather, I let loose a huge gob of stringy saliva that loops out of my mouth, travels a very short distance, becomes aware of its own vast mass and flops onto my shoulder. And manages to be stringy enough to stay connected to my mouth.

Perhaps I'm teething, I think, as the run stops for a laugh break on the part of the more efficient runner. If I was thirty-four years younger, I'd be looking pretty cute right now. Perhaps a photo would be nice.

Ash stands leaning forward, with her hands on her thighs, laughing so much that most of her shakes. She looks around at my shoulder, squawks again, looks away. The spit gob clings on.

Damn seagulls, I say, since it's a moment long past saving.

I should mail Saturday's photos off for cheap processing, but I want to see them now, so I go to Kmart. Somehow even the hour wait for one-hour photoprocessing seems like a major imposition.

Since I have no affinity with shopping, I figure I might as well drop in on work to check my e-mails. And the Window Weasel says:

> Yo! Sleepy! People pay for this, you know. So go click YES!! I LOVE MY WEASEL!! and you can register to use Window Weasel for life for only $30! Click LATER to register later.

Okay, I don't like the tone, I don't even know what it is that the people are paying for and, to be honest, I'm pretty sure I hate being called Sleepy. No way do I LOVE MY WEASEL.

And what an e-mail harvest I get. There's an update from a laser surgery Web site, but when I go there it's not much more than an ad for someone's latest attempt at the laser-that-does-everything. Which is actually just a new version of the laser that does a couple of things and costs a lot.

Then there are two from my father. One headed "Could be time to buy BHP?" and the other "NEW this week at Jim's Fractal Gallery!!!" My father, whose day-to-day life almost never calls for the exclamation mark, has almost as much judgment as George out in the parallel cyber universe.

George, who has today sent me a joke forward about the capacity of dogs to lick their own genitals, and one of those stupid games where you write down the numbers one to six and put various names next to them, and this somehow predicts your future. I did one of them once, I still haven't slept with my mother, and I really don't expect that to change.

No, e-mail's essential, George said, when we decided to computerize properly. And he demonstrates it almost every day, doesn't he?

I go back to Kmart, I beg them to reduce the one-hour wait to forty minutes, but the woman tells me the process is automated.

Once the spitting episode was over, the run went a little better. We found a pace I could maintain and that might have constituted some form of exercise for Ash. And from then on I spat early and decisively, and wore none of it.

You've got a baby seat in the car, she said as she did a hamstring stretch on my bumper. *Does that mean you've got a baby?*

And I told her, No, I'm just prepared for anything. I've got snow shoes in the boot. And that sounded dumb, so I said, Maybe I've got a baby, as though there might be some intrigue about the issue.

Could have been that previous owner, she said, and looked down at the number plate. *MLB. But people don't usually leave baby seats behind, I guess.*

And what an attractive baby she is, too, I'm thinking in Kmart as I look through the photos. What a thoughtful face, what a laugh, and could that perhaps be just a hint of tooth?

Katie's already in the café when I get there. She's reading a newspaper, but I can see her hair over the top of it, all foofed up and kept there with a limp, hot-pink bow.

Hey there, I say, when I get close enough to see her face.

And she says, *Hi,* as though she's been taken slightly by surprise. And she blushes—or does something that looks a lot like blushing—and tries to fold the newspaper in a way it isn't meant to go. *I've ordered already. It seemed like that kind of place.*

It is that kind of place.

So I put my order in and sit down opposite her. I start talking—rattling on in the way I would at the keyboard—and Katie fumbles a few replies. She's still swamped by newspaper, probably wishing she'd gone tabloid instead of broadsheet.

Damn thing, she mutters, giving up and setting it on an empty chair, leaving it like a half-made pirate hat.

My mother used to fold it that way for fire starters, I tell her.

What?

Old newspaper. She used it to start fires.

Pause. It occurs to me that I might be making my mother look like a pyromaniac.

In the fireplace.

Oh. We never had a fireplace.

Well, most people don't, do they?

Pause. Okay, now I guess I've gone for something rhetorical. Not a good choice. This isn't easy.

It's to do with coming from England, I tell her, pushing on. When we came out here my parents looked around for ages for a house with a fireplace. You'd think that, after the first couple of dozen didn't have one, they'd have worked it out.

Yeah.

They don't have one now though. They're in a flat.

She nods. There's still no eye contact. I start to wonder if she's had a bad experience with a fireplace, or if there's something hanging out my nose, then I realize it's probably me who hasn't worked it out. We actually don't know each other very well. Not in a face-to-face way, and I'd forgotten that. Face-to-face we only know how to say "Hi" over colored cake at kids' birthdays, and not much more. I'm going in with the mild detached boldness of text, Katie's hanging back, missing the modesty-screen of e-mail now that she can see the person she's talking to.

And, if the talk troubles her, she seems even more tense in the pauses when no one talks, as though they're abnormal, and that only keeps me trying to fill them.

I tell her about my tedious weekend, and ask about hers. It wasn't bad, apparently. And that's that out of the way.

I tell her about running with someone this morning and spitting all over myself, and she's supposed to laugh but instead she says—using a therapeutic low tone and sudden serious eye contact—*But how are you doing, really? With everything? How are you doing?*

Fine. I'm doing fine, I tell her. The Bean gives me plenty to do, though. Want to see some photos?

And, since she's already Auntie Katie twice over, this puts us into territory where she's altogether more comfortable. She knows baby photos, she knows the noises to make, she knows just when to make them.

Look at that stare, I tell her, glad that the photos have saved the conversation. Don't you think that suggests high intelligence?

I'm sure it does. I wonder what she's thinking about. Can you remember anything of what you thought about at that age? She flicks through a couple more. *I can't remember anything till I was three. At least three. Can you remember when you looked like that?* She holds the photo up—Lily, the straining-to-poo face, the drool on the shoulder.

Well, yeah. About seven-thirty this morning, but I don't think I was thinking the same things.

I can't believe you spat on yourself, she says, and shakes her head. *That is just so . . . spastic. Did the guy you were running with notice?*

It was a lot of spit. An unmissable amount of spit. I tried to put it down to a seagull, but that was never going to work.

She laughs, and says, *Hey, since we're sharing, how about this?* She rummages around in her bag and pulls out a photo of a very fluffy cat. *Here's Flag.*

Which is an interesting name for a cat. Why Flag?

I just liked the sound of it, really.

You're aware that it's a noun, though? That out in the real world it's got some kind of meaning attached?

She goes red again, and says, *Do you have any pets, or anything?*

Yeah. A dog. Called Elvis, actually. Which, out in the real world means big fat dead megastar often sighted in Seven Elevens.

She nods, stays red.

And my daughter was named after a flower, but I seem

to have got into the habit of referring to her as a legume. So I can't be too picky about nouns, can I?

I guess not.

She puts the photo back in her bag, nods again, looks at the door, seems to be enduring something uncomfortable. This time I hold off, figuring I've used words as filler for pauses more than enough in this conversation.

Wendy says things are a bit quiet this month for you. At work. Or did I say that already?

She pulls a tissue out of her bag, wrenches it slowly apart under the table.

Mid-afternoon I have a no-show. George passes my open door with coffee while I'm checking some lab results.

Hey, he says, coming back and standing in the doorway. *How was the date?*

Date? There was no date.

People say you've been lunching with, he looks around, checks the corridor, *chicks with eighties hair.*

I should never have said that. I should never have said eighties hair.

And you think if you hadn't no one would have noticed?

Oh, it's all so *Flashdance.*

So how was the date? You did go, didn't you? Remember, no one leaves Baby in the corner.

What?

It's a Flashdance *quote.*

Shit you're good with that stuff.

Hey, there were generations that quoted Shakespeare. I'm part of a long tradition.

And regardless of that, it wasn't a date.

Okay, but if it's not a date, why would Wendy mention it to me?

Why wouldn't she? It wasn't a secret. Did she mention it in any particular way?

Should she have?

She might have. I think you've got this one wrong, Porge. If Katie said anything to Wendy afterward she would just have been calling to tell her she works with a fuckwit.

Can't see why she'd bother to do that. Wendy's known you for years.

It wasn't the best lunch.

What do you mean?

I think Katie doesn't get out much. I talked a lot. I think it's having a baby. It makes you disinhibited. I talked a lot, and she didn't. So I talked more. I told her about fireplaces. I told her about spitting on myself today. I told her I named my child after a legume. Those things would not have happened had it been either a reasonable social occasion or a date. I think we both know that.

I think we do, he says, and laughs. *Spat on yourself, hey? You sure know how to get them horny.*

It's a long story. And entirely without horn. And lunch was just lunch. You know lunch? I have lunch with you sometimes. And I think a lot of you, but it's no date. I have lunch with people. It's something I do.

No it's not.

Look, you tell me all the time, everyone tells me all the time. Get out and do things. Even if it's only lunch with people. Katie actually does something more dynamic than the rest of you, we agree on a time and place and suddenly it's a date. You weren't there. It was no date. It was a casual suggestion made in an e-mail. Lunch, coffee, casual. The suggestion, anyway. It was just a sort of coffee-friend thing to do.

Is that a category? Coffee friend?

Of course it's a category. And it's a nice, supportive, non-date category. And the fact that she went from coffee—which was the original suggestion—to lunch, just like that, actually shows how much of a big deal it isn't. I've been on dates, you know. In the eighties, back when Katie got the hair. I've been on dates, and they weren't like today.

No, this is the thing. You've been out of the loop a while. My guess is you were on a mid-thirties date. It doesn't work the same.

No, no. No date. We showed each other photos. Bean photos, cat photos. What does that sound like to you?

Oh, north African fruit, grows on a palm, dark brown, sticky, sweet. No idea what it sounds like to me. It's a mid-thirties date.

Oh no. If that's a date this entire demographic sucks. If that's what happens to you on dates, stick to the goodwill of your own two hands. George, that can't be a date. We can't be so bloody old that we accept that that's a date. What about even a minor undercurrent of seething sexual tension?

Hold out for it, Jon Boy. I want you in there batting for us. For the guys who hold out for dates the way they used to be when we were young. Or even partly young. That moment of date competence that hung there for a second or two be-

tween adolescent dysfunction and the mid-thirties photo-swap lunch.

But I don't even want that either. And I'm pretty sure I never had the moment of competence. Look, I'm not in the market for dates. I'm so not in the market for dates that I don't know how it'd be if I was. If I was, I wouldn't want the photo-swap date because it's just not a date, and I wouldn't want the eighties date, either. I do *not* have fond memories of eighties dates, even beyond the first half of the decade when I didn't get any. Eighties dates—and maybe this was just me—seemed to be about hanging around uninteresting people long enough to have sex with them a few times. They didn't necessarily know that, of course, and I might have pissed one or two of them off. So I'm hoping that's not the competence you've got in mind. It doesn't sound great now.

Sylvia appears next to George, holding files.

You both have dates, she says. *And quite loud voices. Nigel's got everything ready to go, Jon. And I don't know if you're interested in my opinion, but I think you're probably a nicer man than you used to be. So I'm sure it'll be all right in the end.*

At least George waits till he's back in his room to laugh.

His mid-thirties date concept preoccupies me most of the rest of the afternoon. It shouldn't, of course. I should be doing much more to take into account where these opinions are coming from.

I remember George had a crush on a girl at college for months because she used an asterisk when she wanted to add something to the bottom of her lecture notes, but a cross of Lorraine if she wanted to add something else. The asterisk was an obvious choice, but the cross of Lorraine spoke to George. I remember him telling me, *Jon Boy, she uses a cross of Lorraine to mark something in notes. Like, how smart is that?*

Fortunately, this was one of those rare crushes that you have the luxury of bringing to a close yourself. After a couple of months of sitting nearby hoping to be noticed, and a snatched second here and there of tense casual conversation, he actually dealt with it head on and asked her how she came to be using the cross of Lorraine in notes. She had no idea what he was talking about. So he pointed to one, and she said, *Oh, that. I guess I got it from somewhere.* And then he could get over her.

And in the end he was glad he'd never quite got around to showing her his own system (cross of Jerusalem, papal cross, cross of Saint Catherine). But George always footnoted far too much for his own good.

After work, we swim. Nigel's a regular, and George decided he should get into some kind of exercise, so he told Nigel we'd join him. How it became a "we" issue I'm not sure, but my parents said they'd be happy to have Lily a bit longer this afternoon, so it looks as though I'm in.

Nigel takes his shirt off to reveal a swimmer's kind of body, and one of those mystical, new-age tatts on his arm. George takes his shirt off, too, but it's not the same. The swimmer's body is lost somewhere deep inside George. Plus, he's a pretty hairy guy. For George, skin is just the biological equivalent of underlay, and he could hide a lot of tatts in there beneath all that fuzz. In fact, there was a time when he won a hairy-chest competition without having to show the judges anything more than his back.

We hit the water, and it's harder on my arms than I'd expected. Nigel turns over lap after lap without visible effort. George swims one length, then part of another, then maneuvers himself to the non-lapping section of the pool and crouches low in the water, bobbing up and down as the bow waves of swimmers come his way, and looking like something that could scare salmon.

A few laps later I go over.

Don't want to overdo it, he says. *Not the first time.*

That was really hard on my arms. Did you find that?

No. I found it hard everywhere.

How about a popsicle?

We get out and sit on the concrete steps of the stand, eating popsicles and watching Nigel swim on.

Do you think he gets bored doing that? George says.

Who knows? I think he gets bored with lots of things.

None of us really gets Nigel. He's good at what he does at work and he's nice enough, but he can be intense about things when you least expect it. It's no surprise that he laps the pool the way he does. He's got a homemade vegetarian curry that he often brings in for lunch and reheats in the microwave. It always smells great, and someone once pointed that out to him. As a casual remark, a passing minor-league compliment, but Nigel came straight back at them with, *The key to it all's not skimping on ingredients. If it says galangal, you get galangal. You don't make it easy for yourself and use ginger.* As though he'd be annoyed if we even thought about it.

When do you have to pick up Lily? George says.

Not for a while. I allowed an hour for this. Kind of hard to believe now.

Yeah, good one. How long does it take to eat a popsicle?

Yeah. That date stuff earlier . . . What you're suggesting is the beginning of middle-age. You realize that, don't you?

I didn't tell you half of it. I didn't mention the dinner-at-her-place option. The froufy nibbly things from the deli du jour or the good hope-chest china or the ice bucket. I didn't say candles, and I didn't say Celine, Kenny G, Easy Listening format.

What?

I didn't say Sinatra.

Sinatra? You are fucking joking with this. Tell me now that you're joking. It's like, if my father didn't exist and my mother went on a date, that might be what she was up for.

Your mother thinks Sinatra's a tosser. Always preferred Bing. But, really, if I went for your mother, I'd be going with something more like Simon and Garfunkel.

George, I don't like the way that sounds as though you've thought it through.

He sings the opening lines of "Sounds of Silence." *Or maybe even some Elvis,* he says. *You know, one of those love-ballad albums.*

George, these are bad jokes. You are being evil to my mind. There could be no Elvis. Not on dates. With my mother or anyone.

Your dog is called Elvis.

As a joke. He's got the brain of a whippet and even he

can recognize it's ironic. Please, don't make the whole thing sound so horribly historic.

So, millennium man, tell me about date mechanics then. How would it work for you? Should that kind of thing be on the cards?

Okay, I haven't thought about this, so it'll be a bit rudimentary. What I'm thinking is that I should capitalize on what I've learned, but it's still got to be fun. It's got to have some sense of the contemporary. And nothing hinting that my best years are behind me, or anything. Because they'd really better not be. So, I'm sorry, there's not only no Easy Listening, but there's no Classic Hits format. This is the eighties hair issue. If I was back at someone's place, okay, and they put on, like, Dead or Alive, and even thought about reminiscing, I'd know there was no chance.

Or Nik Kershaw, or Paul Young.

Oh, Jesus, there'd be *No Parlez* of any kind. Out the door.

Or Haircut 100.

Shit, Porge. I wouldn't have fucked anyone who played Haircut 100 in the eighties. That's never going to change.

Good call. I probably would have, though. Okay, Kajagoogoo. Limahl. Culture Club. Haysi Fantayzee.

Porge, I'm not feeling well. Quit it with the eighties. Eighties songs should be left entirely alone until after the tenth beer on New Year's Eve. At which time the words come back to you automatically and you can't be held responsible.

As I'm well aware. Don't think I've forgotten New Year's Eve 1989 and the large number of appalling songs you seemed to know word for word.

It was a weak moment. I've been better since. You know I was about to go overseas then. It was just pre-departure nostalgia. I was kind of tense. I wouldn't have sung more than a handful of songs on the last few New Year's Eves.

But on the platform at Central Station? In 1997?

People liked it. Anyway, it was New Year's Eve. Besides, what about you on New Year's Eve 1989, with most of the guests tripping over your tongue while you spent the whole night ogling one of my housemates?

That wasn't ogling. It was much classier than ogling. I dropped over quite a bit after that—after you left—specifically because of her. It was a crush, a proper crush, not just some lazy, drunken piece of New Year's Eve perving, you know. I wanted her, all bloody January. Anyway, you've got us off on a deliberate tangent. Stop shirking the issue. Get back to the date. Tell me about it. Begin the date.

Okay, I get to her place—this is happening at her place, like your scenario—she gives me a glass of wine. . . .

What kind of wine?

I don't want to argue with you about wine now.

Yeah, but it's not a chardonnay anymore, is it?

She gives me a glass of wine. And I can't believe you'd dare fuss about the grape, when you're playing such shit music on your date.

Hey, that's her, not me.

Okay. She gives me a glass of wine. The whole thing is casual. No glory-box items involved. She plays—here's the music part—maybe Jeff Buckley. That'd be okay. Ben Folds Five. If it was my place, she'd be getting some *Best of the Lemonheads* at the moment, or some Grant Mc-Lennan.

And if you started singing along by accident?

Oh, fuck, I really am doing that a lot, aren't I?

If you start singing along by accident, you just blame it on the Bean, like always.

Thanks.

Just getting you ready for it, champ.

Okay. Wine, music, then there's conversation. That's when she dazzles me with her brain. Brains are good, George. I'm a sucker for a quality brain.

And for the first time in ages, the concept actually finds a place for itself in my own brain, and seems kind of nice.

See, you can do it. I'd go on that, on that kind of date. You wouldn't have to ask me twice if that was on offer.

And I suppose I could even take a passing reference to the eighties, if it was clear there was irony involved.

Good. Very good. I like your prognosis, fella. Anyway, I'm shitting with you. Do what you want. I think we're the generation that's getting to invent the mid-thirties date. Think about it. Thirtysomething and single used to be aberrant. Maiden-aunt territory. Now it's what most of us seem to be, for one reason or another. And a lot of us don't score enough dates to know much about what's what, anyway. Look at me. Visibly not getting younger, and still I'm holding out for the right kind of offer. Call me fussy, but you're nothing when you stop being fussy. Even if it means I'm the only person I know who buys condoms based on their shelf life.

Later, I have an awkward moment when I realize I honestly couldn't get involved with a person with eighties hair. Not that I'm seeking involvement, but eighties hair couldn't end at eighties hair. It's what it says. Katie goes to a lot of trouble for that effect, and what does that mean? How far does it go? Eighties hair is a symptom, not a disease. What's going on in her mind? How much of all the years since is she yet to notice?

And then there's the idea of the person with eighties hair bearing down on you with all that blue eye shadow, and you know that somewhere in her wardrobe she's got leg warmers, waiting. Right next to the "Choose Life" T-shirt.

But what am I thinking? It's not as though I could ever promise to be at the cutting edge of fashion myself. And anyone with eighties hair is really only one good haircut away from crossing the line, and being a contender.

I don't think I've been this shallow for, seriously, maybe ten years.

6

Do you want to come in for some water? Ash says, when we've finished the run and we're back outside her house.

On either side of the path, the grass is knee-high with some stalks shooting up much higher and bending under the weight of seed with the recent rain. If it wasn't for the car parked in the driveway you'd be sure no one lived here.

In the kitchen, she takes water from the fridge and pours it into two plastic cups. I get the red one.

I think they are Waterford, or something, she says, just as I was thinking I'd accepted my plastic cup impassively. *I'd show you around the place, but this is the best bit.*

There's not much to say to that. Behind the fridge I can see the shitty wiring, and it's probably worse in the places I can't see. When I look down, there's a crack of daylight coming through between the linoleum floor tiles. I want to say things like, Have you had the wiring checked? and Are you sure this floor's okay?, but that sounds too much like my father's territory. And there's no point. She won't have had the wiring checked, for a start.

I got this place through a family friend, she says, obviously figuring it needs some explanation. *Rent-free. They'll build town houses here eventually. Or units. But that'll take a while to happen. They've got a dive-boat business out of Cairns that keeps them busy.*

Is that where you're from?

Yeah. Well, Atherton, not far from Atherton. But I've been in Cairns for college. She stops to refill my cup. *I've been doing psychology and sociology at James Cook and I've transferred down here to do my honors thesis. To work with a particular supervisor. And maybe convert it into a masters. We'll see.*

So are you going to get other people in here to live with?

I don't know. I don't know if that's really feasible. I don't know if the place is up to it.

Do you know a lot of people around here?

No. But school hasn't started yet, so . . . She stops, drinks water. *Things'll get busy soon enough, I guess.*

She finishes her water, and the sweat runs from the ends of her dark hair and down her neck, soaks into today's ten-K fun-run tank top. She does have blue eyes, I notice, even though I thought I'd made that up. Natalie Imbruglia—that's who I thought she looked like. Even though she doesn't, really, so that's even more embarrassing than having thought it in the first place. She doesn't have the same mouth.

She doesn't have the same mouth as Natalie Imbruglia—that's what I'm thinking, standing here in her kitchen, drinking water from her best red plastic cup. Not that the fact that it's different means there's anything wrong with her mouth, but . . .

School starts next week, she says. *It's probably good to have a quiet week or two before getting into that.*

Yeah. If you wanted to do something in the meantime,

we could have coffee. Or something. If you wanted. Look, I could just give you my details and then you could call, or whatever. If you had time on your hands.

Sure.

I've got it all on a card. A business card. How about I give you one?

On the way to the car, it crosses my mind that she's not likely to be faxing me from here, and that maybe a couple of phone numbers would have sufficed. And that going the business card will probably look like the wanker option. I'm really not having an interpersonally gifted week. I think I wanted to offer her some social interaction, but with no pressure to go along with it if she didn't want to, and all of a sudden I was coming across completely sixteen. Pre-competent and caught in a knot of embarrassment. Because she reminded me vaguely of Natalie Imbruglia, and surely that's only a problem if I tell someone. Or stand there staring at her mouth, in the interest of thorough comparison. As if I've got any real idea of what I'm comparing her with. I've never paid any attention to Natalie Imbruglia.

And I sounded cringingly unsure, when all I wanted to do was avoid pushing her into an arrangement she didn't want. Next I should sing, maybe. Or spit on myself again. That always takes the pressure off.

Somewhere in the glove box, under the cell phone and the baby photos and an assortment of small toys and a couple of pens, I find a business card. Which doesn't have my home number on it, so it's not exactly as comprehensive as I'd promised. Lucky I found the pens.

Lots of ways of contacting you, she says when she looks

at it, once I've added my home number. *Hey, your mobile isn't on there either.*

Oh, yeah. It's not mine, actually. It's a work one, but it's no one's in particular at the moment. I just seem to have it for now. For baby emergencies, mainly. Except I'm a bit slack about carrying it. I'm not sure if I'll keep it. But I'll give you the number anyway.

So there is a baby, she says as I'm writing on the card.

There is a baby. Hey, want to see her? I've got photos.

Sure.

So I show her the photos of Lily, aged five months and then six. Lying down, sitting up, reaching out, putting together a wobbly smile or two, showing an imprecise hint of tooth. Ash lacks Katie's baby experience, so she doesn't make the same noises. She makes the noises of someone a long way shy of nieces, nephews and any ticking clocks, which could mean this is boring her, but she seems okay with it.

I like this one, she says. *This confused one in particular. It's like she's saying, "I can't believe you're taking my photo again."*

I did take a few, didn't I?

Yeah, but why not? And, besides, look at her. How could you not want to take a lot of photos?

My thoughts, exactly. And she feels the same way, really. She's faking it with that photo. She's not confused. You should meet her. I think you'd get on.

Yeah, we probably would. So how about the weekend?

I'm sorry?

The weekend. How about the weekend? Coffee, lunch,

something? Remember? What you said in the kitchen. Is that
still on?

I'm late for work, having shown Ash the photos. And
arranged to have lunch with her on Saturday. As I park
the car, that's the part of the conversation I'm still running
through my head. I hadn't thought it was going there. By
then I was thinking I'd made a stupid offer in the kitchen,
and I thought that it wasn't going to go too far at all. I
was sure we were having one of those times when you
suggest something and the person talks about something
else, and you both pretend the suggestion was never made.
Obviously I've spent too much time lately talking to
George about the eighties. I had a lot of conversations back
then that went just like that.

I start work behind, and I manage to stay behind all
day. I don't even get to check my e-mails till after my last
patient's gone and George and Nigel are leaving for the
pool. And the Window Weasel says:

Listen, my friend. You said you wanted the weasel. And now
things wouldn't be the same without it, would they? So go
click YES!! I LOVE MY WEASEL!! and you can register
to use Window Weasel for life for only $30! Click LATER
to register later.

I don't even know what the fucking weasel is, I tell the
screen in a tone that doesn't hide my annoyance. So how
do I know how things would be without it?

I've got one e-mail. It's from Katie.

Jon,

Lunch was fun on Monday. Have to do it again sometime.
Actually, how about dinner? I've just had someone in to redo
the kitchen, so I was thinking it'd be nice to do something
to "launch" the new one. I was thinking Saturday. How are
you placed?

Could she have been at lunch on Monday? Which part
was the fun part? And suddenly, evening baby-sitting arrangements pending, Saturday's looking full for me.

Katie can't have a lot of friends if I manage to be on
her dinner-party list right now, so I should probably try
to go. Maybe she wants to push beyond Monday, pretend
it never happened, re-establish some social equilibrium
where we actually can have coffee, and no one goes red
or wrecks the paper.

But I shouldn't think it's about normalizing things with
me. I expect I'll be there to round up an odd number, or
that it'll be one of those dinner parties where you delib-
erately invite a bunch of people who don't know each
other. To subject them to an evening of protracted awkwardness, or whatever it is that you're supposed to get out
of those events. Why do I think it'll be like that? How
do I already know that the whole night will be character-
ized by the eighties, and by awkwardness?

Tonight, book club is at George and Oscar's. I set Lily up
to sleep in George's bedroom. He got it air-conditioned
one summer in the hope that it would make him more
attractive. *For sex,* he once announced, *I can promise you*

seventy-two degrees. It sounded horribly like the first draft of a line in the personal ads.

You've really got into this running, haven't you? Oscar says, while we're serving the food. *George says it's practically every day now. There's you and the running, him and the swimming.*

George takes his plate, and says, *I think I could be starting to tone. I think that's the feeling I'm getting.*

So how many times have you gone now?

Well, Monday and today. So when I go on Friday that'll be a three-times-a-week routine. That's my plan. And today I felt less comprehensively screwed on the second lap. I'm sure I can call that progress. Hey, are you going to that thing on Saturday night?

At Katie's?

No.

Oh. What thing?

But it's too late. He's smiling, and I know he's completely lost interest in his question.

Katie's?

Yeah. Just some dinner party she's having. What are you doing?

It's a college thing. College of Dermatologists. Of which you aren't a member, so it was a stupid question. He stops there. They both look at me.

Katie's nice, Oscar says.

Yeah.

So what is it? You and a bunch of Jungian therapists? Or just you?

I've got no idea who's going to be there. I don't even

know the collective noun for Jungian therapists. I hope that's not what it's like. I've only ever read *Synchronicity,* and I don't really think that's going to be helpful.

But you bandy Jung's name about all the time, George says.

Yeah, but I'm faking it. You know I am. Not totally faking it, but pretty close. And have you noticed how, if I get specific, it's usually one of only a handful of references?

Like the fish one. The seven references to fish in one afternoon.

Exactly, and how much of an impact do you think that has on Katie's day? It's not going to get me too far on Saturday. Let's face it. Whatever a Jungian therapist does—if there is such a thing, and it's not just a concept one of us came up with in a past conversation—it doesn't involve sitting there reviewing your clients' lives by demonstrating the acausal connectedness of things. She's not sitting there going, "So, fish come up a lot in conversation today, then?" That can't be Jungian therapy. It can't actually help anybody, can it?

Not that they'll be talking shop on Saturday, necessarily. If that's the kind of people who are there.

Maybe I shouldn't have said yes. I only read *Synchronicity* because it was thin. You know that.

Hey, we're talking about books, he says, as though he's just worked it out. *We're talking about books at book club.*

I had a thin-book phase in college. I've known people who have publicly gone through fat-book phases, when they've read one blockbuster after another, but I don't know anyone else who's admitted to a thin-book phase. It's as though you'd be admitting to cutting corners, which isn't fair, since it'd be a pretty rare fat-book phase that'd lead to a person's betterment.

It was a reaction to alcohol, largely. I had a habit of drinking to excess at friends' houses—nothing unique in that—and becoming paradoxically awake around three a.m. I worked out the first couple of times that there was no point in lying there trying to persuade myself to sleep, so after that I read something instead. And I found that picking the biggest, most boring book didn't help (unless it was Patrick White), and I'd still be there at dawn and my body would be confused for days. Sleep, I found, came only with completion. So my best chance came with the smallest book in the house.

I got to read *Synchronicity* that way. And Marquez's *Chronicle of a Death Foretold* and Calvino's *Invisible Cities* and Conrad's *Heart of Darkness*. Which lets me cover quite a lot of territory, if the conversation demands it, but in a way that's a bit haphazard. As a system it's good, but it's not perfect. Its main limitations are the serious expert (who is likely to assume that you might have tried one or two of the larger books of the same authors) or the person who assumes that your thin-book habit suggests a greater acquaintance with the western canon generally. And if you happen to be dropping the references in to impress, you can end up telling a lot of lies about Tolstoy, or Proust or some other fat-book person you've heard George go on about.

I'm beginning to think it's no surprise that I didn't get a lot of sex back then. With the aid of hindsight, I'm sure

I seemed like a wanker most of the time and a charlatan the rest. I'm amazed I could have had such a low capacity to identify a lose–lose situation.

After we've eaten, Oscar changes his shirt for a black turtleneck top.

Do you think this is the look? he says, mainly to George, and he pats the plump turtleneck part of it.

Oscar's going on a date, George says.

It's not a date.

George calls anything a date, I tell him. I wouldn't worry about it.

It's just a reading. A poetry thing.

George, you never mentioned poetry to me in the date scenario.

I was assuming you wouldn't be dating Justin.

It's not a date. You know I've got my own event on in a few weeks. All that new material I've been working on. It's good to see what everyone else is doing first. And to be supportive. Get out there and go to other people's things. And Justin just happens to like that kind of thing, too. Besides, any time I call anything a date we get our hopes up, don't we? I can't work under that kind of pressure.

Well, George says, allowing a decent pause for reconsideration. *I think the top looks good.*

Oscar fidgets—fidgets as though it might be a date—when Justin is three minutes late and still not here. He walks around the room, polishes imaginary marks from his glasses.

So what's your new material like? I ask him.

Oh, more of the same, he says. *But I'm hoping to take it to a new level. A new level of performance, but also a more*

cohesive set of material. I think I do it on the twelfth. You'll
be there, won't you?

Oh, sure.

Oscar is preparing his new material with the aid of an
Arts Queensland grant. The last time I saw him perform,
he wore hair extensions and sat in a large cardboard box
surrounded by dead flowers. I'm not certain why. It was
supposed to be something urban. I can't say I completely
understood the poetry, but it did seem very angry, and
people seemed to like that. Lots of spitting. My kind of
show.

He writes poetry on Mondays, works in general practice
on Tuesdays and Fridays, and does sessions with us on
Wednesdays and Thursdays. He says that one day he'll get
himself a business card that reflects all of that, but he's
still not sure which order the different jobs should go in.
And he'd like to open a bistro too, so there's no point in
rushing with the card.

A car turns into the driveway and Oscar says, *Finally,*
with a gesture that's unnecessarily large. *Now, should I go
meet him, or should I wait for him to come to the door?*

Wait, George tells him, like a big brother who knows.
You don't want to look anxious about poetry.

Right. Right, Oscar says, an element of psyching-up going on as he fiddles with his cuffs.

And get back from the door, Oz Man.

*Oh, yeah, relaxed. I'll be relaxed. I'll be . . . in another
room. Doing other things.*

Good call.

Oscar turns, and walks away from us. He's almost at
the kitchen when the bell rings. George answers the door.

He's about to introduce me to Justin when Oscar reappears with a whisk in his hand and says, *Oh, Justin, is it that time already?*

Hi, Justin says, as they move in a way that makes them face each other a bit like prize fighters, and turns the rest of us into an audience. Justin is wearing a black top as well, and snug-fitting new jeans. *That's a cool look, Oscar,* he says. *It really works for you.*

Ah, thank you. I was thinking it was good for a night of poetry.

Yeah.

Oscar moves the whisk from his right hand to his left, reciprocates the shameless checking-out that's going on, swings the whisk back to his right hand, holds it in both, in a coy kind of way.

Um, George, he says, when the silence has gone on a little too long. *Is this what you were looking for?*

As, yes, my whisk. Now I can make that nice fluffy icing I said I'd make for your cake.

Thank you. I'll look forward to it. Um, we should be going now, I think. For the poetry.

Of course, George says, and Oscar and Justin hurry out the door and down the front steps. *And this is our invisible friend, Jon, though why bother noticing that he's here when you've got a whisk? Honestly, I thought he was going to pin it on him like a fucking corsage.*

Yeah. Where was "I'll be relaxed" when we needed it? It was all rather school formal. What kind of boy are we bringing up here?

Well, a poet for a start. And you should see the new stuff. Prepare to be entertained. But sit at the back. It's a wet show. Lots of energy from that little mouth.

We load the plates into the dishwasher and he boils water for coffee. *I'd be offering you cake, obviously,* he says, *if only we'd found my whisk in time. Where on earth did he get the idea that the whisk was the prop he needed?* He scoops the coffee into the plunger.

So, this Katie thing, he says. *Are you sure it's a dinner party?*

That's certainly the impression I got. I'm thinking six or eight people. Or seven or nine, even.

Did she say that?

Why would she?

It'd only be fair. It's all to do with the signals you send out. It's how you invite that makes it clear what's going on. Is it just you? Is there any suggestion of intimacy . . .

Fuck, no. No intimacy. I don't need to have that sprung on me. Give me a break.

Okay, I'm just saying, be ready. She will be sending you signals, and you have to read them. That's only fair, even if you've been out of the game for a while. And if she's going, "Hey, there'll be nine of us, a really mixed bunch of people, could be fun, why not come?," then that's fine. That's a particular kind of thing. Not that it necessarily means there could never be other things.

Well, that's the kind of thing I'm thinking it probably is.

George just looks at me. We both know she said none of that. We both know that his next question should deal with that, put it in its place, raise the date specter once again. But we also know I've had enough.

It'll be fine, I tell him. Here's what I think, right? She's a coffee friend, and coffee friends can invite people around to dinner parties. And there's none of your highly structured signaling business going on. This is all casual. I'm probably just there to make up the numbers. You can do that with a coffee friend.

I'm glad to hear it. I'm glad to hear that in the absence of socially responsible signaling, there's still a sophisticated conceptual framework underlying this.

Sure. Always. And why not? What's wrong with the coffee-friend concept? That stuff can work, you know. I've got a running buddy now too.

A running buddy?

Yeah. Someone else who does laps of the campus, so we go together in the mornings now. You know how that is. It's like you and Nigel and the swimming.

Yeah. Is it? Who's your running buddy?

She lives near campus. Right where I park my car.

Good, he says. *Convenient.* He stirs the sugar in my coffee, taps the spoon twice on the side and hands me the cup.

She happens to like to run at the same kind of time as I do. And she likes to run in groups.

So there's a group of you?

Well, there's just the two of us at the moment, but there could be other people some time. It's a good time of day to run.

A running buddy and a coffee friend. It's sounding very compartmentalized, this life of yours.

Which isn't a problem, is it?

No. He drinks a mouthful of coffee. *Did I tell you I've downloaded some new software that could be good for work? For the records side of things?*

No.

I've got the demo going. It's pretty good. Do you want to see it?

Okay. Yeah.

We go into his study, and his tropical fish screen saver is bubbling away calmly on his computer.

Synchronicity, he says. *Weren't we talking about Jung's fish references earlier?*

He flips around from one page of the new records software to another, but I'm not paying much attention. I shouldn't have mentioned Ash. I should have known he wouldn't get it, but it seemed like a good chance to bring her up. And I couldn't have said I think she's lonely, or anything like that. So we're running together. And having lunch on Saturday. It's definitely good I didn't say that.

He's showing me how the software recommends dosages, raises possible drug interactions.

Here, he says, *Try it. Prescribe something. Give John Doe a really stupid dose of Amoxil.*

He steps aside so I can get to the keyboard. I fumble around trying to find the right tools on the toolbar.

No, no, it's that one, he says. *Like I showed you before.* And he goes on trying to be helpful, but using software words.

You're teching me out here, George, I tell him.

What do you mean?

You're losing me. Any time you're about to use a word that has a capital letter in the middle or ends in a little R in a circle, replace it with something bland and old-fashioned. Luddite-friendly.

You are so behind, aren't you? I'd like to call it retro, but it's just behind.

George loves technology. Not long after we started school, he noticed that I was the only person in our social medicine seminar whose assignments were done on a word processor. Soon enough he was over at our place pretty regularly, talking hardware and software with my father and then angling for a turn at the keyboard in the study downstairs. Word processing, experimenting, taking the kind of interest I never could. He tried programming, in a very basic way, and designed a totally non-visual golf game that relied on advice from a wisecracking invisible caddie, a random number generator and blind luck. George had never been on a golf course in his life and the game obviously sucked, but my father got quite excited. Particularly when he shot a course record fifty-eight on only his third or fourth go.

It was that kind of thing that made me feel as though I was letting the team down. Letting both sides down. Being an inadequate friend, unable to muster enthusiasm for the world's most unappealing computer game, and an inadequate son, finding myself unable to care much about computers in general (and the record round in particular).

In our fourth year, my father got George a cheap, secondhand computer through work, and George got excited about its very limited graphics potential. He repaid us by doing up a particularly eye-catching flier that read, "[✓] YES!!! I want good head from a friendly person with no serious diseases" and about twenty tabs at the bottom with my name and phone number.

There were several calls. Enough, in fact, that I had to

explain it to my parents. I came home from class one day to find my mother on the phone, calmly telling someone that this was a bit of a mistake, that she wasn't sure I was looking for that sort of thing, really, *But thank you for your interest.*

So we had to have a talk. Not that it was her business what I was looking for, of course—and she was pretty clear that she didn't want to know—but was there anything I wanted to tell her? Was I lonely? Was I looking for what these men were offering? And if I wanted their numbers, they were on the pad next to the phone.

When I explained, my father said, *The lad just likes his new computer. Got a bit excited, obviously. Nothing wrong with that.*

The next morning, I ignore the weasel completely. I have the cursor hovering over the part of the screen where the LATER box will be, and I stare straight at it to make sure the weasel doesn't catch my eye. I click as soon as I see the outline.

I check all my e-mails from Katie to see if there's a hint from her one way or the other. I'm sure there's nothing going on. Then when I go on-line there's a new one, but it's only confirming the time for Saturday and telling me to bring nothing, or wine if I really want to. Not even George could find a signal in that. Damn it, why has he got me thinking this way?

When I go past on the way to the water cooler, Wendy's door is open, and she's going through some reports.

Are you going to be at Katie's on Saturday? I ask her, and I think I make the question sound strictly social.

For dinner? No. I don't think so, she says, and gives a small laugh. *She doesn't need me to hold her hand.*

She said she's had her kitchen redone, I say, as though that might deflect any emerging sibling issues (as though it's all right not to invite Wendy and Steve if there's a kitchen being launched).

Yes, I've seen it. They've done a good job. But you'll see it for yourself on Saturday, won't you? Anyway, I saw Lily was first at day care again this morning. You're really into this running now, aren't you?

It's become part of my routine, I guess. There's a group of us who run now. Well, the beginnings of a group. It makes it easier to stick with it.

7

Okay, it wasn't such a smart way of putting it. Depending on how George handles the conversation of the night before.

Not that I assume people are talking about me behind my back, but it's the kind of thing George mightn't keep to himself. But if I'm not ready for it to be public—even if it's only running—I shouldn't have told him. I've known him long enough to know that.

Then Wendy turned at a right angle in the middle of the conversation about Katie's kitchen, and day care arrival times suddenly seemed competitive and my running public knowledge. And out the explanation came again, or a version of it. The downplaying, covering-up, group-running version. I think I actually am assuming people are talking about me behind my back. And is it too paranoid of me that, without much effort, I can imagine every word of it?

By Saturday I've run with Ash twice more since the conversation with George. We're going further now, and that was my idea. It is better, running with someone. You do push yourself.

On Saturday morning we don't run. I aim for a sleep-in, but I'm not sure why. Lily doesn't yet observe weekends, so I'm up when I usually am and feeding her, and getting more time than I need with the paper. She and Elvis and I go out for a walk before the day gets too hot. I take the mobile with me, since I'm half-expecting Ash to cancel lunch.

She doesn't cancel lunch. She turns up when I've killed more time, got to the café early, found a shady table, bought coffee and read half of another newspaper.

Hey, she says, and makes me look up. She smiles and pushes her sunglasses back on her head. *I thought I'd go all out with the regular clothes. I even wore a dress.*

And there's a second when I'm acutely aware of how much time has passed since I was in pursuit of women this age, and how many fashion cycles have come and gone. No, it's not a generation, I have to tell myself. More like half a generation. And it's just clothes, and she's a friend I run with. There'll be no crushing embarrassment here.

Ash isn't having this lurch. She's already moved around beside me and she's lifting Lily out of her stroller, saying, *Let me take a look at you.* Lifting her up onto her hip and making close eye contact with the baffled Bean, who I'm willing not to cry. *Aren't you nice?* Ash says to her. *I'm Ashley. Can you say that? Ash-lee.*

Probably not yet, I tell her. Words are probably still quite a few months away. But I'm sure she appreciates the introduction. She's Lily, by the way. If I haven't told you.

Then things get stranger than the fashion problem. I watch the Bean adjust, Ash lift her and plonk her feet onto the stone table, play around with her. I wasn't ready for that. Ash in her regular clothes, doing this regular thing, playing with a baby. I was ready for her to call and cancel, but I wasn't ready for this. Or the awkward surge of something like loneliness that comes with it.

Shall we get something to eat?

Yeah. Good idea.

We join the line, Ash still holding Lily, now on her hip again. Lily, not wary the way I thought she might be, kicking her blue-booted leg against Ash's front, pointing at things and babbling, giving them new monosyllabic names.

She talks, Ash says to me, and then turns back to Lily. *What did you say that was again?*

And Lily waves her arm, gives Ash a thump in the right breast and grabs for her dress strap.

You've got to watch her, I warn her. There's lots of discovery starting to go on, and she's not too aware of the boundaries.

When we sit down again, I buckle Lily back into her stroller and I give her a saltine.

This is a relatively new part of her diet, I tell Ash. She got her first tooth last week, so she's into gnawing at the moment. She seems pretty keen on the dog's Bonios, which might be okay, but I don't think it'd look good.

So who does she take after? Who does she look like?

Not like anyone. I don't think. Just like herself. Hey, Bean? And I think that's fine. It's good if she gets to do her own thing.

Yeah. I hadn't thought of it that way.

So, what are you doing at school exactly? What is it that you had to come down here for?

You're not allowed to laugh.

You can't actually say that. Particularly if you're about to tell me a thesis topic. They're all either incomprehensible or funny or both. It's a rule.

Okay. I'm looking at retail. The psychology and sociology of retail. I transferred here to be with a particular supervisor. I'd read some things she'd written on cycle times in calendar-driven retail.

Calendar-driven retail?

Sure. There are a lot of different ways it's described, but the idea is that, spread out across the year, there are specific sale points, on top of general commerce. Some of them are demographically focused, some aren't. My supervisor has an interest in Fathers' Day. Me? I went right for the big one. Christmas.

So, what about Christmas exactly?

Exactly? She stops, smiles. *Okay, I've got a working title of "Christmas retail cycle times seen from the perspective of the rise and fall of Tickle-Me-Elmo."*

You can't tell me this is the bit where I'm not allowed to laugh.

But I do get to explain. You have to let me explain.

Don't worry. I'd like to hear you explain. Any time anyone travels a thousand miles to study Tickle-Me-Elmo, I do like to know why.

Are you still going to run with me after this?

I'm still going to run with you. With this thesis topic I'd only want to run with you more. But explain. Surprise me.

Okay. Here's the thing with Tickle-Me-Elmo. You've got two extremes, right? Father's Day is, like, offensively stable. Power tools, angle buffers, year after year.

The last bastion of fifties stereotypes. Big chunky submarine-under-the-ice novels, a boxed set of Rocky videos. I know what you're saying.

But I don't tell her I'm so out of the Fathers' Day league that I thought it was angle buffers for years (the ads always shout in that bloke-frequency voice, which I can't hear clearly). Not that I'm anymore certain now about what angle buffers are for. Which angles they buff, for instance. I've got plenty of angles around the house, but I haven't seen one that could be improved by buffing.

Exactly, she's saying. *As opposed to all the crap Mothers' Day stuff. A different set of stuff, but also stable. But Christmas is constructed in a different way. Partly, obviously, because everyone's supposed to score a present, but it's also less stable than it used to be when it comes to present choices. Monopoly, for example, was the archetypal Christmas gift for a couple of generations. You probably got given it yourself.*

Well, yeah, but don't make me feel historic about it.

What we see now is the fad Christmas. You get one shot at it if you're a manufacturer. You pitch your brilliant, new idea into the pre-Christmas market. Hype it as hard as you can. You've got a couple of weeks to create anticipation, then another couple of weeks to start shifting it. One technique is to under-supply. Empty shelves make news. And the smart thing to do is target the under-sixes. They're much better networked than they used to be, and no one likes to disappoint them. They get really excited about Christmas, and they're not good at putting disappointment into perspective. So, in 1997, they all wanted Tickle-Me-Elmo, she says, and I love the intensity of it, the way it's coming out like a pitch. The way she's completely over the fact that saying Tickle-Me-Elmo with even half this earnestness should be very funny. *It cost sixty bucks then, but the black-market price hit several hundred. In 1998, they were twenty-nine ninety-five. Their time had passed.*

So what you're saying is, if Lily was a few years older, and I'd bought her one in 1997 I'd be a present-buying god, but if I bought her one in 1998 I'd only be showing her how past it I was.

That's it exactly. Might as well get her Monopoly. Don't tell me you didn't think all this through before you became a parent?

Look, I might still buy her Monopoly. In a few years, admittedly, but it could still happen. Is that a problem?

Well, we'll see. That Christmas is probably many fads away, and classic might be in that year.

This isn't sounding easy.

Surely you weren't expecting it to be easy. She takes a mouthful of coffee. *But enough about me and Elmo. What do you do? Other than the bits I got from the card, the laser company name and the medical degree.*

Laser surgery. Skin laser surgery. And, by the way, I'm not sure we've had anything like enough about you and Elmo. I think you were just warming up.

Maybe. But maybe I stopped just in time. So, what's the company you work for?

It's a group practice, a group medical practice. Dermatologists—or, at the moment, one dermatologist—and GPs with special training in laser surgery. It's mainly medical stuff that we do, though—treating disease, skin lesions—not generally all the cosmetic things you see advertised.

Our lunch comes, and I tell her more. How we thought we'd do more cosmetic work until the patients started coming in, and so many of the people interested in it wanted the impossible, or just wanted an expert opinion that would help them sue their last doctor.

It works for fine wrinkles, I tell her, thinking all the time that Tickle-Me-Elmo had far less capacity to bore than this. But it's not so good for expression lines. Like here, between your nose and mouth. But they're normal. You'd look weird without them. If they get pronounced some people want to do something about them. Some people want to do something about them anyway. But we mainly end up treating skin cancers and sun damage and acne scarring. And then we've got another laser that does blood vessel lesions, spidery veins, things like that.

What about tattoos?

Not as easy as they should be. It's a strange thing, really. Tattoos were designed to be permanent, and now that people are getting kind of excited about lasers there's this idea that they aren't anymore. As though you just get them wiped off, or something. And it's not that straightforward.

Do you want another coffee? she says, picking up her cup to drink and seeing that it's empty. *I thought I might have another.*

I'm being boring, aren't I?

No. No, if you were being boring I'd just sit here and suffer. I thought I might have another coffee. And then I expect you to tell me why tattoos aren't that straightforward.

I am boring you. It's fine. You won't hear another word about tattoos. So how about that rugby tournament?

She shakes her head. *Tattoos. Lack of straightforwardness.*

I expect to hear more. In the meantime, and for the third and final time, do you want another tall black?

Thanks.

She walks off to the counter. What am I doing? It's been years since I cared if I was boring someone. I assume I bore people regularly, but I'm not used to minding. Most people bore me, so it's only fair. Ash, I realize, doesn't bore me. She could go on at length about Tickle-Me-Elmo and keep me interested.

I hadn't expected I'd like her. I thought she was too good a runner to have much of a personality. But I do rather compartmentalize the world, don't I, and that's a pretty ridiculous view to have about runners. And maybe it's just all the talking with George lately, but this is operating more the way a date would than I'd expected it to. And I also think the idea of runners not having much of a personality is a George opinion, some big-guy defense for that sedentary life of his. I wonder what he thinks about swimmers. I wonder if he went yesterday.

I'd braced myself for something brief today, awkward silences, little common ground. I was going to try not to rant about my mother, or fireplaces—whatever Ash did to the paper—but I wasn't prepared for the Tickle-Me-Elmo side of her world. This was just a chance for her to get out of the house, not to get semi-dressed-up, play with my baby, be interesting.

Tattoos, she says, when she comes back over. *You were starting to tell me about tattoos.*

Okay. Here's the strange thing. You'd think tattoos'd be the easiest part of the job, but they aren't. They can need quite a few treatments, and there aren't any lasers that cover all the colors effectively. So you can need several different machines to treat the one tattoo. And you can really only justify having multiple machines if you're doing an awful lot of business. You also don't know for sure how many different components modern tattoo inks are made of. Some of them are pure, some of them are a mixture. So very occasionally you'll see a bizarre response, where the laser changes the tattoo ink to another color instead of making it go away. Another issue, at least in this part of the world, is that almost nobody has white skin. As in, actually close to white. And the laser you use for blue or black ink also picks out pigment cells. It depigments the area so—if you imagine it treating your reasonably tanned skin—you could end up with a white tattoo ghost if you had one removed. Whereas, with a lot of diseases, you're much more likely to get a good result. Those farmers who are sixty and look ninety because of all the sun damage to their faces.

Like my father.

That kind of thing can come up really well. It looks like they've had their wrinkles done, even though you're actually doing it to treat premalignant skin change.

It's strange that something like a cancer can be easy to get rid of and a tattoo's harder.

It's all to do with how the skin works. And the laser, too, I guess. People think skin is easy. They think it's a really simple organ. Probably just because it's on the outside and they can see it. It's much more subtle than they realize. There's a lot to it, and most of it's not on show. It's got quite a few layers, and different components to it, and different cell types. Laser's good because it takes that into account. You can shave off layers microns thick, or you can target particular things.

Our second coffees arrive, and I know we need a change of subject. I'm right on the brink of doing what I used to watch old housemates do when they brought women home, told them all about work and made sure we'd never see them again. And they never actually say, *Yes, you're being boring,* do they?

Lily's awake and talking again, wanting to be part of things. I pick her up and let her bounce around on my thigh. Ash smooths out a mint wrapper and turns it into a goblet.

Is that all right, or is it too small for her? she says as she holds it up and Lily reaches for it.

I think we'll notice if she does anything risky with it. It's a neat goblet. You look like you've done that before.

Hey, I've drunk wine from them before.

You know what fun is, don't you?

Well, there goes your chance of getting a set of six for your birthday.

Sorry. It was just envy. The dexterity of it all . . .

My mobile rings. It's somewhere down in the baby bag, so it takes me a while to recognize it and then to find it. It's a medical receptionist and she's saying, *It's Doctor Mendoza's office calling for Doctor Brand.*

Calling for Melissa.

Calling now as I'm sitting here, having my attention caught by a student and her neat, mint-wrapper goblet, halfway through a long discussion about all kinds of things. Complacent, and I told myself I wouldn't be complacent.

The receptionist hasn't heard. It's not her fault that she hasn't heard.

It's been weeks since we last had one of these calls. Weeks and weeks.

I was sure they were over.

Doctor Mendoza's office calling for Doctor Brand.

I'm sorry, I tell her. She died a few months ago, actually. There's no fancy way to say it, no point in trying. I've worked that out. Better to say it clearly, and as though it's just the way things are. But it sounds horribly strange, still, every time. The receptionist apologizes—hurries into some kind of apology—and then she's gone.

Tough business you're in, Ash says. *I hope you don't get too many calls like that.*

Sorry? What do you mean?

Calls about patients who have died. I wouldn't have thought that happened often with laser surgery.

No, no. It doesn't. That was something else.

I'm giving Lily her bath later when the *who does she take after* remark comes back into my mind. She's splashing, sinking ships, grabbing my face with her wet hands and laughing at the expressions she thinks she's molding into it.

She's her own person, even when she's this young. I think sometimes we give too much credit to our simplistic assessments of where people and their parts come from, playing Mister Potato Head with them, as if all their features can be drawn from the small set their parents can give. People have their own noses, their own chins. Sometimes there might be similarities to someone else, but that doesn't mean the part came as a gift, or slipped in as the work of one gene.

In fact, that's one of the best bits of the process. Here's a new person. No one chose the parts to make her with. She's already complex, and thoughtful, and surprising.

We watch the water gurgle down the plug hole, and Lily says something that sounds like *Yeah,* and claps her hands. I flip a towel over her head and we play the hiding game we've made of hair drying. She probably has no idea this is all about getting clean.

In the car we get most of the way through the Lemonheads' "Into Your Arms" on the short drive to my parents' place.

And I'm singing, maybe louder than usual, and wishing that call hadn't come through today. I thought everyone knew now, everyone who might possibly have a need to know. I thought Wendy and Sylvia had a system for letting everyone know, and that they were handling it. I don't even know why a GP would be trying to call on a Saturday. Who could need a dermatologist on a Saturday. I suppose there are some reasons you might. Maybe I should have put them onto George. Not that I really got the chance. The receptionist got off the line pretty quickly.

I lift the Bean out of the baby capsule, and she's warm and clean and a bundle of kicking and noise.

Oh, yeah, we're at the oldies', aren't we? I say to her. Let the fun begin.

My mother takes her at the door, and slips into babble mode right away. Walks down the corridor copying the Bean's every noise and naming furniture and fittings.

And here's Grandpa, she says, drawing out the "here's" as long as possible and swinging into the kind of build-up that might have worked for the host of a TV variety show, but that doesn't make my father entirely comfortable.

He stands there like a man who was about to do a well-rehearsed piece of stage magic, only to discover he's lost his rabbit at the last moment.

Hello, love, he says, sounding altogether too low-key. And then he suddenly becomes animated and says, *Hey, I've got some new screen savers. I think she might like them.*

And we always did want another computer geek in the family, I tell him. You're just starting work on her early, aren't you?

No. I think she might like them. There's the dancing baby from that American television program, and one with pieces of pasta. They're dancing as well. Lots of movement. I think she'll like it.

Ally McBeal, my mother footnotes as he rushes the Bean into his study, *and the pasta is macaroni doing the macarena.*

And he hasn't a clue, has he?

Not a clue. I once asked if he knew South Park, *and his best guesses were that if I looked at the map I'd probably find it somewhere below North Park, or that it might be the old name of a stadium renamed as part of a corporate sponsorship deal.*

Well, you can't say he didn't try.

No, no. Always prepared to give things a go. You know your father. Now, did I tell you we were thinking of going away next weekend? Just for a few days. Maybe a week.

No.

Just the usual kind of thing. Bushwalking and all that. So you'll be all right then?

Sure. You don't actually have to ask my permission to take a vacation, but . . .

No, I was thinking Lily. Your arrangements. Can you make arrangements for her, since we won't be here on the eighth and ninth? If it's too short notice, we could reschedule.

I'm sure it'll be fine.

We go back along the corridor, and through my father's open study door I can see the Bean slapping spit-covered hands all over his computer screen as it plays the zany Guinness screen saver that's a perennial favorite of George's.

Go on, give him another whack, my father says, with some enthusiasm.

Before you ask, my mother says quietly, *the answer is no, you would never have got to do that. He's being a grandparent. Now, is it Katie Watts's place you're going to?*

Yeah, dinner. A dinner party. I don't know who's going to be there.

Well then, new people. That's not so bad.

Depends on the new people, I suppose.

And you'll be back for Lily in the morning, then?

That's the plan.

If you wanted to have a few drinks and catch a cab home, one of us could drive you back there in the morning to get your car.

I think I'll keep it to a couple of glasses. But thanks.

And I can tell from her expression that she gets right to the edge of giving me some of her old "let your hair down" advice, before deciding to hold back. It's advice that should never be trusted anyway. For years at college I didn't get a lot of chances to make the most of it, and took it no further than drinking on Saturday nights at other people's houses and reading the great, thin works of literature.

Then, one night in about fifth year, George took me along to a Trivial Pursuit party at someone's flat. I played like an absolute bandit. I punned with flair, I told engaging stories about myself and, when the questions came up, I could name ferry ports on the south coast of England, pre-war American baseball stars, all the tributaries of the Orinoco. I owned the board that night. And I completely misread the signals from our host—mistaking them for friendship—and ended up in her bed a few hours later, with her throwing her clothes off and talking through the various options available to me. Several of them would have required at least one of us to have dislocatable hips (something I was learning to test for at the time, but it didn't seem prudent to mention it).

I tried to pick a really slow option, but she thought it meant I was sensitive rather than baffled as to how I came to be there, and she made it clear that far more complicated things were on offer. And if the whole interaction wasn't enough like *Porky's* already, that's when her fiancé, a man not previously mentioned that night, turned up. And I got to spend several hours under her bed, being closer to many of the previously mentioned activity options than I would have liked.

I caught a bus home at seven a.m., wearing the day before's clothes. Feeling proud about having let my hair down, but seriously disorientated at the same time. And my parents, who had urged me for years to have nights like this, were pacing the den having not slept for hours, thinking I'd come to grief and supposedly on the brink of calling the police.

It's kind of sad when you're in your twenties and your mother thinks a night out is more likely to end with your death on the roads than it is to end in sex.

My father couldn't stop the pacing, even when he'd adjusted to the fact that I'd made it home alive.

Your mother was so worried, he kept saying, long after she'd brought out tea and a plateful of biscuits.

I wonder how I'll be the first time I confront the same issue, Lily coming home long after she's supposed to. I won't get to project in quite my father's way. Pacing while clutching a dizzy whippet and telling her, Elvis was so worried, just isn't going to work.

But I hope that moment's twenty years away, and I can't know how things'll be then. I'm the full set of parents now, so there's no projection, no buck passing, no taking turns. Maybe that'll change, maybe it won't. But that's all too odd to think about for now. It's George and his date talk that's got me here, thinking about this kind of thing—my life and Lily's in the future—when I should be dealing with each day as it comes.

And sometimes I actually want to keep her to myself.

Katie's street is empty, other than two cars parked near the top of the hill, about ten houses away from hers.

I ring the doorbell and she's there in seconds, wearing slightly more makeup than I'd expected. Slightly more makeup, large interesting earrings and several bangles. Katie has gone for that "splash of color" and her Little Black Dress is going under for the third time.

Australian champagne equivalent, I say, and hand over the bottle I've brought. For launching the kitchen.

Oh, how nice. You didn't have to do that. I might pop it in the fridge for now. I've just opened some wine. Would you like a glass?

Why not? Thanks.

We walk down the hall and she says, *Don't look in there,* as we pass the bedroom, where most of the contents of her wardrobe appear to have been tipped onto her bed.

She sits me down on a vast overfilled sofa, gives me my glass of wine, nudges the bottle back down into the ice bucket with a rattle of bangles and watches me take a sip. It seems as though a comment might be in order.

That's nice, I say, since I can't go for wine-wanker words. What is it? Is it all chardonnay?

Um, yes, is that okay? It's unwooded.

It's very nice. And chardonnay is good. I've got no time for those wine gurus and their temporary attachment to Riesling, or whatever. Besides, I'm no expert. I'm sort of out of the habit of drinking wine much anyway.

Oh, sorry, she says, as though she's forced me into it.

No, this is good. It's just a health thing, like eating better and running more. It doesn't mean I never drink. It's not as if wine's bad for you. It's probably more that the only other person in the house is underage by about seventeen-and-a-half years, so it's not as though we share wine over dinner.

No. Pistachio? she says, leaning forward and holding up

a bowl. *Vine leaves stuffed with semi-dried roasted red peppers and capers? They're from Angelo's. You know Angelo's?*

No.

At West End?

Not really my side of town.

Oh.

But I'm sure they're great. They look great.

Flag, she says with a pressured kind of glee, as though the moment's been saved by the arrival of a cat, and my deli ignorance is instantly less of an obstacle.

Flag jumps up onto the arm of the sofa and checks me out. I pat his head and he drops down onto the cushion next to me. I bite into one of Angelo's vine-leaf creations and make the right kind of Mmm noise, but a little too quickly. Flag stretches his front paws into my lap, pushes his claws out and starts kneading. I wonder if this is a territorial gesture, a gender-based warning that I shouldn't be getting any big ideas here. But Flag can't know I've got no ideas at all, and that the other guests are probably arriving any minute.

Don't worry, Katie says. *It's only a problem if you don't have a couple of layers of fabric.*

At that second, Flag proves her wrong and prongs me in the groin, making me wince. And I'm not sure if it's best to tell Katie that I actually do have underpants on, or not. It could affect the dynamics of the conversation. Maybe, for future reference, she needs to know that Flag finds two layers of fabric relatively easy.

Um, no Flaggy, she says quietly, *Be nice to Jon . . . Oh, god, music. I've forgotten to put music on.*

She goes to the corner of the room, flicks through some

CDs. *Ah ha,* she says, and just as I'm fearful she's about to play a Scandinavian one-hit wonder from the eighties (or, at best, early nineties) Elvis comes out of four speakers. "Love Me Tender."

This must be a joke. She and George must have colluded. Froufy nibbly things, ice bucket, an Elvis love-ballad album. Pulled out with an *Ah ha,* as though it's quite the perfect choice. Any moment now, George will lurch from a cupboard laughing. That's what I'm telling myself. Or maybe just hoping. Katie's wardrobe maybe, which would explain why all her clothes were on the bed. Or, alternatively, half-a-dozen Jungian therapists will arrive, talk shop all night, and I'll never be brave enough to mention seven references to fish in one afternoon, and I'll never get invited back. And that'll all be for the best.

I miss home, bath time, little plastic boats, a stern but silent dog, quiet battles over apple puree.

But no, we're onto Elvis, talking Elvis now. Katie's saying, *So what do you think of Elvis?* and I can only answer, He's the best dog I've ever had.

I tell her the story of how I wanted a dog and Mel didn't, so we did a deal over naming rights. I could have the dog if I was prepared to accept the name she would give it, and certain other conditions. So I said fine, and she said the name was Motherfucker. And my father had to call it in for dinner.

She won that time. No dog. But months later, in a less-considered moment, she suggested Elvis, thinking there was no way I'd go for that either.

And I've always got laughs out of that story before, but not this time.

Katie goes into the kitchen. I pour myself some more chardonnay, even though my head's feeling out of practice with this stuff, and I go to take a look at her CDs. They're on a rotating stand, and the side facing out is all Elvis. I've probably seen enough.

This isn't going well. I shouldn't have mentioned Melissa. And one Elvis song should have been enough to make me cautious. I shouldn't have told a story that suggested that anyone who knew me well would know that naming a dog Elvis was something I'd rank only marginally ahead of naming it Motherfucker and having my father call it in for dinner.

I go to the kitchen to apologize, figuring this is best cleared up now. On the way, I pass the dining room. Which has candles, and is set for two.

There will be no Jungian therapists arriving here this evening. No opportunity to be useful in making up numbers, or to contribute an eighth of the dinner-party conversation before slipping discreetly into the night. Flag runs past me on the way into the kitchen, tags my ankle and I almost trip.

See, Katie says, a quick recovery from the Elvis disappointment in progress. *Flaggy likes you. He loves a game, but he wouldn't play if he didn't like you. And don't worry. He's not a big Elvis fan either. More an eighties man.*

I've got nothing against Elvis, I tell her, as the prelude to the apology. He did some great stuff. A lot of that old stuff is great. It's just an embarrassing name to call your dog. Any time we go out for a walk anywhere and he runs off, I'm standing there shouting Elvis, Elvis. It doesn't look good.

I hadn't thought of it that way, Katie says, and it seems fixed up. *Linguini con . . . what's Italian for prawns?*

She fusses me toward my seat, serves the meal, says something about dinner music and goes off to change the CD. Sinatra's singing before she's back in the room.

You know, I really like some of this old stuff too.

Yeah. It's timeless, some of it. Isn't it?

We begin forced conversation. We do what we can with Sinatra, which isn't much. I drink more than I should, and by eight-thirty I know I'll be taking a cab home and coming back for the car in the morning. I don't want to drink, but Katie keeps pouring wine for both of us and, with the ambient anxiety she's generating, there's a sense that I'd wreck the evening if I said no to anything. More wine, more linguini, another piece of homemade crusty bread. We force the conversation like a Jenny Craig ad director forcing a before-photo fat ball player into a too-small suit. There's something cruel and uncomfortable about it, and no one gets to laugh. I encourage Katie to tell me about her renovating, and I realize I should have fussed more about the kitchen.

I never wanted to be in this position. I realize that as she's telling me how much thought goes into bench heights and how many times she had to get the ceiling-fan guy back. I never wanted to be thirtysomething and sitting here in the middle of summer with too much chardonnay in me (unwooded or otherwise), some old crooner droning in the next room, and a ceiling fan misfiring above my head. Feeling sweat run down my back and watching it carry the makeup quietly off the face of the person who's deciding the evening will be fine if there are no pauses and every minute of her renovations is thoroughly discussed.

She tells me she's thinking of having her bedroom air-conditioned. She tells me some rooms are completely finished, but that other rooms still have slatted pantry doors instead of solid timber, and she doesn't know what kind of person would have done that. She tells me it's so good that she's met me properly now, so good she's getting to know me when, all these years, I've just been Wendy's friend. And who would have guessed this kind of thing could start happening?

Which is when I choke, and a chunk of dinner flies up into my nasopharynx.

I excuse myself, go to the bathroom. Choke and snort and cough, and eventually a rather soiled piece of prawn flips out of my nose.

From this point, the evening gets worse.

I return to the dining room and Katie stares at me, unable to come to terms with the beastly sounds I've subjected her to. I think I've spoiled her new bathroom, maybe forever. I drink more. So does she.

There are two things I can't believe. I can't believe I'm on a date and I can't believe I'm so bad at it. Three things. I can't believe she went to the trouble to try to translate her prawn dish into Italian, and I left the room to blow it out my nose. I didn't think it was going this way. I thought we were coffee friends. I thought there'd be Jungian therapists.

We adjourn to the lounge room. Katie brings coffee and a plate of little chocolates, handmade by a very delicate man from yet another part of town. If she had traveled any further to put this dinner together she'd have scored frequent-flyer points. She probably met the prawn trawlers on their way back in from the bay this morning too. If Katie came over to my place for dinner, I'd know just which Thai take-out would be my first choice. It's not the same.

She puts the chocolates in front of me, presumably watching to see which orifice I bung them into, then which I blow them out of.

Shit, there's dessert wine, she says. She fetches a bottle, and starts to drink it. *Oh Jon, I just want you to be happy,* she says, in a particularly melancholy way. *Should I have bought a cigar?*

What? I'm not sure that's what my happiness is depending on.

No, I just thought, people are into them at the moment. Separate thought to the happiness. You have to move quickly.

Right. I don't smoke. It was smoking it that you were thinking about? It's like grape varieties. Even if cigars are temporarily in, I don't smoke. So no cigars was perfect.

Excellent. The conversation pauses there. She looks at me, intently. Drinks more of the dessert wine. *You're not always an easy person to read, you know that? You showed me baby photos. You have to realize that.* She takes Sinatra off and puts on Men Without Hats, "The Safety Dance." *Not a lot of people have this album, you know,* she says, implying some angry kind of exclusivity that I don't really understand.

I get up to go to the toilet, and Flag tags my ankle again. Twice, and then he follows me in there. I've had too much to drink and so has Katie, but she's kept pouring, making sure the evening won't fail through an insufficiency of wine. Flag winds his way between my legs, purring, and it's here, standing up in the glaringly bright bathroom, away from Katie's discourse on renovations and the big sofa and the mood-lit lounge, that I realize it's all too difficult, and I know I have to go home. Apologize for the misunderstanding, for anything I've done wrong, and leave before anyone's dignity is put seriously on the line.

I wonder what's going on in Katie's mind out there, with the disjointed statements she's making that seem to add up to suggest I've misled her, and harmed her in some way. And that she was expecting this evening to go very differently. She'd gone for special, without knowing that special was never my thing. But it's overwhelmed me tonight. Katie and her eighties hair, conjuring up one gourmet moment after another and making the night feel like such a big deal. And completely the wrong kind of big deal.

Flag, being a cat, gets curious. He knows that something out of the ordinary is happening, involving a stream of yellow fluid flying down into a bowl.

Not a lot of men in the place, hey Flaggy, I say to him quietly, as he pushes between my legs again.

His tail flicks dangerously by as he passes. He circles, then stands up on his back legs with his front paws on the edge of the bowl.

Flag, be careful there. I know I've still got a young man's prostate, but what's happening is honestly not that impressive.

But Flag is impressed. And I'm mid-stream, so it's not as though I can push him aside. He's looking down into the bowl, looking up at where it's coming from, looking down into the bowl again.

Okay, Flag, stay right there and we all get out of here alive. No sudden movements.

He crouches down, and looks like he's about to clamber into the bowl.

No, Flag, I say in the no-shit, firm voice I've been practicing for the day when Lily takes an interest in the electric outlet.

And that's when he jumps.

Jumps for the urine stream and grabs at it with both paws, spraying it everywhere. This surprises him. He has no grasp of simple physics and obviously expected a different outcome. Worse, it makes me recoil backward, changing the simple physics and directing the stream right at his head before I can stop it. He jumps away, shakes himself, manages to spread it around more. Tonight's dinner had not been going well. And now I've pissed on her cat. Every other grim moment seems inconceivably subtle in comparison.

Flag runs little catty pee footprints around the room as I try to catch him. And Flaggy, as Katie said, loves a game. It takes a lot of pursuit and two bath towels before I pin him to the floor near the door. He purrs like a buzz saw, licks my face.

Katie doesn't play this one with you enough, does she? I say to him quietly, and he licks me again.

I wrestle him up to the sink to try to wash him. I get the water running, and that's when he goes crazy. Being urinated on he didn't mind so much, tap water could be the end of him. He wrestles, slips out of my hands, slurps out of the sink and into the bath and out the window.

Urine is dispersed over most of the bathroom. Fortunately, I've already ruined two towels trying to catch Flag, so it's not hard to work out what I should use to mop up. My pants and my shirt front are wet, but I'm telling myself it's at least eighty percent water. I replace the towels with fresh ones from the cupboard when I've finished, and I ball the urine-stained ones up as tightly as I can and fling them out the window, as close to the road as I can get them.

I do up my fly, I walk back into the lounge room and I tell Katie, Thanks, it's been great, but I might call a cab now.

8

Listen, Jon, this is going to sound kind of weird, Wendy says, when I get to work at lunchtime on Monday. *But it probably needs to be sorted out.* She leads me into her room, shuts the door. *Katie called me yesterday. She's a bit worried about you. And maybe I'm a bit worried about her. Jon, I don't know where she's got this idea from . . . she thinks you might have urinated on Flag.* The look on my face is probably horror, since behind the look it's horror I'm feeling. *I know. It's all very embarrassing. Katie can get herself . . . worked up, if you know what I mean. But this . . .*

Yeah.

I don't know what we're going to do, Jon.

Yeah, I know. He just followed me in there.

And now Katie's got this idea . . .

He just followed me in there, and I'd had a couple of drinks by then. A few drinks. And I haven't been drinking much lately.

Wendy's watching me. She's stopped interrupting. She's now taken over the look of horror. Just as I'm realizing she thought this was all in Katie's head, Wendy works out she's hearing the preamble to a confession.

It wasn't intentional.

Oh god, Jon, I told her no way. I told her you didn't do that sort of thing.

Of course I don't do that sort of thing. I might not have been concentrating particularly well though.

She makes a teeth-gritting motion and nods.

I'd had a couple of drinks. And he moved very quickly.

She looks like someone who's about to up their level of care again. Someone who thought I was handling things all right, allowed her attention to lapse, and now look what I've done. Jon's not coping well at all. We thought he was doing okay, but . . .

It was the fucking cat's fault.

The cat's fault.

Totally. I was standing there, minding my own business, directing my stream with nothing less than the required competence. Not concentrating particularly well, as I said, but it is something I've done a few times before. But I don't think Flag's seen a lot of men in that position.

Men not concentrating particularly well?

Urinating. The standing-up version. He got a bit excited. And he sort of jumped me. And I tried to clean him up . . .

Now, wait a second. I think you've missed a bit.

The bit where I pissed on his head? Is that the bit? Or the bit where he waved his paws around in it first when he was trying to catch it?

Wendy starts to laugh.

Or the bit where I had to chase him around the room to catch him.

Oh, any of those, she says, as the truth of it starts to sink in. *I can't believe you pissed on Flag. Katie's had some bad dates before, but as far as I know you are the first to piss on her cat.*

I didn't know it was a date.

Hardly seems to matter now, does it? Anyway, the date rhetoric's all just ridiculous Georgespeak. Call it what you want. It's the outcome that's the interesting bit. You think you know someone . . . She laughs again. *You dark horse, you. You operator.*

Oh god, Katie was so intense, and she kept topping up my wine.

Well, you pretty much have to piss on people's cats if they're intense and they give you wine.

Do you have to keep saying it? In such a frank way?

I think I do. I think this is a once-in-a-lifetime opportunity. You were dorky at school, and I was worried over the last, you know, decade or so that you were getting your shit together. This is good. Hey, you should get a ping-pong ball to put in your toilet at home. It's great for the aim. I used it with Patrick when he was toilet training. Simple, but effective. And one of the many reasons to be glad you've got a daughter.

Thanks.

That's okay. Oh, sorry, one other thing. This is pretty embarrassing. I think—okay, I get the peeing bit and the extenuating circumstances—but I think it's affected Katie's judgment. You know the way she can be a bit . . . Doesn't matter. What I'm saying is . . . She stops to laugh, as though even she can't believe this story might have anymore left in it. *This is just a small thing we'll have to sort out with her and I'm sure, when we tell her the rest of it, she'll realize she's got this wrong. Katie thinks you steal things. She thinks you went back to her place yesterday morning and took a couple of towels.*

Later, after my last patient has gone, I'm sitting in my room and telling myself it's not so much a lie as something that simply can't be explained properly.

Okay, I caught the cab home. I slept poorly, but there was nothing paradoxical about it, and no reading. My father is an early riser, so it was easy to get back to Katie's place while she should still have been asleep. And to thank my father for the lift, wave him off and foray briefly into her garden, pull the peed-on towels out of the bushes and drive away. They're in my bin now. And they're never going back.

Katie thinks she heard someone in her bushes around dawn, Wendy told me. *And then a car driving off. Your car. She went to change her towels late yesterday and noticed there were two missing from the cupboard.*

Fortunately, I know Wendy well enough that I got the sense she was presenting this to me as a piece of mad supposition on Katie's part. And when I said, Obviously the only reason I'd agreed to go there for dinner was to pick myself up a couple of towels, she said, *Exactly,* and apologized on Katie's behalf.

And as if she'd know what a Corolla engine sounded like.
I was in the Beemer, actually.

Well, there you go. She's getting bars on her windows now, you know.

Who wouldn't be, with all this towel-thieving going on?

Oh, she'll find them in the laundry, or somewhere. She loses things all the time and thinks people have taken them. And she was way out of line when she asked if I thought you were somewhere in the kleptomaniac spectrum, or if it was just a personality disorder.

And with that excellent backhander, Katie was dismissed.

So I might get away with it. But it's hard to believe that I'm telling myself it's a good outcome, any kind of win at all. That I'm now known to a close friend and workmate as a cat pisser, but not a towel thief, so that's okay.

I know I have to apologize to Katie, but how do I begin? With an e-mail, obviously. I will begin (and hopefully end) the apology with a single well-composed e-mail. It might not look as good as handling it face-to-face, but this is hardly a time to begin worrying about appearances.

Today, I get a weasel with attitude.

Hey. I don't know that I like you so much anymore. I thought you were one of the good guys, Jon. Not one of those folk always expecting something for nothing. Now go click YES!! I LOVE MY WEASEL!! and you can register to use Window Weasel for life for only $30! Click LATER to register later.

So I'm no longer one of the good guys. As if that's news. I open one of the ktnflag e-mails in my in-box, and I hit Reply. I delete the text that's there, and then I'm faced by the large rectangular space that has to be filled by apology. Maybe I should try to keep it light.

Katie, Just a note to say thanks for Saturday night. Had a great time. Sorry for pissing on the cat though.

And if it sounded frivolous in my head—which it did—it looks simply stupid when reduced to the nuance-free, semi-formality of text.

Katie, It's like this. I suspect Flag hasn't seen a lot of men peeing before.

No.

Katie, It's probably not possible to explain the events of Saturday night in a way that seems reasonable, or perhaps even plausible. (I'd settle for plausible.) I don't think I even told you how much I'd enjoyed the dinner, horrified as I was at the accident in the bathroom. Flag and I did seem to be getting on well and he is, as you know, a very playful cat. He happened to lunge at a rather unfortunate moment, and this created a small mess. When I tried to catch him so that I could clean him, he jumped out the window. I must have used an entire roll of paper cleaning up. I'm sure you can imagine how embarrassed I was, and that I just didn't know how to explain it to you.

I go on-line to send, and I have two new e-mails. A joke forward from George that I'm sure he forwarded weeks ago, but that must have come back around, and one called "calendar-driven e-mail" from a student at Queensland University. Nothing from Katie. That's probably for the best.

I open the student one.

Hey, just got my e-mail access here sorted out. Trying to learn how to use it (not used to the software). Which is why my address has my student no. in it and nothing more friendly. I've tried attaching a document, just to see if it works. So let me know.

A

It works, it's Ash's school timetable. I e-mail her right back, and I tell her Tuesdays suck.

I send the Katie e-mail, get off-line and decide I'd rather pick up the Bean from my parents than take on my in-box. Wendy, who has stayed back taking on her in-box, gets to the lift at the same time as I do.

Katie is e-mailed, I tell her. It took a bit of thought, but it's done.

And I'm up on the paperwork, so a big elephant stamp for each of us then.

No, I think you get the elephant stamp. I didn't do any paperwork. But then, you didn't pee on anything, did you? It does make a person start the week behind.

Well, you've done the e-mail now. You've cleared the decks.

And I'm assuming Saturday night is something we can keep to ourselves.

There's a pause, and that can't be good. She jiggles her car keys in her hand.

Jon, you went over to my sister's place for dinner and you urinated on her cat. Was there one day in your life when you would have kept that kind of thing to yourself if it had been someone else?

It was the dinner. I was thinking it was a dinner party. I was caught unawares. I'm not ready for this stuff, for nights like that.

Jon, that bit of it's fine. That stuff happens. Being not ready is quite okay. I don't plan to go there. You know that. The bit I want to tell people is the urinating bit. Let me put it another way. The bit I've been telling people is the urinating bit.

Tonight, there's more teething. It's probably more teething. Not much sleep, anyway. A fussy baby, a worried dog and, out there in the world, who knows how many people who have already heard about my Saturday night.

The Bean works up a sweat with the effort she's putting in. I wipe her face and head with a wet washrag, but the game I try to turn that into isn't good enough to end in sleep. It's time for the car, the soothing rhythm of driving, the air-conditioning, the Lemonheads.

We drive, I sing, the Bean chews away at the wet rag. The CD ends, I talk. About the heat, about summer and winter, temporarily about the long-term implications of climate change, about traffic lights, about Ash's house where the lights are all off, about the rowing sheds at the college, about the City Cat ferry stop, the route I run every weekday, about the sugarcane farm that was here in this pocket of the river before they built the campus. About her mother.

Somehow I'm talking about Mel, about how we hardly knew each other when we were here at school. That we really met afterward.

I'm listening to some tour-guide voice telling Lily about Mel, and it's me and I want to throw up. I have to stop the car.

It's just the surprise of it. I was commentating, in the

usual bland way, and she crept in. I take a few deep breaths. Usually I think advice to take a few deep breaths is crap, but this time it helps. I should pay more attention to what I'm saying. I hit the play button, and the Lemonheads come on. I sing, and drive.

I've got to watch for that sort of thing. I've got to handle it better. I have to work it out first, rather than just let it out. Kids take things in, even really early on, and I'm not ready to put that in the Bean's world yet. It's hard enough, anyway, fitting it into its place in a lot of other worlds, but I don't know when she'll know enough about life to understand it.

I took Wendy's kids to McDonald's a few weeks ago, and Emily started talking about birds, birds taking away babies. I think she was worried about Lily. It took a while to work out what she was on about, and it was only when I asked her if the birds were storks that I had a chance of fixing it. I told her not to worry. That birds never took babies away. That there's a very old story about where babies come from that says storks carry them here in their beaks. But even that's just an old story, and everything's okay.

I told Wendy and she said, *Bloody grandparents. The deprogramming I have to do . . .*

But that one was easy to fix. It was far harder months ago, working out how to explain why Mel wouldn't be coming around any more. Why it was me and a baby instead. Actually, it was impossible. Beyond me. I decided I couldn't see them, because I knew it'd be the first question and I knew it wouldn't go well.

But Wendy came over. She came over a lot anyway, but

one day she came over to talk about this—as though she could read my mind to tell me that Emily had been talking about Mel. Jon and Mel. *Where are Jon and Mel?*

So I told her, she said. *I told them. And, I'm sorry, but I've done it in a kind of strange way. I couldn't work out how to do it. So, for the moment, I've told them Mel's gone away. And—I should probably have planned it better—Steve's the only person they know who goes away. To Mount Isa with work. So they're assuming Mel's in Mount Isa, and that's kind of where I left it.*

And I said to her, That's fine. Lots of skin cancers in the Isa.

That's what I told her, and that way she smiled instead of crying. Crying was a distinct possibility, as though she'd let me down by being unable to find a tellable truth in what had happened.

She smiled and nodded. Asked how I was, and we both waited for the moment to pass. She said, *It's all so strange,* and I said, I know. And she went into my kitchen, blew her nose on a paper towel and made us both coffee. She'd never made coffee at my place before. That was always a thing I did. And I couldn't believe that, in some peculiar way, I was secretly annoyed with her for making coffee, because it just made things stranger.

When she left, I said I'd go to their place for a barbecue the next day, now that we had a plan that would do for the moment, an explanation that could buffer, temporarily, the inexplicable truth.

And I wanted to say to her—then, and plenty of times since—How the fuck do you explain this stuff? If only the hassles with explaining it ended when the person was five or six or whatever age you needed to be to have some comprehension of it all. As if it's something you can tell even the people who can understand what you're saying. I haven't told a new person for months. It's just too big. It's not like it's the size of a piece of information yet. It'd be more like turning myself inside out than telling a person something.

It's the shadow I'm standing in, a rock I can't push past. I don't have it down to tellable size, so I don't meet people. That's how I work. And it works for now, and I'll move on in my own time. So people shouldn't ask me to dinner and think it's some kind of date, particularly if they already know. They shouldn't muscle in on my runs and play with my baby and tell me about their thesis topics. And make me like them and want to see more of them. Because I'll lie by omission, and that's not fair to any of us.

I'm doing fine, in so many ways, but it's still so hard to tell people. And I'm terrified of the moment when Lily is suddenly old enough to understand it. This horrible injustice that's been done her. But that's not yet. It's telling people I meet now that's become the issue.

Ash. I mean Ash. Telling Ash. She's becoming a test of this, and some measure of how little I've traveled these last six months. Not that I have any compulsion to rush beyond the people around me. I just hadn't realized I'd been quite this insular. Lily keeps me busy. That's genuinely part of it, and a good part of it. And work is too, the re-imposed routines of work. Three half days and two full days a week. Not completely like it used to be, but the right amount for now.

We had to look at the business structure after Mel died, since I owned two quarters of it all of a sudden and I didn't want to. We had to think about getting someone else to cover Mel's share of the work, and we had to decide whether we'd do that with part-timers or get a new person to buy in.

And I sat there, not really listening, and we'd stop the meetings when I'd visibly stopped caring, and we'd take it slowly. I'd sit there, remember a couple of years before, when we were putting it all together the first time, and it didn't make sense to be having to go through so much of that again so soon.

It probably wasn't easy for the others, either, but I can't say I noticed that.

If I think back now to the meetings a few months ago, I can see the strain on their faces. I don't think I'm inventing it, even if I didn't register it at the time. And it's different, still different here now. For them as well as me, and I'm not sure I knew that. They knew Mel too, after all.

I remember when we set the practice up and how, if we hadn't known each other so well, there might have been concerns about the structure, since a couple technically controlled half of it. But, from before we started, everyone knew it wouldn't be a problem. We knew Mel and I would disagree on most things, since that's what we did. It turned out that the four of us disagreed on plenty of things, but Mel and I had the advantage of being able to argue about it in the car afterward, and at home for as long as we wanted.

And, as a business devoted to laser surgery of the skin,

we argued most about music. We argued about sound systems, then the types of music that might be played, then their implications. George said it worried him, that he could see where it was all heading. That, if we agreed on Vivaldi (to pick one extreme), someone some day could demand Metallica, and what would we do? Most of us would draw a line in there somewhere, but we'd all draw it in different places.

We're heading for middle-of-the-road, he said. *We have to fight against that. We're negotiating blandification. It's the Classic Hits format. It's stagnation. It's a slow death. It's emblematic of a civilization in decay. In the years before the Roman Empire fell, they reverted to a Classic Hits format.*

And Mel said whatever music was played we had to be able to control the volume in each room, because she'd probably want it off most of the time.

Then there was the issue of whether LaserWest would be one word or two. And if it was one, whether or not the "W" would be capped.

We agreed on which lasers we wanted without much debate, and they cost one hundred thousand dollars each.

Then, after Mel died and I went back, it wasn't like the same place. Patients weren't even like the same phenomenon for a while. I could do the surgical things. I liked the parts of the job where the people shut up and I was down there close to the skin, working in microns. It was the talking parts I couldn't handle. I'd find myself explaining and explaining before the procedure, working toward some kind of informed consent and suddenly I'd wonder why the hell these details mattered. And then I'd tell myself to stick to it, I'd remember the next detail and

I'd be rolling again, with hardly a pause on the outside. It's normal for there to be some mild redness and swelling around the treated area . . .

I'd remember, you have to tell people things. You have to get them ready for the common things, and let them know the likelihood of others. Uncommon things happen. Medicine can be like that, sometimes even when it's almost guaranteed to work out well.

But it's not guaranteed, and even when the odds are something massive to one, there's still the one.

The first forty weeks of Mel's pregnancy were uneventful. It was the last hour when it went wrong.

There was commotion first. Or concern, then commotion, then desperate measures, then a time on life support. Academic signs of death while ventilation was going on. Automatic-piloted decisions, and a brand new baby. I was there when things stopped. I remember the Intensive Care guy who talked to me so long it must have been an explanation. But it was like tinnitus. Like a sound that was ugly and nonsensical. With its content so impossible to put together that it was already a blur when it left his mouth, incomprehensible noise. And I noticed his hair. I noticed that he could at least have combed his hair.

And we didn't know what she'd be called. Lily was Mel's choice, but I was never drawn to it. I don't know how many alternatives I'd suggested. And then she was born, and Mel was dead.

Months later I think I like it, even though I'm in the habit of something less formal.

And we're miles now from the campus, but she's asleep. The car clock says two fifty-two. I turn the music down, and head for home.

9

I run anyway. Usually I start so slowly after one of these interrupted nights that I don't even try to persuade my body to do anything at speed. I tell Ash about the teething, and not to expect much from me. She tells me she'll be gentle.

There's been rain just before dawn, and we run around campus with wet smells lifting from the grass and the sun glinting from leaves, from droplets of water that will soon burn away. We run past the rowing sheds, past the City Cat ferry stop, past the colleges and the lakes.

I get to work, I shower, I'm glad it's a half day.

There are ping-pong balls in my in-box. There's an e-mail from George, entitled "International sign of disrespect." It's something to do with urinating on flags, and the UN Security Council. And George isn't even here. Yesterday he was at the campus and he's back there today, re-enrolling in the part-time philosophy degree he's been doing for the last couple of years. George says he needs to keep his levels of mental stimulation high. As demonstrated by his willingness to devote energy to tangents. What did he do to get this UN thing? Go to a search engine and key in "urinate"? I hope they work him hard in that degree.

I go to thank Wendy for telling him, and for the ping-pong balls.

That was actually Sylvia, she says, and fakes a look of contrition.

What? Sylvia's my parents' age. She wears her hair in a bun every day. She's not supposed to be making jokes about my ability to control my stream.

Don't be so ageist. Your mother would do it.

She doesn't have the bun.

Don't be so bunnist. Now, about Katie . . . She pauses. I wait. I'm not going to blow it now. *I thought that was a nice e-mail you sent her.*

Well, thanks. I hoped you'd like it. Should I have Cc'd you in? Except, when I was sending it, I had the idea it was just between her and me.

Um, she forwarded it to me. I didn't ask her to. She'd like to see you, for coffee, maybe. Casual. Just to clear the air, she said. So that everything's all right between the two of you.

And you can't say no to that, since it'd mean everything wasn't all right between the two of you. And when you're the one who's soiled the other person's pet you have to be prepared to go to some trouble to make up for it.

But the day is better when I've got the whole issue out of my head, and I'm working on skin again. Into the rhythm of the laser as it zaps its way precisely into a skin cancer, working off the layers. And the vacuum hums away and Nigel talks to the patient, describing what's happening, or chatting. Leaving me alone, moving precisely between shots, stripping away what I need to.

My memories of six months ago are patchy. I wonder

if they always will be. If it's due to a receptive issue at the time—an inability to take much in—or if it's all there, stored, linear and whole, waiting its turn to be accessed. The simplest things were complicated. Eating a meal all the way to the end, sleeping. A wild tiny baby needing care so often. All a blur. The cremation. The paperwork I had to go through. Looking up at the timber ceiling of the crematorium and seeing what appeared to be a couple of pieces of sticky tape, as though someone had once put a poster up there.

I like the baby, now that I've adjusted. Even today I like her, after a night of moderate shittiness. I like her sense of adventure, her attachment to detail as she studies a broken Bonio or a plastic cup, like someone preparing for an exam on it. We're quite a household. The three of us. The Bean, me and a dog that's only just smart enough to blame me for rain, but not smart enough to know how dumb that is. Who insists on eating the corners of any piece of fruit toast in the vicinity. Who ignores his own name when he chooses to, but never ignores the word "cheese."

Now, everything's organized for next week then? my mother says when I get there after lunch.

I think so.

We'll be back o. .e eleventh or twelfth, so everything's back to usual on Monday the fifteenth.

It's in the diary. I think Sylvia's pretty keen about having Lily at work for a couple of half days next week, after that day not so long ago. She's novelty value. And a good reason not to do the boring bits of the job for a couple of days.

I don't mention the ping-pong balls I have to put up with as the downside of the deal. My mother gets out her bushwalking books and shows me where they'll be going. *And your father's printed off some information about the wineries in the area, so that's the afternoons taken care of.*

When I call Ash, I get her answering machine. I'd forgotten she's at school all day on Tuesdays.

Suddenly the outgoing message is over, I've got the beep and the tape's recording. I wonder if I should have had a reason to call her. So I invite her to dinner, tomorrow night.

I might be going to tell her about Mel. Or I might not. I might actually be wanting all that out of my head again and replaced with human company of the adult kind, but someone outside my too-close circle. It's like, piss on one cat, everyone knows. Everyone thinks you're not on top of your life until you've told them, in some detail, how you came to urinate on a coffee-friend's much-loved pet.

Still, it's better that they're giving me ping-pong balls than trying to rush me off into therapy. How could you bring that story up in therapy without precipitating a grim search for meaning? *Now, Jon, suppose I put it to you this way. Perhaps now that you're in the sole-parenting role, some issues are coming to the surface. Perhaps there's something with your parents, your own toilet training. How do you feel about your mother? Really. And tell me, how do you feel when people are late for their appointments?*

Fine, I feel fine. Another moment's treasured laziness. A chance to address my in-box. Gaze at the horizon. Pass a little urine, maintaining surgical accuracy at all times. Woe betide any cats that cross my path, but I feel fine. And when

I run in the mornings with Ash, she's the only one fit enough to talk. I called her because I felt like conversation, but you can't tell that to an answering machine.

And on the subject of therapists, what's Katie thinking about it? How do Jungians feel when you pee on their cats?

The phone wakes me. I've fallen asleep on the sofa with the Bean on my chest.

I swivel around and pick up, and my outgoing message cuts in. I press all the wrong buttons and the phone screams and wails before I can fix it. It's Ash.

Do you know how to use that thing?

No. No one ever told me. So I hit all the buttons until the noise stops.

Good system.

Um, I called you, I say to her, still waking up. I was going to invite you to dinner tomorrow night.

Yeah . . . um . . . I think you did if I heard the message correctly. So, is it still on?

Yes. If you can make it.

I can make it. It'd be nice. Do you want me to bring anything?

No, I don't think so.

Okay. Now, could I ask you a favor? And if it's not convenient say no, and it's fine.

Sure.

Are you going straight home after work? Because if you are, my car's got a few problems and I need to get some groceries. I wondered maybe if I could meet you at Toowong Village when you finish work and I could buy them and we could take them to my place.

Yeah, that's fine.

If it's not feasible that's okay. If there's a problem with day care, or something.

No. It should be all right. I've got some stuff to buy too. I was going to be there anyway.

So dinner is on. With her head still on my chest, the Bean is looking up at me with her woken-too-quickly face and she's unsure if she should get upset or not. I do some quick talking, anything to force a laugh, then we're okay.

I can't even use the answering machine. Mel died before telling me how to use the answering machine. She set it up when we first got it, and any time we call-screened she cracked before I did.

It's not as though I'm useless. She couldn't use the video or the blender, and I was the only one who could operate the dishwasher without the cups ending up with grungy sediment appliquéd to the bottom. There are too many machines in life now for it to make sense for everyone to try to master them all. Mastery of a new machine, in a couple, must sensibly fall to one party or the other. And then, if you're uncoupled, you have to face taking up the slack or you have to decide not to couple again until you meet someone whose skills exactly match your deficits. I'm learning. I'm fearless at programming the CD player now, embarrassed at how easy it is to do rice in the microwave.

But I still can't use the answering machine. The instructions must be somewhere.

I O

Coffee with Katie. Why did I say yes to coffee with Katie?

The garbage truck comes early in the morning while I'm feeding Lily before taking her to day care. The evidence of towel theft is now permanently disposed of.

I thought the e-mail would be enough. I thought we could leave it there. But I don't suppose I could duck Katie forever, so maybe she's got the right idea. Maybe it is best if we clear the air now. All morning, as I see patient after patient, I don't want to. It's on my mind most of the time, coming back to me as one archetypal dread-filled scenario after another. Being at school and having to think about facing the principal and telling him it was a once-only error of judgment and won't be happening again, whatever it was. Being sprung wanking in your bedroom by your mother, who's just coming in to put your laundry away, or offer you a drink.

Okay, maybe that's a little too specific to count as archetypal. I think it's a friend-of-a-friend story I heard when we lived in England for a year. One afternoon, when the friend of a friend was about sixteen and his mother was making dinner downstairs, he told her he had homework to do and retired to the privacy of his room. He shut the door, lay on his bed, took in a few pages of a porn mag perhaps, put his headphones on and started listening to the Stranglers. And an onanistic thought crossed his mind. He closed his eyes, allowed the onanistic thought some breathing space and tossed himself off something stupid. Then opened his eyes and glanced at his bedside table, only to notice a steaming mug of tea.

So, I'm telling myself as I catch the lift to ground at lunchtime, things could be worse. Maybe the air-clearing moment of reckoning isn't so bad.

When I get to the café, the air-conditioning's broken down. Katie's at the same table as last time, with today's *Courier-Mail*. She has already put a row of nervous little rips along the edge of the front page, each of them reaching as far as the text but no further. Is she actually trying to freak me out, or am I getting there myself?

Hi, she says, in a truncated kind of way. *I got you water. I didn't get you coffee though. It would have gone cold. Could have gone cold. Depending on when you got here.*

I order a tall black, and I sit down.

It's hot in here without the air-conditioning. Really stifling. Don't you think? Sweat beads on her upper lip. *I didn't know it'd be like this. Do you think we'll get a storm later?*

Maybe. It'd be good if we did. It'd get rid of that humidity.

Yes. So . . . how's work today?

Its usual self. No ping-pong balls in the in-box today, so that's good.

We're supposed to laugh at this, share a laugh over it. We don't. Sweat is now beading on Katie's forehead as well.

You play table tennis? I didn't know that. Just as a hobby, or . . .

Not very often, actually. It's a long story.

Snorkels. Sometimes you see them in the tops of snorkels, she says, gripping onto the ping-pong-ball idea with all the appeal of a bull mastiff grabbing you around about mid-calf. *Is that it?*

No, it is more to do with table tennis. It's an old joke. And not a very good one. And it involves some of the biophysics of lasers. Wendy might have told you. You know how the CO_2 laser has a wavelength of 10,600 nanometers?

Um, no. It's okay. Don't worry about it. And Flag's all right. In case you were wondering.

Good.

I think he liked you. He was a bit funny on Sunday, though, but I think cats can detect anxiety. They can detect lots of things. They're quite perceptive.

I think I'd heard that.

Katie takes her cup in both hands, stares down at the table. Whatever's going on, it looks vaguely religious.

I'm sorry about mentioning the towels, she says. To Wendy. I had no cause to add things up that way. No cause. I knew there had been . . . an incident, but just because I've misplaced some towels, and I heard a car and heard something in the bushes . . . of approximately human size . . . There's no excuse for it. There are some big dogs in my part of town, and I should have remembered that. All I can say is, I was distressed at the time I spoke to Wendy. My bathroom was in a bit of a state and Flag wasn't himself. He spends time in there now, and he didn't used to before Saturday. And maybe I just have to adjust to that.

I'm sure it'll be okay.

Yes, but I don't want you to think I'm spreading allegations about you all over the place.

No, that wouldn't be like you. I wasn't thinking that for a second.

That's good. Thank you. Thank you, Jon. But I would have understood if you'd had some concerns like that. And it was wrong of me to think it, and to say it to Wendy. And that's been playing on my mind. So I wanted to see you. To clear the air.

About the towels?

Yes.

Consider it clear.

In the end, there are very few parallels between coffee with Katie and being sprung wanking by your mother and her load of clean laundry or steaming mug of tea.

There's thunder somewhere far away as I cross the road, but at Toowong the air is definitely clear. And I wiped up my own urine with another person's towels, then stole the towels, and I seem to have completely got away with it.

Okay, there's the mild guilt that comes with all the lying, but nothing would have improved if I'd told the truth, to Wendy or Katie. And I feel like a bit of a bastard for letting Katie off the hook with such grand magnanimity, but I'm sure that's how she wanted it.

I'm going to stop rationalizing now, before I'm actually proud of my behavior.

Everyone's about to see their two o'clocks when I get

back to work. They're talking about something, a drug company function tonight, and how dare the company put it on the same night as everyone's book clubs.

We thought we'd get a cab, George says. *Do you want us to pick you up on the way?*

I think I've got something on, actually.

Yes, this. It's in your diary. Has been for weeks. Remember? This is one of the ones you always say yes to. Small group thing, minimal drug bullshit, expensive restaurant, good wine?

Oh, okay.

Sylvia hands him a file and he goes into the vascular-laser room, humming to himself. Oscar calls in his next patient. In my room, I pretend to check my diary. I find it and open it at today's date, to kill the right amount of time. I buzz George on the intercom.

I do actually have something else on tonight, I tell him. I must have written the dinner down in the wrong place.

Oh, really? Something else on? So you were going to be a no-show at book club anyway?

Yeah. And . . . um, it's good you reminded me, since I had a favor to ask. I wondered if you could take my last patient today. I've got something to do after work and I want to do it at five, so that I don't get to day care late.

That's a lot of somethings you've got on. Two already, at least. One at five, one tonight.

Yeah.

You're not planning to tell me what they are, are you?

That's the real favor part of it. Call me oversensitive, but I am a man who's had ping-pong balls in his in-box this week.

And if you urinate on anyone or anything tonight, you'd rather we didn't all know?

That's right.

Do you really think that's fair?

But he agrees to it. The storm grumbles in from the west and passes, dumping its rain on the city and the northern suburbs.

At five, I meet Ash outside Coles.

She says, *Hi,* and smiles, and leaving work early to meet her feels like wagging school.

You get quite dressed up for that job of yours, don't you?

What were you expecting? I can take the tie off.

I didn't know there'd be a tie.

Ninety percent of people expect a tie, if you're going to be lasering the shit out of their skin. Don't ask me why. You've got a problem, buying groceries with someone who works in a tie job?

I can probably get around it.

Just wait. You'll be corporatised before you know it. I wouldn't be so smug if I were you.

I'm not getting corporatised.

You're doing a thesis on retail. Where do you plan to head?

A PhD. Maybe.

You are heading for such a tie job. You and your cargo pants and your exposed midriff and your tableland hippy-chick sensibilities.

She laughs, gives me large amounts of mock indignation. *You wouldn't know a tableland if it fell on you, city boy. Obviously. Or a hippy.*

Your turn'll come. Tie job. That's all I've got to say. Tie job. You have been warned.

We cruise around among the fruit, neither of us devoting a lot of attention to purchasing.

What is it with grapes in Coles? I say to her, when I see someone standing there and sampling about twenty of them. Why do people eat them? Don't they know what a shop is?

What's your worry? Are you a shareholder, or something?

Well, maybe I am. But not in a big way.

Tie job, she says slowly. *You have a go at me when you wear a tie to buy groceries, and I bet you're standing there with a wallet stuffed with shareholder discount cards.*

It's the principle I'm arguing here. This is theft we're talking about.

Go. Go. Make a citizen's arrest. There's another one doing it now.

I'm busy. I'm very busy with the coriander. There's planning going on. For your dinner.

I have a recipe in mind for tonight, but I haven't cooked it in a while. I should have written it down. I need fresh chillies, and ginger. I'm trying to remember how much ginger when a large man pushes past me with a baby in his cart, about the same age as Lily. He's setting up a brown paper mushroom bag on the baby's head and chatting away, paying so little attention to anything else that his thigh drives me into the onions without him realizing.

Let's go and show Mummy, he says.

Ten minutes later I see them again, still charging along, now among the frozen foods, the gleeful baby with its paper-bag crown still in place.

So are you going to have a go at me about the sour cream again? Ash says when we reach dairy.

We'll see. How much are you going to get?

Look, the options are limited when you live by yourself.
The idea of nachos comes up pretty regularly.

How many people do you think there are at my place?
Or do you think that maybe one night I do a curry, the
next night Lily knocks up a saffron and chive risotto, with
fiddly bits of shit wrapped in vine leaves as hors
d'oeuvres? I think she's a hell of a clever baby, but she's
not that good. You'll notice that formula powder and a
rather uninspiring range of purees figure prominently in
my cart.

Which is a shame, since I wouldn't have minded the saffron
and chive risotto.

Give her twenty years. Meanwhile, it's just me and the
wok.

We queue for a checkout, and I'm wondering if I
should offer Ash a go of my shareholder discount card, or
if it would seem patronizing. Or rude not to. Obviously
I'm not confident where cargo-pant-wearing, tableland
hippy chicks stand on these things. And that was a dumb,
spur-of-the-moment thing to say, for a start. I can't believe
it sounded smart in my head. I go through first, and take
the card out of my wallet so it can be swiped. Ash looks
at me wryly.

Look, two hundred thousand people own Coles Myer
shares, I tell her. It's not such an unreasonable thing to
do. If you were nicer I might let you use this.

Really? She pulls a wallet from her back pocket and
takes out a shareholder discount card.

Like I said, two hundred thousand people own Coles
Myer shares. And you're one of them too.

We take the groceries down to the car.

You do a lot of painting? she says, when I open the trunk and move a paint-spattered blue bedsheet aside.

It's my stabilizing sheet.

It's got a name?

It didn't have at first. But it's good. It arose kind of by chance—on one of those rare occasions when I might have been doing some painting—but, trust me, it's the best way to stop everything sliding around in the back.

That sheet? It actually does something?

Cover and tuck. Cover and tuck. That's all there is to it.

You're going to tough this one out, aren't you?

Yes, I am, damn it. On behalf of stabilizing sheets everywhere. Which might be just this one but that's not the point. Innovation provokes such skepticism, doesn't it? And stop looking at me like someone with a psych degree. It's not as though I don't know it's slightly anally retentive.

And down here, do you park in the same spot every time?

Every time.

Are you worried about that?

Less worried than the people wandering around the car park with their keys, wondering where the hell they've left it this time.

Can I feed her? Ash says, when I line up the chopping I have to do.

That'd be great. Do you want to go for the solids first while I warm up the formula?

I give her a jar of apple puree and Lily's spoon. She takes the lid off and says, *This is solids?*

Don't worry. Our solids'll be more solid than that. And right now solids are so recent for her that the concept alone's pretty exciting. An interesting solid would be too much for her to grasp.

I start chopping, but I pay more attention to Lily and Ash. I shouldn't. Wendy's fed Lily and my parents have fed Lily and George has bounced Lily up and down on his knee so thoroughly he's ended up with curdled milk on his shoes and handed her right back, but this isn't the same. At least, it doesn't look the same. It looks like an evening in the suburbs, someone feeding a baby, someone else making dinner. The faithful hound with the begging eyes nearby in the kitchen, patiently urging that all scraps should be his. All of it looking like someone's definition of average, normal, and I've never had a night like it in my life. And most days my definition of normal is fine, but some days it's not. Shit. Where do these ideas come from?

I've done the chicken. I move on to the coriander, and the smell of it comes up from the board. I don't know how long it's been since I chopped coriander. Yes I do. Two months. Two months ago I decided to show how okay I was, so I had some people over and I made this then. And the time before that was about six months and two weeks ago.

It's a recipe of Mel's. A favorite of hers that was her first choice any time she'd have to cook anything. I started doing it when she was pregnant. Particularly on the days when she was feeling really tired and big. There's a certain amount of guilt attached to being the partner who isn't tired and big, and a need to do any small thing that might make up for it.

Easy, Ash says, coming back in with an empty jar and Lily on her hip. *We liked it. So, milk now?*

Well, complex off-white chemical formula-based drink, yes. You don't mind?

She gives me a look that implies that people who mind don't offer. As if the world's that straightforward.

Do you want to put some music on while you're doing it? Unless you want to watch TV. She's not quick.

Let's have music.

She hands Lily over to me and goes to the stereo. She clatters around among my CDs. What's she going to play, I wonder? I'm not expecting Debussy, my one Debussy CD that I'd forgotten about years ago, but that's what she picks.

I was sure you'd have Fleetwood Mac, she says, when she comes back into the kitchen.

I'm going to pretend you didn't say that.

Are you going to pretend you never had a Fleetwood Mac CD? Or never at least liked Fleetwood Mac?

That might be what I'm going to pretend. And you're going to let me.

Besides, there's an era issue she hasn't worked out. I owned Fleetwood Mac on vinyl. Own Fleetwood Mac on vinyl still, perhaps, tucked away somewhere. That's where she went wrong.

I've never owned a Fleetwood Mac CD, I tell her. Now that I think about it, I can say that pretty confidently.

What was the first album you ever bought?

Do we have to go there?

The Cranberries, the album with "Linger" on it, she says. *But I'm over them now.* Then she nods at me, in case I didn't already know it was my turn next.

Tubeway Army, Tubeway Army. But I'm over them now. And don't look at me like you've just noticed my second and third heads. You were definitely alive then. Probably alive then.

Tubeway Army, Tubeway Army, she says, as she goes back into the lounge room with Lily and her bottle. *What is a tubeway, and why does it need an army?*

Hey, this looks impressive, she says, as I'm hurling things around in the wok.

It's all show.

So is this indicative of your kitchen talents?

No, this is the extent of my kitchen talents. Me and the wok. I only do bite-size.

You only do bite-size?

Yeah. The idea of cooking a roast, a whole potato even, is quite beyond me. I've got no idea how people can be confident enough to cook something so big it wouldn't fit in their own mouth.

She picks up a fork, stabs a piece of chicken and then says, *Can I try it?*

Looks like it.

I'm sorry. This is pretty exciting. It smells good. And I don't get out much. So what I mean is, it doesn't smell like nachos. This'd be the first time anyone's cooked a meal for me since I moved.

So are you meeting lots of people in your year?

Not really. Which is maybe what happens when you transfer to do your thesis. You're sort of in between. You're not as in with the department as you would be if it was a PhD, but it's not like you're an undergraduate either, so you don't have a lot of course time with other people. And when I do have lectures and seminars, I'm with different people for each subject. That's how it looks anyway.

School hasn't really got going yet though, has it?

No. This is the first proper week.

It'll be good once you've met some people. It's a nice campus to be at.

Yeah. And I'm thinking of getting a job, too. Looking for a part-time job. So I'll have plenty to do.

Good. It'll be good once it's all sorted out. It's quite a move you've made though.

Yeah, I guess.

Now, this is ready to serve. Do you want some wine? I've got wine in the fridge.

Yeah, thank you.

I open it once I've scooped noodles into two bowls and, damn it, it's a chardonnay. We toast. Ash says we should toast, then clinks my glass and doesn't seem to know where to go next.

Thanks, she says, and then, *To home-cooked meals. Bite-size.*

And a good year. A year that settles down and makes some sense.

And I wonder when I'm going to tell her about Mel. I know it won't be tonight. What is she thinking? What does she think is going on? Where does she think the source of the other half of Lily is, and does she wonder why she hasn't been told? Maybe she doesn't. We don't know much about each other and, since she doesn't know about Mel, she can't know what a big thing it is not to have been told about.

She picked Lily up without holding back, got involved. I watched her and I'm sure she knew I was watching her, as though she was being tested, but that wasn't it at all. I couldn't help watching her, and that's why I watched. The feeding, the bathing—my turn to do something, but Ash came in anyway, and both of us got splashed and stood there in our splashed-on shirts while I cooked dinner. I like the way she got involved, the energy and fearlessness and something like curiosity, the new range of boat noises. I always held back with other people's babies, before I had one. I think I was afraid of breaking them.

We eat on the veranda, with bats fighting in the trees and Debussy coming out through the French doors. There's lightning far off, a silent storm lighting up clouds, but the air is thick and windless here.

I complain about the heat, but she says, *It's not so bad. Or maybe it's what I'm used to.*

Sorry. I've got English parents. Complaining about the heat's a sort of lifestyle choice if you've got English parents. Every summer catches my father unawares.

She tells me about her family. About how they grow tea on the Atherton Tableland. And the house she's living in now belongs to a family friend and spent years being rented to students through an agent. The people who owned it thought everything was fine, and then suddenly it couldn't get approval to be tenanted anymore. Since they'd planned to build town houses on the block, they didn't fight the decision. They didn't even look into the reasons behind it. They knew Ash was coming down here, and if she lived in the house that'd keep out squatters. And her father remembered it from his time at college as a grand, old, riverfront house, a little past its best. He'd slept under it in a hammock after balls, or on a mattress on the bare floor, one of those kinds of stories (of which I've got a million, having a father who was brought up in the war).

So she'd heard about the house and the grandparents of the family friend, the people who had owned it back then but been dead her whole life. And she'd seen a photo—her father had got her a photo of the place, so she could know where she was going—and for some stupid reason she even had the old curtains in her mind when she drove down here.

It was pretty bad arriving, she says. *They've got no idea what the place is like. It was good you turned up. You and your mysterious car that belonged to someone else.*

Yeah. I'd forgotten about that. So are you okay there now? Is it at least safe?

Like I'm an expert. I've been okay so far. There's a room at one end that's got tiles off the roof above it, so the rain's come in there and some of the ceiling's rotted through. And there are birds nesting in there.

That doesn't sound good.

It's a big house. I keep the door shut. Unless I want to talk to the birds, of course.

Have you told the people who own it? Or your family?

No. I can't see the point. They're going to pull it down anyway. I think I said in an e-mail that it's not in a really good way, but there's no point in going into detail. I don't want to worry them.

You communicate with your family by e-mail?

Mainly, now that I'm set up. They wouldn't let me leave home without a lap-top and a modem. Oh sorry, that's right, that'd conflict with those strange, far-north sensibilities, wouldn't it? she says, emphasising "sensibilities" as though I've done her wrong and think them something she's really not entitled to.

I'm over that now. I realize that was just regionalism on my part. Some bad "ism," anyway.

Tableland hippy chick.

Okay. Let me come clean. Never been to the Atherton Tableland. Don't know what I'm talking about. I have seen a few hippies, though, and I've got to admit they tend to have much more hair. And a different approach to personal hygiene.

Which leaves us with chick.

Yeah. I hope it does. It's going to spin me out if I'm wrong there.

Okay, I might give you that one. Chick, she says, and shakes her head. *And my family has its own home page, you know.*

Really?

Halliday Tea.

Halliday Tea? I don't know that I buy a lot of tea, so . . .

We're a medium-sized operation, and for years we didn't have our own brand. We just supplied to other people. We're small enough to be well short of a household name, but big enough to have the occasional tour group come through.

The occasional tour group?

Yeah. I did tours. That was my weekend job. I never really got into the serious cultivation side of things. My father, you can see him rubbing the leaves between his thumb and his finger and you know he's got it pegged. In a second he knows just how good the tea is. I've only got it covered at the tour-info level, really. But still, you wouldn't believe the amount of crap I could tell you about tea, from the effects of soil type on the growth of Camellia sinensis *to the best biscuits to have with it.*

There should be a particular biscuit preference?

Depending on the tea type and how you have it, why not? With a reasonable-quality regular tea—if you simplify things and assume there is such a thing as a regular tea—and a mainstream tea drinker who is interested in putting some thought into the biscuit, we'd recommend something like a Gingernut. But that might be because of some minor sponsorship deal my father did, so I can't tell you it's completely straight. But, yeah, Gingernut. Not the most fashionable choice maybe, but if you're interested in complementing the tea . . .

Gingernut.

Queensland Gingernut.

Queensland Gingernut? You're not saying there's regional variation in Gingernuts, are you?

I certainly am. It's a historic thing. Arnott's was formed by an amalgamation of state-based companies when you were just a youngster. They tried to enforce a standardized Gingernut. Miserable failure. National revolt. There are four different Gingernuts. Always will be. The Queensland Gingernut is, in my view, indisputably the finest. It's the darkest. It's the most brittle. New South Wales's is the hardest. The Victorian

Gingernut's a bit disappointing when it comes to the ginger. But they'd argue that too much ginger overpowers the tea. Very sensitive people, Victorians.

I always thought I was just getting old biscuits at interstate conferences.

And it's not that simple at all. Now you can see how I got interested in the psychology of retail.

It's scary, though, isn't it? If something as friendly as the Gingernut biscuit is so complicated, what is there going on that we don't know? How many times a day are we being subtly and painlessly manipulated?

Go on. Be the first person to come up with a conspiracy theory based on the Gingernut biscuit.

I'm completely socialized to the Queensland Gingernut. And so, I suspect, are you. We've been nobbled. And how could it end at biscuits?

Would it have been better if I hadn't told you?

I think I needed to know.

On the tours—just so you understand how other people handle the information—the tourists generally find the Gingernut story mildly interesting. You know, quirky. Not stressful.

Yes, well, they're obviously not thinking it through.

We take our empty bowls into the kitchen and Elvis jogs out of the Bean's room. He stares at me, makes the familiar initial grumbling overture for Bonios. This, perhaps, is not the time to play the entire Bonio game.

He stares, grumbles. He trots across the room and tries the same with Ash. *Something's going on,* she says. *He's expecting something.* More grumbling. Elvis thinks it's the perfect time for the Bonio game. *What does he want?*

Why don't you ask him? Why don't you ask him what he wants? Just try "What do you want, Elvis?"

What do you want, Elvis?

Some pawing of the ground, more grumbling.

Again, louder, like you really mean it, I tell her.

What do you want, Elvis?

More pawing, louder grumbling, sounding like one of those spooky reincarnated mummy voices from a *Scooby Doo* cartoon. And, if Ash knew what she was listening for, at this point she would start to hear the word "Bonio."

Say it again. Say it again.

What do you want, Elvis? Louder, more enthusiastic, like she knows the game already.

And Elvis comes back louder, too, just as he knows he's supposed to.

Okay, you have to go with me on this one. The next line is, "Do you want a cheeseburger, Elvis?"

She laughs, bends forward to get closer to his face, brushes hair away from her eyes as it falls forward. *Do you want a cheeseburger, Elvis?*

And Elvis moans like the *Scooby Doo* mummy venting its spleen at the far end of a long tunnel, lifts his front paws from the floor, then drops back down again.

And now, "Do you want a fried peanut butter and jelly sandwich, Elvis?"

You are insane, Ash says, still bending forward, her hands on her knees. *Okay, here we go.* She takes a breath in, musters up a huge amount of pretend enthusiasm for the offer she's about to make. *Do you want a fried peanut butter and jelly sandwich, Elvis?*

Elvis goes down low to the floor, moans *Bonio* long and mournfully and several times.

Okay, here's the big one. And you've got to do this one sort of innocently, as though you've just worked it out. "Do you want a"—and I mouth the next word very carefully—"Bonio, Elvis?"

Ah, she says. *I've got it now.* She pauses. He looks at her. Stares. She holds the pause and then, just as he's about to get very confused, says briskly, *Do you want a Bonio, Elvis?*

He dances around on his back legs, says *Bonio* like someone who knows he's close to the prize, nudges his shoulder into Ash's calf to urge her in the right direction, pushes her over to the corner of the room where the Bonio jar is waiting.

And now?

Now you give him one. And don't worry, he'll be completely polite, even though he's pretty excited. And he won't eat it. He'll take it away somewhere for later. The treat is having the Bonio. Eating it is a separate treat. It's surprising how much joy a small-brained creature can get out of a dense, wheaty biscuit. But I guess you know all about tea drinkers and Gingernuts, so . . .

Don't be rude.

It's all right. I come from a long line of tea drinkers. I can say that.

She takes the Bonio out of the jar, Elvis reaches up and it clunks into his mouth. He jogs out of the kitchen. Ash follows.

We're going down a hall now, I hear her say. *Looking in a door. Not going in. Looking in another door. Going in there. It's a bedroom, double bed. Pushing the Bonio under a pillow with our nose . . .*

She says a few more things that are too muffled to hear, then Elvis's toenails are back on the wooden floor of the hall, moving at jogging speed, and he reappears in the kitchen. Ash is behind him. Wearing a slim green silver-and-black swirly tie.

You must have been Mister Trendy in the eighties, she says, treating the discovery like a victory. *And someone's done them all up too.*

It's just easier that way.

Oh no, you're defending it.

Well, what choice have I got? You've found them now. Besides, it makes sense.

And it makes sense to keep every tie you've ever had?

Yes it does. They take up very little space, and that style will be back, you know. I'm quite attached to that tie, and I'd be depressed if I chucked it out and then it came back in. It got me through a lot, you know. Back in the dark Dickensian days when I was a resident and they'd work us sixteen hours on a Sunday. There were days when my fashion sense was all that got me through. I used to have these excellent black pointy shoes that went with that tie perfectly, but they got a bit fungoid so they had to go. They laced up at the side.

Bet you got a lot of action in those.

Well, maybe I did. But they were strange times. I also had an excellent skinny black leather tie, but it got fungoid as well. I think I got the idea from the Knack. Who also inspired me to learn guitar. You know the Knack?

Do I know the Knack? How old do you think I am? Six? "My Sharona" is a classic.

A classic? "Smoke on the Water" is a classic. The

Stones' "Satisfaction" is a classic. "My Sharona," attached as I am to it, can't have been around long enough to be a classic.

It's a classic. Live with it. And anyway, this is a cycle-time issue. Who knows when a song's a classic? Soon a song'll be a classic if two people talk about it after it drops out of the charts. That's all it'll take. And, by the way, before we move right along, that's quite a game you've got going with the dog.

Hey, you seemed happy to play it.

How long have you lived alone, exactly? With your knotted-up ties and your dog rituals.

Six months. But the dog rituals go back at least a few years, and the tie knotting about ten. Or so. I'll have you know I haven't developed a new eccentricity in ages. So I'm stable, at least. And I stand by the tie knotting.

I know you do. And I bet you never trash e-mails.

Why would you trash e-mails?

I pour more wine and we sit down. I decide that tonight a glass and a half will be the limit. I don't really know what's happening here, but it wouldn't be improved if I went to the toilet with Elvis and peed on him.

"My Sharona" has been around at least twenty years, she says.

All right, it's a classic.

About 1977, I think.

Surely not. It's not even their best song anyway.

No. "Good Girls Don't" was their best song.

Okay, we agree on something.

Elvis climbs onto the sofa next to Ash and stares at her again.

A "My Sharona" fan from way back, I tell her. Don't

worry. It's a whippet thing. I spent years trying to work out if he was being really thoughtful or just intensely blank. Then someone pointed out to me that his brain is actually the size of a walnut. So I think it's better to err on the side of not brilliant.

I don't know, she says, taking his face in her hands and pushing his ears back. *He looks kind of smart.*

He looks like a seal if you do that, maybe, but I don't think he looks terribly smart. Just one example—he blames me for rain.

He blames you for rain? How do you know?

It's the way he stares when it rains.

He's got more than one way of staring?

You get to work these things out after a while. You work out most about the mechanisms of the walnut brain if you take him for a walk. If you go along just behind him and imagine watching the world through whippet cam. Motoring along, with your ears back, all these instances of unexpected distractability, when one tuft of grass that looks just like any other tuft of grass compels you to sniff. And rub yourself in it. And then chug along like the smallest freight train in the world to catch up with your human again. It seems to be fun, but I don't think it's sophisticated.

When Ash has finished her wine, I drive her back to her place.

I'd better get going, she said as she drank the last mouthful and put the glass down on the coffee table. *I've got a few things to look at for class tomorrow.*

When I'm home again, and the Bean's out of the car

and back in her cot and I'm loading the dishwasher, I wish the evening wasn't over. Over in the car outside Ash's house with her calm, *See you tomorrow.* Over back here with the silence, the sleeping baby and the quiet, watching dog. The weight that had lifted all evening without me knowing is back on me.

I couldn't tell her about Mel tonight, even though it's the one crucial thing about me that she doesn't know. I could show off, I could go on at length about the dog, I could embarrass myself with the Bonio game and be embarrassed by my ancient pre-knotted ties, I could find myself sitting there listening to that biscuit story. But not just listening. Being drawn in by it and thinking, does she know how that kind of thing appeals to me? So could she please stop? But I couldn't tell her about Mel.

What am I doing? How do I get to be playing this game without thinking it through?

11

I didn't expect to be here, playing anything. I didn't think my life would be like this. As naïve as it seems, when I was in school I think I assumed that everything would be sorted out long before I was thirty. And by thirty-four I'd be years into marriage, I'd have two children, all would be going well and we'd be happy that two was enough.

I suppose I thought my big stresses would be how long the grass got between Saturday mowings, and people not turning the light off when they left the room. That's how much it looks like an uncontested assumption that I'd be replicating my parents' lives.

So it was wrong from the outset. But even if it hadn't been, it would be far too simplistic to say that it was Melissa's death that stopped it. The whole situation was much more complicated.

In so many ways, it just wasn't working. I don't know if I can say that it never worked, but it stopped working.

I think it was in England that we decided we'd be together, share the pursuit of the lives we expected, and bad jobs and a shitty winter that got us thinking that way. But maybe that's too dissected, too clinical. Maybe I should be remembering something properly passionate, but it's long ago and there's too much in between. I can remember days and things we did and things I said, but when I try to remember how I felt, I can't quite get there.

Mel was doing a year of her dermatology training in Cambridge. She'd always planned that, since before we started going out. We'd talked about it as though it gave us the safety of something finite, a relationship with an end point. We weren't committing. We were clear on that with each other. We were filling in time. Six months. I kept telling myself not to get attached. But at the three-month mark, when she said something like, *What are your plans for next year, really? You don't seem to be making any,* I realized she was right. I'd gone into general practice. I'd decided I wouldn't do that forever. That was the extent of my plan.

I suppose I could come over to England for a while, I said. It's been a few years since I've been back there.

I think I even called it a change of scene.

I went with her. I stayed. I did GP, so it wasn't much of a change of scene. Then a non-accredited laser surgical position came up at the hospital. Temporary Clinical Assistant to the Director of Dermatology. There were weeks when I did more laser work than Mel did. Those also tended to be the weeks when she'd tell me about rare diseases that she'd seen (and that I'd never even heard of), or some small technical point she'd discussed with someone important. *While you're doing the hack work,* she never actually said.

But I liked the work. I'd found a kind of work that I liked and, surprisingly, it was the focused practical challenge of it that I liked best. And I knew I'd never care that I didn't know the three-word Latin name for yet another skin rash, so I was happy for her to put me in my place. I even recast it as a plus, being with someone who had that kind of ambition. I decided to see her as assertive, positive, a more positive person than me. I told myself it was a good thing, and that I respected it. And that it wasn't a competition.

And any time it really shitted me off, all I had to do was wait until she'd finished the last long Latin word of the disease name and then say something like, *Doesn't it just respond to steroids?* as if, for the veteran GP, it was all everyday stuff.

But it wasn't like that all the time, and it's wrong to remember it that way.

There were times when we were on the same side, like the morning when the heating had gone out and I was outside long before dawn, shoveling coal and thinking, Why the fuck am I here? and wanting to kiss my father's balding head for accepting that job in Australia in the early seventies. I went back into the house to find that Mel had got up as well, and made hot chocolate. She had woken with the cold, as I had not long before. She had heard me outside, my vigorous swearing and my almost as vigorous shoveling. And she had decided, at a time when it would have been more than reasonable to roll over, close her eyes and wait for the heat to kick in, that she'd get up and heat milk on the gas and have hot chocolate ready for me. And we'd share the moment of acute homesickness.

It snowed that same day, and we ran around in it like kids, built a dirty knee-high snowman and laughed at how

shitty I'd been just hours earlier. There are photos somewhere. Mel, rosy-cheeked in the beanie she'd bought for
skiing, poking an old, discolored potato into the snowman,
around about mid-face. *There's his nose,* she said. *He's that
actor, that actor from the forties, with the voice.* She meant
WC Fields. She was wearing her entire ski wardrobe and
making a grubby mini–WC Fields.

We only went skiing once. She didn't like the way the
boots felt. She probably also didn't like not being good at
it right away, but she didn't say that.

By the time it was spring and the weather was sometimes better, we seemed quite sure that we were together.
So we were together when we got back to Brisbane, in a
way that we hadn't been when we'd left.

We rented a flat, and started looking around for a place
to buy. And we decided—we both decided, as far as I can
recall—that we didn't want people to think this was something we had stumbled into. We wanted to show them it
was more than that. We decided to get married. It went
exactly as expected. Mel had clear ideas, I had none, so it
suited us both to go with hers. My mother gave up her
hold on calm in stages. First, there was, *It's your wedding,
so you make all the decisions.* Then there was, *It's your wedding, so you make all the decisions,* but said accompanied by
the sound of grinding molars. Then we moved to, *It's not
quite how I'd do it . . .* and finally to her strident decision
that the cut of Mel's dress was *morally wrong.*

And next your head spins, I told her, and green vomit
comes out.

My father brokered a fragile peace the next afternoon.

It was all very odd. My mother and I weren't used to arguing at all.

And I don't know if my edginess on our wedding day was more than the average and, if it was, I don't know if my mother's madness was to blame. Again, I'm looking for signs. Signs that all was not quite right. But it's too late, far too late, to look back fairly on the day we got married. And perhaps the certainty and uncertainty of it all was nothing more nor less than normal.

Mel did dermatology coverage work when we got back from the UK, and was still doing that when we got married. I got a job with a laser surgery group, but it was mainly cosmetic work and that wasn't really the direction I wanted to take. Meanwhile, George was thinking of setting up his own dermatology practice, focusing on laser, and Wendy—who was a year or two older than us—was finishing her MBA, about to have Emily and aiming to resume her clinical career the following year.

So we got together and planned. Wendy and Mel seemed to get on pretty well from the start and, in a way, that counterbalanced the fact that George and I had been friends at school in the eighties and had enough in-jokes to last us for years. With two of the four of us being married to each other, we'd all started off wary that that relationship would intrude but, when each meeting began, it seemed easier to leave the marriage at the door than George's projectile vomiting stories. I can remember Wendy arguing with him, and insisting that the Med Ball of 1986 couldn't possibly be as legendary as he was making out, and George coming back with something along the lines of, *You graduated in eighty-five, didn't you?*

Mel and I were on the same side that day, the side that could remember the legendary Med Ball of 1986, but valued neutrality a little more. And we were already putting any problems we had—and they seemed to be small problems—down to the stress of investing large amounts of money in a business together, and taking on a new mortgage, and any other good reason going.

Maybe that's when we started to agree on less and less. In the context of setting up the business, a context in which we'd all made it clear that we had to speak our minds, be up front, hold nothing back. But Mel and I would go home and do the same, and it came to characterise our interactions. We both dealt with any issue as though the argument concerned only the issue itself, and the incompatibility that was starting to gape between us became something we were good at turning away from, a big dark space that we put our backs to and pretended wasn't there.

And you can't do that forever but, by the time we started looking at it seriously, the relationship was used up, all of it. If I'm going to be honest. Long ago we'd used up all the affection. We'd used up most of the arguments. We'd used up even the simple differences of opinion.

We'd used up each other's faces, senses of humor, presence in the house. We had become blanks to each other, each of us the only person in the other's life who had taken on a kind of invisibility. A heartless, but not cruel, invisibility.

We had descended to the mathematical part of the relationship. The co-ownership of things. The arithmetic of partnership, mortgages, leases. Documents to do with money and bearing both our names.

Punctuated by desperate attempts to take history by the collar, pull it around, stare into its eyes and change its mind. Therapy, consideration, compromise on the smallest things. Cooking Mel's noodle dish when she was feeling big and tired in the late weeks of pregnancy. But that's not love, however decent it might be for an evening. However much I might have wanted to fix the situation as she paced with her hands on her sore back and the unbalanceable bulge out the front and the near desperation some nights that it all be over soon. And she'd slump into the sofa and put her feet up and look down at the bulge and tell me there must be a better way. I'd do what I could to help and that only led to misunderstandings, the idea that things might be better than they were. An idea that always had its wings clipped soon enough. She'd find some energy somewhere and we'd discover the capacity to argue again, or talk differences up instead of down, or simply not like each other and do separate things.

It's all that normal stuff that happened to us—two people who have made a simple mistake and actually shouldn't be together, who are drawn together by things that don't work in the long term. Back then I blamed it on Mel, but therapy genuinely made me realize I wasn't as right as I'd thought. We were just different, and it had become problematic when put to the test. Mel did hold views dogmatically, and it did make arguments hell. And

I did avoid conflict about anything that mattered, and I also stirred it up sometimes to prove the contrary, and to prove that Mel was the unreasonable one.

But she was also the spontaneous one, the risk taker. They were all parts of the same package. They were actually the same thing. I admired it sometimes, and sometimes I battled against it, and how could that make sense to her? Her ambitious ideas and her dogged pursuit of them could take us places, or take us nowhere but a fight. They took me to England and turned me into a laser surgeon. They came, irrevocably, between us. I'm allowed, I think, to feel ambivalent about them now.

Too many things worked like that, worked for us and against us.

In return, I gave her a kind of support I think she'd never had. The last year of her training, the year in England, wasn't easy. There seemed to be some resentment that she'd won her place ahead of someone local, and she had a pretty rough time. I was there for her to talk things through with, night after night, one injustice after another. I'd be on her side. Quietly, steadily on her side, and I'd talk her down, and she'd go back the next day. *You got me through that,* she said, on the plane heading home. *I wouldn't be—I might not be—a dermatologist now, if you hadn't been there for me to whine to.*

And if I tried the same tactic in an argument between us, it only made things much worse. It'd be called patronizing. I'd be told I shouldn't think I was always right.

Our differences showed themselves in antagonism, and then showed themselves less and less. As we each learned how to be better in relationships, we each became less inclined to try what we'd learned on each other. And maybe people could see it, but they gave us space. Besides, we were at our best with other people. At work, for instance. Our different opinions on some things made us seem independent—something we were supposed to be— and the four of us worked well as a group, setting up and running the practice. Another source of false hope.

Like everything else, our differences can't be interpreted simply. They could have been the making of us, or the breaking. They brought out the best in each of us, sometimes, and brought our flaws right to the surface.

Separation loomed like something caught in headlights, and any time we looked at it we'd try to swerve. But not as a team. We were fighting for the wheel or both letting go of it, too tired to fight, so the view ahead of us didn't change. It still loomed. It got bigger, closer.

And here's the hard thing. Lily was conceived one drunken, reconciliatory night. The night of the last try. The night we blew off therapy and spent the hundred bucks at the pub instead. What a sad story to have. How unlike *Birds 'n' Bees* version 1.0, where two people make a baby because they love each other. So how do I handle that when she's five or eight or however old they're supposed to be to hear it? Actually, no. We didn't make you out of love. We just got so tired of arguing, we had a truce one night and made you out of beer. So you became our last try. Our last try that wouldn't have worked.

Is this how all those stork and cabbage-patch stories came about? To mask that kind of history? No. I still want to believe that many—maybe even most—conceptions involve acts of great affection. Not just drunken, misshapen, impossible reconciliations. Or some sense that it's the thing to do, or that time's running out.

During the pregnancy, we still talked through the options. I think we could have come up with something workable. We could have held the business partnership together and let the life one go. Something like that. That's where we were heading. It feels wrong to even think it now, of course. It's odd in every conceivable way. Right down to the price on her head. Mel's insurance has paid out our mortgage, and much more. I'm worth a million bucks now, at least, but only because she's dead.

All the questions I had about my life were answered at once, but each of them given an answer I'd never thought of. Would Mel and I break up? Suddenly the answer was no. An emphatic no that was more than a no. A never. It had been the big question, and now it couldn't be a question anymore. We would never break up, but I was single anyway, and a parent. We'd stuck to the promise when it looked like we couldn't, been parted only by death, and here's how it was going to work.

The house freaked me out and I talked about selling it, but it would have been too much change. Besides, selling it would have involved so many steps, and explanations, and more finalities. My parents moved in. We had plenty of room, so that was easy. And less strange than me trying to move to their place since they've only got a three-bedroom unit now, and too much computer hardware to fit guests in comfortably.

We had a stupidly big house. That was a Mel plan. Don't be an only child. Mel had been an only child, and born long after her parents had stopped being young. So she wanted four to six, which seemed ridiculous to me. We never sorted that out. We just agreed we could review it with each child. I was going to go in hard after two, regardless of gender balance, but I'd kept that to myself. It was as though, if we bought a big place and filled it with children, we'd be kept so busy all would have to be well.

And then it didn't happen. Another doubt rendered pointless.

I bummed around. I couldn't work, couldn't look at a lesion for at least weeks without being baffled about my life. I stayed at home, stayed with friends, pestered friends, added myself on to their holidays. Me, at my most distracted, and a new baby whose every noise left me panicked and confused. Whatever good advice came my way, whoever it came from, whatever bestselling books I read by pediatricians with regional English accents.

I can remember a town house at the beach, walking over the bridge behind the Sheraton around about dawn, the Bean on my front, me singing Blondie's "In the Flesh." I'm not even sure who I was staying with. I took her into the National Park, all the way to Hell's Gates where the wind whipped madly up off the sea, pulling at me with such strength I had to stand with my arms around her to stop the fear that she might be blown away.

It was just us there—it was winter and early—and before we turned back to the track a gust whacked a bug into the corner of my mouth. The thought that it could have gone down my airway nearly panicked me, and all the way back I breathed through my teeth. And imagined myself asphyxiated among the rocks, Lily struggling to pull herself free from the pouch on my chest. Or, still tiny, not trying, not having any idea she should try, making no effort other than noises about hunger.

Then I remember being back at a café looking out over the beach. It might have been the same day, or it might not. Wendy—so now I remember who I was with—pointed out the old guy with the metal detector on his slow patrol along the sand and said, *Hey, your dad in ten years' time* ... And anyone who knows him would back her up.

We'd planned the trip. I remember now. So it wasn't me gate-crashing someone's week away. Not that time, at least. We'd planned a holiday at the beach for when Lily was a few weeks old. We were going to share a town house out along the sound. Because Wendy and Steve wouldn't be scared off by the presence of a new baby. Because Wendy always worked hard at being a friend to both of us and would have mediated once or twice, or laughed at us, or argued with Steve a couple of times, just to show us we were normal. I'm sure she did that.

It was in that café looking out over the beach that Wendy asked me if I wanted to talk. Asked me in a way that tried to be conversational but didn't make it, and came out sounding very premeditated. Steve was up at the counter, organizing some more drinks. That's when she asked. And he didn't need to go to the counter because there was table service. There were even signs saying that. And I thought about talking, and about what mattered to me that minute. And it was the same day as the walk to Hell's Gates, because I thought about the bug. My fear of choking on the bug, and that Lily might be abandoned there, that this whole wrenching story might come to a close among those rocks.

I thought back to the night that it all went wrong. And I said, No. I said I was fine. I looked away, and Wendy looked away. That's when she pointed to the beach, to the old guy with the metal detector.

So, I can remember much more than I thought. Maybe Lily could have fixed something, or at least made us think. Put us on the same team, got us trying out that way of doing things. It sounds like such a big deal, the problems we were having, but we were just two people who didn't get on, and that happens all the time. And, shit, it complicates things afterward. Not that anyone, ever, could have this notion of afterward in their heads at the time.

But it's what happened, and it's why my mother made at least some kind of issue of checking with me before leaving this week. This is the first time my parents have gone away for longer than a weekend since all that.

12

I've told Ash about learning guitar because of the Knack.
I've let her in on my dog-feeding secrets, and she's had
my best bad eighties tie around her neck. I run with her
every day and I don't tell her about Mel and, even though
I've known her only a couple of weeks, she's become someone I think should be told.

In which case, the issue is telling her. How to tell her.
I think of myself telling her, and all the words for it are
so horrible I have to stop. And the whole thing so inexplicable. Once I start telling, how much do I tell? Does
the story end with Mel being dead, or only begin with it?
I've got no idea, because it's not a story. It's something that
gapes there, off in the dark, and I try not to look.

Even with my friends, how much can I tell? Which day
is the right day to talk? There are no two successive days
when I feel exactly the same about it all, and out there
there's an assumption about how I should feel, every day.

Not long ago, I saw an interview with Marc Rosset, the
Swiss tennis player, at the Australian Open. A few months
before, he'd changed a flight booking to stay in the US
and practice after the US Open, and the flight he should
have been on went down into the sea off Nova Scotia.
Everyone was killed. And the interviewer said something

like, *Every day must feel like a bonus after that. Every day you must feel lucky to be alive. It must really put it into perspective when you lose matches now.*

And Rosset said that everyone said that, and that's how he'd expected it would be. But he still gets angry whenever he loses a match, just as angry as always. He gets annoyed when he double-faults. And most days are just like they used to be, and his lucky break is something that seems to be behind him now.

Half an hour later, during his match, he double-faulted. And the commentator said only, *Every day feels like a bonus for Marc Rosset now, after not getting on that plane that went down off Nova Scotia.*

So Marc Rosset thought he'd fought off the cliché, but no one was listening. No-one actually wanted to know how he felt. He'd had a life-changing experience—that's what they'd decided—and it was a story that wasn't to be spoiled by how things were. But Rosset hadn't noticed. He hadn't noticed that the interviewer had said *must* three times, had told him three times how he *must* feel.

Of course, there are ways in which that's very different to my situation. Some things did change for me. Plenty of things changed. But it'd be wrong to think that every one of those changes was for the worse, or that I felt the same obvious way about anything, day after day. It's complicated by the fact that no one really knows how things were before. There was a lot that we told no one, and that I can't go telling people now. And it'd shock people if I told them even one thing was better than it used to be. It'd be as though I wanted Mel dead. It's absurd.

———

Ash has no weekend plans. Some reading for school, but nothing other than that.

I'll go mad if that's all I do, she says on Friday morning after we run.

So on Saturday afternoon, late in the afternoon when it's not so hot, we take Elvis and the Bean for a walk around the campus.

What was this place like when you were here? she says.

Mainly like it is now, I guess. I suppose there are a few new buildings. More gourmet cafés, but the whole city's like that. Mid-eighties you couldn't get a good cup of coffee here, then suddenly a few years later there were coffee shops everywhere. The campus looks more corporatised now. The dining parts of it anyway.

Much like yourself.

Obviously. Thank you. I can't escape that tie job, can I? But you would have liked it here back then. The main question in any campus dining hall was "How would you like your nachos?" You would have been right at home. As opposed to now when it's a hundred and one things to do with pannini, and they can't make a pizza without tossing on a handful of capers and some semi-dried, sun-dried, oven-roasted something.

Wood-smoked. You left out wood-smoked. Or at least a reference to a wood-fired oven.

And the cheese of an entirely unanticipated mammal. I always like that. We live in very cowist times. I really don't think that, as a society, we should be so bored with ourselves that we go to the trouble we do, trying to find new mammals to milk in case their cheese might be more interesting. I've even been to a place that offered yogurt from four different mammalian species, but specifically not a cow. They had yak's yoghurt there. And as far as I'm concerned, "What color is yak's milk?" should have remained a Trivial Pursuit oddity. There's no reason for it to be making its way into suburban life.

What color is yak's milk?

Pink. Presumably to make the yogurt more attractive when matched with rhubarb and a compote of summer fruits.

And I bet they chopped their own coriander as well, and took ages to pick the right bunch in Coles.

That's different. I don't know how, but it's different. I think there was a while there when I ended up eating at yak's-milk joints more than I would've expected.

That was after you left here, though.

Yeah. As far as I know, yak's milk still hasn't penetrated here. But it's not the nachos joint that it was. It was a good time to be here, despite the fact that it was somewhat cuisine impaired. It was sort of in between seventies radicalism and the nineties pressure to treat the study part seriously. If that's actually how it is. It's how the papers think it is. But maybe it doesn't feel particularly different here to me because I've kept coming to the place. I've always lived nearby, so I come here to see movies. And to run, obviously. Things like that. I think it was more interesting before I was here. I think it probably did have a phase where there was a no-shoes, tie-dye dress code. For all the people being radical and individual, anyway. And the student activists were actually active. Someone once told me that, since the student union owns the cinema and that whole retail area, they got to give all the buildings their names. And the Schonell Cinema—the big one upstairs—is apparently officially called the Ho Chi Minh Theater. And there was an extraordinary union meeting in the eighties when they'd just sacked an official and he was fighting them about it and they voted to rename the whole student union complex the Whatever-his-name-was Persecution Complex. I think that's all fairly indicative of how things had changed from the seventies to the eighties.

We walk up the hill and through the Persecution Complex, and more has changed since then than I'd thought. It might be my preferred movie venue, but I now realize I haven't been to a movie in a long time.

You've never played Trivial Pursuit, have you? I ask Ash, thinking back to her ignorance about yak's milk.

No.

I think it probably had a few years of being a hot Christmas selection. In between the historic longevity of Monopoly and the fleeting attention we pay things now.

She's never played Trivial Pursuit. Even though they still sell boxes of new cards, maybe they're only selling to the converted. The mid-eighties TP fans, sitting back waiting for more, wanting to be quizzed harder, getting a bit older, a bit larger. Not realizing that their game is history. That the newer kids played Pictionary, and the even newer kids didn't. Not realizing that the whole world hadn't learned from their era's favorite game that yak's milk was pink. Maybe Ash is right and cycle times are shorter, but I wish that didn't seem to put quite so many cycles between us. I want us to know the same things, or at least a lot of the same things.

We keep walking, into the Great Court where, since it's a Saturday, there are wedding parties having photos taken.

I hadn't expected this, she says.

You haven't been here before on a weekend then, have you?

No.

This is about average. Three different wedding parties. People meet here, or have pasts here. So if this is where it all started they often come back here for photos, if they're getting married nearby. And the sandstone looks good too, I suppose.

Actually, I have a whole album of photos at home that look just like these will, if you're interested. But that's the part I don't say.

It's only when the moment's properly gone that I realize it was an opportunity, some kind of opportunity. An opening to begin a conversation about Mel, in some way other than starting with an awkward pause, then moving on to throat-clearing and the tough part.

Two rainbow lorikeets fly into a nearby tree and start fighting about berries. The Bean's head whips around in the pouch to follow the action, but they're out of the tree and gone before she's got them into focus. She looks back at me.

Too quick for you, hey? Don't worry. There'll be plenty more of them. And they're just like the ones at home anyway.

Maybe they even are the ones at home. It's not like you live far away.

Yeah. I wonder how much territory they cover? No I

don't. That sounds far too much like a Trivial Pursuit question.

Except, if it was a Trivial Pursuit question, I bet you'd know the answer.

Thanks. Do you want to sit down for a while? I think Elvis could do with a break and the kicking going on in the pouch right now suggests some ground time could be popular.

We sit under the tree. Elvis flops to the ground and pants. A lorikeet lands on a branch, and I manage not to wonder anything about it. I take the Bean from the pouch and she wriggles. Soon she'll crawl. For now she flaps, rolls, stares at the nearest blades of grass, as though they need a lot of working out. Ash offers her a hand and she takes it, grabs hold of a finger and starts wrestling with its ring.

Go on, Ash says. *Bet you can't get it off.* And with her other hand she gives Lily's fine sweaty hair a stroke. *It's weird sitting in the middle of all this, as though it's not really happening.* She looks around, her free hand still stroking. *The big dresses and the old cars and guys in tails.*

Not like your last campus?

I don't think so. But I was doing tea tours on weekends, remember? It's a bit surreal, watching it in triplicate. And how does it feel for them? You turn up, having your special day, and it turns out it's special in the same way as everybody else's.

They're probably not even noticing each other.

And look at the drivers, having a smoke over there. One of them's even eating a banana.

It's not supposed to be special for them. I don't think

he's wrecking anyone's day by eating a banana.

No. Okay, I'll let the banana go. It's just the rest of it that's strange then. Wearing clothes you'll never wear again, spending all that money, standing up in front of people and declaring things. It's like you're giving a guarantee that you'll never change your mind. Life's already complicated enough without that. But it's a nice idea, I suppose, in some ways. And maybe sometimes . . . sorry, I'm rambling. As if I'd know.

No, I know what you mean. Sometimes I think people complicate things more than they should. It's like, one of the people at work, Nigel, the nurse we've got, he's got this life that seems to be exactly the way he wants it, and there's no apparent relationship involved. He's got his motor bike and his diving, and he goes to Asia pretty often. And it seems to work for him. I guess it's an individual thing, though. Wendy, one of the other medical staff at work, seems really happy being married and having two children and barbecues and all that.

I think there's too much pressure to be in relationships sometimes. If you're not going out with someone, people assume you want to be and that you're probably depressed that you aren't. And I don't think that's what life has to be about. It's fine if it happens but, you know, I don't think you should kill yourself trying to make it happen. The idea of having friends I completely understand—I hate it when I have to go a whole day without a conversation—but, like you said, people complicate things. They can't help themselves.

Yeah. I think my parents look at my friends and can't believe how many of them are single. As though part of what we definitely should have been doing at school was pairing off. No, that's probably a bit harsh. I think they thought women should have been taking more interest in me, but that's a different issue. And they probably figured that some time at school, or not long after, we'd all be getting our shit together and embarking on the next phase. Little did they know. I think the next phase is career, marriage and children, but I don't know a lot of people who have the set. But my parents are even pre–baby boomer, so they've got no chance of getting it, really. There have been far too many shifts of expectations since they met in the fifties.

The sixties, for a start. The decade of baby-boomer glory.

When the post-war kids invented the world but didn't inhale? Yeah.

I'm really not convinced that the sixties meant all they say it did.

Absolutely. Highly overrated. Always thought that.

So what were the sixties like?

What were the sixties like? How would I know? I was born in the middle. For me the sixties were about teething and sphincter control. I don't know what they were like. All I remember is the lunar landing. And one Beatles song. Other than that, I've probably seen the same footage as you have. So I'm not really personally any more familiar with most of the decade than I am with the Battle of Agincourt.

So what was the Battle of Agincourt like?

Well, a defining moment in archery if you were British, I suppose. And a really bad day at the office if you were French cavalry. But I was young then. There's really not much of the thirteenth century I can remember.

Obviously. Or the fifteenth.

Yeah? It's all a blur. You mean I lost a couple of hundred years, just like that? Anyway, I don't think the sixties were properly invented till the eighties, when all those people started turning forty and needed to think they'd had some glory days. Changed the world. I plan to do the same about the eighties, of course. All I have to come up with is an event where a million people voluntarily wallowed in mud and a war that we stopped.

How about the Cold War?

Excellent. The job's half done. And we were all there. That's the thing. We were all there when the Berlin Wall came down. I know I was, and my grandchildren will, too.

And where were you, really?

At work, I suppose. No, probably in bed. And I saw it on the *Today* show when I was having breakfast. Then I went to work. And changed the world. That's the order it happened in.

Well, well done. I'm proud of you. I think I helped bring it down, too. Even though I was only about ten. I was very aware of the big issues at the time.

You always struck me as socially responsible.

So back then were you doing any of what you're doing now?

No. I didn't even see a laser until a few years ago, in England. I think I'd just graduated around Berlin Wall time, so I was in a hospital.

Does it feel strange to study so much for so long and then end up working in one small area that you didn't even study in the first place?

No. Not if you like what you're doing, I suppose. And

it's not like you forget all the rest of it. You'd be surprised when it comes up. It's a very useful degree.

Yeah?

Yeah.

Okay. Tell me two useful things.

Two useful things from my degree?

Yeah.

Okay. Let me show you something. This is number one.

I move in front of her, and sit cross-legged the way she's doing, with the Bean in my lap. I take Ash's hand and make her index finger point and I guide it to just above my right eye, to the edge of the eye socket, where it starts to curve down to my nose.

Feel here.

Then I move it over to the other side.

Then feel here.

Hey.

They're different. There's a notch on one side, but not on the other. I noticed that when I was young. Maybe even as early as the sixties. And I didn't say anything about it to anyone. Because they hadn't said anything to me. So I thought something was wrong, and they were keeping it from me. I thought something had happened and they weren't telling me about it. And then I started reading the kind of story where the child—the main character— has a mark that means something. They're a witch or an alien or there's been some terrible incident that they're repressing. You know the kind of thing?

Yeah. Scary stuff.

Exactly. And part of the problem was that I read a lot, so I was reading books for people who were much older.

Anyway, the sign means that something's going to happen. One night, someone's going to come for you. Which didn't make it easy for me to sleep. And a notch seemed definitely abnormal, plus it was only on one side. And if I pressed on it too hard, I'd get a flash of pain. Definite alien. I came to terms with it eventually, but I still kept it to myself. Then I did anatomy at school. It's normal variation. Totally normal. It's where the supraorbital nerve goes through, and that's why you get the pain with pressure. And it goes through either a notch or a foramen— a hole. And if you've got the foramen there's no discontinuity at the orbital margin, the edge that you're feeling. I've got a foramen on the right side, and a notch on the left. So there it was. When I was about eight it had been a big, secret part of my identity and ten years later, there I was, finding out it was just normal asymmetry. So my degree was useful.

You poor thing, being so scared about it, she says. *And I bet your friends at med school weren't at all supportive.*

You think I told them? I've never told anyone about it in my life.

Let me have another feel.

I lean forward, and Ash does too. She puts her left hand on my shoulder.

Don't want to jab you in the eye, she says, and she puts her right index finger on my right eyebrow and moves it gently down. Then she does the same on the left. Concentrating, looking at me but looking deep to the skin, looking at the anatomy. Feeling the contours of the bone, smiling, thinking she might laugh with the strangeness of us doing this, concentrating again. *Well,* she says when she's done both sides. *There you go. I wonder what I'm like?*

She sits part of the way back, but only part of the way and, with her elbow on her shin, she puts her index finger up to her own right eye.

And?

Wait. I've got two sides to do. She checks the other side and says, *Hey.* She takes my right hand, makes its index finger point and says, *Tell me what you think.*

She guides my finger up to her eye. I move in closer, put my left hand on the side of her head.

Okay. On the right I think you've got . . . a notch. And on the left . . . a foramen.

That's what I thought. A mirror image of you.

Yeah. I think our parents could still tell us apart, though.

Very funny, she says. *So what does it mean?*

Oh, lots of things. Both of us can expect a visit from aliens, probably.

Oh no, she whispers. *Not the anal probe.*

And my left hand has moved down to her shoulder, and we're still close, closer than a social distance apart. And as I'm looking at her, strangely, as I'm watching her mouth say "anal probe" so conspiratorially—as I'm watching her blue eyes watch me—I could kiss her. I could travel the last short distance between us and kiss her. It's an urge that comes upon me, not from any place of reason, not a thing I can anticipate. But then all the reason comes in, comes back, battens the rush down and I'm in control.

Anything but the anal probe, I say to her, and take my face back a little, and move my hand.

I'm looking at her differently, and I shouldn't. I still

want to kiss her. I want to tell her about Mel, I want to pretend several years of my life never happened, I want to put it all in its place, but I don't know what its place is. I want to shake all this out of my head. I want her to stop looking at me, or kiss me, or something.

And Lily? she says. *Where does she fit in with this?*

So I test the Bean's eyes, and she treats it like a new game. Takes the approaching finger with both hands, as though she's steering it down and it's some lever, making her more and more cross-eyed as it approaches.

Okay, I think foramen and on the other side . . . also foramen. Hard to tell, but that's what I think. So that means we don't have to have the talk that my parents— had they been half-reasonable—would have had with me, immediately before that age when you think asymmetry means you've either been abused or the anal probe is just a matter of time.

It's amazing. Really. It feels so obvious, when you feel it. It's surprising what you don't know, just because of skin.

Most of the time it's probably a good thing. Our bodies would look pretty bizarre without it. Without an opaque outer layer there'd be a lot of distraction. We'd be showing each other all kinds of things that are better left unseen. Facial muscles, laid bare, would look very mechanical. It'd take all the real, subtle purpose out of expression. There'd be no mystery.

She laughs. *And there's just not enough mystery in the world, is there?*

No way. I think we spend far too much time trying to make things obvious, and not enough appreciating the chance to discover them slowly. Skin is good for that. It's expressive, but it doesn't give it all away. And it has many properties people take for granted. It can heal itself, and that's not easy. Have you noticed how, most of the time when you injure skin and it has to grow to fill a defect, it not only knows that it has to grow, but it knows when to stop? So that's why lasering it isn't like stripping paint from a door. The skin is waiting. Waiting for an attack and ready to fix up the damage. So you use that when you're working on it. You know how far you can go and keep the skin on your side. And if you don't know that, you'll damage it so that it'll scar when it doesn't need to, or scar more than it needs to. So there's a second useful thing from all that time at school. Now, how about you?

That second one sounds to me like a work issue. So I think I only have to come up with one to match the notch discovery.

Okay. You can start with one, but I'm assuming it's going to be good.

Okay. Erikson.

Erikson?

Erik Erikson. Childhood and Society. *Part three, chapter seven. I did a child development subject, and the lecturer was big on Erikson. And when you look at it—when you look at the eight stages part—it applies to everyone. And just when people tell you adolescence is the turbulent time, bang, you sort it out—Stage Five, identity versus role confusion—and suddenly you're into Stage Six, intimacy versus isolation. But you would have done that at school too, wouldn't you? Erikson?*

Yeah.

So you know what I mean, then.

It was a while ago but, yeah, I think I know what you mean.

Good. So, we're even. Unless I have to come up with a work-related one too. Hey, I meant to tell you—I got a job. At Bagelos. A few shifts a week for a few hours each, starting Monday afternoon. Making bagels.

I think I know what you mean.

So how long has it been since I did Erikson? Mid-eighties. I can vaguely remember it, but not even enough to drop his name in conversation. Therefore I probably shouldn't go around pretending I know what people mean when they start talking stages.

Why can't I just admit it when I don't know something? Is there something unresolved in one of those early Eriksonian stages (and who knows which one) that means I can't admit it when I don't know something? In case people might like me less? I even hated it—quietly hated it—when I got the century of the Battle of Agincourt wrong. And no one ever liked anyone even slightly less for that, surely.

It's probably my parents' fault. Those kinds of things usually are. They were probably too supportive, gave too much reinforcement to me when I got things right or did well. Plus, I have to remember that I was a notch child, stricken with a secret asymmetry, living in fear that my fate was always just one wrong answer away.

I should never go into therapy (real capital-T, couch-based therapy, as opposed to the relationship-fixing kind). I'm sure it'd only do me harm. My poor parents. They were so encouraging when it came to me knowing things. As if you can be critical of people for that, for fostering a chronic sense of excitement at having the right answer. I think my father once even gave me fifty cents for knowing the capital of Zaire.

But Erikson's stages are lost somewhere, back in the huge vault of early school knowledge that got archived at the end of each semester. The only stages of anything I remember from the recent past were in an e-mail from George a few weeks ago, and they were stages of drunkenness. Stage one was something about becoming an expert on every subject in the known universe, and wanting to pass your knowledge on to anyone who will listen. To which George had added some *Who needs alcohol?* kind of remark.

Bread. I also learned to cut bread when I was at school. This number two non-work-related useful thing crosses my mind as I'm slicing into a fresh loaf on Sunday morning.

We were generally a sliced-white family back then, so I didn't cut much bread at the time, but I picked up the principles of cutting when I did surgery. One of the keys to a neat incision is never cutting a moving target. Hold the skin to cut it, put it slightly on the stretch and ensure that the only moving thing is the knife. Same with a big crusty loaf of bread, or the knife finds its way anywhere.

But what do I know? I try to impress a girl by poking her in the eye, and she comes back at me with comments on the uneasy transition between Erikson stages Five and Six.

13

I know I should have planned ahead more effectively when my parents told me they were going away, but I didn't. So it's not until late Sunday night that I work out I haven't made any day care arrangements that would allow me to keep up the usual running plans over the next couple of days.

I call Ash just before I'm due at her place in the morning.

That's okay, she says. *I think I know the way by now. Of course, it might not take me as long, so I'll probably have to go a bit further.*

Thanks. Hey, how's your car?

I have to call them tomorrow.

You're starting work today, aren't you?

Yeah, this afternoon.

I start at two, so I could give you a lift before then, if you'd like. If the time works out for you.

Um, yeah, that'd be great, if it's no trouble.

No, it's no trouble. I'll be in the neighborhood. I've got a few things to do, so it'd be easy to drop by.

A few things to do. Mid-morning I'm in the neighborhood, at the campus libraries to read some Erikson. And I didn't know half of it when I was talking on the weekend about how much this place had changed.

For a start, where I'm sitting is underground and surely used to be dirt below a path when I was studying here. Back in a time I'm now thinking I should be referring to as the old days. The old days when the microfiche machines were cutting-edge technology and everyone got a tutorial on how to use them.

I sit inconspicuously at a terminal around the middle of the fifth row. I stumble through the catalogue, trying out keywords that take me off on tangents. Remembering the name of the book would help. In the distance I can see librarians sitting at a counter and I wonder if I should e-mail them and identify myself as the person floundering back here, needing to be saved. I'm prepared to wave to direct them to me if it'd help, even though it'd be an uncommonly public admission of my ignorance.

Eventually I stumble upon *Childhood and Society,* and I remember that's the name Ash mentioned. I click in the box that offers geographical directions, and I send the directions to print. Somewhere.

I listen for the noise of printing. No. Of course there's no printer nearby.

Somewhere near a printer, someone is being told where the library keeps its copies of *Childhood and Society,* while I'm staring at the screen, memorizing each step of the directions and the first bit of the call number. Good planning. I didn't even bring a pen. Why? Would it have made the process too formal? As if, without a pen, I'd be doing something casual that I do all the time, dropping in here for a bit of a read?

But at least I get there. Through places that are so new

they even smell it, up stairs I walked up in my first year here, through a doorway I've never seen and finally among shelves that smell just as they always have, and books.

And what am I doing here, anyway? What am I on about with this woman? If I was putting on any more of a performance I'd be obliged to do curtain calls. Yak's milk and notches, and why the fuck do I need to know a thing about Erikson on the off-chance that he'll come up again in conversation?

Conversation. We're good together in conversation. I get to use my brain with her, actually use it, think. And of course I want more of that.

On Saturday, Ash said, *Do you think all disease occurs at a biomolecular level?* and I almost said something like, You should get out more, before I realized she wasn't George and she genuinely wanted to discuss it. And then I wanted to as well, more than I wanted to tell her she should get out more. And we talked about the biochemistry at nerve synapses, the molecules that send signals, the immune system and clotting mechanisms, each as a series of molecular events. She said she'd wondered about the question for a while, since she'd been sick once, but she'd had no one to ask before.

There was a time when I had conversations like that with George and other people. When more of our talk was actually about things than it has been lately. Maybe we've known each other too long, talked them all through too many times. Maybe it's just where we are now.

It's the reading Proust joke. At school, George would have loved it if we'd all read the big stuff and talked about it. Debated it all night over cheap wine, sitting on someone's den floor. Now, our book club that reads Proust but reads nothing is only a game we play with Wendy's mind. And the wine is much improved, and we go to bed early. I haven't had an argument about a French film, or a Czech novel or the cultural or biological or sociological significance of anything in years.

Erikson says—I know he says it because I've got it in front of me—that the adolescent mind is an ideological mind positioned between the morality of childhood and the ethics of adulthood. So maybe the ideological stage was the time when we had to talk everything through, when the big questions were worth asking, and now we're just cruising ethically along. Or maybe that's not what Erikson means at all, but Ash did suggest he was applicable to everything.

None of which helps explain the several seconds when I wanted to kiss her. When I clunked back a stage or two myself and nearly made the move. I'm almost expecting to break out in acne and bad clothes, just sitting here thinking about it.

Stage One is basic trust versus basic mistrust. Forms of comfort and people associated with them become familiar. And teething is perhaps the first crucial test of that trust, and where mistrust begins.

And didn't I need to learn that right now? I thought it was just a few tough nights we were having. I didn't realize we were creating mistrust during this lost sleep. I have the Bean with me now, sound asleep in her pouch. I can't believe there's any mistrust, even if I couldn't fix the teething completely.

I think it's Stage Six where things went wrong with

Mel. Intimacy versus isolation, in which the young adult, having won identity, looks to fuse that identity with others. So maybe we were both looking for fusion and picked the nearest feasible identity. We should have paid more attention to Erikson then. There are dangers in Stage Six, and he doesn't hold back from spelling it out. First, when intimate, competitive and combative relationships exist between the same people. And that certainly sounds like us, though we wouldn't have admitted it. And also the "isolation *à deux*," where—if I'm reading it properly—two people share the avoidance of contacts that would lead to a commitment to intimacy, and thereby protect themselves from addressing the big Stage Seven issue, generativity. Establishing and guiding the next generation.

Of course, we ended up addressing it by accident. Or putting ourselves in a position where we were about to address it, at least. And maybe Mel's houseful-of-kids scenario was a desperate hope that we could stake some claim to Stage Seven, while leaving Six in a shambles behind us. But, shit, we tried so hard, and does Erikson give us any credit for that? We must have believed in something, believed at least some days that the intimate would outlast the competitive and the combative. But maybe it's not so easily negotiated, and trying hard doesn't always fix it. Maybe I'm too Stage Six for any plunge into Stage Seven to have worked, even though I was genuinely prepared to try to force myself there.

I think Ash is Six as well. How long can you be Stage Six?

Or maybe I'm not. I haven't felt any biological need to establish the next generation, so technically I'm not Seven, but there's something about having the Bean around that's different, and that I'm growing accustomed to, and that I'd fight a lot to keep.

Perhaps I shouldn't get too hung up on the numbers. Perhaps this is all a little knowledge being a dangerous thing. And it scares me, looking at the early stages, to see how much of an issue parenting is when it comes to getting through them intact. I wonder how Mel's death will mess Lily up developmentally. I wonder how I'm going to tell her, how I'm going to measure it out in the right doses. Erikson doesn't let you know that, and neither does the baby book. There isn't a chapter called "How to explain that the other parent has always been dead."

Lily doesn't even have a concept of life yet. That's years away. And maybe you get to understand life and death together, and before then you just assume. Food will come, diapers will be changed, you will be kept from harm. Then you're out in the world, learning things one at a time. The noises blocks make when you whack them together, how rain feels on your face, words, simple maths, impermanence. How old are you when you realize for the first time that some of your assumptions have let you down, and there might be harm out there?

Can I guess the phases Lily will go through? Can I guess how she'll feel about Mel's death, even some of the time? The bits she'll tell me, and the bits she won't? The times when she'll blame herself? Can I preempt any of it at all? What's it like to win the Electra war on day one? Or am I getting that wrong too, just fooling around with Freud and Jung and Erikson, and plenty more names I don't know?

How do I even feel? I have to keep my own head straight to be much good to her.

Wake up, I whisper down into her ear on the way out of the library. Wake up. Let's play now.

We'll make it up as we go along, I decide. That's what we'll do most of the time.

We sit under the shade of a poinciana tree, and Lily flaps a seed pod around. The dry seeds rattle inside it, and that's enough to give it toy status. She's happy.

I call Wendy on the cell to follow up a few things while she's got some scheduled admin time, in case we don't get the chance to talk between patients later.

I should check your e-mails, she says, about someone who hasn't called back. *They might have tried that way.*

Yeah, good idea.

Hang on and I'll go to your room. She puts me on hold— thirty seconds of something that might be Tchaikovsky (another issue of pointless partnership dissent)—and then she picks up my phone. *Okay. What's your password?*

Oh, yeah, I'd forgotten about that.

Too many letters.

Okay, um, it's B, I, G, B, O, Y.

And you're thinking that by spelling it I won't know that your password is bigboy?

Well, they have to be six letters long. Or six alphanumeric characters, anyway. And I needed to have a word I'd remember.

And "dahlia" or something would have been beyond you.

Definitely. I'd never remember dahlia.

Bigboy. Short for big boy who'll never grow up, I suppose.

You all probably have passwords to do with your penises, don't you? And you think it's so subversive. Okay. First there's something about a Window Weasel.

Yeah, skip that.

Should I? It's not happy with you.

Just hit LATER.

Okay, now onto your e-mails. I'm dialing in, typing in bigboy, and here they come. You've got a few, but I don't see anything like what we were looking for. You've got a couple of joke forwards from George. I got them too. Nothing particularly new. Another New Zealander's fucked a sheep or something, but been caught out by a vacationing Australian ventriloquist.

Some of these things don't really deconstruct well, do they?

No. And they're not always brilliantly funny, either, but he keeps on sending them. You've got a couple of notifications of Web site updates. Looks dull. One's a laser one, the other's about airfares to New York. When are you going to New York?

I'm not. That was ages ago. There's this complicated unsubscribe process you have to go through to get them to stop.

Okay. There's one from your father with the title "made good time heading south." I might leave that one for you. And there's one from Katie. No title. Let's have a look. She double-clicks. *And it says, "Jon, I know the timing's not right, but I can't keep it to myself any longer. I'm developing strong feelings for you and there's no denying it" . . . Etcetera, etcetera . . . "Please, please tell no one. Particularly Wendy" . . . So, what do you want me to do with that one?*

Probably better leave that for me to take a good look at later, as well.

Sure. Now, one from Southside Surgical about a discount on cotton buds this month. Do you think you're up to that?

Depends how they're feeling about me, I suppose. Do you think there's any chance we could keep the Katie one to ourselves? It's not the same as peeing on the cat, is it?

No, it's not. It'd be the kind of thing I'd carry to my grave, except . . . There's a noise, somewhere in the background. A human noise, being muffled.

Um, are you alone at the moment?

No. George is standing right here. Heard the whole thing. That's the laughing sound.

Doesn't he have a seminar this morning?

Apparently not. There's a pause. *What?* Wendy laughs. *He says he thought you'd done enough to put her off by pissing on her cat. And I'd have to say I thought the same. Perhaps you really did need to steal from her as well.*

I have to fix things with Katie. I know I have to fix things with Katie, and soon. I pick Lily up and we go to the car.

Why does it get complicated? I say to her, as she pokes the seed pod into my chin. Wasn't I minding my own business enough?

I drive to Ash's place. There's music on when I get there, I can hear it from the path.

Hi, she says from inside, when I get to the top of the steps. *What's the time?*

I'm early. Sorry. I was nearby, so . . .

Early's fine. You had me thinking I'd be late for my first shift for a second. It'd be pretty sad to get sacked from a bagel joint on your first day.

Sorry. There's plenty of time. I thought we could have lunch before you start work, maybe.

Yeah, good. I just have to change into my . . . um, overalls, first.

Overalls? That'll be a nice look. Heavy work, bagels.

At least there's no tie, she says, when she's in her bedroom with the door shut. *Couldn't stand to have one of those jobs.*

The CD player randomizes, picks another track.

I should work out how to get to the airfare site and unsubscribe, rather than just trashing the e-mails unopened out of habit. New York was my plan. Travel was not uncommonly one of my fixing-things strategies. Mel would happily have stayed at home if I hadn't pushed her into it most years, but she liked it once we were on the plane. She was big on galleries. They gave us a chance to argue about art, instead of life. And there was something—temporarily—very okay about arguing about art. Never have I seen one person get so shitty about another person's view of Jackson Pollock, but for once I could laugh at her shittiness and she'd laugh back.

Or maybe a tie wouldn't have been such a bad thing, Ash says as she comes out of her room in overalls that have the bagginess and color of a sack. *I'm sure this wasn't the pair I tried on. What do you think?*

Well, they're very gender neutral.

That's good to know. At least they're not expecting me to use sex to sell bagels. They're practically species-neutral. She picks up her keys from the kitchen bench and says, *Let's go. Let's listen to that Lemonheads album one more time, shall we?*

You've got a problem with the Lemonheads album?

As soon as the engine's running, she cues up track two—"Into Your Arms"—and she sings along quite loudly and not very well.

I do this, don't I? I ask her. I sing when you're in the car.

Sometimes. Sometimes you just hum.

I don't hum.

You hum.

Humming is such a grandpa thing to do. Don't tell me I hum. Okay, I have a book, a baby book, that recommends singing. And humming. Some humming, I think it says, as well as the singing. Or there's no way the child gets to Erikson Two intact.

Poor Bean. Wouldn't want her to be sorting out that basic trust stuff forever.

Exactly. So now you understand. On occasions, there must be humming. Particularly since we're having bouts of teething at the moment and mistrust has therefore, for the first time, reared its ugly head.

We pull up at traffic lights. I look around to the back and Lily's asleep in the car seat.

I haven't told you everything, I find myself saying, as I turn back to the front.

It was a thought in my head, but now it's coming out. I was thinking of how much I haven't said, wondering again about how to say it, and now I am saying it. Starting to say some of it, anyway.

I haven't told you about Lily's mother.

That's okay. I figured she had one.

Yeah. Here's what happened. It's a complicated situation, and I won't try to get into the whole thing right now, but . . .

The lights change. We drive off.

This is her car, actually. MLB, the vanity plates, they were her vanity license plates. Melissa Brand.

Yeah . . .

Okay. It's complicated. I'm giving the car back when the lease runs out.

To Lily's mother?

No, to the company, the leasing company. There's an amazing amount of stuff you have to sort out, so it's easiest if I just keep it till the lease is up. It's her phone that I've got too. She was a dermatologist. She was one of the other partners in the practice. We met at school. But she died when Lily was born.

It falls into a silence, that last sentence. It doesn't follow the rest in the way I thought it might. It was an explanation that I was attempting, me hurling myself at the shortest possible way of telling Ash everything, setting things straight. I just want them straight. So I needed her to know. The problem started with the introduction of the past tense. She *was* a dermatologist. I was committed at that point, and I had to get it over with. But that's not the problem. There was no other way.

And now we've driven two blocks since, and we're both staring straight ahead.

Oh, she says, then takes a breath in. *I didn't think that was what you were going to say.*

Yeah. It was unexpected.

I'm feeling sick now, and my mouth is dry. In the back, Lily poos loudly.

I just changed her at the campus, I say, thinking aloud again. But I knew there'd be more. Sometimes you can tell.

Ash rubs her eyes and sniffs. *I don't know what to say. That's so awful.*

Um, yeah. But it happens, you know? There are a few days there that'll probably never make sense to me, but I'm on top of things now, I think. It's different, of course.

Yeah.

I'm okay now, really. I'm doing okay.

Yeah. Oh god, I thought you just broke up, or something. Sorry.

I didn't tell you. It's not an easy thing to tell, you know? So you don't tell people, in case they can't get past it. It's like, the last few weeks, running together and things, that's been good. Because you didn't know. Because you didn't spend the whole time being careful, or treating me like I was abnormal. So, if it's okay, please don't change that now.

All right.

But the immediate issue is that poo smell, which will kill us if we don't put all the windows down.

It will. She smiles. *How do they make those smells? What are you feeding her?*

The blandest diet in the world. And somehow it gets incredibly putragenic in there. Not all the time, though. That's what I don't get. Sometimes it's okay, sometimes it's disgusting.

The windows whir and slide down and the air comes in, hot and smelling of cars and cut grass as we go past a school playing field.

I won't be careful, Ash tells me. *I won't change things.*

We get to the shopping center and find a space in the parking lot. I carry the Bean, since no one else should have to when she's in this state, and Ash walks on the other side of me carrying the baby bag.

And no debate about disposables versus cloth diapers, I say, when we're in the change room. I've got to do this four thousand times.

Plus, whatever she's done in that diaper really needs to be disposed of, and I'm talking toxic waste facility, a long way out of town.

Ash stands well back. I accomplish most of the job with one long, held breath.

Now, lunch?

I'll get there. Give me a few minutes, but I'll get there.

The car still smells badly of poo when I get back to it after we've eaten, so I put the windows down again for the drive to work. Ash is now with her overalled co-workers, though looking more baggy than most of them.

I'll see you, she said, when I left her at Bagelos in the food court. *My four-to-six Tuesday seminar hasn't started yet, so call me if you want to do something tomorrow.*

Sylvia takes the Bean from me as I walk into work.

Hello, you lovely thing, she says. *Let's get you away from that daddy of yours. Bad, late daddy. You two have been out playing, haven't you?*

We have. And she's got practically no concept of time. You get her started on one of her favorite topics and there's no stopping her. There we were playing with a seed pod and suddenly she said, "Do you think all disease occurs at a biomolecular level?" and we were off. First, of course, I argued that it was a bit of a reductionist approach, but I have to say she was talking me around toward the end.

It's a shame she can't do laser surgery, too. There's a bit of that here this afternoon for anyone who wants it.

I work hard, but I'm behind for the rest of the day.

Between patients three and four I take a look at this morning's e-mails. Wendy's left them sitting on my screen, and for three patients I've been trying not to be distracted by the one sent by ktnflag. Waiting there, benignly untitled.

It's worse when I read it. Text buffers nothing, softens no edges, gives it right to you. And the part that Wendy quickly etcetera'd away on the phone this morning is no better than the *I'm developing strong feelings for you and there's no denying it* part that precedes it.

At least I've been straight with Ash now. And I think I've known her long enough, or at least seen her often enough, that that'll be okay. We've talked about too many other things, surely, to get stuck on this one. I think that's been my worry, why Mel has been on my mind lately. I haven't been meeting new people, and I haven't told this enough yet that I know how to tell it. Eventually, enough time will have passed that it won't hit people the same way—won't whack into them like an air bag, the way it did with Ash—but we're not there yet. But she had to know some normal things first, before I tossed in the big abnormal one.

14

Now, how do I fix things up with Katie? How do I make it clear, but look after the dignity issues too? I don't want to do that "It's not you, it's me" line. I could do it. It is partly me, but she'd make assumptions straight away. Tell me she was prepared to wait. That's my guess. And I don't want her waiting for something that's not going to happen.

So, what's the right way for Katie? It'll take a gesture. Katie went for the ice bucket and the fancy hors d'oeuvres when she made dinner, so gestures work for her. Flowers. How about flowers? Flowers and a card. And some smart way of saying you're fine, but it's not happening and I'm sorry, it's just not happening, it's not how I feel, but being friends would be good. Because you're fine.

What sort of message do you want to send? the florist asks me at six o'clock, when I've finished my paperwork, persuaded Sylvia to give Lily back to me and gone down into the shopping center as the last of today's flowers are being redistributed into as few buckets as possible for overnight storage. *Who are you giving them to? Is there an occasion? Some flowers are better for some things than others. Like love, or an anniversary, or sympathy, or what? What kind of message have you got in mind?*

Um, it's just a sort of friendly thing, I tell her, thinking that, on the scale of options available, my message probably falls somewhere between "sympathy" and "what."

Flowers seemed like a good idea, but as I stand here going through the buckets to make my choice I realize that I don't know a thing about buying them. The "I don't want you" flowers—would it have been too inappropriate to ask for those? Or did they go earlier in the day? "I don't want you" flowers turning up on doorsteps all over town. With nice, affirming, you're-fine, thanks-but-no-thanks cards.

I've never bought flowers before, other than a corsage for a school formal in 1981, and I wasn't even brave enough to pin that on. In case it would take me slightly too close to my intended victim's breast in front of her mother. I think that was the reason. Not that I ever got any closer. The evening ended outside a nightclub when we were both refused admission because of our age, and she told me her cab home would cost about ten dollars. And I handed the cash over, and that was that. Life's so much better, being twice that old.

Once I've bought a noncommittal but friendly, medium-sized bunch of something multi-colored, I sit in the car to write the card. The card itself is excellently noncommittal. A black-and-white photo of three ducks on a seat. It's the words that are the problem. I do really want to get this right. Katie, though she might be painfully shy and, ultimately, not my type, deserves a better run than she's been having.

But can you ever say that? Can you ever say the type thing? Do people believe you? What does it mean, anyway? I'm simply not attracted to her.

So I open with an apology. First for that awkward Flag issue again, then for sending out the wrong signals, if that's what I've done. And I tell her she matters to me as a friend, but I don't think it'd work any other way. And I don't want to complicate things and risk the friendship. So . . .

Then we drive across town, the Bean gurgling in the back in a way that sounds contented, the flowers and card next to me on the passenger seat.

Why do I feel like such a bastard? I say out loud, but no one answers. Such a gutless bastard, for that matter.

We turn off the freeway, and it's dark now. I don't feel like playing music at the moment. I want to get this over with. And I'm not feeling proud about doing it this way, but it's a conversation I couldn't handle. I don't think Katie would want to deal with it face-to-face, either.

Does that sound too much like a rationalization?

I park outside her house. Her car's underneath and there's a light on down the side, the kitchen light, probably.

Back soon, I tell the Bean. Then home for dinner.

I shut the car door as quietly as I can. In the light from the apartments next-door I can make out a hose across Katie's path, and I step over it carefully. As I get closer to the house I can hear her TV, a commercial break during the news. I sneak up the front steps, my guilt at this commando approach increasing with each one. I set the flowers down at the top and rest the card against them.

What if she always uses the back door? I'm thinking, as I sneak down again. What if she doesn't find this for days, and thinks I'm rude for not responding to her e-mail, then thinks I've left a bunch of dead flowers as some horrible fuck-right-off gesture? Should I have put the date on the card? It's too late to change the plan now. I'm halfway to the car, stepping over the hose again.

And that's when the plan goes wrong.

Flag flies out from under a bush, ready for play. First I don't even know it's him. It's too dark. There's noise on the grass, and a blur, and I don't know what's happening. Then my foot comes down, and little animal ribs crunch like a box of pencils. He squirms away and I fall over, trying so hard to take the weight off him that I forget to stand at all. I hit the path, land on my knees and skin my hands, and Flag stumbles off to the right, out of the dim light, and slumps heavily onto some tan bark.

I go after him. I can hear him struggling under a bush, trying to get away, then I see him on the other side. Just as he falls into a hole not far over the property line, where someone's been gardening at the front of the block of apartments. There's a spade in the hole and he hits it with a soft clunk, probably with his head. He no longer has the capacity to land like a cat.

I get over there as quickly as I can, still madly hoping that he might be all right. I kneel down beside the hole, and it's hard to see him in there.

It's okay, Flag, I tell him. It'll be okay.

There are sounds of difficult breathing coming from the hole, and I try to tell myself it's just the exertion from his run across the garden. I reach down. He tries to bite me, but he doesn't have the breath for it. He's lying against the shovel, lying with one side on the blade of the shovel.

I'm going to lift you out now, I tell him, in my calmest

possible don't-worry-I-haven't-killed-you voice. And I'm going to lift you out on the shovel to protect your spine. And then we're going to work out what the hell to do.

Retrieve the flowers, leave him by the roadside, flee. Go straight to the door, confess all. This is such a morality test. Flee. Flee is good. No, I have to face it. I can't duck it. Can I?

No, I can't.

Katie's outside light goes on, illuminating us with an alarming brightness. Her front door opens. She doesn't notice the flowers, but she does see me, kneeling next door. Next to a cat-sized hole, with Flag slumped semi-conscious across a shovel. And she screams.

No, no, it's fine, I shout out to her, using my calmest possible voice again. I'm just protecting his spine.

Flag, of course, is fucked, something that the bright light makes horribly apparent, but that I choose to disregard completely as I run toward her front door, hoping to fix this. Showing her Flag on a spade, as though it's a great first step. As he wheezily exhales blood through his nostrils, his head bobbing like a rear-window plastic dog until I put my other hand there to support it.

Katie screams and screams, slams the door. Through the window next to it, I can see her go for the phone, and she's got to be calling Wendy.

I shovel Flag down next to the flowers and I grab my mobile from my belt. I punch Wendy's number in as quickly as possible, but Katie's obviously got her on speed dial. Through the window I can see her talking, hear the screeching. And I'm getting put through to voice mail.

She sets the phone down, disappears for a second, comes

back with the biggest knife I've seen come out of a kitchen. And she holds it in both hands and looks along the blade at me, as though she's lining me up in a gun sight. What does she do in there? Slaughter buffalo?

And I don't want to know what sick thing you've done with my towels, you bastard, she screams. She's distracted by her phone again, someone saying something, and she picks it up. *Yeah, he's still here. Shall I call the police? . . . Okay . . . But I'm keeping the knife.*

She hangs up, glares at me along the knife again.

I can explain, I tell her pathetically, as I hit Redial. I get Wendy in her car.

Jon, hi, she says. *How's it going?* In just the soothing voice you'd use to chat to a slathering cat murderer. *Might be seeing you shortly . . .*

Wendy, let me explain. I know Katie will have sounded pretty stressed on the phone. Fuck, I can tell from the enormous knife that she's not the best, but this is a total accident. You have to understand that. Let me explain.

I'm listening.

Okay. I just dropped over here, I was visiting, in a totally normal way, and Flag ran out of the bushes and under my feet. You know that cat game where they tag you? Flag does that, when he likes people, doesn't he?

Yeah . . .

But unfortunately he's not as gifted at it as Katie thinks. And maybe the dark confused him. So he sort of got under my feet. And I stepped on him. A bit.

So you were just dropping over there?

Yeah.

To see Katie?

Well, yeah, kind of.

And you happen to have killed her cat? Accidentally. She tries not to laugh, I can hear it. *She thinks you've killed him.*

Possibly. I have to admit that. He's certainly not well.

That's pretty bad luck, Jon.

Well, it's worse luck for Flag.

I look down at the floppy Flag, gurgling short breaths in and out at my feet. Inside, I hear Katie moving furniture against the door.

He could do with a chest tube, I suspect.

Katie thinks you went over there to kill him.

Yeah, well that was kind of unfortunate. What happened was, after I stepped on him, he ran off and fell into a hole, just outside the apartments next door. You know how there's some work being done in the garden there? Well, there is. And there was a hole. With a shovel in it. And Flag fell onto the shovel, so I lifted him out. Still on the shovel. Protect the spine, you know? And that's when Katie came out.

When you were standing next to a hole, with Flag on a shovel . . .

Well, kneeling, but yes.

Kneeling? Finally there's a squawk as she can't hold back and laughs properly.

Kneeling, with Flag kind of hanging off the edges of a shovel, yeah. So it's easy to see how misunderstandings might arise.

Look, I'm going to have to stop talking now, or I could seriously wet the seat. You know my pelvic floor hasn't been the same since Emily. I might have to pull over for a couple of minutes, but I'll be there as quickly as I can.

Please, she's got a very big knife.

Another squawk, and the line goes dead.

Soon enough, the voice of mediation is ringing out across the neighborhood. Wendy calmly and clearly saying things like, *Now, Katie, don't you think it'd be better if the three of us could talk about this? On the same side of the door?* and, *You'll have to move the sideboard before we can help you . . .*

But Katie menaces on, keeping a firm grip on the knife and making sure the point is always angled my way.

She has so lost it, Wendy says in a low voice, her hand to her face as she struggles to stop a laugh breaking through, a battle that Katie interprets as emotion.

See? She cares, you bastard, she shouts. *And you're not a kleptomaniac at all. You're just a straightforward psychopath, like the rest of them.*

Katie, it was an accident, I try. It was just an accident. The hole was there already.

Oh yeah? Holes don't dig themselves.

The gardener next door did it.

He likes Flag. He'd never touch him.

No, that was me, but it was an accident. Honestly. But for now the main thing is getting Flag some help, isn't it?

Wendy and I both look down at the slumped bundle of fur, and Flag looks back up at us, glassy-eyed and panting noisily.

How is he, like, neurologically? Wendy says, again keeping it at murmur level. *Are those back legs doing much? If you've transected his spinal cord the vet's probably not going to be too interested, and we might as well head back next door . . .*

Don't. Don't even say that quietly.

It might be an idea to check, though.

Okay.

I kneel down next to Flag, and Katie screams. I look up and her face, and the knife, are pressed against the glass.

Just a quick medical check, Katie. I asked Jon to do it, Wendy says, and then she whispers to me, *I'd skip checking sphincter tone if I were you. She'd be likely to take it the wrong way.*

Don't make me laugh, Wend. I'm going nowhere near his sphincter and you know it. Okay, his lower limbs withdraw from pain, so that's good enough for me. His tail moves. I figure it's the fractured ribs and the possible pneumothorax we've got to deal with.

Possible pneumothorax?

Yeah. Flag is in trouble here. I have done a bad thing. We've got to try and fix it.

Yes. Sorry, it's just . . . not what I was expecting to be doing tonight. And Katie's so . . . worked up about it. Where did she get that knife? She raises her eyebrows, sighs. *Okay, Katie, I'm coming in,* she says, like a person who's watched far too many cop shows. *Push the sideboard away and put down the knife.*

But what about . . .

Katie, it's all okay. It's a misunderstanding. It's an accident. Flag was playing and got tangled in Jon's feet and the hole next door was already there. Jon was just . . . protecting Flag's spine by keeping him on the shovel. That's what you saw. The sideboard starts scraping back along the hall, Wendy eases the door open. *We've got to go, now. We've got to get Flag some help.*

Are you sure?

Yes, I'm sure.

Katie puts the knife down next to the phone and comes closer to the door.

I'm sorry, Jon, she says. *I just saw what I saw, and didn't react very well.*

Perfectly understandable.

I'm a single woman. I live alone in a dangerous world.

And now, Wendy says, *you two can take Flag to the vet hospital, so you can finish sorting this out.*

We'll go in my car, I tell Katie. You can look after Flag on the way and I'll drive.

And look, Katie, Wendy says, pointing. *Jon came over here to bring you flowers. That's why he was here.*

Yes, yes, that's why I came over. See? To give you flowers. Nothing to do with Flag.

You were bringing me flowers?

Yes.

And that's when I start to remember what the flowers were about.

Um, yes. Let's get Flag sorted out now though. That's the important thing at the moment.

You were bringing me flowers and just leaving them on my doorstep? That's sweet.

This could be a tension pneumothorax here, Katie. Do you know what a tension pneumothorax is?

I'll put the flowers in water, Wendy says, starting to beam

misguidedly, like someone who's stumbled upon something rather nice, as opposed to a dumping-by-gutless-
bouquet plus cat-trampling event. *Why don't the two of you
go and get Flag sorted out?*

I'll get his blanket, Katie says. *He'll be better wrapped in
his blanket.*

She runs down the hall and Wendy keeps looking at
the flowers and maintaining the low-key beaming.

*Flowers are a nice thought, Jon. I wouldn't have picked
you as being that kind of guy.*

Actually . . .

Then Katie's back. *Okay. Let's go.* She crouches down,
wraps Flag up delicately. *Flaggy, it's your blanket. It's your
favorite, sweetie. The one Mummy got you from Acapulco.
You're going to be okay.* He makes a spluttering noise, but
keeps breathing. *And I might have mentioned the missing
towels again back there. In the heat of the moment . . .*

It's no problem.

I'll get some water for the flowers, Wendy says. *You can
leave me to lock up.*

*No, it's okay. We'll take the flowers with us. Flaggy likes
flowers.*

We turn to go to the car, and I wonder how the situation can be saved from here. I'm not in a strong position,
having crushed her cat in a way that may yet prove fatal.
The flowers are sending entirely the wrong signal right
now, and the only thing that will send the right signal is
the card that's tucked in there somewhere—among the
stems and near the wheezing, gurgling cat—but it somehow has to disappear before Katie sees it tonight.

Shit, Lily, I realize, and say it aloud. I've left her in the
car all this time.

You were just leaving the flowers on the doorstep . . .
I run down the path and jump the steps at the bottom.
I get to the car door and pull it open. And Lily looks at
me. I think I've woken her. I think it's okay.
I'm sorry, I say to her. I'm sorry. I was only going to
be a minute. I can't believe I left you here.
I'm sure it's okay, Jon, Katie says. *It really wasn't long.*
She lowers herself into the passenger seat, cradles Flag like
a baby. *And there was the knife. I think that had you distracted for a while. I'm really sorry about the knife . . . See
Flaggy? It's all a mistake. Just an accident in a game.* Her
voice, in its attempt to reassure, is taking on more of the
tone of a mad person than I'd like it to. *You'll have to be
more careful in the dark, won't you?*
Wheeze wheeze, gurgle gurgle. I'm reckoning Flaggy's
chances of seeing any more dark beyond this night are
fifty-fifty, at best.
Where should we go? I ask her. Is that one near the
PA Hospital the nearest one that'd be open?
That's where Flag always goes, she says, and strokes his
head. *Poor little guy. We don't have your very clever night
vision, do we? Not enough carrots, hey Flaggy, that's us humans. Jon brought us some nice flowers, though. We like flowers, don't we? We sometimes wait years between bunches of
flowers, don't we, Flaggy? And there's a nice card to cheer
us up.*
She pulls the card out, whips it out of the envelope and
snaps the passenger-seat reading light on before I can even
think about how to stop her.
Um, Flag's eyes . . . the light might not be a good idea
at the moment.

The vet's not going to examine him in the dark, Jon. Now don't be embarrassed. I know you wanted to leave this on the step and drive away, but . . . She stops talking, reads the card, smiling. Then goes completely still, and the smile freeze-frames itself on her face, flickers like an old video. There's a sharp intake of breath.

Um . . .

Oh, I thought that'd make me feel better. Another sharp breath in. *Oh, you bastard. You maybe kill my cat, and then you give me this to read.*

I didn't . . . I'm sorry. I'm sorry.

You hurt my cat. And you peed on him. Sob. *It changed him, you know. And you . . .* Sob. *I thought we were getting on so well.*

Sorry. I'm really sorry.

She says nothing, wipes her face with the corner of the blanket, the "O" in Acapulco, and stares grimly at the back of the car in front of us.

Look, you know it's about me at the moment, don't you?

But the card . . .

I know. I know what I said in the card. I just don't want to mislead you. It's too easy to give people the wrong idea and cause harm, and that's not what I want to do. Really.

Yeah. There's a pause, and I mistakenly take it to mean that she's absorbing what I've just said. *Um, everyone tells me you make jokes about my hair.*

What?

Eighties hair.

What?

It's only cause my ears stick out a bit. I wanted to cover them, she says, in a wobbly, quivery voice as we drive into the vet hospital and park.

Why don't you take Flag? I suggest, and I'll carry Lily. And we'll leave the flowers in the car for now.

She sniffs loudly and takes a final, firm wipe at her face with the blanket.

I'm not desperate, you know, she says, as we go through the sliding doors and into the bright flourescent lights of the reception area. *I might have turned thirty and be single almost all the time, but I'm not desperate. And we can't all be as together as bloody Wendy.*

Yeah, I know.

So you didn't say the eighties hair stuff?

I think we've got to focus on Flag tonight, Katie. I don't think it's a night to get too deep into the personal issues.

Eighties hair, she says, and starts to sob again.

No one's as together as bloody Wendy. Certainly not me. So don't worry about that. And I know you're not desperate. Katie, your hair's fine.

Really?

Yeah, it's fine. I like your hair.

Do you like the eighties? she says, totally pushing the friendship.

And she looks at me in a way that says she really needs me to like the eighties, just for now, just to get through this moment, so I have to say, Sure.

Good, she says. *Cause I think they're pretty good too.*

———

So that's one of the high points of our evening behind us, this flimsy agreement about a decade best forgotten, and after that reality cuts in all too often.

The vet doesn't like the look of Flag at all. She agrees it's probably a pneumothorax, and she works quickly to get a tube in there. The emergency X-rays confirm the diagnosis, the second set of X-rays show that the tube's in the right position. My Visa card gets a good working over. Flag gets wheeled to Intensive Care.

The vet talks about Flag's ribs, and assumes there was a car involved. This makes no one feel better. She points to the fractures on the X-ray, and I tell her it's what we'd call, in humans, a flail segment, where you've broken enough ribs in two places that there's a section of the rib cage that doesn't work in the normal way. She tells me it's the same deal in animals, unfortunately.

There is more sobbing from Katie, several more outbreaks of sobbing. Sometimes linked to particular increments of bad news, sometimes out of the blue. Her eyes go red and stay that way. Her nose starts to run and, with all the wailing going on and Katie oblivious to most things, I take to it instinctively with tissues. She keeps talking without making much sense, her nose steps its contribution up a notch and I find myself saying, Come on, give it a good blow, before I realize that the vet is staring at us like we're one fucked-up family.

Lily is wailing too, with all the distress around and the shambles this has made of mealtime, and the vet fetches more tissues so that I can get to her nose before major problems start.

They're glad when we leave.

There's not much talk in the car on the way back to Katie's. When we get there she tells me she'd rather not take the flowers, and she runs inside.

I drive back onto the freeway, and Lily keeps up the wailing. And we might have got through the recent teething intact, but tonight I've shut her in a car, deprived her of dinner and exposed her to way too much unhinged human emotion. The concept of basic mistrust should be kicking in right now, just as Erikson knew it would, and it'll be years before I'll get to explain any notion as sophisticated as extenuating circumstances.

And the vet said she'd do her best, but she could make no promises. Katie let go a lot of facial fluid at that point.

Soon, very soon, I say to Lily, but it does no good.

The wailing is with us the whole way home, and all the music and soothing talk only adds to the noise. And I think back to the occasional e-mails Katie and I exchanged until not long ago, and how simple it seemed. And now I think I might have killed half her e-mail address.

15

I get to work early on Tuesday, and put in some quality time with the pathology reports and build-up of junk in my in-box. The sensation of cat thorax underfoot is hard to keep out of my mind, though. It's hard not to feel awful about Katie and Flag, ktnflag, the whole e-mail address.

Other people start to arrive. Elevator doors start pinging open and the phone starts ringing. I hear conversation in the corridor, Wendy laughing.

George comes to my door and says in a deeper-than-usual, CNN-anchorman voice, *It's Flag, Jon. Katie just called to say he could still go either way.*

Look . . . Quit the voice, okay? It was an accident.

Yeah, I'm sure it was. Gotta hand it to you. You know how to turn 'em down. You've got this dating thing so under control, haven't you?

It wasn't a date. And I've got to get to work now. I've got to make some positive contribution to the world.

I stand and walk past him to take my first file from Sylvia.

And it wasn't a date.

And she knows it now, doesn't she? Hi, honey, he says, slipping into something less comfortable (but more like

Darren from *Bewitched,* this time), *just turned up to trample the livestock.*

I never called anyone "honey." Not in my whole life.

I can see my first patient listening, looking less than confident about the hands he's in.

And until yesterday, George goes on, *you could have said, I never killed a chick's pet to put her off. The world's a more dynamic place than you give it credit for.*

You bastards. You're all being so insensitive. Katie's really attached to that cat. And Flag is still fighting the good fight. I've put him in Intensive Care, I know that, but I haven't killed him. Not yet.

Hey, you're good. You trample on a cat, and you call everyone else insensitive. But I do admire you for this, you know. You were actually making a move to sort things out, even if it did misfire a little. There might have been a time when you would have juggled two chicks, but you're pretty clear that's not happening now. Sorry, not two chicks. One coffee friend, one running buddy.

And no juggling. You know that's not where I am. This is not about juggling. I just didn't want to be misleading people.

Yeah, I know, he says, after pausing and deciding to ease back on the game. *I'm sure it's just bloody envy on my part.* He squeezes my shoulder, gives me a pat on the back, beefy but gentle, and picks up his own next file. *You and that sleek runner's body of yours. It's a weapon out there. That's what they're all saying.*

Yeah, yeah.

I call my patient in, and try to assume something like

a professional demeanor. I try not to let it show that my body's a weapon out there. What is it with everybody here? Is nothing my business? Why do they seem to be paying such close attention to my spare time? Because I piss on cats, put them in the hospital, get it wrong with flowers, find myself a running buddy, somehow. But I guess if it was George doing it I'd be paying plenty of attention, and cutting him no slack at all.

Two patients into the day, I go to check my e-mails. The Window Weasel looks really cranky this time, and says:

Bad Weasel. Bad Weasel. I s'pose you steal stuff from people all the time, Jon. Pay up, bud. Go click YES!! I LOVE MY WEASEL!! and you can register to use Window Weasel for life for only $30! Click LATER to register later.

That's it. I've had enough. George is in the vascular-laser room. I buzz him on the intercom.

Did you put all the software on these computers?

Yeah.

Well, what the fuck is a Window Weasel?

Um, I'm doing a procedure in here. On a patient.

I don't mind which one of you tells me.

Um, it's those really cool icons you've got. And stuff. And that shloopy noise when you open and shut things, or move them around.

That shloopy noise?

Yeah, the one that goes . . . shloop.

Ah, shloop. It's much clearer when you put a bit of effort in. Now I get it. The shloopy noise. Thanks.

Yeah, well, it's all that stuff. I lined it up for you a while back.

Oh, I wondered where it had come from. I thought you'd just done a general software upgrade for everyone.

No, just you. Well, you and me.

Oh, thanks.

I thought you'd like it.

Yeah, I do. I do like it. It's just that this weasel's started appearing. I didn't know what was going on.

The trial period must be up. Just click LATER and it'll leave you alone.

I've been clicking LATER for weeks now. It's starting to get really cranky with me.

Yeah, I've got a strategy for that. That's when I tell myself it's a cartoon. I think you'll find that helps. The whole thing gets a lot less stressful then.

Thanks a lot, George. I'm sure I'll be fine now.

What icons? What shloopy noise? The only difference I noticed was the weasel, coming out to bug me every day and hit me for thirty bucks. Was there no shloopy noise before I took the time off? Surely there was. Surely there was some kind of noise, at least. And was there really any call for an upgrade? Is my day improved at all by a change in tone of the shloopy noise when I move things or open them? Is there some extra whoosh to it now? Some extra spring in my step as a result? How many of my precious megabytes are now devoted to things as purposeless as shlooping?

I've got no idea about this stuff. When people say "icon" the first thing that comes into my mind is still the Ortho-dox Church.

Wendy comes into the kitchen when I'm making coffee.

Hi, she says, and then leaves it to me to say something.

Hi. Just thought I'd make some coffee.

Me too. She goes to fill the kettle, gets her mug from the cupboard. She still has her back to me when she starts to crack up laughing. *I'm sorry,* she says when she turns. *Last night was the strangest night I've had in my life, I think.*

It'd be at least in my top ten too. Do you think it's stranger than going around to someone's house for dinner and pissing on the cat?

The hole next door, the shovel, that's what made it for me. It was those finishing touches that made it special. The kettle boils. *I shouldn't say that, should I? Flag's really not well.*

No. He doesn't sound well.

I thought it was nice that you went around there.

Somehow I think that, even in time, Katie won't come to feel the same.

No, I mean, going around to tell her . . .

I wasn't going around to tell her. I was going around to be gutless. Sneak up, leave a card explaining things and a bunch of flowers as some kind of stupid gesture. That was the plan. And I'd put thought into it. It was my best plan. I thought face-to-face would be even more uncomfortable from Katie's perspective.

Which it would have been.

Which it was. She did get to read the card in the car, remember. We got to do face-to-face. I don't think she liked it.

No, she told me. I'm sorry if I did anything that contributed to this.

What do you mean?

Well, I might have accidentally contributed to her expectations. I got the impression . . . It doesn't matter what impression I got. Katie just has to adjust to the idea that you aren't interested, and that's what I'll be working on.

Um, it's . . .

No. I don't need to know the details. You're my friend, she's my crazy sister. You pissed on her cat, you stepped on her cat—all of it accidental, that stuff happens. Then there's that business about the bath towels, and I never want to talk about it again either. These are two worlds that were not meant to collide. I realized that last night. And I realized, when I saw Katie with that knife, that there's a lot I don't need to know.

I hope she's all right. How is she today?

Mental. Don't call her.

Do you really think I was going to call her? You could beg me and I wouldn't call her. I'm hoping she's all right from afar.

Well, let's see what happens to Flag. She presses the plunger, pours her coffee. *Is anyone, ever, going to tell her he's only a cat?*

No, obviously. If someone stepped on my dog, I'd feel terrible. You are so not a pet person. I know she pushes it a bit with the Acapulco blanket . . .

Jon, she sent Flag postcards from Mexico. Four of them. She sent us one.

I'm sure she would have handled it differently if she'd known you were counting. Oh god, it was such a charmed life for Flag until last night, wasn't it? How is she about me today?

Not good. I could lie, but she's not good. She's still pretty angry. And not entirely coherent.

What does that mean? What's she said?

Something about how you seem to have it in for everything she stands for. I don't know quite what that's about.

Neither do I. What does she stand for?

She mentioned hair at the same time. But I don't get the connection. Did something happen to her hair? Did she cry last night?

Yeah, but . . .

Did she get . . . she can get a bit messy about the face, a bit snuffly, when she cries. And when she cries a lot . . .

She cried a lot.

Damn. Poor Katie. And it got in her hair again?

No. There were tissues. It wasn't a problem. Anyway, you know what it's like. We've both got kids. Fluids'll never put me off a person again. And you have to respect someone who doesn't hold back.

Yeah. What a disaster. Have you got the sugar?

Sure.

She taps her single, carefully measured spoonful against the side of the Tupperware container, *Hey, George says you've got a running buddy.*

Yeah.

I thought you told me you ran with a group.

That's sort of the idea, but it's supposed to be flexible. This might surprise you, but we don't have roll call, or anything. No-one does a head count. It's just running.

So there are lots of you, then?

Not lots.

So how big would the group be at its biggest?

So far?

No, next year. Yes, so far.

Still mainly the two of us. Me and the running buddy. You know the buddy theory with exercise? How it makes you better at sticking to the routine?

You were sticking to the routine already.

Well, maybe it gives her a routine. She's a student from up north, a postgrad student, and she used to run with people there. She prefers to run with people.

You poor, powerless man. A young woman comes along and forces herself on you like that . . . Your pants are so on fire.

No one forced anyone. It's a series of coincidences. It's healthy. And people should stop reading things into it.

And she's butt ugly, right?

Look . . .

She stirs her coffee and laughs at me.

Too easy. She shakes her head. *Way too easy. And I'll take that as a "No, she's not butt ugly," shall I?*

We just go running. She's got a runner's body, I suppose.

Whatever. Having someone to run with is nice. And, let's face it, it wasn't going to be one of us. She pauses, and I'm bracing myself for some more reassurance that it's okay that I'm not with Katie. *How are you doing really?*

I'm fine. Really. And I'm going. Things are moving along all right. Don't think I'm stalled, or anything. I've got Lily for a start, and we're okay. And I know it seems odd to start running with someone and then see them suddenly practically every day, but that's how running works, if you think about it. You do it practically every day. So it could be that it's not as complicated as George might like to think.

He doesn't mean . . .

I know he doesn't mean.

It's just you that we're thinking about. You know that, don't you? With all of this interfering . . .

Yeah, I know. And it's not interfering. But don't make too much of the running. Please.

Okay. But sometimes you have to tell us what we should make of things. This, the last six months, it's all been different for us, too. I wish things could be the way they were, but they can't. So all I can wish, really, is that things work out for the best. That's what we all want.

I know.

Sylvia's at the door, holding a handful of files. *We've got a couple waiting. Just thought I'd let you know.*

My shirt wilts as I get out of the car at Ash's place. From my east-facing window at work I could see nothing but clear sky, but the western storm clouds have been building most of the afternoon. They're not here yet though, and the air's still thick and hot and humid in the world beyond air-conditioning. In the distance, a City Cat hums along the river, behind Ash's house.

Ash comes down the steps, her hair wet and slick. She's wearing the dress she wore when we had lunch on campus a week and a half ago. She jumps into the car, swings the door shut behind her, and before I'm back in there she's leaning over to the car seat, saying hello to Lily. Reaching to let Lily's small hand take her finger, and asking her what kind of day she's had.

Then she flops into the front seat and says, *I've just been swimming. Thought it'd be a good day for a few laps.*

And she smells like a clean, well-chlorinated pool as she

sits there, transferring some of the damp in her hair to the headrest, wrapping her arms around herself as the sudden temperature change springs goosebumps up on them. And last night seems like a long and complicated nightmare I could have done without.

I shouldn't feel that. When I think of last night, I should think more of the distress I've caused Katie and the harm I've caused Flag, but now that Ash is in the car it all seems to matter less. Or to be less real, or more in the past or another place.

Running buddy. Am I thinking "running buddy?" This is not how it's supposed to be.

So what were you doing around there with flowers in the first place? she says, as she kneels on the floor with the Bean. She gives her fingers to hold again, this time one for each hand, and says, *Go on, stand. Stand.*

I put her glass of mineral water down beside her and I turn the ceiling fan up a level. There's a grumble in the distance, thunder somewhere.

Ash lifts Lily so that she stands on her wobbly bow legs and then says, *Nah.*

I think she said "stand."

I think she said "nah." But nah is good, too. Not everyone gets nah.

Why am I getting a song about a drunken sailor in my head? Ash says, as Lily keeps wobbling. *And what was that about the flowers?*

It was all to do with a misunderstanding. After we had our usual approximately annual conversation a few weeks ago, she e-mailed me. I e-mailed back. Then we had coffee.

You know, just coffee. Then suddenly it got out of control. I hadn't given the slightest flicker of interest—I'm sure I hadn't—then suddenly she's got the candles out for dinner and we've got this big misunderstanding happening. So I went over there to clear it up. And I thought I'd take some flowers. She wasn't expecting me, so she didn't have the front lights on. And her cat rushed out, and I stepped on him. Then there's the hole, her coming out, the light going on, and you know the rest.

Couldn't she have misunderstood the flowers, too?

No, there was a card with them.

You were going to give her this on a card, too? A summary of the conversation you were going to have?

No. I was going to leave it on her top step. The flowers and the card.

You were going to just leave them and run off? That's not very brave.

I never said it was an act of bravery. She's a very private person. I thought it'd work better that way.

Ash gives me a look that suggests that a certain lack of bravery is still an issue, and that I could have done better. She moves to sit with her legs crossed and steers Lily into a sitting position on her right thigh, in a way that leaves Lily's pale feet resting on one of her tanned ankles.

There we go. Enough of that standing. She looks back at me, drinks some of her mineral water. *I'm sure you had good reasons.*

Even her sister backed me up on it today. She said face-to-face would have been a mistake. It was part of the difficulty all the way along. Katie never said much, and then she'd spring things on me. And I wasn't saying much because I thought there wasn't much to say. I was just cruising along and then suddenly, bang, she's got these feelings for me, and she's probably thinking I've got them for her, too. Or at least some kind of feelings.

Why do people do that?

I've got no idea. It's so unfortunate. She's nice enough but, really, it was never going to happen. But I shouldn't be talking about it now, should I?

Why? It sounds as though there's quite a bit of talk going on behind your back. And at least some of it was to do with setting the two of you up, surely. That's what it sounds like to me.

Maybe. She's just—and I know this sounds kind of dismissive—but she's just not my type. We don't have common ground. I really wish it hadn't escalated and ended up how it did—she must feel pretty bad now—but we haven't ever had a conversation that hasn't been crushingly awkward, for god's sake. And, you know, where I come from that's not a good sign.

Were the conversations less awkward before the feelings cropped up?

Yeah, probably. Never easy. Always awkward, but less awkward before.

See, it's that unnecessary complication business again, she says, and there's more thunder, closer. *You had me worried before. When you called and told me you were out hurting animals and having knives pulled on you. I thought you must have had some dark side.*

Yeah, that was it. The call was my other side warning you about the dark side. And the dark side likes to be clear with people on the issue of feelings. If they ignore the cat crushing, they get a horse's head in their bed.

Well, that's something to watch out for.

I'm sure you're quite safe. Shall we order some take-out before the storm breaks?

I don't know that I'm up to take-out. I haven't been paid yet. I only started work yesterday.

That's fine. I'll pay.

You shouldn't pay for me.

Why not? I started work ten years ago. I've been paid several times. And I wasn't thinking anything wildly extravagant.

As long as I pay next time.

Sure.

No, I mean it.

Fine, mean it as much as you like. Now, let's have an argument about which take-out instead. That'd be more worthwhile.

I fetch my binder of take-out menus without even thinking about it.

Ash laughs. *You file these? Oh my god, you've got them in plastic. They're in individual plastic sleeves.*

They're easier to read that way.

I can't believe you.

What's wrong with it? They put these things in your mailbox. They make them all letter size. Do you think that's by chance? They're practically inviting you to have a system. I think this is smart.

You do, don't you? You think it's damn smart.

Yeah, I do. It may be just a little anally retentive as well, but it's bloody useful.

And I bet you've got particular favorites from each place, haven't you? Things you just reorder and reorder.

Well, yeah. But it'd be chaos otherwise. There must be two thousand meals in this thing.

But isn't spontaneity a part of take-out? Isn't it spur-of-the-moment? Don't you just make up your mind on the spot?

No. Not at all. Spontaneity is the enemy of clear thinking. The more shit you have to be spontaneous about, the more you use up the limited thinking power of your brain. There's far too much emphasis placed on spontaneity. If every decision in life was treated like a new experience—like the first time you confront a Chinese restaurant menu and it seems to go forever—you'd get nothing done.

Okay. Well, give it to me. I'm going to choose, she says, and takes the menu. *And it's going to be very spontaneous.*

But no weird bits of animals, all right? No feet, no noses, none of that.

She picks Indian, and orders more than we could ever eat. Enough that we qualify for free home delivery, so we don't even have to go out to get it. And, without knowing it, she also happens to order things I regularly order.

We drink more mineral water. Ash feeds Lily and I put some laundry on. Elvis trots in from outside, drooping with the heat, and folds himself across my feet in his usual bony-limbed way.

The storm builds and builds, and it breaks right after dinner gets here.

It comes in like a night coming early, black as an eclipse, and the cicadas go wild. The hot air that has waited all day to turn to something becomes wind, slipping in under the guard of the tree canopies, swirling the loose leaves, rushing them, scraping them along the veranda. And from the west a wall of rain comes at us, with a lumbering sound like a street-sweeping truck, erasing all but the outline of the next hill, collapsing onto the roof. We stand in the kitchen, Ash, Lily and me, wrapped up in this noise and the thrashing rain. Elvis, implacable before in the face of thunder, now stares me down, holds me responsible.

Ash sees the look this time, points to him and shouts at me, *Your fault.*

And then, fifteen minutes after it began, the storm is gone, marauding elsewhere, east of here, and the rain tails off and stops.

I pour us wine. Ash opens the food containers and acknowledges her rank over-ordering by saying, *Hmmm, won't be going hungry tonight.*

No. But it was spontaneous. Very spontaneous. And that's always good.

We sit out on the veranda in the relative cool. Somewhere not far away, fire alarms are ringing, then there's the sound of sirens.

You feel bad about the person with the cat, don't you?

Yeah, I do. It's not a good situation, even apart from what I did to the cat. It's not as if I haven't had my share of unrequited interest in people. I know what it's like. And it's bad enough just having it, but it's worse when it gets public. You feel like such a loser.

It's difficult, the love business, she says, and lifts a forkful of lamb rogan josh to her mouth.

Fortunately, I don't think the "L" word came up in this situation. I headed that one off at the pass.

I meant generally.

Yeah, but when is it the love business? When is something more than just a dumb crush or infatuation? I don't know where the boundary between love and major enthusiasm lies.

Well, if you're thinking boundaries, it's probably not it. I guess you could maybe think of when it gets you physically, so it's sort of beyond reason. When you feel it in the pit of your stomach and you get ... what's the name for it when your heart goes fast?

Tachycardia.

No.

Well, I obviously wasted those years of med school.

Palpitations. It's palpitations.

Well, close, yeah.

What do you mean?

Tachycardia means fast heart. A palpitation is a sort of subjective thump when your heart suddenly does something you're not expecting it to.

Has anyone ever told you you might be a bit pedantic?

Oh, yeah. But it doesn't bother me. I'm fine with it. And I can control it, you know. Some more naan?

I push the oily brown paper bag her way and she says, *Thanks,* and takes the last garlic piece. *Hey, the CD's finished. Is it your turn to pick one?*

I go inside to change the music. It's getting dark again, night this time. I flip through the CDs and settle on some old Go Betweens.

Do you have that thing, I say to Ash when I'm back outside, where some songs get linked to events? Or people?

How do you mean?

Sorry, this is related to the topic. I mean where you're having one of those days when there's a heightened sense of reality—to do with something great or really shitty—and the next song you hear is permanently associated with that day, any time you hear it, or even think about it. It's like, the first massive crush I had, nothing got to happen. And then suddenly, when it looked like it might, the girl left town. We were going to be doing something that day, and I got a call from her friend to say she'd gone. Some family problem in Adelaide, or somewhere. And she never came back. And I went into my bedroom and turned on the radio, and the first thing I heard was a Phoebe Snow song. And it's now stuck in my mind as part of that day. Fortunately it wasn't her big hit, though, so I'm relatively safe.

Who's Phoebe Snow?

Safer than I thought. But you're right. It's not as though I can even name the big hit anymore, is it? Anyway, she probably wasn't such a big deal, really. The girl. Mild tachycardia at the most. No palpitations.

Have you wrecked a lot of songs that way?

A few. I managed a few seething, silent crushes in my time. At school and, tragically, still when I got to med school. After that I had a rather bad phase.

A being-single phase?

No. No, that'd been the easy stuff. I'd had a lifetime of that. Hence the bad phase afterward. I'd become too good at desperately wanting people to take an interest in me, so I was hopelessly unprepared when they did. And I sort of got into this "shoot first and ask questions afterward" mode of operating, and it's not a popular way to conduct relationships. One way or another, I didn't handle things particularly well. The word "thoughtless" comes to mind. And then I was kind of involved with someone I really liked, or thought I might be about to really like . . .

Sounds like you put a lot on the line with that one, if you were thinking that you might be about to really like her.

Yeah. I wasn't exactly big at risking things then. She was an OT, an occupational therapist. And I'd got into this cycle where, in the face of impending commitment, I'd get people to dump me.

Some seriously unresolved Erikson Six issues then?

Really? You mean none of it was my fault?

It sounds like all of it was your fault. It doesn't mean Erikson wouldn't have had a view on why you were doing it.

He's a tough man. But that was it. I was Erikson Five and playing with the Erikson Six crowd. And I hadn't got it sorted out when I met this OT, so I freaked out a bit—probably because of the possibility of some serious liking happening—and she didn't take a lot of shit from anybody, really. So, before I'd thought it through, I was gone. Dumped and suddenly feeling seriously dumped. And after that there was just Mel.

Well, you loved her.

Yeah.

And it catches me like a surprise, someone coming out and saying that. Almost as though it's an accusation, an attempt to catch me off guard. It's not what people say. People who know ask me if I'm all right, really, and usually they leave it at that.

So what about you?

I think I might have met a couple of guys like you in that postgrad bastard phase.

I'm not sure that I said "bastard." And I didn't know it was a phase. I thought it was just me.

No, I think it goes loser at college, then postgrad bastard.

I'm sensing you don't approve. I'm sure it's just normal development.

Well, of course you're sure. You wouldn't want to have to accept responsibility, would you?

Never. There's not a crappy act in my life that I can't at least link to extenuating circumstances.

She laughs, and asks me to pass the butter chicken. *Perhaps I'm just oversensitive. I think I've had my share of postgrad bastards. So, now I'm down here and away from all that. Much safer. But anyway, you don't seem like someone who commits a lot of crappy acts to me.*

I'm reformed. I think I was getting better, anyway, but it's surprising how having another person depend on you completely makes you think of things differently, and stop always putting yourself first. Last night, I had this horrifying moment when things had just come back under control and I realized I'd left Lily in the car. And it hadn't been for long, and nothing happened, but I'd forgotten about her and that really scared me. It made me scared that I might forget her again sometime. That something might actually happen.

Is this when you'd had the knife pulled on you by the cat woman?

Yeah. I shouldn't have put that cat-woman idea in your head either. I've made her sound insane.

I think it's fine to be distracted when something completely out of the ordinary happens. You're great with Lily. Don't doubt that for a second.

Yeah, but I *have* to be great with her, don't I? And I have to be great all the time. But I want to be too. And it's not like I don't get a lot out of it. Think about it. She's an amazing opportunity. The best chance I'll ever have to pass on a whole bunch of crappy opinions as wisdom, to explain the simple mechanics behind things happening, to teach someone switch-hitting from the day they can stand, in case getting in early makes a difference. I'm going to bore her.

I pick her up from her rug and she wriggles in my arms, twists around until I let her stand on my lap, looking at Ash across the table.

You probably won't bore her all the time.

Thanks. You know what's bad? I'll be at my worst when I'm meaning well. And I'll embarrass her. I understand my own father a lot better now. He's very embarrassing, and I'm going to be just the same. From when I was about four he told me that footwork was the key to batting in cricket, and we put in a lot of time on the footwork. So what if the bat was up to my chest? My footwork was sound. What he didn't take into account was that I was naturally utterly talentless, and my footwork fell to pieces any time a ball got involved. Shit, we worked at it though.

So what makes you think you're going to do the same things with Lily?

I just am. I already want to throw things to her to see if she can catch.

Ash laughs at me, at this confession of dorkiness.

Just soft things. I sit there thinking, Yes, baby genius, you can catch this squishy toy. You can play for Australia. You can make movies and cure disease, be a senator with influence. But no pressure, you know?

Lily stops standing, thumps back into my chest.

Sure. No pressure.

But the nice thing, actually, is that she knows who I am. Look at her. She stands up—with assistance—till she forgets she's standing and then she falls over. She can't even trust gravity yet, but she trusts me. And she laughs at things. Boats in the bath. Thinks they're hilarious. And I don't get it, but I like it. This is all great, this stuff. And you get to see it happening, evolving right in front of you. You get to see her develop new levels of sophistication every week. I'm pretty keen for her to talk though. That'll be good. You know the picture on the fridge? That big one stuck on there with magnets?

You're not telling me she did that?

No, no.

Good, cause I'd probably have to go with your baby genius idea if she'd done that by six months.

That was Emily. The daughter of Wendy at work. She's three, but she's one of the first people I've seen while they've been developing language. And do you know what she says when she's mad with you? "I'm not your friend." That's what she says. She doesn't say she's mad. She withdraws her friendship, since she knows that's a much bigger deal. How sophisticated is that? And in the same day you can realize how many things she doesn't get. She asks me lots of things. Some of them are buggers too. Like, what's a parsnip? What do you say to that?

What did you say to that?

I said it was like a pale carrot that tasted funny.

You're totally ready for this. What's your problem?

Lily pulls a piece of bubble wrap from a parcel that's lying on the table, and starts flapping it about. Waving it and saying *Wah,* and squishing the bubbles with her fingers.

Hey, is that . . .

Proof that bubble wrap is indeed a toy, despite what they say. Don't worry. I've got a good grip on the other end. We won't be putting it in our mouths. You know, I think the first sign that a child is growing up is that they can tell which bit's the present and which bit's the packing material.

And somehow that puts them only a matter of days away from an appreciation of brand-name specificity and gender stereotypes.

All that Lily talk. Where did that come from? That's what I'm wondering later, when I'm by myself mixing formula and hanging out the load of laundry from hours ago.

It just came out of me and came out of me. And came out of me. Was I boring Ash by talking about boring Lily? I'm turning into one of those mad baby people. Those people who don't have lives. Who have photos of drooling and sleepless-night stories instead.

Years ago, Mel and I talked about how we wouldn't get like that. How we'd be the kind of people who take reproduction in their stride and make sure they keep going out to do things. *You'll have to make sure you still make time for the two of you,* the therapist said, as recently as thirty-eight weeks into the pregnancy, so it was part of that process, too.

Perhaps tonight was just another manifestation of what George warned me about—the strange disinhibition that's part of all the singing and talking recommended by the baby book. No way would I have blathered on so much until very recently.

But maybe it was also the first chance I'd had to work some of it out. And all the nights when it's just me and laundry and formula-mixing and a quiet, big-eyed dog, I'm fixed on the processes—the mundane, repetitive cycles that underpin each day. That have changed the way I look at time, and use time, and notice that large amounts of it have suddenly gone without me knowing.

All those Lily things I said tonight. I don't think I've said them before. And it's far from the whole story—it does no justice to teething and inexplicably bad diapers and fussiness with food and bouts of undiagnosable grumpiness—but it is part of the story.

Fortunately, I'm not completely without judgment when it comes to what I say and don't say. When Lily picked up the bubble wrap, I was on the brink of slipping into another piece of inappropriate self-disclosure, but for once I pulled up short. Ash doesn't need to know my father's bubble-wrap car-bumper plan. Not yet. She knows my stabilizing sheet and the take-out menu folder, and that's enough innovation for now.

Months ago, my father nudged another car in a car park. His bumper clipping the corner of its bumper, and inflicting an easy eight hundred dollars' worth of damage. I can remember him fuming about it, about car companies and how they wanted this to happen, how they wanted the most minor of accidents to require the replacement of major parts. He was going to write to the papers, but then he came up with the bubble-wrap bumper plan.

It's still at the prototype stage. He's sure there'll be millions in it, when it takes off. It involves a long wad of bubble wrap, several centimeters thick, attached along the length of the car bumper, with a very cheap (but aesthetically acceptable) plastic cover over it. On the classic minor car-park impact, the bubbles burst. You feel (and maybe even hear) the impact, but you have those several centimeters in which to pull up, and prevent real damage.

And it's matte black, my father said. *Very discreet.*

So I didn't tell Ash that tonight but, in my disinhibited state, it's safe to assume I came close. My father, inventor of the bubble-wrap bumper, curator of Jim's Fractal Gallery ("the place in the virtual world where art and maths collide"). There's a lot she doesn't need to know yet.

Besides, I'd talked enough. I wanted to hear more about her. Tickle-Me-Elmo, Gingernut biscuits, whatever. I wanted to listen to her brain work, like a brain that's not yet cluttered too much by twenties and thirties and other years of opportunities and obstacles, compromises and lessons learned. The realities that can see imagination too much tempered or put safely away.

I admire her. She has ideas. She's unafraid to have ideas and put them out there. And I'm now too well aware of what I don't know to take chances like that most of the time. A few dubious remarks to do with Erikson is about the limit for me, and I had to go reading to manage that. And sometimes it feels as though, when I'm not with her, there's no prospect of excitement at all.

I hang out my last pair of underpants. The house is quiet. I'd like her to still be here. I don't know if that's smart.

16

Of course, if I'm being consistent, I should also be admiring my father for getting out there with the bubble-wrap bumper. Or at least for showing that imagination doesn't have to fade at twentysomething. On the other hand, who on earth decided that art and math should collide? What is the man on about? As some Italian duke probably said about Leonardo da Vinci...

Tonight it's me who doesn't sleep well, though there's no real reason for it. Lightning flickers, off in the distance. Another storm cell moving through, but so far away that there's no noise. It's like the weather on the night Mel moved out early last summer, two weeks before Christmas. She was gone two days, and no one knew but us. So now no one knows but me.

She left work early, and I got home to a message on the answering machine. She said she had gone to think, to spend time alone. I wasn't to call her on her mobile. She couldn't say when she'd be back. If she'd be back. I remember pacing around the house followed by Elvis, who knew something was wrong. I remember the conversations I had with her in her absence. Rehearsals for fast talking, for anger, for distress, for my own clear-headed leaving.

I wasn't sure how to handle work the next day, how to tell the others that Mel, all of a sudden, wouldn't be turning up. But she did turn up. She was there at work, in new clothes, and she kept herself away from me all day. And again the next day, again in new clothes. And if we passed in the corridor she'd look down, and look at the wall, and walk faster. The one time I went to speak, I'd said no more than her name before her hand was up, signaling me to stop.

I canceled therapy. She turned up at home. She apologized.

She said, *I always thought we'd be happier than this.*

And that didn't work for any of the things I had ready to say to her. She cried and I said none of them. We went out, to the nearest pub to home, the RE. We listened to a band, bought a pitcher of beer and then another. It was Mel's idea to go there. It wasn't the usual kind of place she'd choose to go to, nothing like it. We'd both spent some time there when we were at school, but never with each other. So it wasn't about reminiscing. I could remember—can remember—noticing her back then, but only a couple of times and in the distance, and as one of a group of people I recognized from my year but didn't really know. So we were each revisiting our separate student days, perhaps as though we were meeting for the first time. In case, in some unspoken way, that could be like starting again.

So I looked at her that night, took a fresh look at her, as best I could. At the mess that crying had made of her face and that she hadn't quite been able to fix up. Mel, staring at the band, willing things to be better, her hair clipped tightly back. The sideways looks she'd give that had a kind of smile in them. That said, *We're on a break from all that fighting, and no one knows. We're playing at normal, and maybe we can play some more.*

Nothing had changed in the RE beer garden since our college days, as far as I could tell. Except for the new red chairs (replacing the old red chairs) and the crowd. They've turned over a few generations of college students since we were there, and the band, of course, was younger too. I can remember Mel saying, *Hey, that girl singing, she's young enough to be our daughter, just about.*

That was fifteen months ago, maybe slightly more, now. Lily was conceived that night, almost certainly.

And I can remember the strange horror of the answering machine message two days before. The thought of Oh my god, it might actually be over. The weight that lifted, and the weight it dropped on me. The times during that sleepless night that I wanted her to come back, and the times I didn't. And she did come back, and I kept every thought from that night to myself, since we both agreed to try again, and to call it a new start. And we told, as far as I know, absolutely no one.

After Christmas, the bills came in on our joint credit card. Her two nights at the Sheraton and all those clothes. *I couldn't think here,* she said. *And then I found out I couldn't think there.*

In the morning, I take Lily to day care and drive back to campus to run. Ash is there waiting. I apologize for my ramblings last night and tell her that I hope I didn't come across as one of those baby-obsessed people.

And she says, *That's okay. You whipped out that packet of photos on about the second time we met. It's not like I didn't know what I was up for.* I must look horrified, because she laughs, and then says, *God, you're paranoid.*

Who's clean? I'm saying to Lily when the doorbell rings after bath time that evening. Who's the cleanest person in the house? Oh yeah, you know who it is.

Elvis jogs off to check the door and I hear him being called by name, Ash's voice.

Hi, she says, when I get there. *I got bored. I've been in the library the whole afternoon and I couldn't stay there any longer. I needed some kind of human interaction.* Then she notices the baby bag near the door. *And you're going out, aren't you?*

Yeah, but . . .

Sorry. I must have forgotten that you had a life. Maybe I should have called first.

You don't have to call. And I wouldn't exactly say that I had a life. In fact, the more I've been thinking about it lately, the more sure I've been that I don't have one. So drop in any time. And come along tonight.

What are you doing?

Just going over to someone's house. A couple of the people from work. It's a habit we've got into on Wednesdays.

I'd be in the way.

How? Come along. You might get bored, but you won't be in the way.

Will the cat woman be there?

No. It's her sister that I work with, and she won't be

there either. And stop scaring me by saying "cat woman." You know it'll get stuck in my head and I'll come out and say it at the worst time. And Flag's not out of the woods yet.

Well, if you're sure...

I'm sure.

I'm sure until we're about halfway there. I'm amazed it takes me that long to work out what I'm doing. I am introducing George to my running buddy. As recently as yesterday I was full of denials, clear on the boundaries. And though this technically breaches none of them it does take us outside the running-buddy definition, and there will be assumptions. She doesn't even look like a running buddy tonight. She's come straight from the library, which means it's the cargo pants part of her wardrobe that's in use this evening. She even has pens in one of the pockets, around about mid-thigh. She looks... I was thinking that she looks about nineteen but, since she isn't a lot older than that anyway, it's not much of a stretch.

You're sure I won't be in the way?

I think they'll be pretty happy with the idea of you being there. You certainly won't be in the way.

When we get there, Ash takes the baby bag and I carry the sleeping Bean up the steps in her car seat, her little hands bunched into fists and resting by her sides.

Now, they could get a bit excited, I tell Ash on the way in. These two get out even less than we do. They don't meet a lot of new people. So if I use the term "running buddy" to put you in context, don't be surprised.

Running buddy? She laughs. *Well, why not?*

Sorry, it's a long story. Or maybe just a stupid one.

We get to the door and George sees us. Or, in fact, sees me and gives a regular, uninspired, *Hi,* and then sees there's someone behind me. *I didn't realize the Bean needed to come with her own entourage,* he says, as Ash walks in with the bag. And our expressions must tell him something, since he then says, *Faux pas,* and looks at me, with a grin building on one side of his mouth. *This must be your . . .*

Running buddy, Ash says, and moves forward to shake his hand. *I'm the running buddy.*

George immediately thinks of more glib, testosterone-driven remarks about running buddies than even a bad e-mail joke could handle, and uses none of them. *George,* he says instead, and reaches his hand out. *I'm the George. Ash.*

Girls at book club, Jon, he says. *It's new, but it could work.*

Ash turns to me, looking puzzled, misinformed. *You told me this was casual. You didn't say I should have read a book.*

You've been reading books all afternoon.

Over-qualified, George says.

What book are you doing? Ash asks him, still not unreasonably expecting that there's a book club going on.

Most recently? Some Hegel. I'm doing a philosophy degree. Oscar, who's in the kitchen—yes, Jon, a meal is actually being prepared tonight—he's doing poetry. Mainly his own. It's new. As yet unpublished. But it's performance based anyway. Oscar believes there's too much emphasis placed on publication. Jon? You?

Seuss, Doctor, *Green Eggs and Ham.* It's a bit performance based, too, if you're prepared to commit to it. But at least it's quick. Did it a couple of times this afternoon.

Does she get it yet? George says. *The Bean. Do you think she gets it?*

Green Eggs and Ham? No. She still gets mush for food, so even the basics elude her. She doesn't understand ham, so what chance has the story got? I think it's up to me to broaden her diet before she can work out what it's really about.

Which is?

Well, this is just my reading of it, but I see it as being about the diminishing willingness to take risks with age. To take the plunge. To leap into the unknown on the off-chance that there's something there to bring back. The old grumpy guy with the silly hat, he keeps insisting he doesn't like green eggs and ham, regardless of circumstances, and you know what? He's never even tried them. Then he does, and . . .

He loves them, George says. *Yeah, I remember now. I'm sure the Bean gets it. She's just pre-verbal, so it'll be a while before she tells you.*

I didn't think book clubs were like this, Ash says.

George nods, thoughtfully. *I don't know. That'd be the first time we've got heavily into a book. Just then. Or the second, at most. We don't like to force things. But you should meet Oscar. Come and meet Oscar while Jon's dropping the Bean off in the spare room.*

He takes her into the kitchen, and from the spare room I can catch some of the introductions. The term "running buddy" is used at least once or twice. By the time I get back to them, Oscar is completely ignoring his simmering risotto and they're standing talking, holding glasses of wine.

The others are asking Ash how she's liking Brisbane, questions like that (that sound obvious, but that I've never directly asked).

Well, it's bigger, she says. *Bigger than any place I've been before. So I'm trying to get used to this part of it before branching out and getting to know the rest. And trying to get used to school here too. It's pretty big as well. I still need a map to get anywhere on the campus, and I really hope I get over that soon.*

Something makes me want to jump in and shout loudly, But she's not a freshman. She is a postgraduate. But I hold back. I give Oscar's risotto a stir, since I think it's getting stuck, and he says, *Thanks, mate.* George agrees with Ash about the campus, and talks about when we were there. And could he possibly make our college days seem more ancient? We sound as though we must have hung out in pantaloons and drunk mead, the way he talks about it.

The campus is not that baffling, I tell him. It's not that different. It wasn't that long ago. There are one or two new buildings since we were there, but you'd still be able to find your way around.

The whole city's changed since then, he says, defensively. *When we were at school the only take-out choice was whether you went for the sweet-and-sour pork at the Sunny Garden or the chow mein.*

And now you could write a book on the take-out options in this neighborhood alone, Ash says, giving me a sly half-smile. *Couldn't you, Jon?*

She's seen it, hasn't she? She's seen the fantastic plastic cuisine guide to the whole region.

Anyone want to talk about a book now?

Aren't we?

And so it goes. A bunch of guys in their mid-thirties showing off in front of a girl. That, when you look at it, is really all it is. Ash leans against the counter, drinks her wine, and doesn't seem to mind in the slightest. George treats her Bagelos job as fascinating, calls her Tickle-Me-Elmo thesis topic *outstanding.*

Oscar declares himself to have *a certain interest in that kind of thing. The sociology of contemporary iconic constructs. So we'll have to talk more.*

But for now, luckily, he leaves it at that, and he finally gives his risotto some attention. George clears the table, quietly elevating this evening to special-occasion status, and Oscar says, *The good bowls, Porge. The good bowls.*

I was getting the good bowls, Oz.

And the level of fuss going on is at least two hundred percent above normal, even before Oscar says, *I would have liked a little sprig of something. Just as garnish.*

It looks very exotic as it is, Ash says, taking her bowl and looking down at the pine nuts and slivers of sun-dried tomato.

Oscar, George declares, *lives in an exotic world. For me this whole town is not half as exotic as the guys Oscar brings home.*

Oh, come on, Oscar says, but quite proudly.

Ramone. Ramone and his lap-lap.

Well, okay. Ramone was exotic. A little bit exotic.

Ramone was the kind of guy who could make concepts like Ramone and the Solid Gold Dancers seem perfectly reasonable.

Yeah, but underneath it all he was lacking in substance. We both know that.

Charles.

Charles was not exotic.

He was fifty times more exotic than me, fella.

Don't be down on yourself, Porge. You've got your own thing going.

And what about Justin? Don't tell me you weren't practicing this risotto with Justin in mind. Justin's exotic, in a gentle sort of way.

Maybe he is, but that's a different thing. And the risotto was not to do with Justin, just a good idea I had. Its time is yet to come. Next time there'd be chives. And Justin's not a bringing-home guy. With him it's more like just a mutual interest in poetry.

Suspicious enough in itself.

Hey, I've got my thing on this Friday, remember? You've got to be nice about poetry this week.

His event at that West End bookstore, George clarifies. *Where we get to see exactly what Arts Queensland gets for its grant money.*

I think you'd like it, Ashley, Oscar says. *It's very sociological. Very influenced by the icons of our contemporary consumerist digital society.*

Sounds good, Ash says, and convincingly too, though we all know that Oscar delved a little too deep into the adjective bucket to make complete sense.

I want to relax this evening, but I can't. I want this kind of thing to feel normal. But all the time I'm watching Ash, watching this incursion of hers into my regular world, and I'm suddenly conscious of how George and Oscar must look to a marginally postgrad outsider.

She asks how long we've known each other, and George

says, *We were friends at college. I suppose that's where it started. Jon and I used to spend a lot of time together then. After that we ended up at different hospitals when we graduated. And you sort of get caught up in that—in your hospital—particularly if it's a big one. It can be a big part of your social life too, when you can fit one in. Then when Jon's . . . um . . . time in England happened, I was finishing off my dermatology training here, and heading in the same sort of direction as he was. And the next year there were four of us looking to set up a practice. It took a couple of years to get that happening though. But I guess we would have known each other since 1982.*

Which, Oscar adds, *might have been the year you both gave exotic your best shot.*

I don't think we're going there tonight, Oscar. No 1982 stories.

We talked about me and exotic. In the nineties. It's only fair that you get acknowledged. You guys had a thing happening in the eighties. The shirts. Remember the shirts?

That's exactly where we're not going.

These guys had these shirts, he says, identifying clearly where we're going. *I didn't even know them at the time, but we all knew the shirts. No, Jon, I think Ashley needs to know you've got some exotic cred, even if it was a while ago.*

And even if you copied, George adds.

That's where I stop them, and claim the right to at least fall on my own sword.

The year 1982 was a special one for fashion, I explain, as if going for documentary-style might stop them interrupting. That's how I remember it. It was the year that shirts around here took on a fancy look, and stopped buttoning up the middle. Of course, we couldn't afford the ones in the shops. George bought some curtain material off-cuts—to create contrast between the panels—and designed one that buttoned up diagonally. And I'm sadder than that, for two reasons. First, I thought his was great, and I copied the idea. Second, I gave it my own spin. George's shirt, for example, wasn't bottle green, with a row of big way-off-center gold buttons and gold piping. And epaulettes. I explained it to my mother, and got her to make it for me. I thought it was superb.

But you both look so regular now, Ash says. *And that's all so . . .*

Duran Duran? George suggests. *Flock of Seagulls?*

Well, except for the hair, yeah. Very Flock of Seagulls.

And who, exactly, said we paid no attention to the hair?

Porge, the hour of your death approaches.

Jon, you owned the Flock of Seagulls album. I only had a pirate tape from it. Don't go into denial on me now. Chock-full of hits, I think you called it.

No I did not. You are lying now, making it up. No-one called that album chock-full of hits.

Don't come over all nasty and anti-eighties again. Did you know Jon has a problem with eighties music?

It's not eighties music that's the issue.

It's the people with the hair to go with it?

It's the people who think there's only eighties music that I worry about. Eighties music is fine, in its place.

Which is?

The eighties, for god's sake. No, some of it's okay. But forgive me for not loving the eighties. It's a decade I managed to begin and end as an adolescent, so it was never likely to be my favorite. From the entire eighties I'd be happy to keep about ten songs and my pointy, side-lacing shoes. The rest can go. Maybe I should keep the shirt as well, in case anyone ever does a musical about the Napoleonic Wars.

There should be a museum of the eighties where those things can go, George says, sounding disconcertingly genuine. *Shirts like that shouldn't be forgotten.*

No. No museum. Shirts like that should have been forgotten right after Waterloo, George.

No. You could begin with them and go all the way through to "Choose Life" T-shirts, via leg warmers. You could even have a section on eighties hair. There are people we know who'd go for that.

Me for a start, Ash says. *Eighties hair can be hilarious. I think a museum of the eighties'd be cool. Anyway, Jon, you could have the Knack there. You'd like that.*

What?

Jon and the Knack. He's a big fan, remember? You know how they inspired him to learn guitar? How he thought he could be in a band like the Knack?

No, Ash, actually they didn't know that. And the Knack might be late seventies, so . . .

I think we'd let them in, George says. *Jon, you've been holding out on us all these years. Did you learn all three chords?*

All three.

Oh, it's tragic, isn't it? The desperate attempts we made to turn ourselves into objects of desire.

All the way to those skinny ties, Ash adds. *Like that green swirly shiny one that Jon's got.*

Remember when you wondered if you'd be in the way this evening?

You don't still have that, do you? George says, jumping in with something approaching glee. *You got that at school.*

At the very end of school.

But you've still got it?

You said you were keeping it in case it came back in, Ash says, completely merciless tonight.

The swirly tie, Oscar says. *I remember you in the swirly tie at Mount Stephens General. You were a bad man in those days, you and your dirty-dog phase.*

George can't resist jumping right back in, treating the whole conversation with the enthusiasm of a young first-timer in an inflatable castle. *What about that time we bumped into that nurse in Coles, ages later? What was her name?*

Kelly.

And you just ignored her and ignored her, and she actually came up and took you on about it. And the best excuse you could manage was that you can't recognize people from side on.

It had been years.

And now it's been a few more, but I can remember it vividly. I can remember her saying something like, *You haven't learned a thing, have you?* But I'm sure I'd learned a lot by then, which was exactly why I had to be so embarrassed about seeing her.

Those were the days, George says. *Those swirly-tie, dirty-dog days. Why didn't I have them?*

Trust me, Porge. They weren't the days. Even when I was at my dirtiest, and the closest you got to the action was drooling on my housemate, the way I recall it there's not much to be nostalgic about.

You're not telling me these are the days, and I'm not even aware that I'm missing out? I can't remember anything I've done that I'd call close to halcyon, ever. The drooling was the best of it. She was a hell of a housemate. And you know that thing, that moment, where you suddenly realize your body's on the slide? Where you start getting the odd inexplicable ache or pain, and you realize they'll now come and go forever?

No.

Yes you do. I think I had it one day in the middle of last year. It was like my whole body just fell. With a clunk. And there I was, older. I'm getting older, Jon Boy, and far too gracefully.

That's crap. It doesn't work that way, or at least it doesn't have to. I run. I get twinges because of running but, other than that, I'm fine. Don't scare me, George. Be graceful, but don't get older on me just yet. I'm assuming these are the days. And those weren't. I'm assuming the days are starting any day now.

So am I, Ash says. *That's what I came down here for. I'm here for my days. If it turns out I missed them by ten years, I won't be happy.*

Oh, youth, George says, with the sternness of an old and weary magistrate. *You can afford to be so glib.*

I haven't noticed the slide, the clunk of my body falling. And I'm sure that's not through inattention. My body's changed these past six months, but for the better. This running is getting me somewhere. Not in a competitive way, but that wasn't the plan. I can go further now, and my times might be better than they once were, but I'll never be good. Actually, if I can maintain my present best five-K time for about forty-one years, I could be looking at a world over-seventy-five age-group record, or close to it, so it's lucky I'm not doing it for the glory. I've never had that kind of patience.

But it is about the long term, I guess. Delaying my body's fall, and its clunk. Piloting it to a soft landing. Staying well. What surprises me is the changes I can feel. I can feel my body working, and I used to take it for granted. Before, where I had the smoothed-out contours of skin, I'm now marked with the shapes of muscles. Muscles, working just under the surface, dense bundles of muscle, like the pictures in *Grant's Atlas of Anatomy*.

In our surface-anatomy seminar in first-year med school, I was all bony prominences and tendons. Now I've filled in the rest, given substance to it, at least in my legs. I could stand in one of those tutes demonstrating the different parts of the quadriceps femoris, or two clear heads of gastrocnemius, instead of being a fine example of the nobbliness of knees.

When I started running, I felt like crap every time. Every wheezy, mucusy second. Now I can get a rhythm going, a sense of my own mechanics. Working parts, working like a machine, carrying me along, clearing my head. It's as though I've never operated inside my body before, never understood it or known its signals, until now. Just got through the day in it, and paid it no regard.

But I can't tell George that. It'd be like an alien language, so I have to keep it to myself. George, it feels good. It's endorphins, it's physiology. I don't know what it is, but it feels good. It's like feeling more alive. And one day I'll go further.

So my belt's in two notches, my thighs are half like runners' thighs. I'm the same weight, but it's better weight. I'll make myself into some lean old running man forty-one years from now. I'll shake that over-seventy-five record yet, if my knees last. I can see myself out there, a snowy-haired, ropey old codger, trotting along.

Mel hated gray hair. Hated the thought of it, hated each one she found as gray hairs broke out all over her head.

I don't mind gray, and I told her I was fine about the gray bits at my temples, happy to leave them alone. It's a better hair color than people give it credit for, I said to her, but she wouldn't hear of it.

I want it to look natural, she said, *but not old.* I told her it didn't matter—not to me, anyway. It simply didn't matter. And, if she wanted to know, I actually thought it looked pretty good. She experimented with dyes, tentatively with semi-permanents, then committed to permanents, every six weeks calling herself a skunk as gray appeared around her center part. And then she'd dye again. *I don't want to look old.*

17

Anyway, I remember George's clunk in the middle of last year. The only clunk he had then was nothing to do with age and, at the time, he even tried to call it sports medicine.

One day there'll be Nintendo at the Olympics, he said defiantly, as he went off to a P.T. appointment. *And who'll be laughing then?*

He had four treatments before the frozen shoulder got much better, and he was instructed never to stay up playing video games till three a.m. again.

But I was in the groove, he told the physical therapist. *In the zone. You don't think I meant to stay up till three a.m., do you?*

At lunchtime on Thursday, Flag's still hanging on, still racking up excellent cat ICU bills of hundreds of dollars a night. With Katie maintaining a vigil, reading him stories, playing him his favorite music. And, yes, Wendy used the word "vigil." And said, *I don't have to tell you which decade it is that's pulsing through the Walkman and into that little feline brain.*

George tells me *Oscar's got a lunch thing,* when the two of us sit down to eat. *So he won't be joining us today.*

Probably just one of those lunch-friend events, not a date. It's Justin, so not a date. Oz still wants to pretend there's nothing going on there but poetry. So maybe it's a poetry-friend thing. Is that a category?

I don't know. I'm not the category expert. Poetry and cake-making, maybe? All I know is that there's no category where you should turn up in darkness to dump flowers. Where's Nigel?

Swimming.

By himself?

I'm having a day off.

So how many times have you been now?

In total?

Yeah.

Two. Or thereabouts. But I don't think it helps to count. I'm sure I read that in a book about exercise. Hey, I liked your running buddy.

I figured we'd get around to that.

Well, why not? You will go bringing her along . . .

She just turned up. She was bored. She doesn't know a lot of people. Bringing her along doesn't mean anything.

Then don't go crazy and make it look like it does. I was just saying I liked her. Smart kind of girl. Knew how to put shit on you about that swirly-tie phase. Even if it finished when she was about ten.

Started when she was about ten, I correct him, and he laughs. Look, she's in her twenties. Or around that. And you're getting it wrong, anyway. This is not some *Lolita* thing.

Well, no. Not that you've read Lolita, *since it'd be slightly too big.*

Good point.

You could at least have seen the film.

I was busy.

If you'd seen it you'd know there's a critical difference, as far as the age issue goes. Yours is technically an adult. People might still think you're a dirty old scumbag, but they'd be way out of line if they mentioned Nabokov.

Thanks for the support. But it's not like that anyway.

Why not? You can't say she's not your type.

I don't have a type.

Sure you do.

The whole business of "type" sucks. It's discriminatory.

So, what, you just pick anyone at random? Is that how it's supposed to work? Raffle yourself? Give them all a turn?

Yeah, right, and that'd take ages. You're flattering me with the concept of "all." And look at the women I've been involved with. There's no type.

There's a type. It's just bimodal in distribution. You've got the petite, dark-haired type, then you've got the taller, willow-ier, blond type.

Doesn't that mean I don't have a type?

No, you're just confusing people by having two. You look like someone without a type, but you've always had them both.

Yeah, but it's not as simple as type at the moment, any-way, is it? And you've got it wrong. It's not happening. That's actually the best thing about it. It's not happen-ing. There's no pressure to make it happen.

Don't have to squish any of her pets . . .

Hey, they've got to learn. If they keep e-mailing.

Such a waste of a good fantasy if it's not happening. Some young pony takes an interest and you let her down.

This isn't about an interest. You don't get it, and don't waste your time trying to. And her demographic isn't even part of my fantasy landscape.

Okay, so who's there in the fantasy landscape?

God, I don't know. Helen Hunt, I suppose, if I've got to name someone. Yeah. She projects that kind of appealing vulnerability, she's smart, very high babe coefficient, and she's even my age. How respectable is that?

It's pretty respectable. And a type-two fantasy for you.

Jodie Foster.

Also type-two.

Helen Hunt or Jodie Foster early on a bad-hair day in men's flannel pajamas . . . Or is that a bit more specific than you'd like?

No. No, it's good. It was slightly more specific than I was expecting, but it's not bad at all. Of course, I'm assuming you wouldn't actually enforce the dress code. I mean, I'd take either of them if they turned up dressed like a high school gym teacher.

What about you, then? Fantasy-landscape-wise?

We're not sure where we stand at the moment at our place. Since Brad Pitt and Gwyneth Paltrow broke up, and that's ages ago. The Oz Man and I had a double-date fantasy thing happening.

I check my e-mails after lunch, for the first time today. The weasel stamps his foot, but all I can see of his complaints before I click LATER is, *I've tried everything with you . . .*

Go away till later, I'm thinking, but more calmly this time. Let me work you out later, when I can work out exactly what it is I get from a Window Weasel, and decide whether or not I want it. I'm too busy now to fit it into my head. To work out if I want the shloopy noise.

I have three e-mails, one from George, one from my father, one about a Web site update. Am I on the Web site mailing lists because of George too? I don't ever recall being interested enough to put myself on them.

I open his e-mail first because it has *You'll really have to do this* in the subject column. Which I'm sure I won't, but the others looked even less compelling.

You must follow the rules on this one exactly, otherwise it won't work. It's really scary how this works out. NO CHEAT-ING!!!!

First, get a pen and paper.

Second, write the numbers one through six, leaving some space in between the numbers.

Next to number one, write any number . . .

Next to number two, write the name of anyone you are really attracted to . . .

Next to three, write down the first color you can think of . . .

Next to number four, write the name of your first pet . . .

Next to numbers five and six, write down the name of a family member . . .

Remember . . . no cheating . . .

Keep scrolling down . . .

Don't cheat, or you'll be upset . . .

Here's the answers . . .

So why do I really have to do this one, after the trouble I've gone to not to do the last dozen or so?

I open the e-mail from my father, and it's mainly about a particularly good unwooded chardonnay. As if I haven't had more than enough trouble with those lately. He tells me they'll be back tonight.

Out of routine, I check again as I'm going off-line. There's one from Ash that's just come through.

Hey Jon, thanks for including me last night. Had a great time. I think you've known your friends too long for your own good though. Particularly George.

I've been—maybe you noticed this, maybe you didn't—in a pretty bad mood sometimes the last couple of days. If I'm bugging you being around a lot, you have to tell me. I'm trying to meet more people down here, but it's not working out yet. So most of the time it's just me hanging around this big, old, crappy house. If I've pushed into your life you have to let me know.

If I'm getting this wrong, let me know that too.
A

I call her right away but she's still on-line, so I can't get through.

I take another look at the George e-mail, the test I *really have to do*. I get a pen and paper and write the numbers one to six on it, and I keep hitting Redial. Eventually she answers.

You're getting it wrong, I tell her. As someone who spends a lot of his time hanging around a big, old, moderately crappy house, I know it's not the most fun thing to do. And you're not pushing in anywhere.

Good. That's good. I was just . . . hmmm, you know.

Well, don't worry. And don't stop bugging me, whatever you do.

Okay.

What are you doing this evening?

I've got lectures till six. I'm just about to go back to school now.

Well, how about I meet you after that? After your last lecture. I think I've got your schedule on my desktop, so I should be able to find you.

There's a short silence, and then she says, *Yeah, that'd be nice.*

Once she's hung up, I read through her e-mail again. I want to be with her now, rather than wait till six. I click it shut, and George's test is sitting open underneath.

So I go to my piece of paper and I put six, Ash, red, Fish (I was very young then, and not good with names—if only Fish had been something other than a fish, the whole process would look much cleverer), Lily, Jim, and I check the answers.

The number next to number one shows how many times you should be smashed over the head with a baseball bat for thinking that stupid e-mails like this actually mean anything.

The person named next to number two is someone who will never sleep with you because you're stupid enough to waste your time on something like this.

The color you picked means nothing. It's a friggin' color, for Christ's sake.

Number four gives you the name of a dead animal.

Numbers five and six represent family members who are embarrassed to be related to you.

Pass this on to everyone you know, so they can feel like a gobshite too.

Thanks very much, George.

But it's true enough, I suppose. At least in part. Fish didn't end up doing so well. My parents already had a cat before I came along, and Fish's tenure at our place was brief. Hubble was not a nice cat. He was tough and amoral and unfriendly, and could have worn the name "Motherfucker" better than any pet I've known since.

Okay, it's answer number two I'm steering clear of. She was on my mind at the time, the obvious choice. And how could I not be drawn to her in some way? How could she not start to matter in some way?

Fuck. It was like a secret, being kept from me until I

wrote it down. I could tell myself I wasn't thinking about her every day, because I was with her for part of every day, so it didn't count. You have to think about people you're with. George—I think about George practically every day.

Mainly, I wonder why he keeps e-mailing me this shit. But George doesn't cross my mind at night. George isn't part of the turbulence, all this wondering what I'm supposed to feel, entitled to feel, going to feel. George isn't someone whose happiness came to matter to me in three weeks. I am not, whatever happens, in any danger of falling for George at all.

I go back on-line, get to a search engine and find my way to Halliday Tea. I order a pound, I click the Express box, I give them my Visa card number.

Then Sylvia's at my door. *Jon, you've been quite good all week.*

Just checking e-mail, I say quickly, like someone who's been caught writing notes in class.

Ash's lecture is over when I get there.

Hi, she says. *We finished at five-to. Hi, Bean.* And she offers a finger for Lily's waving hand to clutch. *What am I doing? Am I getting anywhere with all this?* She waves to the huge sandstone buildings around the Great Court. *Do you have days when you wonder that?*

Plenty. Plenty of my days are the same as all my other days and therefore, by definition, get me nowhere. That "every day in every way I'm getting better and better" thing? It's not possible. You can't even keep it up till you're a month old. I've had, like, ten thousand days now, and I must have improved on twenty of them at most. Three or four of them while at this campus.

And none in your first few weeks?

Exactly. Let me show you my favorite thing here, I say to her, as though I'll win the hand by playing an ace. Well, maybe that's creating a bit much of an air of excitement, but come and see it anyway.

I take her across the Great Court, to the Parnell Building, to the display case just inside the door. The pitch experiment set up in the twenties by the university's first physics professor. He mixed the pitch and sealed it until it cooled and was apparently set, then he upturned the funnel and began a 170-year demonstration that pitch isn't solid. That it looks completely hard, but it's still viscous and flowing. In the experiment it drips out of the bottom of the funnel, but years pass between drips.

I got my whole degree between the third last and the second last, I tell her. It often falls on weekends, and no one's ever seen one fall. For the last year or so, it's been about to go.

So what was he thinking? Ash says. *He knew his physics. He must have known his great-grandchildren wouldn't see the end of this experiment.*

I hold the Bean up to the glass, and she slaps it with her hands, and makes a noise that says she knows there's something going on. Something in the case that I think's worthy of attention.

So was that to demonstrate the virtues of patience? Showing me this?

No. I'm not a demonstrator of virtues. It was me showing you something I liked.

Good. I like it. It's sort of like a very slow black lava lamp.
This was about the speed Professor Parnell liked his lava lamps, I hear. The sight of grass growing used to really trouble him.

She laughs at this try-hard joke. *Thanks. Thanks for coming out here. I'm going to sound like such a ... I don't know. I come from a pretty small place, so people know each other there. Automatically. Sometimes too well, but ... Okay, Cairns wasn't like that, but it wasn't like this. And it wasn't far from home, and I got to know people there. I come from a place with a couple of hundred people. Not even Atherton, which has a few thousand. And we didn't have famous hippy craft markets, or anything. It was agricultural. And my weekend tours were pretty simple. The only souvenir we sold was tea. We've been debating for a year now about whether there'd be enough business to make it worth doing our own postcard. So all this, down here, is taking more adjusting to than I'd expected. That's what I was trying to say earlier. Of course, now you've shown me the black blob thing, so ...*

Okay, so it didn't fix much.

No, I'm kidding. I'm glad you showed me the black blob thing. I like it. Enough of my mood. What did you do today?

I'll show you. Let me show you.

I take her to work. I take her to buy a large bunch of bananas in Coles, and then I take her to work.

Okay, she says. *I'm guessing, but I think you played with a monkey today.*

No, I had my usual kind of day, and this is how it goes.

I fit a new handpiece to the laser, give her glasses to wear and put mine on too, and I laser a banana.

It's what I started on, I tell her. This is what you get to do before they let you loose on humans.

She asks me how I know how deep to go, how to set the machine, what pattern to make, how I handle skin when it's a person rather than fruit at one ninety-nine a pound.

I drop dots of laser of different sizes onto the banana and it develops a sheen where I hit it, and then it starts to brown up. I resurface one side till it's so smooth it's almost shiny, and it feels like an old, smooth glove.

Ash takes the handpiece, recoils when she zaps with it the first time. But she keeps going, working at it till she's got control. On her second banana, she gets me to narrow the beam and she writes her name, like the first proud word of a child with a crayon. I try to show off and tell her I'll do eighteen-point Times Roman with my name, but the end result isn't much like it. Our bananas are both more like the work of kids taking a knife to a tree trunk, or scratching into the paint on a station seat.

She takes another banana and writes "apple." I take one and write "fish." She takes one and writes "rama."

I ask her if she means the Hindu god, and she says, *No, Bananarama. It's an eighties concept.*

And by now the room is filled with the smell of scorched peel, and the Bean, in her car seat, is hungry.

Can I take them home? Ash says, collecting the bananas.

Sure. But they mightn't look that way for long.

I was planning to eat them. I mean, I love them, but I was also planning to eat them. I don't get paid till next week.

18

On Friday morning, Wendy says, *We think Flag's going to make it, Jon. He'll never be quite the Flag he was before, but he'll be okay.*

In the afternoon I take Lily to my parents' place, where my father's already racking the new wine in the garage.

It's funny, my mother says, as she gets out Lily's third or fourth present while we're drinking tea. *There seemed to be things that were just right for her, everywhere we looked on the whole trip.*

It's probably better if you don't talk to him beforehand, I warn Ash, as we go into the West End bookstore for Oscar's performance. He can get a bit short with us before he goes on. We've learned that.

The bookstore is long and narrow, and it's hot and humid in there with a few dozen people fitted in, lounging against shelves, waiting.

George sees us and comes over, wearing black jeans and a black shirt, and looking defiantly not-quite-right.

Very Neil Diamond, I tell him. I like it.

Thanks so much. And good to see you tried so bloody hard. He turns to Ash. *I suppose you made him take the tie off after work, to give him that contemporary, casual, evening look.*

Yeah, but he didn't undo the knot.

Seriously? You're not still . . . He laughs. He looks like a man who just robbed the Roy Orbison museum for his clothes, but somehow he's the winner because of my tie habits.

So glad you're here, I tell Ash. How's the poet, Porge?

Tonight? Shocking. Not an easy night. New material, you know? He's been clearing his throat all evening and asking if I've taken his "Scruffing Lotion 3½" creme. As If I'm not more than scruffy enough.

George knows as much—or as little—about sophisticated male grooming products as I do. He's had three different minor skin rashes on his face in just the last couple of years, and he's treated each one as if it's nothing worse than an acceptable untidiness. After giving it its three-word Latin name. It's Oscar who gets stressed about it. Oscar with the multi-level trolley of grooming products, who's forever telling George he could make more of himself. Not much more, but more.

Just before start time, George points to the door as Justin sneaks in. Wearing a black beanie and with a jewel—probably a ruby—in the side of his nose. I didn't notice that the other night. I wonder if it's a regular feature, or something he holds back for special occasions. Maybe I never saw him from the left.

Justin, George says, when he comes over. *I'm not sure you know Jon and Ash. You might have met Jon before, but you probably don't recognize him without one of his ties on.*

I want to take him aside now and I want to say to him,

How the fuck has it become a problem that I wear ties to work when you do too and Justin's wearing a goddamn beanie in a room that's rapidly approaching body temperature?

There's a pop from the microphone at the small stage down at the far end, a yowl of feedback as the host starts to talk.

Welcome, he says, like a grand old showman, or perhaps a parody of one. *Welcome everyone, back to this seething hotbed of the new, to the latest in our series of experimental performance poetry, Words Let Loose, where some of Brisbane's and Australia's finest let loose their newest and boldest on the second Friday of every month. And tonight, like every night, we've got a special treat in store. One of last season's success stories is back. Back with something very new. Back with the fruits of his labors on an Arts Queensland grant. So tonight, here it is, his grant acquittal reading. Please make welcome Oscar Wong and his . . . "Millennium Suite."*

There's muted applause—not exactly what the razzamatazz intro was calling for—then silence.

Then a thump from the stock room out the back, an empty cardboard box falling over. From Oscar this would usually be part of the performance, but I think tonight it's incidental. He surges from the stock room in a glittering, gold-embroidered gown, looking like a marginally oversized Christmas tree decoration. He strikes a pose and fires something down each sleeve and into his hands. Fans, bright yellow fans, and he snaps them open, then shut again, then places his head between them, turning them into a pair of thin jaws. He hisses. Four times, once to each point of the compass, rotating with a slow and practiced elegance. It's as if someone has lifted the lid of a rather creepy music box.

I should have known it'd be like this. I'm not sure if it's worse than I remember from last time (hair extensions, box, dead flowers), or if there just seemed to be less at stake then. George and me standing up the back in our work clothes going, Oh my god, where did this come from? Now George has gone the Big O with the wardrobe, and I've brought a girl. I can't believe I brought Ash to this. I can't have thought it through at all.

The poetry begins. Words let loose, but fighting to get out sometimes, piling on top of each other, rushing out, staccato and spitting. The audience leans back, out of range wherever possible.

> *Yes children*
> *The forest is large and all of it*
> *Forest*
>
> *There is no playground there*
> *No swings, roundabout, monkey bars*
> *No unfettered pleasure in any*
> *Of its brightnesses*
>
> *There are paths that are not paths*
> *Not paths that are paths*
> *Paths to nowhere and*
> *To rectangular corners and*
> *To reckoning*

There is the appearance of
Creatures and
Food
Bright in small orbits
Harvestable

But look
While you gorge yourself
On golden globes of possibility
Even while the leaves are still
The wind gone
Danger sets to tap
Any shoulder

Oscar twitches among dialects and demeanors, hisses and scowls, sweeps low with his fans. And his gown slips open, giving us a good look at his Mickey Mouse boxer shorts. (Is that part of the show?) *Up* his Mickey Mouse boxer shorts, actually, and for a fraction of a second there's a little too much performance happening tonight.

Sweat runs down his face, and that's when I realize there's makeup involved, a hint of gold about his cheeks. He rattles on, dangerous and amorphous and confrontational, and the crowd stands silent, in fear of what might happen next, or simply in fear of the next dose of spit or view up the shorts.

Death that stalks
On jelly legs is
No less death
Even in bright hues

Death comes in
The color of your children's clothes
With a sad smile
And from any portal

And all is gone
On the third chance
All untoward and
Unavoidable

Play while you can
Embrace the moment and
Play
Some days there is no
Smoking gun
Only life and
Death

He digresses into bewildering similes and then machine noises, chops with the closed fans, swings his arms like pistons, flaps the fans open like wings, comes right back rhyming like a bandit when you least expect it.

There are pauses for bowing. They might be the ends of individual pieces, but no one knows. Except George, who starts the applause each time with a few whacks of his solid hands, and the audience, relieved to get a clear signal of some kind, bursts out clapping too.

There's been a lot of rehearsal at our place this week, George says. *I know the score. I hope you're keeping track of what it's about.*

It's about something?

There's not a scrap of poetry in you, is there?

I concentrate hard, and in the slower, quiet parts I can make out the words, but that doesn't seem to help.

> *Go checking*
> *Take all your hands and mouths and*
> *Get to work*
>
> *This bird will brook you*
> *No fair clutch of eggs*
> *Should you delay*
>
> *Their pleasure's simple*
> *In your cup-shaped hand*
> *But hurry*
>
> *Collect them as a child might*
> *This season*
> *This quick season*
> *Just before breakfast*
> *And they will give you*
> *Life*

And then he speeds up and I'm sure he says *Pac-Man* at one point, and cheese (or possibly lozenge). Anyway, it's very powerful, whatever it's about. I can talk about the power later. And the costume, I suppose, if that's the right word. This must be how deaf grandparents feel at elementary school musicals.

The end is climactic. Much spit, much sweat, much shouting. And he freezes with the fans snapped open in front of his face, their two bright semicircles forming a circle and hiding him.

Wow, I hear myself saying inadvertently, as the clapping begins.

And someone near me says, *Yeah,* in the same hushed, slightly overwhelmed tone of voice.

Some of the crowd rush Oscar, most of them rush the door. By the time we get to the front he's having a very serious discussion with someone about *going CD ROM on this one.*

Like it, Oscar, George says, when it's our turn. *Very non-traditional. Very . . .* He shakes his head, as though there can't be words.

Political? Oscar suggests.

Very political.

And very powerful, I say. Very powerful.

Good, very good, he says, and nods. He wipes his sweaty brow and a streak of gold comes off on the back of his hand. *So, a success then.*

Oh, absolutely.

Then let's eat. It really takes it out of you up here.

He starts to move for the door, still in costume.

Oz, the gear, George says. *You haven't changed.*

Porge, I'm on a roll. Don't stop me now.

It's a different world beyond that door, Oz Man, George says, and shepherds him back to the stock room, where he's left his non-performance clothes.

I don't think I got all that, Ash tells me while he's changing. *Everything Oscar was doing in his . . . show. What was it about exactly?*

It was poetry. There's no "about" in poetry.

Sometimes there's an "about." Plenty of times. Sylvia Plath. And he seemed like such a quiet person the other night.

Yes, but maybe lurking deep in all of us there's some scary performance piece waiting to be poetry-slammed out.

Oscar re-emerges, taking the last of the makeup off with a baby wipe and looking much more like his normal self (and far less likely to spit). On the short walk to the restaurant, though, I notice that his gestures are still a little more flamboyant than usual, everything's scaled up twenty percent, as if he hasn't slowed down completely from his performance high. And sometimes—by accident, I hope— he slips into rhyming couplets.

I wonder, he says, as we wait for our entrees, *if I could take it somewhere. Take it on public access television, maybe. Particularly now, or in the next nine months, since that's when it will be at its most meaningful, obviously. Do you think?*

Well, yeah, George says. *You see a broad range of stuff on public access.*

Of course, it's still evolving. Tonight was just the start. Already there are things I'd do differently, one or two. He taps the ends of his chopsticks on the table, jogs his knee up and down. *I'm still reaching out with some of it. Still trying to get in touch with the other side of me.*

Is that why you've got the traditional costume? Ash asks him.

Traditional costume? No. I just saw this in a thrift store one day, and there's so much gold. It's pretty special. George thinks it might be from The Mikado.

And what's your other side, exactly?

Other side, he says, like the far side of a canyon bouncing it back to me but making it no plainer. *The other side. The other. The side that is the other.*

George interrupts. *This is a big thing of Oscar's. He thinks you should be able to hear that he's got inverted commas around "other."*

Oh, other, Ash says. *That other. The side of you that represents the other, the outsider side.*

Yes, but when you do it the inverted commas are quite audible.

And how does the costume represent the other?

Well, Oscar begins, *that's a very good question, Ashley, since the choice, I know, is somewhat atypical. For a start, it doesn't represent every regular day of my life. I mean, look at Jon. Imagine him just the way he is now, but with a tie.*

I can do that.

Well, that's where I am most of the time. That, but just a bit more stylish. No offense.

Since when did I take offense?

You're always taking offense. But, anyway, I can't explore the other from there. There needs to be more . . . let out. It's got to be bold. It's got to be unafraid to be honest. I have to liberate myself to allow the words to surge out of me, with the writing and with the performance. That's what any creative process is about, the surge. And maybe a small amount of glamour. I think that's me. Deep down, I mean. There should be glamor there. It should be just a bit . . .

Shimmery? George suggests.

Oscar goes *Mmmm,* and gives a small, satisfied nod. Shimmery is, I suspect, a nuance he'd like to call his own. *And from there, you see, the poetry begins. I can be bold.*

Unafraid. I can create my "Millennium Suite," again and again.

And the section about the "golden globe of possibility," Ash says. *Is that to do with getting in touch with the other, or is it something specific?*

Oh, both of those things. Very definitely, both. But it's also about good and evil. And I know that's a little reductionist, but I quite like the starkness of that contrast sometimes. Don't you? The innocence that's behind it, behind that uncomplicated view of the world. It's quite special. And very millennium, I think. That's what I'd call it. Millennium.

And what exactly is the "golden globe of possibility?"

At a non-metaphorical level? It's pretty much about Pac-Man. There's a pause, as this takes us all neatly by surprise. *You don't know Pac-Man, Ash?*

It's the . . .

I know Pac-Man, she says.

Okay, it's like this. This is where your thesis comes in, I think, he says, but he could just be doing it to scare her. *I believe when any new technology comes along, we first try to interpret it in terms of the fundamental struggle, the struggle between good and evil. So the early video games, before they got all fancy, that's what they were all about. Two classic examples—Space Invaders and Pac-Man. So most of my poetry is about them. But particularly Pac-Man. Cause there you have the innocence. You see?*

Um, not totally.

I was worried about that. The clarity of it in performance in particular, since the imagery has a certain density to it. I thought perhaps I should wear a glove, a single white glove on my left hand, and hold it this way. He cocks his hand into a very poetic shape. *But even then it's in the eyes, you see. And in what the other hand is doing. It's that dichotomy of knob hand and button hand. Gloved hand and naked hand. Let me show you. Here's another one. I didn't do this tonight. It's a little unfinished.* He pulls a sheet of paper out of his folded *Mikado* costume, arranges his napkin on his raised left hand like an imaginary friend, shouts out a few bizarre lines, ending with, *Redolent, fabulous, yes mother, yes mother earth, your children are gone and all by these small hands.* Like someone who's remastered a recording of the poetry of seventies legend Rod McKuen, with intent to do harm.

He looks at her as though she must now understand. There's clapping from a nearby table—people who were at the reading—and Oscar gives a nod their way, turns his napkined hand to a small but majestic wave. From most other tables there's silence, and staring.

George clears his throat, leans forward. *What I think Oscar's saying—I don't mean to butt in here, Oscar, but sometimes, as you've said, your work's a little elusive—is that there is something very innocent about Pac-Man, at least about the player's role. You chug around munching, engulfing the, um . . .*

Golden globes of possibility.

And you confront these very finite nasties along the way.

But isn't that just promoting consumption? Ash says. *The fact that you're rewarded for eating the yellow dots?*

No. It's not a commodity, you see, Oscar explains. *It's a kind of life force.*

But doesn't evil triumph in the end? Don't you always, like, get munched, or something?

In the end, yes, but the struggle is heroic. And the ultimate victory over evil will only come through such sacrifice. But maybe, at another level, it's also nature, a cycle. And it doesn't end. The globes give life to the Pac-Man, the Pac-Man gives life to the other creatures. And when it's all done, you can press Start again. There's a lot to find in there. Big, enduring issues. But this millennium, it makes us hurry. From another perspective, as you heard earlier, Pac-Man is like Star Wars . . .

And here are the entrees, George says. *The food perspective.*

Oscar takes a spring roll and taps it against the side of his bowl. *And the government, for this work it gives me money. It recognizes the importance.*

And you let that man laser people? Ash says, when we're back in the car.

He's very metaphorical, isn't he? That side doesn't come out at work. At work he's a quiet man, interested in small things.

You never know what people have got going on beneath the surface.

Until you give them a *Mikado* costume and a bit of encouragement.

She laughs, and puts the Lemonheads back in the CD player.

Different song. She cues up "Outdoor Type," sings along with the first two lines in a way that seems to constitute a threat to go the distance.

There's five bucks in my wallet. It's yours if you stop.

Don't you like it? I can't believe you liked that poetry, but you don't like my singing.

Your singing's very . . . enthusiastic.

I'm sure it's more than that. Go on.

It's powerful. Political, shimmery, stop me when you find one you like. Your singing doesn't have anything to do with Pac-Man. I appreciate that, a lot.

Okay, I believe the last one.

I just thought a little quiet time wouldn't be bad. Nothing to do with your singing. Oscar's a bit of an assault on the senses, when he gets going.

I think that's what he's trying for.

Who knows? I've got no idea what he's trying for. You have to realize tonight's not indicative of what goes on in my life.

I think I'm aware of that. We pull up at a red light halfway along Coronation Drive. *And quiet time wouldn't be bad. I must have eaten too much. I'm not feeling very well. Are you okay?*

I'm fine.

Maybe it's not dinner, then. Maybe it's the six bananas I had for breakfast and the four I had for lunch.

Maybe we should get you some food.

I liked the bananas. I'm sure I'll be fine.

She doesn't look well. She's starting to look pale under the streetlights. Not that they flatter anybody, but she doesn't look the way she usually does.

We park at her house and she leans over to me, puts her arms around me and hugs me and says, *Thanks for tonight.*

Ash, that was surely some of the worst poetry you've ever heard.

Definitely. But it gives me a clear idea of one thing I don't want to be. If I ever start hanging around thrift stores looking for Mikado *costumes, you will shoot me, won't you?*

I promise I'll at least pay for the therapy, however long it takes.

She smiles. The CD has randomly picked "Into Your Arms," and I stop myself on the brink of humming, or singing along. Since she's at close range, I think it was going to be humming.

Might see you tomorrow then.

Yeah. Actually, Lily's at my parents' tonight, so we could run, if you want, before I pick her up in the morning. Maybe eight or eight-thirty.

Good. And the streetlight shines in at an angle, catches her left cheek and her mouth. She's still half-turned toward me. *Eight or eight-thirty then,* she says, just when I think she's about to say more than that.

Yeah.

And what happens if I move now? What happens? Nothing. I don't move. It's been so long since I've known how to read this kind of situation, so long since I had any idea what to do, that I don't move.

Not before she says, *Okay,* and by then it's too late. *Well, I'll see you.*

She turns and the seat leather creaks, and she opens the door and goes. Steps out into the light, into the warm night air. And she's through her front gate, halfway along the path, when she pulls her keys out of her bag and turns to wave.

19

I'm reaching out across the bed, most of the way to the other side. It's not long after dawn, and something has hit the front steps with a thump. That's what's woken me. Since it's a Lily-sized thump, that's what it becomes in the next dream. The Bean, tumbling down onto the first of too many steps, falling under my feet.

There's no point in trying to sleep after that. I need to show myself she's not here. I need to show myself it's not her.

Her room is empty, as it's supposed to be, and on the step there's a pound of tea. Halliday Tea.

It's vacuum sealed, like a large, light brick.

I don't understand last night, the end of last night. All of last night, but it's acceptable not to understand the Oscar part. But what happened at the end? I don't even know what kind of situation it was. If it was a situation.

That's all I can think of as I turn the block of tea over in my hands and see the label, the sketch of a homestead, the description of the blend. It's Ash's voice I hear when I read it. Ash's voice turned to advertising, with gusto and a hint of irony that almost no one will get.

Last night I didn't want to leave her. I didn't want to watch her run off up the path, and then drive home.

Which doesn't mean I'm sure of what I did want, but I didn't want the night to end then. I wanted to take hold of her, tell her she meant something. I don't want her to struggle with money and loneliness. I don't, but that's only one side of it. One small part, and the rest of it's less valiant and much more about me. I wanted to cross those last few inches between us, but I froze. I'm not sure what I was waiting for, if I was expecting some kind of sign. I don't know what to do anymore. It's been so long.

But I never knew what to do, from the night of my prom on. Who am I trying to kid? What do you do? Eighty percent of what you're going in with is the hope that you won't look like an idiot, whatever the outcome. That's the dominant feeling in that instant and, until the need to make the move becomes greater, becomes compelling, nothing can happen. The instant passes, to the catalog of missed opportunities.

I take the tea to the car and I drive to Ash's in my running gear.

She's waiting at her door, but her shoes are off and she says, *I really don't know that I'm up to it today.*

Is it more of what was wrong with you last night?
Yeah.

Do you think you should do something about it? What do you think it is?

She swings her shoes by the laces, and they seem too big for her. She's not looking the way she usually does. She looks younger, delicate rather than compact.

Preservatives in last night's dinner, maybe? I've always been a bit allergic to MSG. So, why don't you run without me?

No, it's okay.

Well, do you want a drink or anything?

That'd be good, thanks. Hey, I've got something in the car. I'll be back in a sec. Do you want to put the kettle on?

Oh. Okay, she says, and smiles for the first time today, like someone with a surprise to prepare for.

I go down to the car to fetch the tea, and come back into the house holding it behind my back. She's getting two mugs out of a low cupboard, and she stands and turns. I show her the packet, and there's surprise on her face, but not the look I'd expected. Not the mild pleasure of recognizing something familiar.

Where did you get that?

I thought you might like it. Something from home.

But I left home. And she says it as though there's something wrong, as though I've done something wrong.

Oh. I ordered it on the Internet a couple of days ago. From the Web site.

Oh . . . Thanks. It's a really nice thought. Let's have some. And I can tell you more about the taxonomy of biscuits.

I'd like that.

She laughs at herself. *I'm sorry. I've never been caught off-guard by a tea packet before. I was just dizzy standing up quickly—you know the way it goes—and things were looking a bit wobbly, and suddenly there was this tea from home. When I least expected it.*

The glories of the Internet.

Yeah.

That stuff on the box . . .

The text? "The young leaves picked for maximum tender-

ness"? "Shrouded in Tableland mists"? That's mine. Mainly mine.

I thought so. Shrouded in Tableland mists. Very persuasive. Very mysterious.

Exotic?

Definitely exotic. I could end up drinking a lot of this tea.

Well, it was blended to be your everyday tea, so that would be okay. The best and most exotic everyday tea, of course. She opens the packet, holds it up to her face and takes in the aroma of the leaves. *I nearly drove off the road in one of those damn mists once, I was so shrouded. But let's have some. If only I had a connoisseur's array of biscuits to complement it.*

Or even food for your own breakfast, I'm thinking, as I'm on my way to my parents' later.

She had some sugar, a carton of milk and some Vegemite. Not much else. So it's no wonder she's not feeling well, and dizzy when she stands up quickly. It was hard not to get parental, force money on her. But everything sensible that came to mind sounded like some kind of telling off, and finally all I could say was, You have enough Coles Myer shares for a discount card, but you can't buy a loaf of bread?

And she said, *It's a temporary cash-flow problem. It's the deal I've got going with my family. I get the computer. I get the crap car, but with four new tires. I get the stock portfolio so I can learn about being grown up, but for the day-to-day stuff I fend for myself. I'm on at Bagelos at ten today, and*

I'll scrounge something there. And she sounded almost proud about it. *And then I'll get paid and everything'll be fine.*

So I left when we'd finished the tea, feeling I'd been told that her empty fridge might not be my business. And worrying about her not eating, missing home and not eating. Or just not eating. Trying to think back to my time in psych and remember everything I know about eating disorders. But I don't think that's her. And maybe I shouldn't be overanalyzing someone's interest in self-sufficiency.

And I don't want to be parental. I've already got someone I can be parental with. The best I could do was make sure she'd come around to dinner and let me cook for her again.

How was the poetry? my mother asks, when I get there. But she does it with the look of comic wariness that I'd expect.

You know how it was. You know Oscar's poetry. Give me two fans, a *Mikado* costume and a lot of spit and I could show you the latest.

Wonderful. Knew he wouldn't let you down. What does it all mean, though?

Almost anything if you listen to him explain it for long enough.

I gave your father a copy of Oscar's last book, and I don't think he understood it at all.

And for once we'd agree completely, I tell her. I can't even imagine him reading it. Poor man. Page after page, waiting for Inspector Morse to walk in and the whole thing to start to make sense.

He knows some poetry.

He can recite the chunks of Tennyson they forced him to learn at school.

Tennyson? my father's voice says, as he emerges from his study with the Bean in his arms, and he zips right into the first couple of stanzas of one of the Crimean War poems, turning it into a comical horse ride, and the Bean cackles and grabs what's left of his hair, pulling it till his eyes water. *Oh don't, love,* he says, wincing and gently unfolding her fingers. *I'm just an old cart horse, really. I was only pretending.*

Ash turns up at four-thirty, and tells me she feels better after a day in air-conditioning and a few bagels. She says she's up to walking, so we load Lily and Elvis into the car and drive to the riverbank on campus.

She's quieter than usual, so, as we walk, I find myself lapsing into the baby commentary, naming the obvious out of habit, helping the Bean toward memory.

See? Ash says. *If only someone had given me this kind of campus orientation when I'd arrived, instead of just that big map. If they'd gone, "There's a bird, See the big tree," I'd have known my way around straight off.*

And to the right, Lily, you'll see a new engineering building, and behind that a small brick place where all the rude people get sent. That's where Ashley has meetings with her supervisor.

Look at the big palm tree.

Too late. Did I tell you about my mother, when she was going to a meeting one day? When I was very young?

No.

This was in England, and I think she might have just got her PhD, so I was about one at the time. She was going to something entomological with a few other people and they were driving in her car, and there were fields at the side of the motorway. I think she'd been worried about getting lost, but once she was on the motorway, she knew she was on the right track, so she relaxed. And that's when she started going, "Look at the cows. See the big blackbird in the tree." I think she probably surprised them when she actually presented her paper. She says you get over it. But it takes a few years.

And you're just getting into the habit.

Yeah.

You seem pretty good at it, though.

Thanks.

No, I mean it. In a good way. I think you are good at it.

Like I said before, I think I have to be. I think, since there's just me, I have to be prepared to make a dick of myself naming every object in the vicinity, and singing along to anything that's playing. But it's okay. You don't have to sing badly in front of people too many times for performance anxiety to become a thing of the past. No-one expects quality from me. The Lemonheads they expect, quality they don't. I'm sure you know what I mean.

So what was it like? Dealing with Melissa dying, and the time after? That must have been very difficult.

What?

What was it like?

Um . . .

No one's asked you that, have they?

What do you mean?

No one's directly asked you. About what you've been going through.

They ask me how I am. All the time.

That's not the same.

It's the same if I want it to be. I can tell them whatever I want. They're there for me. I know that. I can talk about anything I want with them.

But you don't, do you?

Yes I do. I don't always tell them all the details, but I could if I wanted to. There's all this bullshit about talking. It doesn't fix things, whatever people say. It's only a small part of fixing things. Sometimes you talk, but there are some things you can't explain. So there are times when you've got to keep it to yourself. Work it out yourself.

And present this calm, coping exterior.

What do you mean? What's wrong with coping?

Nothing's wrong with coping. I'm talking about the exterior. People who show everyone everything's working on the surface, while they hide beneath and try to sort things out.

What are you saying?

I'm saying . . . It's like what you were saying in the Great Court that day, last Saturday, about skin. How it works. Maybe it's like that. If you want to see it that way. An opaque outer layer. The exterior that stops the interior being seen. And she's saying this slowly, as though each word needs weighing and measuring before being let go. *I don't know what gets let in, but you don't seem to let much out.*

What am I supposed to be letting out? Am I supposed to be reaching right in and pulling stuff out for people? What kind of pop-psych stuff are you reading for this degree?

There's a pause. She looks away, shrugs. I should talk. I've taken it too far. I wasn't expecting this. I wasn't expecting her to wade into it the way she has.

All right. My mistake. You're obviously totally fine then.

Sorry. Sorry about the pop-psych thing. For all of that.

She looks back at me. It's almost a glare, but she's letting it pass. She nods.

But, you know, if you'd like to reinterpret my life in terms of "The rise and fall of Tickle-Me-Elmo" I'd be very keen to hear that.

A small laugh, but nothing more said.

What I'm saying is, I don't totally get what you're saying. So much of this is only mine to deal with. I don't know how it would be fixed by wearing it all on the outside.

Which is not what I was saying. You have friends. You have been through something that—correct me if I'm wrong—could reasonably be called a very significant loss. I don't know why you don't talk to them.

I talk to them. All the time. But in a particular way.

I'm shitty with her again. I'm shitty for "correct me if I'm wrong" and for "significant loss." As though she's out-debating me, out-flanking me with technicalities. As though what I'm going through can be reduced to technicalities.

It's not as easy as it seems.

I'm sure it isn't.

How? How can you be sure? How can you know? Look, this is how it works. This is how life works… Sorry, that's really patronizing.

Good pick-up. So go on. She smiles, since she's entitled.

I said the dumb thing, and she's letting me off. *Tell me how life works.*

Yeah, okay. Here's what I think. With all the people you know, you've got this repertoire. There's a range of things you can be. And outside that things feel weird. I've got a history with these people. I've known George half my life, and the others for a while too. Just about as long, even though there was a gap in the middle. There's a way we do things. Over time, you fall into a way of interacting with each other, and supporting each other. And that kind of talk isn't what I want them for. I want to be okay. I want them for when I'm okay, even though I know they'd be there, whatever. They make that clear. George deferred his degree to cover for Mel not being there. We said it was just to cover for Mel, but he's been covering for me too. We both know that. We both know how important it is, in a practical way. And we don't have to keep talking about it. And I don't want to handle that another way. I don't want to change the way I relate to these people. I don't want to remake my relationships based on how I deal with Mel's death. I have the right to try to keep some things the same. What can I say, anyway? I don't know what I'd say.

We walk a few more steps.

I hadn't thought of it that way.

Well, neither had I until I had to. Plus, you have different relationships with all the people you know. There's a lot to take into account when it comes to dealing with this. And I know this situation's not just about me, not just about me and Lily. It's tough for the others too, but I'm not ready for all those conversations. Not yet. And if that's selfish, they'll let me be selfish. They're good that way.

Lily points at a passing car, so I tell her, Car. Blue car.

I've got no idea about this, have I? I'm sorry. I've got a headache. I'm not feeling the best today, so . . .

Okay, sorry. I think I wasn't expecting it, this conversation, and I've handled it like an idiot.

I had this idea that you could tell me things. And then I wondered if you told anyone. If it's not my business to say that, tell me. And tell me how I should handle it. I want to get this right. You told me about Melissa days ago, and ever since then you've steered conversations around her. That's how it seems, whenever I've mentioned her, but George did it too, the other night. So I don't know what I'm supposed to do. She looks away from me, down at the ground in front of her. *And you have to try to tell me what to do. If you don't tell me, I won't know how to talk to you. I'm sorry if that's not like George . . .*

No. No. Don't be like George. I've got one of those already. Okay. This is how weird it was. We went out one night, Mel and me, about a month before. Or a couple of months. It was a slightly pretentious place. I was never into those sort of wanky places, Mel kind of was. Goes with the Beemer, I suppose. Which is fine. I'm not being critical.

Ash looks back at me. It's not fine. Already I've swerved from the truth of the story, or at least failed to meet it directly.

Fuck. Okay. We didn't actually get on. That's what I haven't told you.

I didn't realize.

No, you didn't realize. You couldn't realize. I kept that all back. We didn't tell people. At least, I haven't told people and, as far as I know, Mel didn't say anything either. So that adds to the mess, really. How can I tell them about it now? And how can I talk about any of it without getting into that? It makes it hard. Too hard, to be honest, and that's the real issue. Anyway, there were problems. We were working on them, and one night we went to this restaurant. Wanky place. And what I hate about those places is how they're all about making you feel like an idiot, when that's not what I go out for. If I want to feel like an idiot, I can just sing or name nearby objects, or spit on myself.

My favorite was the spitting.

And you haven't even seen me in action with people's cats. Anyway, these restaurants. It's like they've got a competition going to put as many stupid words as possible on the menu just to let you know who's boss. Well, this one had a pasta dish with lardoons of bacon. I saw it on the menu and I said something about it, because the rest of the description made it sound pretty interesting, so Mel said, "Why don't you have it?" That's very Mel. Order the thing partly because you don't know what it is. It's not me. I always expect those things won't work out, so I don't order things with words I don't know. Mel had a go at me, about how I never take any kind of chances, how I can't even risk it with a meal if there's a new word in there. And I was actually really sick of that—I think there'd been a bit of it around at the time, not that I'm saying I was faultless—so I didn't let it go, which led to an argument, which kind of wrecked the night. Actually, you might have read about it in the paper.

What? Must have been a hell of an argument.

No. It was just, like so many things, misunderstood. I had acutely had enough of it, and I knew the evening was shot, so I decided to go. Leave and catch a cab. Mel followed, and we argued all the way to the cab stand about me and my risk-taking, me and what was my business, all of that. And then we talked all the way to the car park, once we'd decided to go home. And we'd forgotten to pay. And have you seen, in the weekend papers, the articles a couple of times in the last year about people scamming free meals from restaurants? We're the "professional couple having a row" story.

Couldn't that just be anyone?

They named the restaurant, and they described us pretty well. As if we'd gone to some trouble to costume ourselves so that we'd look just like a professional couple. Even the seething that went on between the entree and main, so obviously we hadn't kept that to ourselves as much as we'd thought. And the woman was pregnant, or faking a pregnancy. That's how I really knew it was us. They even speculated about us doing that to draw focus from the scam. But that's off the track. It was also very strange reading the articles, since they came out after she was dead, but that's off the track too. A week or so after she died I was in a pretty bizarre state. She was gone, the Bean was home. I was totally sleep-deprived. I dropped in to work—I don't know why—and I was walking around and I found myself in the bookshop, standing there with the biggest dictionary they had, looking up "lardoon." Which is the fatty cut of bacon used to lard other meats. So I was entirely justified in not ordering it. And I happened to see, I think, someone who looked a bit like Mel in my peripheral vision, and I turned and I told her, with my finger still in the dictionary, what a lardoon was. As though I was the winner. And then I thought, Oh, fuck, she thinks I'm mad, so I tried to explain. And when I explained I said something like, Sorry, you look a bit like my wife. She's around here somewhere. And I think it wasn't a lie. It was wrong, but it wasn't a lie. I think, just in that second, seeing that woman, I thought Mel was somewhere nearby. See? That's how it works. How do you find the right way to tell that to people? Because what's the right way for them to respond?

There's a message on the answering machine when we get home. Wendy, saying that Flag will be discharged in the morning. *Katie's having a welcome-home morning tea. As you might expect. It'd probably be good if you could put in an appearance. It's at ten-thirty. And you know the address.*

Flag's the cat, I tell Ash. The cat I stepped on on Monday.

Do cats like morning tea?

No.

I chop garlic and chilli and basil to go with some linguini, and Ash feeds Lily.

As I'm chopping, my mind won't shift from the restaurant fight, the day in the bookshop. The futility of that night out, the waste of time and money and energy and life. Another game about surfaces, gone wrong. The professional couple, out for dinner close to term. Anger in a double string of pearls. It's anger we were hiding, not an intent to steal. I'd done something. I don't know or care what. It's only every part of it that's futile, so it doesn't matter why we were at the restaurant and not getting on that night.

And maybe, a month later, I had some idea that if I found out what the word meant I could close the story, put it away. Perhaps go back to that night and say, I know what the word means, so let's talk about something else. Not my minuscule sense of adventure. Let's talk about you. Let's talk about what went wrong today. Let's make sure it doesn't happen again. But by the time I looked the word up, nothing could happen again.

Everything from the time of Mel's death is too strange and extreme to explain, and I often don't get it myself. I'd forgotten about the stories in the paper, and the way my brain worked, seeing Mel as I looked up from the dictionary eight days after she was dead. It's all still stuck in the jumble of that time, all too big to make sense of. None of it's even medium-sized, so where and how would I start the talking to make the process of talking do some good?

For several weeks it was like driving in fog. Blank and intense. I think I had my friends there to buffer me, keep me from harm. But I don't even know.

The rules seemed irrevocably different, suddenly. As though everything I'd understood about the world was wrong, everything I'd taken to be certain couldn't be relied upon. Everything I thought I had to argue about or to fix didn't have to be battled over anymore. And it happened with no effort at all.

Death seemed always likely then, in those first few weeks, in a way it hadn't since I'd been a hospital resident, when I saw it all around me during some terms. Even now, Lily scares me when she sleeps. As though it's reckless of her. Sometimes I have to watch and watch.

But I'm doing it again. Standing here, chopping, listening to Ash talk to Lily, and doing it again. Running the tape again in my head, being my own audience of one. Not talking, perhaps trying to wear out the tape, play it so many times it becomes inert.

When Lily's gone to bed, I cook the pasta and I toss it with everything I've chopped. It smells good. The kitchen fills with the smell of garlic and basil. I've known Ash three weeks, three weeks and three days. And I lie awake at night, thinking about her. She's more than ten years younger than me, for god's sake. I've no idea what she wants, what she's thinking, what her life's about.

We eat outside. On the monitor, I can hear Lily making murmuring noises and, just when it sounds like she's building up to something, about to wake properly, she settles.

Well done, I tell her in absentia. Good choice.

It's useful, having that.

Yeah. It's better than checking, getting up to check every few minutes. Which is what I'd do if I didn't have it.

When she's sleeping?

You don't think I'd leave her in peace, do you? I never

slept at first. I'd have to get people over here during the day to mind her so that I could sleep. And I'd have to tell them we'd had a bad night, which we hardly ever did. She's always been a good sleeper. I just couldn't leave her to it. I still can't really relax when she sleeps. However dumb that is.

I don't think it's dumb.

Hmmm. It's not very rational. She scares me when she sleeps, and that's kind of off-putting, potentially. It's a pretty neurotic thing to admit.

Dickhead, she says, in a joking kind of way, and shakes her head. *What have I been saying? I was hassling you about not talking. I can't complain if you do. So what's it about?*

What do you mean?

You're not a neurotic person. What's the problem with her sleeping?

Okay. At first I think I kept trying to convince myself that it was safer to believe that she was temporary. That the whole thing was a phase. Having her was a phase. I tried not to get attached. Just in case. I couldn't believe that someone as comprehensively naive as her could be given something as fragile as life to look after. When her mother was smart and took no shit and paid attention to everything, and she still blew it. But it's not like that, of course. All Lily's parts, I'm told, are in great working order, and any problem would come as a complete surprise. But surprises happen sometimes. So there you go.

Yeah, but . . .

Ash, I now notice, is quite pale. She's been going pale and looking more and more uncomfortable over the last few minutes.

Sorry, should we talk about something else?

No. It's just my headache. It's nothing to do with what we're talking about.

Are you sure?

Yes, I'm sure. I knew you'd think that. She puts her head down on the table. *Which is why I wasn't telling you. Have you got anything I can take? It's getting worse.*

Yeah, probably. Let me go and look. It's just, you know, a regular headache?

Yeah.

I get to the bathroom and I look through the cupboards. I don't know where all that stuff's gone. I pull the drawers open, and there's all kinds of junk, a lot of it not even mine, but nothing useful.

Ash appears in the doorway, looking unwell in the harsh bathroom light. She says, *I'm . . .* and then nothing more, as she goes down on her knees, doubling up, curling up on the floor.

What's happening? Really. What's really going on? You have to tell me.

Um, she says, and takes a sharp breath in. *It's a period thing, I think.*

What?

A period thing. I used to have trouble. I went on the pill and it got better. I've been off it for a while now and it's getting worse. She squeezes up her eyes and clenches her teeth. *And it's been a longer cycle this time, so that makes it worse too.*

A period thing?

Yeah, not a headache. I was planning to keep it to myself, but . . . right now it's better to curl up on the floor and admit it.

I put my hand on her arm. I stroke her hair. I can't remember what to do. I don't know what to do for this now, I've been lasering so long.

You're cold, I say to her, and I pull a towel down and wrap it around her.

She sniffs, wipes her eyes, pulls her knees up higher.

Have you got anything to take for it? Anything at home?

I don't have any money, she says angrily. *You know I don't have any money. How could I get something to take?*

Okay.

Sorry.

Don't be. Let's get this sorted out. I'm getting help. I'm going to call someone who's a gynecologist, and he's pretty nearby.

She doesn't argue. I fetch my mobile so that I can call from the bathroom. That way I don't have to leave her. I tell her Roscoe will know what to do. And he'll have drugs for now and free samples for later and he'll get this fixed. And we can get more of whatever she needs. And all the time, watching her on the floor, curled up, I'm scared and powerless.

You'll be okay.

I know. Jon, it's all right. I've had this before. This is just the worst time. But it's okay.

I move her so that there's a towel under her as well as wrapped around her, and I fetch a pillow for her head.

Sorry, this is stupid.

It's not stupid. And stop apologizing.

I go through the cupboards again and I find a half-full bottle of infant Tylenol. There's nothing I can do but wait. She squeezes my hand hard.

The doorbell rings. It's Ross Donovan.

Jon, what's happening? he says when I get there.

I don't know. I could be overreacting. It's just someone who was here for dinner who . . . she's on the bathroom floor. She thinks it's GYN. She looks like she's really in pain, and I didn't know what to do. I didn't know if I should take her somewhere, because there's Lily to sort out too.

That's okay, he says. *Just take me in there.*

I lead him to the bathroom and he kneels beside Ash, Roscoe Donovan with his wide, rounded shoulders and his big gray head of hair making her look like a broken child.

Could we just have a few minutes? he says to me, when he realizes I'm still anxiously hanging around.

Yeah, sure. I'll be out here.

Now, let's work out what's going on, he says softly as I go.

I wait outside the door, telling myself I'm there in case I'm needed. I hear Ash answering questions. I should stop being so concerned. When I hear him ask if she's been sexually active lately, I realize I do have to go, but I can't stop myself hearing her answer. It's no.

I make tea in the kitchen. I'm not sure why, since I don't want it. I sit and drink it, and the murmur of Roscoe's voice is still calm, questions with spaces for Ash's answers, longer stretches of explanation. Elvis trots in and sits at my feet.

Then I hear Roscoe's footsteps along the hall.

There you are, he says, as he comes into the kitchen and puts his bag on the table. *She's fine, Jon. She wanted me to tell you she's fine. And that it's primary dysmenorrhea.*

So, like, period pain? She's collapsed on my bathroom floor and it's just straight period pain?

Yeah. It sounds a bit better when you say primary dysmenorrhea. It's sometimes this bad in young, thin, healthy women. Occasionally you end up having to look at other possibilities, but not usually. I've got a daughter that age. She got almost that bad. Kept it to herself. You know how they do. You don't know anything's wrong with them when they're that age until you work out the house is being overrun by echinacea and saint someone's bloody wort.

Okay. Thanks. That's good isn't it? I'm sorry. I got you around here for dysmenorrhea?

It's not a problem. It still needed something done about it, even if it's not going to . . . do her serious harm. Why haven't you got her to see anyone before?

This is the first cycle I've known her.

Oh.

She's from up north.

That's the moment when Roscoe realizes he doesn't know who the hell Ash is, and it's followed by the moment when he realizes he's going to take "She's from up north" as a respectable attempt at an answer.

Thanks for coming round.

No problem. I was in the neighborhood, as you probably figured.

Maybe I did, but I didn't call you because you live nearby. I called you because it seemed like it was going to be GYN and, you know, you're the best. Obviously we didn't really need the best for this, as it turns out, but who else would I call? Who else would I hassle about Saturday evening period pain?

Glad I could help. And they're taping The Bill *for me at home so, like I said, it's really not a problem.*

Do you want a drink? How about a scotch?

Only if you're having one.

Sure. Why not?

Why not? Well, several reasons, but I keep them to myself. I don't like scotch for a start. Not on its own, not with anything. Not since a bad Med Ball experience with scotch and dry, many years ago (perhaps even the legendary Med Ball of 1986). Once any drink has mixed with your stomach contents and been passed out your nose, you can't feel the same about it again. But Roscoe likes scotch. He's known to.

Black Label, he says when I find the bottle. *That's a nice one to be offering me. But don't go opening a new one on my account.*

I'm sure it was due to be opened anyway.

I didn't know you were a scotch drinker.

Oh, from time to time.

I sip, and try to take my mind off the Med Ball incident, but the smell is powerful and olfactory memory hard to shake. Ash is okay. She'll be okay. For that I can drink scotch, and recall the disappointment of however many Med Balls I managed to fit in, and not care too much about it.

So how have you been? Roscoe says.

Pretty good.

He turns the tumbler around in his hand and nods. *Good.*

It was tough for a couple of months there, but things are starting to fit into place, I think.

That's good to hear.

The baby's well. Lily. She's doing really well.

He nods at that too.

Roscoe, Mel . . . these things happen.

Yeah . . . I did a term as her father's resident in about 1972. Did I ever tell you that?

Yeah, I think so. On one of our antenatal visits, probably.

Ashley's going to come and see me next week, so that we can get on top of this, he says, and finishes his scotch. *But she'll be right for tonight, and the rest of the weekend. She's in bed now. I thought that was better than the floor.* He forces a smile. *So I might be off. Might go home and watch that tape.*

Okay. Well, thanks for coming. I really appreciate it. I might have overreacted a bit there, calling you, but she looked pretty bad and I didn't want to mess around.

It's no problem. Any time. If you've got any worries, call me. The Bill *can keep. But this'll be okay, so don't be too concerned.* At the door, he shakes my hand and says, *It's good to see you. Good to see you looking all right.*

When he's gone, I go to check how Ash is. She's not in the spare room. I walk in, and the bed is as made as it was after my parents last stayed, and I wonder where she is, if something's not right.

I only get one door down the hall before I see her. In my room, in my bed, the hall light coming in as far as the bedside table, but putting enough diffuse light in there that I can see her, curled up. I walk in—doing a quiet check of her breathing, I realize, once I'm most of the way to the bed. I'm too used to checking on Lily.

I stop, and I watch her. Her head on the pillow, facing this way, but with her hand there to brush the light off, and now half closed with sleep and covering only one eye.

She wakes and sees me, says, *Oh . . . I'm sorry about all this.*

It's quite all right.

No, I should just go home.

That's not likely, really. Now, you're okay? Is there anything you want?

No. I wish I felt better. How can a normal process be so foul?

Well, hopefully Roscoe can do something about that.

I walk over to the bed and she reaches out and takes my hand.

Thanks. He gave me something. It's getting better. It hasn't been this bad before, but it's better now. I was hoping I could keep it to myself earlier, but obviously not. And I think I need to lie down.

Which is exactly why you aren't going home.

So take a seat.

She lets go of my hand and pats the bed. I sit there and she starts to doze. Her hair is spiking up here and there, and I stroke it back into place without thinking. She holds my hand there, and it seems to be a signal. I sit, stroking her hair. She curls up, so that she's almost curled around me. Her knees bump into me and her eyes open again.

Hi.

Hi. I should warn you. If I stay here any longer, there's a risk I could sing.

I wouldn't mind.

When she's properly asleep, I leave the room.

But I don't sleep myself, even when it gets late. I check Lily, I check Ash. Elvis follows me on my rounds.

Chicks hey? I say to him. You've got to watch them.

I make another cup of tea and he sits nearby, staring at me, giving me the stare that says, What madness is this? Where the hell did our routine go tonight? And when did you start liking tea?

I'm becoming my mother, aren't I? I admit to him. This is my third cup today.

I screw the top back on the scotch bottle. I haven't seen Roscoe since the funeral. We probably talked then. I don't remember.

The bottle was his. His well-known favorite, bought to give to him on the day when Mel and the baby would have been discharged from the hospital. A thank-you for seeing us through it all, delivering Lily, making sure everything went to plan. Which it didn't, and the scotch sat there.

Mel's death was nothing to do with Roscoe. It really was just one of those things. I've never seen him respond so quickly. It simply didn't work. He's good. I don't know who's the best (if there needs to be a best), but he's good. I should have talked to him months ago. But that was never going to happen. And that has to be okay.

Mel's father was a surgeon. A surgeon of the old school, a big surgeon. Which meant big incisions, heroic procedures and an expectation that crowded hospital corridors would part before him. Which they did. He died when we were at school, before I really knew Mel and before

I'd heard much about him. He lingered as a phenomenon, in the way patients revered him, in the sweep of his scars across abdomens.

Mel was an only child, born when her parents were both in their forties. She was, it seems, something of a surprise. She was always spoiled, and always destined to do medicine. Mel didn't even know she was spoiled. She thought childhood was about getting everything you wanted, preferably right when you wanted it, and that affection fitted in around that, as part of it, somewhere. So we weren't going to be similar as adults.

She liked my parents, once she worked out that they did things differently. She never quite worked out the basis of the difference, though. They were younger than parents, as far as she was concerned, and that's what she put it down to. She never questioned the way her own mother and father had been.

My parents took a while to adjust to her, but they got there. It was my mother who had named my dirty-dog phase, after all, and Mel was clearly something new. They were amused at the way she organized me. *I always thought you needed one of those,* my father said. And maybe I did, sometimes.

Her mother's death in 1995 was unexpected. She was in her seventies, but she seemed healthy and her family had a history of long life. Longer life than that. So we had one set of parents to share from then on. A set of parents who were particularly good about that. About Mel's birthday, about doing things with her and treating her as more than simply the person I'd married. The "morally wrong" cut of her wedding dress became something she and my mother could laugh about.

Mel inherited everything her mother had owned. We sold the family home. Since we'd come back from England Mel had been trying to get her mother to sell it and move to somewhere smaller, so it didn't surprise me that we didn't keep it. It covered our share of the practice start-up costs. It also let us upgrade from our own small house to something much larger—too many bedrooms, I thought, but it didn't seem fair to get in the way of Mel calling the shots. And it gave her the first of her two BMWs.

So our money was Mel's money. At least, that's how we came upon it. And the last of our debts was paid off by her life insurance.

That's all easier to accept if I tell myself the money's Lily's, not mine. I'm holding it in trust for her, in an informal way.

And Roscoe got no closer to knowing how Ash fitted in than being told she was from up north. And I said it as though I take in strays from there, and it needs no further explanation. How do I deal with that? He's seeing her in a few days. Should I call him? What would I say if I did? No one's forced me to define this relationship before, not seriously. Does any definition, any attempt to define it only lead back to "dirty old man," or is that just George getting to me? I can't see myself calling Roscoe and trying anything about a running buddy.

I watch TV with the sound down, and I've got a choice of old movies. Two black-and-white versions of people falling madly, stupidly in love with each other, and one in color. Epic situations, swollen soundtracks, hardly a regular experience in there.

I channel-surf mindlessly, slide down into the sofa and sleep till my dry, open mouth wakes me, and it's almost light and someone's demonstrating a mop on a home shopping show. The compere says, *That's truly remarkable,* and I miss those old movies, and all their more sincere lies.

20

Next, I wake having one of those trapped dreams. I'm lying on the sofa, with Elvis folded up innocently on my shins, looking at me with a more pleading version of last night's stare. A please-get-things-back-to-normal stare. Please go and sleep in the usual place, so there'll be more room for me.

Lily wakes and makes noise, so I take her out to the veranda. I bounce her up and down. I point to things and name them. She settles. They're all things I've named before. I'm boring her early in life.

I make breakfast for Ash while she's still in bed, another thing I've never done for anyone before. I hope it goes better than the flowers.

I don't get this at home, she says.

It's only toast and coffee and juice. We don't even have a tray. My mother would do it with a tray.

She arranges the pillows into a position for sitting, and she says, *Well, it's very nice. Thank you.*

So how are you today?

Not bad. The guy last night, the doctor . . . what was his name?

Ross Donovan.

He gave me some sample packs of something, and it's

working pretty well. I'm so embarrassed. It just got really bad over a few minutes. I wasn't feeling good for about a day, but then it was like . . . you don't need to know what it was like.

Don't be embarrassed about it. Be embarrassed about the way your hair is sticking right up off the top of your head, but don't be embarrassed about last night.

Oh my god, she says, and grabs the top of her head with both hands. *I must look awful.*

No, you don't look awful. I was kidding. Don't you have it cut so that it sort of sticks out anyway? I mean, I know I'm not particularly stylish, but isn't that, like, a look?

Only when you mean it to be. It's supposed to do it at the sides, but it's not supposed to do it straight up.

That's all too complicated for me.

Every day when I wake up my hair looks ridiculous. It looks like it tried to get away during the night, but it didn't quite make it. You're the doctor. Why does some people's hair go mad overnight, and other people look fine in the morning?

To make you start the day a couple of inches taller?

She takes a bite of toast. *Yeah, thanks. So you're saying I'm too short now.*

I'm sure you're just the right size.

Very diplomatic.

I read it in a women's magazine once. It's the only safe response when it comes to questions of size. Unless you're confident it's something that's supposed to be tiny or enormous.

This is so strange, sitting in bed here in yesterday's clothes, eating toast.

It'll work out fine if you're careful with the crumbs.

Now, I've got to go out to that welcome-home morning tea for the cat I squished. So why don't you stay around?

Are you sure?

Let me put it another way. Why don't you stay around, and that way I don't have to do the time-consuming baby component of a trip across town? I can just get in the car without all the junk, go, suffer for an hour and then come back. All the Lily things are done for the moment, so you'd just have to . . .

Babysit? Sure. Playing, stories, things like that?

You've got it covered.

Katie meets me with a smile so forced that I'm sure she's practiced it with me in mind.

Hello, Jon, she says, with the warmth of an eastern-bloc gymnast executing the next part of a compulsory routine. *Come in. Everybody's here.*

How's Flag?

Recovering.

I don't imagine he'll be particularly pleased to see me.

Well, there might be a bit of ground to make up.

But, much to Katie's displeasure, Flag bears no grudges. Among the dozens of potential laps in the house, it's mine he chooses to sit on. Soon enough he's kneading away at my pants, purring like a slightly more distant buzz saw than usual. Of course, this does turn me into some kind of cat cushion, while other people can move on after making the obligatory fuss.

You have a good time there, boys, George says. *The rest of us'll be out on the deck. And have you seen the catering out there? It's like Flag fought in a war, we're so happy he's home.*

No half measures with our Katie. I'm sure she's been up all night baking.

He leaves me to my servitude. More people arrive. Katie and Wendy's parents, Anita and Ron, take the seats on either side of me.

Someone stepped on him, I hear, Ron says.

Yes.

And his tone is completely noncommittal. It could be a joke, but there's no way of telling.

Seems like a damn clumsy thing to do.

It was nighttime. I think. And you know how he likes to dash around.

Hmmm. Well, won't be much of that for a while, will there? He leans across, gives Flag's head a scratch. *Not too much dashing around for a while, Flag.*

Scratch, scratch. Flag lifts his head, purrs louder, stretches his front legs out and kneads my lap with more vigor.

Easy on the trousers there, Flaggy, I say to him, and he pays no attention.

He's a happy chap, for all that, Ron says, and keeps scratching behind his ears and under his chin. *Yes, a happy fella.* Baby-talking and scratching him into some state of excitement.

I move Flag's paws to the arm of the seat, he moves them back to my pants. I move them to the arm again, he moves them to my groin. Looks up at me with mad eyes and puts a claw through my every defense and into my penis, around about mid-shaft.

There's a good fella, Ron says, as tears come to my eyes and make me blink.

Flag knows he's stuck, and twists his paw like a cork-screw in an obstinate cork. It does no good. It does harm.

Good fella, I say, in an obviously strained way, and I grab his paw and hold it.

I press on his paw to loosen his grip. He digs in deeper. Looks up at me contentedly as he tilts his head to maximize the chin-stroking angle for Ron. Flaggy loves a game, I seem to remember.

Yeah, good fella, Ron says. *Good fella.* Scratching away. *Now, there'd be food, wouldn't there? At one of these?* Two more quick pats. *Good to see you home.* And they go outside.

I moan, but hopefully to myself. I want to be at home, too. I want the pain to go away. I want to check my penis, first chance I get. Oscar's near me, standing just inside the French doors, so I call him over.

You're going to have to help me, I explain. The cat hates me, I think. He's got me pronged around about mid-shaft at the moment.

What?

Stop laughing right now. If we get this wrong, I could blow a corpus. I might never fly straight again. And anything I do just makes it worse. So how about I distract him and you sneak in and whip the claw out? Okay?

Okay.

And be discreet. Pretend you're down there for Flag.

We've never got on.

Put that aside, Oz. Help me here.

He goes down on his knees, maneuvers in close to the seat.

Actually, it's ... It's hard to see exactly which one, which claw . . . He leans in closer, takes the paw delicately in his hand. *We're going to be okay though. I think we're going to be okay.*

I keep talking to Flag, trying to make soothing noises and doing what I can to take the edge of pain from my voice.

No writhing, please. No more writhing, Flaggy. We'll be there any second.

Oscar moves his head onto my thigh, next to Flag.

Why do they make them so fluffy? Okay, got the claw . . . And, here we go.

He pops the claw out, Flag writhes away, rolls off my lap and onto the seat next to me. Anita comes back in through the French doors.

Oh my lord, she says, seeing Oscar's head in my lap, his hand on the front of my pants and Flag's fluffy body obscuring the detail. *I'm sorry.*

She backs out onto the deck, looking flustered.

I've got to go and check this, I tell Oscar. Cover for me. Us.

I run to the bathroom. Or, rather, start running, but change it to a brisk walk. I'm already sending the wrong signals. I don't need to make things worse. How do I get into these situations?

I lock the bathroom door. I check. There's a puncture wound where I knew there would be, but I think it's only superficial. Even if, at the time, it felt as though Flag had pushed it so far it could constitute the kind of body piercing that would allow me to wear a big enough piece of metal to create mystery at airport security.

A dot of blood wells up out of the puncture, and so

does another when I wipe it away. I'd like to avoid ap-
plying pressure to stop this. All Flag's wrenching around
has made the area far from comfortable. I pull off a good
length of toilet paper and improvise something involving
a lot of wrapping. Which, when all is put away, makes
me look like I'm trying to tell everyone I'm hung like a
donkey, but this isn't the time to care.

I go back into the lounge room and Oscar's still there,
or back again.

I don't think he penetrated beyond the deep fascia.
So . . . what do you think?

I think, he says, looking at my pants, *I think you're looking very perky today. Is something happening?*

A big wad of toilet paper. There's active bleeding, you
know. I meant, what did you think Anita thought?

Oh, it's okay, I cleared that up.

You told them about the claw.

No, I just said I was going down on you.

What?

It's okay. I told them it was your birthday.

I'm going to assume you're kidding. That's what I'm
going to assume. And your next birthday, you're still getting socks, okay?

*Sure. I like socks. How about we go outside? And pretend
this never happened.*

Good idea.

*And how about you walk like you haven't spent forty-eight
hours in the saddle.*

Also a good idea, but perhaps not possible. We'll see.

We walk through the French doors. Everyone stops
talking. Oscar gives them a three count. And they sing

"Happy Birthday." Several of them, I'm sure, give my pants a lot of attention, but try to be very open-minded.

There's throbbing down there. Not good throbbing. I just don't understand body piercing, do I? Particularly those bits of the body. I stand at an angle, but there's no angle from which my groin looks small for everybody (a problem I never thought I'd face in my whole life). I should have stayed in the bathroom. Gritted my teeth and applied pressure until the bleeding stopped, and then made do with a simple, non-space-occupying bandaid.

They give three cheers, but I know Katie's faking it.

Someone asks how old I am, and I say, About thirty-five.

Because thirty-four and a half isn't a birthday. But it does mean I'm up for thirty-five next. I hadn't thought of that before. It seems a lot older. There are going to be forms where I have to tick a different box. Thirty-five to forty. Thirty-five to forty-four. That seems like a whole different bunch of people. Men who like jazz and badly groomed beards. Shit like that.

Jon, Anita says, beside me. *I'm sorry about before. I just . . .*

It's okay.

No, I just didn't realize you were both there. I didn't know Oscar had arrived. Um, and . . . that you were in that situation.

Um, I . . .

No, no, it's all right. How are your trousers?

They're okay.

Good. Good. Well, happy birthday.

Thanks.

She smiles and goes to refill her plate. How are my trousers? For parents, these people are much more open-minded than I thought. Was that a Monica-Lewinsky blue-dress joke she was setting up there? I don't think I can stay here, surrounded by cheery people who think I just got a happy-birthday blow job from Oscar in the lounge room. I'm used to living in a much more hung-up world than that. Things have changed while I've been out of circulation.

Hey, Jon, Wendy says. *Your birthday's not till September.*
That's right.

So why did Oscar tell my mother Flag had his claws in your birthday-present pants and was on the brink of doing some serious damage?

They're very special pants. So what if my birthday was months ago? I've only worn them about twice and I didn't want them wrecked. Someone had to get right down there to sort it out, or I would have had big loops of thread hanging everywhere.

I tell her I'm going to get some food, and I go to find Oscar.

Before I talk to anyone else, could you tell me exactly what you told everybody?

Oh, yeah, sure. It got a bit elaborate, didn't it? It was worth it though. I liked it best when the singing started. Your face was good. And you really are Big Jon in your birthday trousers today, aren't you?

George sidles up to us, and I've never seen him even attempt sidling before.

Have you tried these mini quiche? he says, with an almost peculiar enthusiasm. *They're still warm.*

Mini quiches? I haven't ever seen a quichelet get such a warm reception.

Mini quiche are worth it. There's a lot of thought behind this catering.

Good of you to notice. I'm sure Katie'll be pleased.

Yeah. Maybe she is. He wrestles hard to suppress a knowing smile, but it breaks out anyway. *We've, um, got coffee scheduled for Wednesday. She figured I'd get a break for coffee now and then. And I thought, why not? I've completely come to terms with the eighties. Unlike some people. So why not?*

Ash is holding Lily when I get home, rocking her, calming her, singing. Their noses touch, and Lily grabs Ash's ear.

She's been a bit fussy, Ash tells me, as Lily looks at the ear in fascination, and they bump heads. *But I think we're okay at the moment.*

We look okay.

I put her back in her cot for a few minutes and had a quick shower. I borrowed a T-shirt. I hope that's all right. I think it's just the right size. She passes me Lily and holds her arms out to show me how well the T-shirt fits. *What do you think?*

You might not know this, but there are some countries where the convention is to wear the elbow outside the sleeve. But I'd have to say that, to me, it looks just the right size.

That's when I realize I don't want her to go home. That something's missing when she's not here. That if she stopped coming, there'd be another loss to cope with. That's the sum total of what I've stopped myself thinking till now. Till now, walking in the door, seeing her with Lily. I want to tell her. I want to tell her now.

Have you got a hair drier?

No, I don't think so.

That's okay. No big deal. We'll just have to put up with the spiky look.

She stays for lunch, and into the afternoon. She talks about going to do some work in the library, but it doesn't happen.

I make us cups of tea, and she sits there holding hers, both hands around it as though they're cold. Which they can't be. She's looking down into the tea, thinking.

I haven't been completely straight with you either.

What do you mean?

I was going out with the guy who handles the distribution of our tea, runs the Web site, things like that. And suddenly the whole thing turned icky. It ended a few months or so ago. So you surprised me with the tea yesterday. I thought it could have been something to do with him. Which is pretty stupid . . .

Well, it's not rational, but I wouldn't call it stupid. But you did tell me about the home page. It wasn't too hard to get there and click in the right boxes.

Yeah. Which is what I should have been thinking. But you know how things can do that? Trigger things that don't make sense?

Yeah.

He was sort of into the relationship more than me. A lot more. When I talked about coming down here . . . that all became clear. What got to me was that it seemed to piss every-

body off. My family—my father particularly—they like him a lot. "Part of the family," I think the expression goes. So I think there were lots of people more into the relationship than me. It turned into a bit of a mess. It was like, You're going to what? Dump the golden boy, quit the weekend tour groups, move to the other end of the state? What's got into you? You'll worry your father sick? What'll you do for money? What's wrong with everything you've got here? Etcetera, etcetera. I mean, welcome to Erikson Eight, guys. The nest is emptying.

Did you say that? I hope you said it.

Do you think it would have helped? So here I am. After all my bold counterarguments like, Oh yeah? I'll get a job. You'll never hear me asking you for money. So here I am, wearing your T-shirt, having sponged six meals off you in the last few days. That's independent. I can't even have a period now without getting your help. She laughs at her own joke. *And then I hassle you about not opening up, and I tell you none of this. That's not very fair.*

You could have told me.

And it's meant to come out saying just what it says— to mean that I was willing to listen—but it accidentally sounds tougher, maybe critical.

Hey, I have now. It just seemed insignificant compared to what you've gone through.

No, I meant you could. It wasn't compulsory. And I'm sure what you were going through felt pretty significant when it was happening.

It still does. It's not an easy time, going through all that.

I know.

And even that sounds patronizing. I drink my tea. She drinks hers. Before I make a mess of this, I want to tell her how I feel. I have to tell her. Before I say the wrong thing. I have to work out how I feel, the right words for how I feel. How I felt when I walked in the door today.

Do you think she's getting another tooth?

Who?

Who? How many people around here don't have the full set? Lily.

Um, I don't know. Look, we've been seeing a lot of each other lately ...

But that's where I stop, and get stuck mentally rifling through all the things I might say next, suddenly feeling the risk I'm on the brink of taking.

And? she says, as though urging a slow child.

What do you mean?

There's an "and." We've been seeing a lot of each other lately ... I should be paying for more things? Is that what you're going to say?

No.

But? Could it have been a "but"?

No. Give me a chance. Um, I'm not sure ...

That's evident, she says, and I can't believe how awkward I feel, how long it's been since I tried to say anything like this. I don't even know what I'm trying to say—the actual words anyway.

You turned up at a strange time for me. And my mind was on other things. So I don't always know ... we haven't ... I didn't think through anything when we started running. I'd always run by myself. And I know it's a good idea to get into a routine when you exercise with people.

You're slipping back to that non-direct approach again.

What?

The non-direct approach. You're talking about exercise theory.

Yeah, right. And how many weeks did it take you to tell me why you came to Brisbane?

I came to Brisbane to study.

You know what I mean.

At least it didn't start off as a story about car license plates.

Are you kidding? How was I supposed to tell you? I'd never told anyone before, not when it mattered. And you don't exactly make yourself an easy person to tell, with your ands and your buts and your observations about the non-direct approach. And you could have told me that other stuff sooner. It wasn't such a big deal. Relationships end.

I knew that was bugging you. I knew you thought I should have told you.

Fuck. Look, I'm sorry. It was a big deal. Of course it was a big deal. And it doesn't matter when you told me. I just . . . please don't get into the license-plate stuff again. I can really do without it. I mean, that's all to do with the person I married having died, you know.

There's a pause. She looks down at her tea and the muscles in her face clench.

Do you think I'd forgotten that? For a second? How am I supposed to deal with you? How is anyone supposed to deal with you? I've got to be so cautious around all of that. I just forgot how to handle you for a second, okay?

Handle me? What are you? A zoo keeper?

Shit, Jon, what am I supposed to say? There's another mistake. Sometimes you're so far in there, running around, that you don't even know what's happening on the surface. How temperamental you are. How carefully people treat you. How nothing gets sorted out.

Well, there goes the careful handling. This is nice and direct.

I'm sorry. I'm not sure what to say. I'm really sorry that the person you married has died. And I'm sorry that you didn't like her. And I'm sorry that you don't really know how to deal with that, and that no one ever talks about any of it. She stops, leans her forehead forward onto her hand. *What am I doing? I'm sorry I'm saying all this now. It's not my business. I can't know what you feel like.*

Particularly if I don't tell you. And I'm working on that. And I've made it your business. So don't say it's not your business. It's your business now more than it's anybody else's.

I think I'll go home.

What? Don't go.

No, I think I will. She stands up, goes to the coffee table in the lounge room and picks up her keys.

I follow her in, watching this. Watching her being angry, and leaving.

Don't leave. Please.

I'm not leaving. Don't say it that way. I'm just going home for tonight. Because right this minute you are pissing me off. Hugely pissing me off. But I will see you tomorrow, idiot. I'm not feeling very well. I'm not up to this conversation. If we've been seeing too much of each other lately, you can have an evening off tonight and pick a different day to tell me. If there's some problem with the running, then ... She shakes her head.

No, that's not it. That's not it at all. You've got it totally wrong. I don't want to see a minute less of you.

Really?

Really.

Okay. Okay. But I think I should go home, for today. I can't be careful enough right now. I'm not feeling very well, so I'm going to go. I'm going to go, I'm going to take my tablets, I'm going to watch some TV and go to bed early and I'll see you tomorrow.

I don't know that you should drive.

Don't tell me that I shouldn't drive.

I was just . . .

Yeah, I know. And don't ask me to stay, and don't offer me a lift, and for god's sake don't offer me money for a cab or I'll fucking kill you.

Kill me? Is that just the cab one or all three?

She laughs. *Don't. Don't even try to make a joke out of it. Being your . . . friend is very strange. Sometimes too strange. But I kind of have to be, because you're the only person like me that I know. You get me. People don't get me often. Most of the time, I think I get you. I'm going home now, and let's not make a bigger issue of it than that. I will talk to you tomorrow.*

What about food? You don't have any food. Wait. Wait.

Sit, good girl, sit.

That was not my dog voice. That was my sincere for-fuck's-sake-you-need-food voice. Give me a break. I'll be one second.

I run to the kitchen and I wonder what the hell I'm going to give her. What kind of food will make her come back tomorrow? Am I that tragic? Giving myself one second to plunder my kitchen for commitment food? Everything's half-open jars when I look in the fridge, and I yank a bag out of the fruit section at the bottom. It looks like there's a lot in it, but it turns out it's only grapes.

Two pounds of grapes, she says. *Thanks.*

Look, it could have been a two-pound chunk of pumpkin. And if you're anything like me the only thing you'd know to do with that is cook it, mash it and serve with a tiny plastic spoon and a lot of airplane noises.

I can't imagine what you had in mind with two pounds of grapes.

They're bite-size. They're totally ready.

21

It got better toward the end. With or without the aid of my try-hard jokes, it got a little better. But it could only get so good. I blame it on the material. I'm sure I made mashed pumpkin as funny as it can be.

I wish she'd stayed. And I couldn't watch her go. I had to stand where I was and listen to her feet on the steps, her car driving off. Was I supposed to follow? Who knows? With this kind of thing, I always used to pick the wrong option, and I don't suppose that's changing now.

In the middle of the night, I think Ash was right. There's teething going on. Lily sounds restless. Or perhaps it's me not sleeping, and noticing every snuffle on the monitor. I wait, willing the grumbling to settle. It doesn't. She wakes and opens her mouth wide and really lets me hear it.

When I pick her up she's a bundle of tense muscle. I check, and there's a new red bump not far along the gum from tooth one. I give her Tylenol and rub on some teething gel.

Neither of us exactly has our shit together tonight, do we? I say, as we walk up and down the hall.

Soon we're in the car, and I'm saying, You'll like this.

Nice soothing motion, four-speaker sound, as if I'm trying to sell it to her.

See what it looks like out there at night? Look at the streetlights. Look at the trees in the dark. Look at the cows, I add, just for the hell of it. Look at the no traffic. Can you get that kind of thing yet? An absence. Other than the absence of comfort and trust connected with teething. Which, by the way, I do not cause. Like rain. I don't do rain and I don't do teeth. They're both beyond me. Listen to the fire engine. Do you hear that? Fire engines, and they're coming closer. Must be something happening this way.

And the fire engines swoop over the hill behind us and fly past, red light and sound bursting into the car, swamping Lily's brain with stimuli and then vanishing ahead of us and over the next hill.

Wow, they're in a hurry, aren't they? Did you notice the Doppler effect, the subtle change in siren pitch from when they were coming toward us to when they were going away?

From the back she looks at me, quieter now. As if she's just seen the great red flashing teething monsters who hate whining kids, and it's in her best interests to shut up and hope they won't come back.

It's okay. It's nothing to do with us. We haven't done anything wrong. We're just out for a drive and they happened to be passing.

I turn the CD player on.

Why did tonight end the way it did? I'm thinking of Ash again. I can't help it. I don't think I always avoid conflict, or the tough issues. Okay, I'm thinking of Ash, and I'm thinking back on a few therapy sessions. But what's going on? What was I going to tell her anyway? What's happening with us? All this talk about talking, and we don't talk about that. And I don't raise it in case I'm getting it totally wrong.

We're close to campus now, on the edge of my running-track street circuit. I hope Ash is okay with those pounds of grapes. I turn left. I should have given her bread. I look around, and the Bean is peaceful.

We'll just go by Ash's place, and then get you home to bed, I tell her, in the gap between tracks.

But there's a red light somewhere, flashing. I can see it through the trees and on the front of a cream-colored block of units at the T-junction ahead. I turn right when I get there, into Ash's street. The red light fills the car again. From up ahead, red light.

Red lights, lots of them. From right where I park in the mornings. From Ash's house. The fire engines have pulled up outside Ash's house. Through the neighbors' trees I see flames. Ash's kitchen windows with flames spouting out of them, bursting out between the boards of her kitchen wall. The crews are connecting hoses. I can see them, lit by the fire, moving toward the house.

I'm already shouting her name before I get to them. Shouting to let people know there's someone inside. Shouting so that she can answer me back and tell me she's out of there. I'm halfway up the path when I'm grabbed.

Mate, what are doing?

There's someone in there.

No, it's a derelict house. They're going to pull it down.

Someone's in there. Ash.

What? What ash?

Ash. Ashley. Fuck. She's inside.

I break his grip and run for the door. I hit it hard with my shoulder. Something cracks, but I think it's my shoulder. I hit it again, I kick it. I probably start screaming.

One of the fire crew comes past me with an ax, and another takes me by the arms. It's the guy I pushed aside.

We'll get her, he says. *If she's in there we'll get her.*

The ax splits the door with one blow, and they heave it open. Hot smoke billows out onto all of us. I break free again and I push inside. I drop to the carpet and I crawl along the corridor. I have no idea where anything is. There's no air, no air here. I'm as low as I can be, but I'm not below the smoke.

They grab me by the legs, and pull me out. I can't fight them this time. I cough till I throw up in the garden. I'm dizzy and on my knees. My back's hot from the fire in the kitchen above, scorching me through my T-shirt.

We've got her, the guy I've been battling says. *Mate, we've got her. She was around the back.*

Oh, thank god. So she was out?

No. Nearly out. She was on the floor near the back door. But she's out now. And we're giving her oxygen and the ambulance'll be here any second.

I'm a doctor. Maybe I can help.

You're a doctor?

Yeah. Yes. I'm a fucking doctor. This woman means a lot to me and I'm a doctor, so let me help. Please.

I stand up and the coughing starts again. In the black of the trees, I see sparkles and my knees start to bend.

I'm on the ground again. My hands are on Ash's path,

opened wide and holding me up, lit orange from behind by the flames. Oxygen is fitted to my mouth and there's an arm around my shoulders. An ambulance trolley pushes past through the long grass and up the side of the house. I pull the mask off and start hitting the arm that's holding me.

It's okay. I'm okay. I've got to help.

When we get around there, they're checking pupils. I can see Ash, crumpled on the ground, not conscious and, in the smoky haze, the small, white cone of light dropping down onto her eyes, checking each of them.

I can hear a voice say, *We've got a doctor here,* as I move past, toward her, and one of the ambulance crew turns to me and says, *Smoke inhalation. No apparent burns. She's not conscious. We've got her on oxygen now. Her heart rate's one-fifty, we're just checking her BP.*

And the pupils?

Normal. We're about to get her off to the Royal quick smart.

They lift her onto the trolley and fold one flopped arm back out of the way, leaving her half-open hand next to her face, just the way it was last night. I take it to hold it, but it's limp.

Why not the Wesley? It's closer. I'll sign for it, for the cost.

They're on ICU bypass. Full tonight. Big pile-up on Milton Road. But don't worry, doc, you haven't seen how we get to the Royal.

In the light at the back of the ambulance Ash looks gray, streaked with grime on her forehead where she pressed her hands to hold the smoke back.

I start coughing again, and spit some very bad-colored mucus into the gutter.

And one for you, the ambulance guy says, and fits an oxygen mask around my head.

I take the stethoscope and I check Ash's chest. There's air everywhere that there should be, as far as I can tell. But the ambulance is moving now, we're on our way, so it's hard to hear. Then the sirens cut in.

I'm Dane, he shouts over his shoulder as he's sticking on ECG electrodes. *And Julie's the driver.*

I'm Jon. I'm actually a friend of hers. And a doctor. A laser surgeon.

Still, it'd be like riding a bike, this stuff, hey? Hopefully? Shall I get a bag of fluid ready? Are you going to get a line in?

Yeah.

I take a tourniquet and find a vein on Ash's forearm. I rub away at the skin with a swab, cleaning as much of the smudged smoke off as I can, and the vein feels full and plump under my fingers. Almost too good. I've blown veins like this before. But that was years ago, and it was confidence that blew them, inadequate attention to detail.

Streetlights flash by, a car buzzes past going the other way.

I pick the cannula and slip it from its sheath. I palpate the vein again.

We take a corner fast and it throws me down onto one knee. I look out the window. The road will be straight for about ten seconds.

Keep it still, I tell myself. Don't go deep. Nice and steady.

I push the tip forward and the skin dimples, gives. There's a flashback of blood in the cannula. I ease it further in to make certain, unclip the tourniquet.

Here's the line, Dane says, and hands it to me. *And the next corner.*

I brace myself for the turn and, when we're through it, I connect the drip up. It runs. I loop the line down to her wrist and back, and tape it securely.

She's got quite a tachycardia going, he says, and points to the ECG. *Or is that just a problem with the trace?*

No. Fuck. They're ectopics. They look like ectopics, on top of the tachycardia. The wandering baseline just makes it hard to read.

Problem?

Yeah. Could be.

Then there are more.

Jesus, Ash. Don't do this.

More. A couplet. Another couplet.

Have you got all the gear for cardiac things?

Yeah. But you'll be the one using it. I'm not a paramedic. We're just a regular ambulance, not the cardiac one. We've got gear though. Just tell me what you need.

Okay.

And her BP's down to eighty systolic. Maybe seventy. What's normal for her?

She's having couplets now, I tell him. You see those ectopics there? Two in a row. Then another two in a row. That's what it looks like. If this gets more unstable we could be in trouble. Have you got any lignocaine, or bretylium?

Yeah, I'm sure we do. Let me get them.

Thanks.

Another couplet. A run of three in a row. Sailing silent and misshapen from right to left across the monitor, as the siren doubles its frequency and we glide through a red light.

Have you got a defibrillator?

The words even sound as though they're being said by someone in another life, or on TV. I'm out of my depth here. These drug names are just memories for me, and I'm about to go guessing with them. If lignocaine comes in 100 mg ampoules, that'll be my guess. That'll be what she gets. I'm holding her hand as he fetches the drugs. I'm watching the ECG. Watching it tell me heart rates that are swinging around all over the place, all of them too high. We lurch around another corner. I slip, I hit my head, my oxygen mask falls off. We're going through the city now. I can see the lights out the window. One of the defib paddles goes near the sternum. The other I'm not sure. Hopefully it'll say on there. It's been too many years.

And that's when it really hits me. Ash might be going to die. I've seen this before, held the limp hand, watched the monitor go all wrong.

Don't do this, I tell her. Please don't do this.

And I've left Lily in the car.

Lignocaine? It was lignocaine you wanted first?

Whichever.

I've left Lily in the car.

I only need one of them, I tell him.

He hands me something, takes another BP.

Still eightyish.

Good.

I've left Lily in the car, and there's nothing I can do. Nothing I can think of. I watch the monitor. I get ready for it all to get worse, and to demand that I try something. I imagine defibrillating. I imagine it failing, Ash jolting and dying there. And I push that out of my head. I imagine it working, and I imagine the routine, where the paddles go, setting it to three hundred joules and hitting the red button. Sometimes it works, that's what I tell myself.

I let go of Ash's hand. I tear the top from the lignocaine box. I tip the parts out. I remember it from med school. It's a single-dose set. I screw the vial down into the syringe. We're in the Valley now, almost there.

And the couplets settle down. Peter out, like a storm passing.

Single ectopics slide across the screen, then they're gone too. There's a tightness around the fingers of my right hand, Ash squeezing. I'm holding her hand again. She murmurs something inside her mask. She's looking at me.

There's been a fire, I tell her. But it's all going to be okay.

She nods. I keep watching the screen, trusting nothing. I keep the lignocaine in my other hand, just in case.

Dane . . .

It's looking better, isn't it? The ECG?

Yeah, much. I've left my baby in the car.

Shit. Um . . . We've got a phone. Is there anyone you can call?

Yeah. Thanks. What's the time?

Three-ten.

Right. So, well after everybody's bedtime then. Don't know why I asked really.

I swap him the lignocaine for the phone, and I call George and Oscar's number. It rings four times and the answering machine cuts in, George and Oscar sharing the outgoing message, with some lounge music in the background. It beeps and I tell them, Pick up, pick up. Please pick up. It's Jon. I really need you to pick up.

Then George's voice is there, a bleary *Hello.*

George, it's Jon. I need you to do something for me.

Hmmm.

Are you awake?

Yes.

There's been a fire at Ash's place. We're on the way to the Royal. Everything should be all right, except I left Lily in the car.

What?

I need you to go and get Lily out of my car.

But I don't have a key.

Break a window. Now, I'll give you the address.

He takes it down, reads it back to me and sounds more awake now.

I'm on my way.

Thanks.

I'm feeling sick again. I put the mask back on.

We make a left turn, and then sweep into Royal Brisbane Hospital. The doors of the ambulance open, and the back fills with flourescent light.

Let me sit, Ash says, and we click her up into a half-sitting position.

Before they pull her out, she reaches out to me, puts her arms around me and draws me in to her, our oxygen masks nudging each other in a soft plastic clunk, like a collision of two *Star Wars* characters.

Even with the mask on, I can smell the smoke in her shirt, my T-shirt.

Let's get you out of there, someone says.

22

You're wearing a doctor thing, Ash says, when she turns to look at me. She blinks at the bright sky behind me and looks back at the ceiling.

That's because I stink. No, it's routine. Everyone in here wears one of these over the top of their regular gear. It's to do with infection control. Of course, every bug on my skin got smoked out about four or five hours ago.

What happened?

It was probably your wiring, but they'll work it out.

Weren't you at home? How did they know to call you?

They didn't. Lily's teething. We were out driving. I was probably focused on the anti-wailing measures, so I must have automatically found my way onto our running circuit and followed it. The fire engines were getting there when we did. The crew had to keep tackling me to stop me helping. Poor bastards, I'm sure they know what they're doing. And then I left Lily in the car.

She's all right?

Yeah. George got her. Smashed a window. Took her and my phone and my wallet and drove off with the alarm going. I hope those things stop after a while. She's with my parents. He was here not long ago, before work, to see how things were going. So he brought the phone and the wallet. And some grapes for you.

She half smiles, and looks as though the effort tires her. *You guys and your grapes.*

Do you want to get some sleep? Do you want me to go?

No. Oh, have you got to go to work?

No. It's Monday, so I'm off this morning.

I want to sit up. Can you help me sit up?

Sure.

I help her lean forward, I reshape the pillows and I slide her back against them. She sits with her crepe-bandaged drip arm on top of the covers, and she squints out the window.

Where are we?

Royal Brisbane.

Hmmm.

Do you know where that is?

No. Is it a long way from home?

Not too far.

She nods, looks around the room. There are three other beds, two of them with people in, both ventilated.

Oh, what am I going to do?

First, you're going to get well. You were lucky to get out really. And there were a few scary moments in the ambulance. I was pretty worried actually. Your heart was doing some things it shouldn't. Which is why you're in here on a monitor, but it's been normal all night.

What was happening?

Rhythm problems. That's how it looked anyway. It

wasn't easy to read. But they sorted themselves out. There was a minute or two when I was really, really worried that they weren't going to. Shit, even seeing you in a hospital bed scares me. I hate this stuff, you know?

Yeah. She starts to cry. I pass her the tissue box, put my arm around her. She puts her head against my shoulder and says, *You stink. You stink like my mouth tastes.*

Just cause I wasn't sick enough to get bathed.

Oh . . . she groans. *What am I doing? What am I doing here?*

It'll be okay.

Oh, Jon. What's going on? My life is fucked.

It'll be okay.

She lifts her head, looks me in the eye.

You're okay.

Thanks. She puts her head back on my shoulder.

And I want to do whatever I can. I want it to work out for you here.

She pulls tissues out of the box and wipes her face.

Um . . . I don't know what's happening. I mean, I'm here for this year, but I don't know. Maybe for longer. I'm not in love with you. You know that, don't you? I don't know what it is that's going on, but I don't think I'm in love with you.

That's all right.

Is it?

Yeah. I don't think that's what either of us was looking for. So it's fine.

She puts her arms all the way around me, and her IV line hooks itself onto my ear. She smiles, and carefully lifts it free. It's as if the dangers of last night give us a more immediate need for clarity today. I think we both sense it.

That we have to pause, if only momentarily, and actually define things before we move on.

And of course she doesn't love me. We've only known each other a few weeks. And she might think we're like each other—we both might think that—but we can't ignore the differences either. It's good that she's talked about it. Probably good, too, that she doesn't love me. Who knows where that could have led?

So what are you looking for? she asks me.

What do you mean? I don't think I'm doing much looking. I'm looking to get through each day, I guess.

But you're already good at that.

What do you mean?

What I said. You're already good at getting through each day. What's the next phase?

I guess I've been leaving that to work out later.

Yeah. This time I'm not going to say one of those things like "Sometimes you seem to be leaving a lot till later."

I can hear the sigh I let out, but even I'm not sure if it's exasperation, or resignation, or just plain tiredness.

Sorry.

Don't be sorry. Let's not go back to sorry. It seemed to lead to such a crappy night.

She laughs.

You know, no one's put it to me that way before. They haven't—and this is what you've been saying—they haven't dared. They're behaving like people who have come home after they were supposed to, and they're taking their shoes off so that the bad guy in the house doesn't wake. But that's okay, too. They're there for me. I know that. And I wouldn't want them any other way. And, yes, maybe I do leave things. Maybe I can get away without crying my eyes out over this, so why shouldn't I try? And maybe I do keep things in, but what do you want me to do? I'm grinding my way through this, and that's a day-to-day thing, but I am getting through. And you're now a part of that.

Good.

But it's not so much what's happened that I have to deal with. It's what will happen. People think it's the past that I've got to deal with, and I do, but it's only part of it. And it's a part I can't change. It's the future that I've got to think about more. And the past that I have to accept. Find a place for. Take apart piece by piece and put away somewhere. And that hasn't been easy, and it's not going to be easy, and you and everyone else can't tell me it'll be otherwise.

She looks up at me, but she doesn't say anything.

Sorry. You're not trying to tell me that . . . Okay, I'll be honest with you. Totally. This is all knotted up. Fairly knotted up. All the way in. And there are things I haven't told people specifically because they were Mel's friends too. So maybe I can tell you sometime.

Go on.

What?

Tell me.

Now?

I get bored in hospitals.

So I tell her about Lily's conception, Mel's absence and her return. The drinking that night. The desperate hope with which I invested that last chance. How we ran to the taxi stand as rain started to fall, storm rain that drummed on the roof as we drove home, that soaked us when the keys slipped from my hand at the front door.

You idiot, Mel said as they fell between the steps. *You idiot.* But she was laughing.

How it was my idea not to use contraception, even when Mel was clear about the timing. Particularly when Mel was clear about the timing. My excitement when the pregnancy test was positive a couple of weeks later. My hope—having fallen for the hope she'd once had about what a family would do—that this would make everything good. And we argued another nine months, remained two separate people, mostly, had days when we didn't talk, days when we'd find something to agree on, but usually something inconsequential. And days when I'd do something like cook her the noodle dish and wonder again what would become of us.

So the pregnancy, Lily, was my idea. And birth killed her, killed Mel. I couldn't face the fact that our relationship might end, and the last thing I made us try to fix it killed her.

Oh, god, Ash says, and cries again, wiping another dirty mark onto a tissue. *You can't look at it that way.*

And usually I don't. But sometimes I find myself looking at it that way, and I'm not going to pretend I don't. See? See what happens when I speak my mind? See what happens when I actually tell someone the worst five percent of what I feel? And then I had Lily to look after. The most dependent being imaginable. And I had this idea in my head that she'd lost one parent far too easily, and I thought, what happens to her if something happens to me? I was afraid for her, as if she was already halfway to being abandoned. That's dumb, I know, but it's how it felt. And that's when I decided I had to live. Take all possible measures, and do whatever I could for her.

Ash coughs, and I hear it rattle. I pass her the cup on the bedside table and she spits up some sooty mucus.

How long does that go on for? she says, looking into the cup.

I don't know. I do laser skin surgery. I'm next to useless with this stuff.

You couldn't know what was going to happen that night, when you went drinking.

No, I know.

But I can see why you couldn't tell your friends all that. Not yet anyway. So try the risky things out on me first, if you want to. If you don't want to try them on anyone else.

Thanks.

She sighs against my chest, and keeps looking out at the day, at the blue sky tinted darker by the windows.

So let me take a risk then, I say to her, since I seem to be in the mood. Let me tell you some of the best five percent of what I feel. I know you're not in love with me. But I might be in love with you. So does that wreck everything?

No. Not at all. What could it wreck? What could be wrong with it really? Shit. I'm so messed up about all this stuff. I should come with warning signs. You don't know how messed up.

You could tell me.

Yeah. Or I could just demand that you spill everything, and stay nice and quiet myself. That'd be good. You said it was

*so confusing, when we talked about these things, ages ago. Or
you said that things got confused easily.*

They're clear today.

*So don't you run away now. I'm glad you told me. It's a
good kind of thing to know today. Even if that sounds a bit
selfish.*

It doesn't.

Good. Thank you.

She looks at me. She's blinking, frowning, determined
to stay composed. Sitting there, propped up in her hospital
bed in a crumpled white gown with her hair spiking
everywhere, thinking composure might amount to anything today. She moves her arms up around my neck,
breathes out, lets a breath slump out of her. She kisses me
on the mouth. Kisses me and holds her mouth there, and
I can feel her messy hair in my hand, her bare back where
the gown hasn't been done up properly.

Then it's over. Our mouths are apart again, close but
apart, our foreheads touching. Both of us, I'm sure, caught
unawares, not knowing what's next.

I . . .

There's a nurse at the door. *Oh, I'm sorry,* he says. *Your
heart rate just went up on the monitor, and I . . .*

I'm okay, Ash says to him, and shakes her head. *It's like
school in here. You can't get away with anything.*

Sorry. I had to check.

Well, thanks. I'm okay. He goes, and she looks back at
me. *I don't know. I don't know what that was about, so don't
ask me. Not just yet. I'm sorry. Did I mention I was kind of
messed up?*

I think you might have. And I think we both know that I've had a good go at being messed up myself from time to time, so that's not a problem.

She nods, smiles, leans back on her pillows.

I want to go home, she says. *I don't like this place. Fuck, I don't have a home, do I? How bad is it?*

George said there's not much left.

Shit. There's another pause. I should say something. I don't know what. *Thank god I'm poor. Thank god I don't own much.*

Come to my place. I've got plenty of rooms. We can find you a new place while you're there. And we'll buy you some clothes. And don't argue, please. I don't want to argue again just yet. I think we can be clear enough with each other that I can buy you clothes because you need them, and you owe me nothing. And let dealing with how I feel about you be my problem. Your problem is that your house has burned down, and that's a bigger problem.

Yeah. I don't think I own anything at the moment. I even came in in your T-shirt. Shit. I thought my life was bad two days ago, when I had no food, no money and PMS. She laughs. *I could have died in that house. And I didn't.*

The consultant comes by on a ward round and clears Ash to go home tomorrow, or later today.

We might have to do some follow-up tests just to be sure there's no underlying cardiac rhythm problem, he says. *But I think that's very unlikely, and we don't need to keep you in.*

Once he's gone, Ash says she'll sleep.

That was good news, wasn't it? I can take it easy now?

It was good news. The tests are just about being certain.

Tests for this, maybe tests from that Saturday night doctor if things don't get better. I'm falling apart now that I've moved to Brisbane. I'm getting sick of it.

Well, that's healthy. Don't stop being sick of it. And I'm sure it'll be fine. So sleep. I'll be back later. After lunch. Is there anything you need?

What don't I need? I'm the complete damsel in distress. I need one of everything, and two or three of some things. Except grapes. Clothes would be good.

That's a tough one to start with.

You can do it. I'll write down the sizes. See? See how easily I'm giving in to this? she says, visibly annoyed with herself. *And could you phone Bagelos to say I won't be in?*

Yeah. Easy.

Okay, go treat that teething. On to the next patient.

So I hand my gown back, I catch the lift to ground, barefoot and shabby in my T-shirt and shorts, sleep-deprived and rung out. Standing in the lift with a group of white-coated med students who give me lots of space, and are sure I'm a reprobate in from the street overnight to sleep something off. One of plenty of sad stories in this place. I want to tell them, Those people are your patients, too, remember, but I don't. I'm no authority figure at the moment.

The tinted glass doors of the building open, and I'm hit by the glare of daylight, the streams of people coming in and out, moving purposefully past me, taking care of business. Ambulances dropping people off. Two painters with a ladder, clerks with files. The day is bright and warm already, the asphalt hot under my feet. And if I had to pick one relationship in my whole life to get right at the moment, it'd have to be the Bean. That's what occurs to me when I get in the cab, show that I can pay, despite my appearance, and we've turned round, U-turned to head west, to my parents' place.

I'm glad that's over. The night, this morning. I'm glad I told her, and set things straight.

In my whole life I've only told two people that I was in love with them. No one knows that, of course. It's not one of the stats you necessarily share with your friends.

I told Mel. The first time was in Cambridge. It was winter. We wanted to come home. We were drinking red wine and cooking pasta in the kitchen of our flat and all of a sudden I didn't care about the cold, the car that wouldn't start, how early the night came. And I told her I loved her. And what happened to that? Where did it go? What did I actually feel that night? I can't remember. There's too much fuzz in my head today. Or else I just can't remember.

Today. My second time. Ash. In the instant I worked it out, I told her. Maybe I told her even in the instant before I worked it out, and it just came out of me, un-reasoned and unstoppable and I heard it at the same time she did. But it sounded right. It wasn't my plan to tell her. I was going to admit to something, but it wasn't quite supposed to be that. But it is that, I guess, so out it came.

And this time, there was no anxious wait, no moment of deadly freefall while you wait to hear if you're loved back. Because she'd already told me she didn't love me. But I needed her to know anyway. Simply, I think, be-cause it feels true. More than true. Alarming even, that I'm off the rails like this and feeling such a thing, but the best kind of alarming. That I'm suddenly able to feel again. Feeling things I'm not certain I've ever felt, and surely I'm too old for that. I should have felt everything by now.

She told me she didn't love me and then she kissed me anyway, with her mouth and its taste of burnt linoleum, burnt carpets, thick asphyxiating smoke. A different mouth. It's been years since I kissed a different mouth. Not far short of ten years. She has different teeth, a different tongue. It's as though I've done something wrong.

I wasn't ready to be kissed. I'm still not ready, but I'd do it again right now. There's a hint of that taste—the smoke—still in my mouth, and the taste of her and I don't want it to go.

I don't know what happens next. In a different way from not knowing what would happen when Mel died. Today it's about life, fresh despair I can't avoid, but don't even want to. Ash, Ashley, coughing up the last of the smoke, living. Not loving me. But I'm not afraid now. Not afraid to be loved and even not loved. So whatever barrier I might have put up between me and the world, it's far from perfect. This is so odd. It's been years since this stuff's been around and now, this too-bright morning as we run west against commuter traffic, it's all I can think about.

Not all. I'm going to the Bean. And I've got a lot, having her. I want to see her, I want to wake her, I want to play. I want a few of hours of this day when things are as normal as they could possibly be.

I think I'll take her to harass the ducks. I want to see her explore today. I want to be there when she sees brand new things. When she chews on dirt, crawls till her knees are green. Gives me one of those looks that wants information, and trusts me to give it to her. I want her to walk and talk. I want her to get to Erikson Six without a single bad day, and I want to be there for her, every bad day she has. Even if it's today, and even if today is only teething gel and Tylenol and fussing and no fun at all.

I want to tell her about life, and how it never works the way you expect it will, but most of the time it's more good than bad. And I don't care if that's the corniest thought I've ever had. There's more. I want to teach her to write her name, to like the music I like and hit a two-handed backhand, and I want to be there if she falls in love with someone who doesn't love her back. Who gives her only a strong kind of like in return. I want to say to her, if she ever needs it, I know it hurts like you can't believe, but imagine what it means, that you can feel these things, even if they sometimes turn on you. Imagine how it might be if it worked out. I think I can.

The Bean. I can visualize every last thing about her, every detail. Her mother's eyes, her mother's nose. My ears (poor thing). The tiny creases she makes in her hands. They're all her own. But wherever they came from, these parts are hers now, a combination programmed by the genes put together fifteen months ago and worked on, reshaped, by every day since.

We were desperate that night, Mel and me. Both of us desperate not to give in. After the band's last set, after we hurried home, it's desperation I remember as I fought to get the key in the door and wished I'd left the outside light on, wished the storm hadn't opened up when it did.

And there were plenty of days, before and since, when we didn't feel that desperation, but it must mean something that we did that night, when we were both afraid enough that we didn't care about being soaked, about the water we trailed through the house, the clothes that we left in wet disarray on the bedroom floor. And the rain thrashed down on the tin roof and we forgot the debris of the past few years and found something better. At least some echo, some recollection, of love.

And that, then, is the bit the Bean will know when the time comes to deal with this. The Bean, still starting in the world and needing a load of looking after between now and any explanations. She's a very good reason to believe that these are the days. But I should be making them the days anyway, and considering her a bonus.

The cabbie chats, or tries to, but realizes he won't get too far. On the radio, Gene Pitney sings "Trans-Canada Highway."

I decide that, if I'm going to cry, I should make it quick—finish before we get to my parents—or they'll wonder what the hell's going on. They just wouldn't get that.

And now on with more classic hits of the sixties and seventies, the DJ says, not even stretching his definition of the world as far as the "Choose Life" T-shirt. *And some Neil Diamond. Let's hear that "Beautiful Noise."*

Fine, I'm thinking. Wreck a Neil Diamond song for me now. Stitch that onto this morning and see if I care. Thank god I don't share the cabbie's taste in radio. How would I get through it if it had been another station, any track from *The Best of the Lemonheads*?

I call Bagelos on my cell phone before I forget, and I tell them Ash is sick and won't be in for the next couple of days.

And then I call my parents, and I tell them everything's okay. I ask how Lily is and my mother says, *Fine. Slept like a baby. Your father's gone toy shopping, but she's still here. She's looking over this way right now, waving. That's "hello," I think. So how are you, really? You've had quite a night.*

Yeah. I'm fine. Actually, I honestly am. I'll tell you more when I get there. Tell the Bean I'll be there soon. Tell her we're going to play with the ducks.

ACKNOWLEDGMENTS

First, I'd like to thank Mark Saywell, my laser coach, for both his expertise and his willingness to put up with the unappealing smell of scorched banana, just so that I could have a firsthand understanding of Jon Marshall's job. I'd also like to thank the Queensland Ambulance Service for confirming details about training and ambulance outfitting. Naturally, any slip-ups when it comes to the technicalities are mine alone.

I'd like to thank Binker for appearing as Elvis, and the stabilizing sheet for appearing as itself. Also, Helen, Amy, Bek, Marie-Louise and Gina for their insights into Erikson, science, babies in fiction, and sensitive mothers and their steaming mugs of tea.

And I'd like to thank the crew of people who make the draft versions welcome and help me get the most out of each book—particularly Clare Forster and Rachel Scully at Penguin Australia, Fiona Inglis and Jane Bradish-Ellames at Curtis Brown, and everyone at home.

A note concerning violence to pets: readers can be assured that a highly trained stunt double was hired to play the role of Katie's cat, Flag, in chapters seven and fourteen, and that no animals were harmed or put at risk during the concept development, writing, editing, and publication of *Perfect Skin*. Certain scenes in the novel in which Flag's well-being is inadvertently compromised by actions of the central character, Jon Marshall, should not be seen to indicate the type of behavior the author and his publisher feel is suitable when interacting with household pets.